Blue Notes, Still Frames

Colin Bell

 Ward Wood Publishing
www.wardwoodpublishing.co.uk

Published by Ward Wood Publishing
6 The Drive
Golders Green
London NW11 9SR
www.wardwoodpublishing.co.uk

The right of Colin Bell to be identified as the author of this work has been asserted by him in accordance with the Copyright, Designs and Patent Act, 1988. © Colin Bell 2017.

ISBN 978-1-908742-62-9

British Library Cataloguing in Publication Data. A CIP record for this book can be obtained from the British Library.

Designed and typeset in Garamond
by Ward Wood Publishing.

Cover Design and artwork by Kayla Bell
© Kayla Bell 2017

Printed and bound in Great Britain by
Imprint Digital, Seychelles Farm,
Upton Pyne, Exeter EX5 5HY.

The views expressed in this book are those of the author, and do not necessarily represent the opinions of the editors or publishers. All the characters in this book are fictitious and any resemblance to actual persons (living or dead) or to institutions is purely coincidental.

Blue Notes, Still Frames

For Adam Bell and Henry Bell

The man that hath no music in himself,
Nor is not moved with concord of sweet sounds,
Is fit for treasons, stratagems and spoils;
The motions of his spirit are dull as night
And his affections dark as Erebus:
Let no such man be trusted. Mark the music.

(Shakespeare: *The Merchant of Venice* act 5 scene 1)

Chapter One

A melancholy melody is haunting a busy Brighton street. Joe Edevane, an enigmatic young man, stands louchely swaying, leaning against a lamppost, one leg casually crossed over the other. The music is his. He's playing a silver flute, an old *Armstrong 80*, with a beauty of tone that belies his rakish appearance and the mischievous twinkle that animates his deep brown eyes. His flute sparkles in the sunlight, and he attracts a few scattered coins, and some tearful eyes too in the bustling crowd of pedestrians, laden with carrier bags, who are not expecting to find themselves moved on this, the first day of Brighton's summer sales.

A young Asian woman, with inquisitive eyes, snaps him with an expensive camera and rushes off with a man, or maybe it's a woman. They're dressed identically, bright red shorts and yellow t-shirts, children's clothes on young adults. Someone else notices Joe, an angry man. A wounded soldier, perhaps, in a torn camouflage jacket, with a stumbling walk, and eyes that focus on Joe like pinpoints. No one but Joe sees the knife. 'It's music from hell,' the man shouts. 'You are the noise of lamentation.' Joe plays on; there's an exchange of looks, the man steals a handful of coins and runs off, but the flute continues to its crescendo. Alan Norton walks past, blond hair stylishly cut, dressed in the latest summer chic. Unaccountably, Joe and he smile at each other. Alan gives Joe a pound coin. Joe winks and carries on playing.

A Brighton street on a summer's day. It's England in summer 1994 and it's hot – very hot, the hottest temperatures in England since 1911 according to an unreliable newspaper story. The British don't like it hot, but often forget that when they moan about the cold in the winter. It isn't just the heatwave that has made Britain bad-tempered this summer.

There have been demonstrations against perceived injustices – in the government's Criminal Justice Act and plans to privatise the railway network. It's definitely not all sunshine and shopping, a series of twenty-four hour train strikes have left many passengers stranded and frustrated. Irish Republican Army bombs have exploded, killing and maiming, on mainland Britain and in Northern Ireland. The horrors of genocide, this time in Bosnia, haunt Europe again, and thousands, mostly young gay men, are dying of AIDS.

The government in Britain is beginning to fall apart and the new prime minister, quietly-spoken, worry-faced John Major, is losing support. As the Twentieth Century stumbles to an end, the nation may have stopped loving itself or, maybe, it's nervous about the future. Britain isn't sentimental about its politicians and, this year, it has started to look for a change – but maybe not today, it's much too hot. There's bad news out there, but the summer sales are in the headlines, and governments encourage shopping-sprees in times like these. The British have learnt to worship market-place gods, modern Brits are defined by what they can buy. Bargains are everyone's birthright – the poor and the rich, the needy and the greedy.

If he's worried by any of this, he isn't showing it, Joe looks happy – happy enough to a passing stranger but, on closer examination, Joe's face flickers with contradictions. He's playing his flute on a lively thoroughfare in the centre of town only yards from the beach, a famous beach. This is Brighton, a city wannabe by the sea; in love with things urban, Brighton quickly forgets the beach, distanced from the town by its urbanised stone-clad cliffs.

Only the luminous light, the hints of ozone in the air, and the constant neurotic shrieks of herring gulls, make this place feel like the seaside. Brighton folk ignore the sea when everyday life intrudes. Today, shopping is king and the summer heat is unwelcome, merely trapped in narrow streets, irritating bargain-hunters who sweat as they push through the crowd stumbling into revellers, mostly cropped-haired young men and women spilling in and out of pubs. Joe does well to attract attention, sharing his space with discarded litter, cigarette ends and fast food packaging.

Why did they smile at each other, Alan and Joe? Alan is young, Anglo-Saxon, good-looking, golden-skinned, a regular guy expensively clad in designer jeans and a skin-tight white cotton shirt. Joe is not many of those things. Joe is dark and ragged, his medium length curly black hair looks dreadlocked even if it isn't. He's small-boned, maybe of mixed-race, with the unexplained brown pigmentation that had upset and surprised his white parents on the day he was born – or so they'd claimed. He was an unlikely addition to a family proud to be the rare and exclusively English holders of the Edevane name.

His father, a private man, no stranger to confusion, had never referred to his only son's skin colouring. Mrs Edevane had stayed silent too. If she knew something she would rather not have shared, she didn't let it prevent her loving little Joe, and telling him that he was a special child. Special to her, and a gift to the world. He'd believed what she said without understanding it. Children believe what they're told, and Joe had felt something special inside himself. He still does – it sparkles in his eyes. It has seen him through difficult times. Mrs Edevane had cried as she died. 'You're my special child,' she had repeated to her fourteen-year-old boy, but she had taken her secret, if there was one, with her.

Mr Edevane had grieved and remarried. He had found a woman who disliked confusion, so they hadn't spent too long looking, when little Joe Edevane ran away from home with his prized possession, that *Armstrong 80* flute. Family-free, Joe's a man-boy with soft-toy features, a cartoon character down on his luck but, look closer, he's beautiful. A hint of black beard sculpts his jaw-line, and his eyes, vivid and knowing, would be black if they didn't have that hint of mahogany that can beguile instantly. If God had designed mouths, he would have been especially proud of Joe's. It is perfect, the upper lip curves like Cupid's bow, and the lower one is lush to the point of pouting. Whether he means it or not, Joe's mouth naturally smiles, curving upwards quixotically on each side.

He's street dusty from begging, earning some kind of living with his flute. It has brought about a meeting of sorts between Joe and Alan. They are exact contemporaries, the same height, both look about twenty-eight. Maybe that was it, they share something, perhaps, and, seeing it, they smile. Maybe that meeting of smiles was an act of aggression, like rival chimpanzees grinning territorially, just before they bite. The rich man at his gate – Alan might have looked like that to Joe, who is most definitely poor.

Alan didn't know why he'd smiled and, anyway, he's already forgotten about it. He gets out his keys and goes home to his flat, through a nearby smart black door complete with big brass knocker and matching letterbox. The door is his escape route, taking him away from street level squalor to a private space above a hairdressing salon, Scarlet O'Hara's, where the staff, male and female, have bright red hair. Next door, on one side, is a music shop called Wah-Wah, the best place in town for guitars and drums and for informal chatter about the history of rock'n'roll.

On the other side is Smith's Emporium, a specialist in sari materials and incense, which is always kept burning to bring in customers. It also deals in small Hindu statues and, in a room at the back, body piercing practised by Mr Smith himself, a shaven-headed Englishman who wears a skirt-like Indian dhoti, with matching and usually brightly coloured material draped over his shoulders, guru-style. Along the street, there's The Golden Orb, a pub with the best Country and Western music juke box in Brighton, that also sells world-class steak pie and chips.

Joe's flute music stays with Alan; he's humming it as he goes up the stairs and even, irritatingly, while he makes espresso coffee for himself and for the beautiful, yes, she is truly beautiful, Rachel, who sits waiting for him on the white leather sofa. She has been gazing out of the floor-to-ceiling sash windows, that open onto a balcony, that looks across a short street, to the sea. The view, Rachel's passion, fills the window frames with a shimmering mix of blues, as the cloud-free early evening sky imperceptibly joins the sea, now a blend of aquamarine and grey. One day, she hopes, she will take the perfect photograph of her own personal seascape, but from the many that she has taken, nothing, so far, has been good enough. She wants to capture the beauty she feels when she's seduced by sunlight's subtleties.

'For Christ's sake stop humming that fucking tune!' she snaps irritably, but she's lost none of her allure by her foul mouth. She's gained some in fact, silencing him as she draws him down into the soft white cushions. Alan stops humming, his mouth invaded by her pointed, athletic tongue.

The music plays on, not in Alan's head – he's otherwise engaged – but on the beach, down two flights of Victorian stairs, railed with rusting cast-iron, across a road and behind a row of beach huts. It's evening and Joe, the busking young Rastafarian who's not really Rastafarian, is still improvising on his flute – it's a continuation of the melody that has no natural ending. Maybe he will always be looking for that ending, he doesn't know. He's been playing it for years, maybe eternally, elongating, abbreviating, then expanding it in an elaborate and tearful arabesque. He's a denimed pied piper with no followers, but with a song in his head that will not let him go.

He and Victoria sit by their campfire. Victoria Buchanan's a big woman, probably in her late twenties too, statuesque on the shingle. She's smoking a spliff. She's defiant, a faded Goth, always tensed, flexed to defend herself. Her morbidly pale face is a trick with make-up. Black eyeshadow and mascara make her large brown eyes larger, black lipstick, her voluptuous lips more so. Her black clothes have turned grey, her boots are scuffed and dusty under a long ragged skirt. She's watching the sea or looking towards it, her face blank – unable today to live up to her mask. Dusk waves goodbye to the swimmers and sunbathers, then welcomes the night shift – crusty nomads huddled in groups for forbidden pleasures, or just an alternative to sleeping on the streets – a new phenomenon in England, thanks to politics' new cold-hearted economy. The melody continues, a languidly elegant evening hymn, only interrupted when Victoria cracks open two cans of lager.

They have a row, well, Victoria does. About small things that seem big. She's bored, hungry, she feels dirty, unattractive, yes, especially that. Her body's losing condition, beginning to sag; youth won't keep her muscles taut for much longer. She wants to bring him down too, her minstrel boy. 'You're so fucking happy all the time.'

He's too damned happy, he knows that, sitting there with his flute, intense behind those smiling eyes. No fat there on his compact lean body. More small spiteful words do the trick. She creates a summer storm, summons up the forces of evil and wins. Joe's suddenly angry, watery-eyed, she loves that, then he bites back, calls her names. She sees the fire behind the smile, and she's scared. She has never been frightened of him before. He notices and puts it right. He touches her like he did that first time, his hand on the nape of her neck, long musicianly fingers caressing her, loving her. He's a man of joy who recognises and, just maybe, collects the frail and damaged into himself. He wants to make her whole again. His famous grin returns. Later they swim in the darkness, naked in the cool inky sea. The campfire dries them with crackling warmth, and they snuggle down together in their tight, ragged sleeping bag – no room for rows in there. Now she can love his neat little body, and he, secretly, for he'll never tell her, can find a momentary home in those voluptuous curves of moon flesh.

Chapter Two

Harry Pollard had always thought that if you wanted to sit on the beach, you should just sit on the beach. You know, on the pebbles; he would never have thought of hiring a deckchair. Those were his poetic days, when he first dreamt about being a rock'n'roller, or a musician at least. Not that he'd given up exactly but, today, and for the predictable future, his money comes from looking after the deckchairs on a section of Brighton's seafront. It's a key stretch, his part of the beach, in fact, possibly the most important, right next to the pier, where everyone coming to Brighton wants to go, and where most of them congregate – a self-imposed crowd.

It's not too late to make it in the music business at twenty-eight, he knows that; some bands struggle for years before getting there in their thirties but, mostly, he knows this too, bands don't usually last that long. He's still hopeful of getting it together. In some ways the wait has been good. He's changed from the drum kit, and is now more into African drumming. Musically, he thinks, he's come a long way but, psychologically, he knows he's a bit messed up.

He's grown increasingly introverted during his Brighton years. When he first arrived here, an enthusiastic twenty-one-year-old, a bright-eyed kid from Burnley, with his three best friends from school, he was a quarter of the best band that he'd ever heard. It had seemed easy at first; once you were part of the scene, the bookings came in, and you were off. It didn't last. As they say, when new kids join the block, then the old ones must move on. They'd had their first wave, they'd performed all the songs that they'd written at school, their adolescent manifestos, their youthful autobiographies. Then they'd started to look for new material, about their lives now as young adults. They'd worked up some pretty decent songs about late night drinking sessions, inconsequential sexual encounters and morose mornings-after.

Those mornings-after might have been the problem – instead of finding a new seam of originality in their late night drinking binges, they'd just started to write too many songs about waking up, feeling crap and struggling to get out of bed. This had been their second wave. The third wave had begun some time ago, and had been even less productive. Now the four of them are, they claim, working on their own material, looking for new ways of expressing themselves, experimenting with new musical forms. In fact none of them has written a new song for over a year, and they've drifted apart, not needing each other to remind themselves of their failure.

So that's why he's now working on the seafront. It isn't his first job, that had been in a music shop, Wah-Wah, the coolest shop in town, but it hadn't worked out. He'd never mastered the tact of letting customers live with their own lack of taste. If they liked bubble-gum songs, then he'd thought he should put them straight. He'd just split up with his girlfriend too. Vickie, a London Goth who'd come into the shop looking for a tambourine. Now she's with Joe, his best friend.

The relationship had ended amicably enough, in a mildly depressing way. She'd got fed up and he couldn't summon up the energy to keep her interested.

His friend Joe is fine about Vickie's depressive side. Joe is like that, easy-going and, mostly, cheerful. He sleeps rough wherever he can, and used to drop by at Harry's deckchair store, a kind of cave built into the cliff that now supports the promenade. It's a semi-official space, most of the deckchairs are stacked in a container on the pebbles. Harry's store is the ideal hideout for a man hiding from himself. Joe had first come round just for a chat, then he'd started storing a few possessions there. Harry lets him sleep here too when the weather's bad, but that's not very often this hot summer. He hasn't been around recently, since the Vickie thing, but Harry never worries about Joe – they're mates.

Deckchairs. They fit somehow, fit with his life. He feels free. He's free enough. He can spend all day out of doors, wear what he wants, pick up a tan – even sit around on a deckchair if he isn't busy. Deckchairs are great, he's decided. Just a strip of plastic material and two wooden frames hinged together, easy to stack and simple to turn into an outdoor armchair. He was a genius the guy that invented the deckchair. Harry wonders if he'd invented any more outdoor furniture like that. In a hot country, you could live outdoors all the time with the right equipment. Maybe he'd do that one day. Sometimes he doesn't even go home to the room he rents in a multi-occupancy house of bed-sits, or as they're known in estate agent speak, studio flats, preferring just to sleep out on the beach, and bathe in the sea the next morning to wake himself up.

He's now a virtuoso at ricocheting pebbles on the shingle, and he's also built up a considerable knowledge of world affairs through the skilful gleaning of discarded newspapers. He's following the war in Bosnia, depressed that so many people could die just for being, ethnically, the wrong kind of neighbour. He reads about Burnley Football Club too – it's his way of keeping in touch with his roots. Sometimes he misses the guys from his band; they didn't just drink together and do music together, they used to kick a football around pretty neatly too. He has the time, in this new job, to practise his skills; he can kick an empty can over his head and heel it back over again, sometimes three or four times without dropping it.

Recently he's taken to bringing his djembe, his drum, to work with him. He bought it at Wah-Wah and it has become a major obsession. It's an import from West Africa and, Harry likes to think, contains an African soul. It's made from the wood of a lenke tree and a taut goatskin, tuned by a complex of knotted ropes. Joe told him that djembe meant 'gather in peace' – he likes that. Joe knows about those kinds of things, and sometimes he brings his flute along, and they improvise together. He stores the djembe in his attendant's cave when he's busy, but when he has the time, he sits in the sun pounding out African rhythms, sometimes even drumming for peace in Bosnia, or for peace in the pit of his stomach. This is when he's happiest, but that doesn't mean that he's happy.

Harry thinks of himself as an average guy. He knows he's good looking enough to play in a band, but he isn't someone you'd spot in a crowd – he's tall, sinewy in an athletic way, with enough muscle tone to look good without his shirt and, for a white man, he can tan an exceptionally deep brown. He likes his body enough, but he's not a flippant person. He just wants to feel free, so he wears his hair long and dread-locked. He likes a laugh with the lads, the usual innocent anal blokish stuff mostly, but he also gets a kick out of wackier habits, like appearing in other people's holiday snaps.

He's been doing this since he played a starring role sticking out his tongue behind a happy Italian family posing for a photo, on the promenade at Blackpool, when he was nine. Since then, he fancies, his image has adorned photograph albums from Tokyo to Rio. It's his form of graffiti, and his job gives him numerous opportunities to pursue this innocently inane pastime. For a relatively introverted and shy type, his informal career as an impromptu photographic model has led him to extremes of exhibitionism – from gurning to

16

shirtless muscle-pumping and, on one occasion, a nearly perfect cartwheel. Amateur photographers are always much too intent on getting a picture of their beloved, standing squinting into the sun, ever to notice Harry's anarchic behaviour in the background. He's sure that, when the photographs are developed and shown around, he will have made them unique – performance art on a truly international scale.

And so it is today. Dressed down for summer, brown-chested in green surfer shorts and scruffy
trainers, his Rastafarian locks bundled up under an unseasonably woolly hat, he has already made his appearance in a Taiwanese home video, and now he's spotted a young couple, quietly posing for each other, in front of the pier. She has thick black hair pulled back taut into a pig-tail, intense black eyes, and very white teeth. She's wearing bright blue shorts, cut to mid-thigh, and a skinny yellow t-shirt. Her small bra-less breasts aren't so much flaunted as unconcealed – clearly displayed through the thin cotton.

The man, or rather the boy, has dark cropped hair. He too wears a body-hugging yellow t-shirt and blue shorts that reveal most of his thin hairless legs. A Walt Disney couple, Harry thinks. Y-chromosomes and a few bits apart, they look like identical twins. It's the boy-man's turn to pose, this time with his back to the sea, in front of a line of blue and white striped deckchairs. As the young woman changes lenses on her expensive camera, Harry takes up his position, he's ready to spring into a much-practised handstand, in anticipation of the opening shutter. He loves this moment of precision timing: she raises the camera, caresses the long zoom lens and calls out 'OK!' The boy grins, Harry springs into action as the zoom lens purrs and the shutter clicks. He walks away smiling but the girl calls out to him.

'Perfect Mister! You good acrobat.'

The background artist has just gone centre stage.

'My name is Kanti Subhadi,' she says, with quaint formality, offering him her hand. 'And this is my brother Diep. I like taking photographs of typical English persons.'

'I thought you were taking your brother,' Harry replies weakly. He feels like Kanti Subhadi has caught his soul with one click of her camera.

'You English don't like modelling for me, so I pretend to take something else. I don't need pictures of Diep – I see him all the time.'

Diep looks shyly at his feet, but says nothing – happy to live in his sister's aura.

'We're busy this week. Tomorrow morning I'm photographing the naked swimmers at your nudist beach, and this time I have asked for volunteers.'

'Wow!' Harry is silenced, embarrassed that he was about to say something very English like, 'Are you here on holiday?'

'I tried doing it without asking, but naked people can get embarrassed too,' she laughs. 'This time I'm doing it properly, like a professional.'

A flustered woman with two small children and an elderly mother come up and cut across their conversation, asking Harry about deckchair prices. Harry tries to hide his irritation, and points to the notice behind him. It shows all the prices, by the hour or for a day. As he reads the information out to them, he hears the camera shutter again.

'Maile kehi galti gareko chaina,' Kanti says, her voice intense in her native tongue. Diep nods – he too looks suddenly solemn. They take their opportunity to go. Hunting for more victims, Harry thinks, trying to decide whether he felt violated or flattered by Kanti's intrusive camera.

Chapter Three

It's that song again. Alan hears it before he sees Joe playing the flute, sitting on his haunches as if he could pounce at any moment. He's improvising on that melody again, in his usual place between Wah-Wah's guitar shop and The Golden Orb pub, and across the road from Anything Goes, a black windowed sex shop. Alan hesitates, he's a careful man, something he's always regretted. Should he give more money? Once was a friendly gesture but doing it again, that would be patronising, too intimate somehow. No, it's best left. Then he changes his mind. He can't walk by and simply lose himself in the crowd. The music, even if he's never really liked the flute, affects him. It's not exactly jazz, or blues, his personal taste, but today it hits the same spot, cutting through the anonymous civility of the street. He has already walked past, but he goes back and drops a pound into Joe's woolly hat, it makes a satisfying clink as it joins the other coins, coppers mostly, so Joe looks up. Alan grins, embarrassed. That's better, he needed that eye contact. Joe's tune continues without a pause.

A middle-aged woman comes out of the sex shop with a plain black carrier bag. She's homely and wholesome, with hair tied up untidily under a comb and wearing a cardigan, in spite of the heat. She stops to listen for a moment, and smiles at Joe, dropping him a few coins before making her way to The Golden Orb, the locals' local. Before she can get there, an athletic and unquestionably handsome young man, in white running gear, comes up to her, holding an old-fashioned Polaroid 600SE camera, and immediately, without asking, takes her photograph. She shrugs and laughs when he gives her the print-out.

'No thanks,' Rosemary Seymour tells him. As co-proprietor of The Golden Orb, she's used to refusing offers.

'Keep it anyway,' Nico Mellas says, in a distinctive American accent, giving her his business card. 'A gift from the Public Service Photographer.' He nods to Joe and tosses a pound coin into his hat. Joe carries on playing. His eyes, forgetting to blink, follow Nico who hesitates for a moment, before running off towards the seafront.

Alan is home, playing his saxophone, his favourite activity. He loves his second-hand Japanese 'horn', an immaculate *Yamaha YTS-*

61, the best he can afford. It looks decidedly cool in the white and hi-tech flat he shares with Rachel. In crisp red shirt and loose white cotton trousers, he plays his own laid-back jazz in the living area of the open-plan apartment. It's Saturday morning, hot and bright outside, so the windows onto the balcony are open, and the sea view looks like a projected feature film. Alan hangs loose, he likes to feel his body when he's making music. Tapping a bare foot on the laminated wooden floor, he lets his shoulders drop and his spine sag, but his diaphragm is tight, supporting his breath, freeing his soul to roam with the saxophone, or so he likes to think. Rachel's making coffee with their shiny espresso machine – the star gadget in their chrome and gunmetal kitchen area – and she doesn't care that she's making noise over the music.

Rachel Seymour has planned to look perfect in her summer designer gear: she usually succeeds. Crisp cotton is her thing too, she knows how to reveal her body by covering it up. Just enough cleavage – tailored around the bust, of course, and tucked tight at the waist to celebrate her figure. She knows she looks good, and that's the way she'll keep it. Long dark hair, cut to look uncut; evenly tanned skin, easily maintained with her olive complexion, contrasts dramatically with her violet eyes and naturally lustrous lips, highlighted by obsessively-applied bright red lipstick.

She's watching Alan lasciviously but it's not the music that's turning her on. The coffee-making ceremony hisses over the saxophone's song. It irritates him. She likes that. For Rachel Seymour, everything must be perfect, and that only happens when she controls her environment. Today she wants mid-morning sex with a jazzman; Alan isn't the only one living in his own imaginary feature film. For the moment, he's in another world, the mythical sweaty smoke–filled bar of male dreams, where sex is always lurking, but enjoyed all the more after prolonged anticipation. She'll allow him his moment. She'll make the coffee the seduction point – espressos perfectly poured into perfect coffee cups, very retro: Beat Poet glass.

She comes over to the giant, swallow-you-whole sofa and places the cups on the mirrored-metal coffee table. His time is up. She comes up behind him, undoes a couple of his shirt buttons and, slowly and lingeringly, puts her hand inside to feel his warmth. He smiles, it's detectable, even with that saxophone bit in his mouth, but he carries on. She turns the gesture into a pectoral massage then makes to move further down. The game is up, his tongue leaves the reed, he wipes saliva from the mouthpiece and lets the saxophone drop. It hangs round his neck on its strap, like a polished albatross, while he blinks and rubs his slightly swollen lower lip. Naturally she's got her way.

'Oh don't stop. I was beginning to enjoy it.'

Her mockery is eroticised by her south London, or, maybe, Brighton accent. She knows how to make her short vowels and absent consonants sound dirty. She's full of pleasure at a job well done. Alan laughs. His voice is pure Middle-England: 'Do you want me or are you just trying to shut me up?'

Rachel grins purposefully. 'Oh, I know just how to shut you up!'

He unfastens the sax, but she's already got hold of its strap, his leash, and uses it to draw him to the sofa, to pull him down for her caffeine seduction, which begins with a kiss but is almost immediately interrupted by the chic chimes of the doorbell

'Shit!' they cuss simultaneously.

Alan does up one of his shirt buttons; well, he's not quite as free as he thinks, and goes to the door where he meets Joe's eagerly charming grin and, behind him, looking shy and sullen, Vickie. Joe looks cool, Alan thinks, in his filthy crumpled jeans, dirty white t-shirt and ragged trainers. His face is his fortune, as his mother always said, even if his father hadn't wanted to see it. 'You'll get away with murder with that face of yours,' she used to say, laughing at him when she'd meant to be angry. Vickie has new blue highlights in her dreadlocks; she's done them herself, but they've turned out all wrong. They're much too blue, like poster paint daubed on a black and white photograph. She's very unhappy to be here, and it shows.

Joe speaks enthusiastically in his difficult to define accent – subtle Caribbean, with layers of estuary and middle-class English. 'Hi! I'm sorry to disturb you but my girlfriend really needs to borrow a towel.'

Alan is incredulous. 'What?' He looks to Rachel for encouragement, but doesn't get it. She distances herself in the kitchen and Vickie recoils in embarrassment.

'Look, I know it's a bit of a cheek but, really, she needs to have a shower. There's a public one up by the pier. We're sleeping rough and she's got a job interview to go to. We'll bring it back, honestly.'

Alan gives Rachel a desperate look, but she turns away – he knows that look: it's your problem, sort it out.

'Look, you'd better come in,' Alan whimpers pathetically. Joe is delighted, but the surly Vickie cannot believe his cheek – she's already resenting the way she's being presented as a problem.

'Great. Thanks. Wow! You've got a great place! Two people could have a lot of fun in here!'

'Given a chance,' Rachel mutters murderously to the espresso machine.

Alan ignores her imagined look, he's panicking.   'Thanks.'

'No, really. It's so beautiful, you know.' Joe goes straight into the living area, and sees the saxophone.

'Hey, is that yours? Do you play?'

'Yeah. A little.' Alan's weariness is soon seduced by Joe's enthusiasm.

'What sort of stuff?'

'A bit of jazz, you know, and some blues.'

'Great! Who do you like?'

'Oh, Coltrane, the early stuff mostly – Charlie Parker...'

Vickie just stands there, emitting the occasional not-so-involuntary sigh. She has totally frozen, and now believes that you really can die of embarrassment. Rachel puts things away noisily in the kitchen. When the music talk looks like developing ('Yeah! It's a great instrument...what make is it?') she snaps and interrupts, trying to hide the ice in her tone.

'Well, before we all get too carried away, it was a towel you wanted, right?'

Alan is flustered. 'I'll get one, hang on a minute,' and he goes off to the bathroom. Joe turns his attention to Rachel, who now has to play host for a few resented seconds. She flexes her face muscles, giving an insincere impression of a smile, and allows Joe's monologue to continue.

'Sorry, I got carried away.' He's looking around like an estate agent. 'You're being very kind and it's such a great place. Hey! Look at that picture!'

He's looking at a framed photograph on the wall. It's a Brighton seascape; the ruins of the West Pier at sunset, scarlet sky behind the darkened silhouette. 'Brighton is such a great place. We love it here, don't we Vickie?' he says, trying unsuccessfully to engage Vickie in the conversation, but immediately turning back to Rachel. 'Did you take it?'

'Yes. It's good isn't it!'

'You've got the eye!' he enthuses, beaming his focus like a marksman, straight between her eyes.

Rachel smiles – she's almost charmed, but not quite.

'Thanks.'

'You can tell by this flat. I mean this is real design, you know what I mean. What do you think, Vickie?'

'S'pose,' says Vickie. She camouflages her middle-class voice by swallowing her consonants. 'Must've cost you.'

'Well, anyway…' Rachel is giving them go away body language, when Alan returns with a thick pile bath towel, pure white. Rachel flinches when she sees what he's found, but retains her neutral mask.

'Here you are - this should do.'

'Hey, thanks. Look, we're really grateful. Aren't we Vickie?'

Vickie gets ready to go, and tries to warm up her monotone. 'Yeah. Thanks a lot, it's really good of you.'

Alan stumbles on out of politeness, his voice speaking without him. 'Would you like some coffee?'

Rachel can't believe that he's just said that. Vickie looks unsure, but Joe snaps at the offer.

'That would be great, thanks.'

'Rachel's just made some, haven't you, Rachel?'

His question is more of a plea than a question. Silently he's screaming: 'Don't-make-a-scene.'

Rachel obliges and sorts out the coffee, concealing a smile; she would hate Alan to know that she's enjoying this. There's an awkward moment, all four analysing the scene, then Joe and Vickie sit at the Perspex dining table. Alan hovers twitchily, Vickie gazes around while Joe fluently pursues his role as polite principal guest.

'This is so good of you, really. You're real Brighton people, aren't you?'

Alan laughs. 'Are we?'

'Oh yeah. You're very liberal – unprejudiced. We really appreciate it. You don't know us and us being homeless and all that.'

'No. It's fine. You're welcome.'

Rachel brings over the coffees and pointedly remains standing. This is to be a quick drink. Joe takes his cup as if it's the Holy Grail. 'Thanks. Great! You were bound to do great coffee. I knew it!' Now he's laughing gently at them. 'You're both pretty clued up, aren't you?'

Rachel laughs readily and spontaneously – she likes to be appreciated, but doesn't want it to show. She's identified her own style, worked at it and wants it to be admired. Alan may be won over, but Rachel's still playing her game.

Alan fishes for more compliments. 'Clued up? I dunno. Are we?'

'Well, this place must have cost you a fortune. Are you some kind of professional musician or something then?'

'No. This isn't my place, it's Rachel's. I'm just staying here.'

'Well, it's brilliant, man.'

Rachel enters on cue. 'Anyone would think that, if they were living on the street.' She doesn't mean to be unkind, she's just saying it as she sees it.

Joe goes quiet, his face as neutral as it can ever be with those smiling lips. 'Yeah, suppose.' He's thinking this one over, accepting her challenge. 'I like it, yeah, but possessions...' he's laughing again, '...they tie you down. Don't you think?'

Alan is about to agree but Rachel wades in. 'They don't have to. Nothing has to tie you down. If you're good at what you do, and you like it and, even better, if you get a load of money for it – then that's just fine by me.' She believes this, but tries to make it sound light.

'Right! I like that.' Joe has brightened up again. 'What do you do?'

'We're in I.T.' says Alan. 'Computer graphics, that sort of thing.'

'I can see you both doing that. Cool people, cool jobs, you know – do you work together?'

Rachel picks up the cups as she speaks. She's dismissing them. 'Yes, but you'll have to excuse us – we've got a lot on today.'

They get up, Vickie gathers up the towel and hugs it to her chest. She sees Rachel flinch again, and now feels even dirtier. Joe jumps to his feet, spontaneously in tune with the etiquette. 'Yeah, we should be off but thanks again for the towel.'

Vickie echoes his thanks, her eyes already escaping from the room. 'Yeah, thanks again.'

'Well, I hope it brings you luck. For your interview, I mean.'

Rachel is gracious now that they're going, and Alan gives a limp wave as she closes the door on Joe's smiling face.

'Well, we'll never see that again!' she laughs, turning round to her man.

'The towel?'

'Yes.'

'It doesn't matter.'

'I know.'

Alan joins her solicitously as she leans against the door. He snuggles up, gently pushing her against the wood, hoping that she will defrost. 'It really doesn't matter you know,' he says, tenderly, apologetically.

Rachel loosens up at his touch. 'Yes, I know, you don't need to tell me. I was being a bitch.'

Kissing her on the neck, he whispers in her ear, 'You've always said easy come...'

She laughs lasciviously. 'Yes, I know...easy go. Yeah, what the hell! Anyway, we've got unfinished business.' She's her old self again and she's already opened his shirt.

Chapter Four

He's been early morning running on the beach, and to bring down his heart-rate, Nico Mellas practises his Tai chi form extra slowly, balletic, beautiful, but with a hint of martial intent, on the water's edge, facing the pink stained sea in the morning's first light. Nico is an athlete, with an addict's need for the chemical cocktail you only get from physical exertion. He's trained his body since childhood, and it has grown strong and supple in the natural way of all young mammals preparing for adulthood, pushing the boundaries, and delighting in his own physical potential.

On the eve of his thirtieth birthday, he's new to this town, he's never liked staying anywhere for long, but standing here with the tide bathing his feet, he decides to like Brighton. In a new spurt of energy he goes for a swim; there's no one around, so he skinny-dips, swimming at speed out to sea, then lingering in a lazy backstroke, recharging his lungs for the return race, easier now that he's carried along by the incoming tide. Approaching the shore, he sees he's no longer alone but he doesn't care, because he's not the only one who's naked.

Maybe thirty people have gathered there on the shingle, not far from Nico's clothes. Among what he takes to be an all-male gathering, there's near uniformity of age and shape – all the men are middle-aged or older and of ample girth. The men who are not already naked are stripping awkwardly in their hurry to join the others.

'You all look very fine,' a female voice shouts. 'You are very kind to let me have your portraits. I am honoured much by this.'

Kanti Subhadi and her brother Diep, both still very much clothed in their primary coloured t-shirts and shorts, set up the shot, Diep positioning the tripod, and Kanti training her lenses on the willingly proffered nudity. There are a few furtive sidelong looks between the men but, mostly, they're concentrating on pulling their stomachs in, and flexing whatever musculature they can muster for the camera.

'That's great,' Kanti shouts, delighted to have got the whole group's eyes focused in the same direction. Everyone notices Nico, the classic tall dark stranger, seaweed clinging to his hair, lightly panting from the exertion, emerging shamelessly naked from the sea like a Pygmalion statue, another Greek masterpiece bursting into life. He raises a hand in a laid back 'hi guys' kind of greeting, but turns away to slip into his running gear when he realises Kanti is female. She doesn't make it obvious, he thinks, unembarrassed. He's more concerned about the terrible clothes she's wearing. Definitely some work to do there, but he doesn't hang around, leaving the photoshoot with only a couple of amused backward glances. Kanti Subhadi may have blushed. Diep doesn't notice any of this, he's still adjusting the tripod. Very strange, Nico decides as his jog turns into a sprint along the promenade. Brighton is a surprising place. Yes, he'll like it here.

Early the next morning on the nudist beach, there are only two swimmers in the sea, their heads bobbing in the choppy luminous water. It's a warm enough day for an English summer, but a change of wind direction, with just a hint of chill has reminded the regulars that this is still the North of Northern Europe, and summer is England's most untrustworthy season. The beach is deserted, well nearly; Nico has shed his clothes again, and is running over the pebbles, heading for a lonely seawater bath, to wash away his birthday hangover after a drunken night, followed by a recuperative sleep on the beach. The celebration had been accidental, just a few new acquaintances he'd met in a bar when he'd gone there alone wanting a short birthday moment, looking back at his life over a drink. The hangover was an accident too – he must kick the habit of smiling at strangers. He vowed, yet again, to avoid friendly advances from guys mellowed by drink.

He feels sick, maybe he has already vomited, he can't remember. There's no gory evidence, but sea gulls are flocking around the spot where he slept, boisterously competing for breakfast – nothing too repulsive for their insatiable appetites. They move on, shrieking in anticipation, but find nothing of interest among some discarded clothing, placed neatly in two piles on the shingle. Soon they fly away, taking their hunger out to sea. Their discordance is replaced by sweeter sounds coming from further along the beach. Lyrical music from a flute, with a softly persistent drum accompaniment, sounds like a pagan hymn to the rising sun. Joe and Harry are back together, serenading the dawn, the sea, the horizon and the Universe beyond. It softens Nico's gloom and he dives from a breakwater into the sea.

He hadn't chosen to sleep on a nudist beach, in fact he still doesn't know that it is one. It's screened from general view by heaped up shingle that forms a modesty screen, saving the blushes of strollers on the promenade, but provoking curiosity from anyone who wants to catch a sneaky preview of Brighton's most uninhibited location. Apart from the beach's liberal credentials, this is like any other English seaside on a fine summer morning, large flint stone shingle giving way to smaller pebbles, before leading down to dark, clay-like sand and the sea. Even so early in the morning, the temperature's now rising to Grecian proportions, continuing this English summer's radical change of character.

The two swimmers are unremarkable enough, progressing backwards and forwards in a relentless if not exhausting breast-stroke. There's no one around to take any interest in their mundane daily habit, the traditional early morning swim. Nico has already made it out into the depths and they pay him no attention. Eventually, instinctively perhaps because no words are exchanged, the two swimmers emerge simultaneously from the bad-tempered waves and clamber over the pebbles towards the twin piles of clothes at the base of the shingle wall. They are men of mature years, in their fifties, or sixties. One fat and one lean, like a music hall act, a pair of comedians, perhaps, both red from the cold water, seaweed bespattered, and both as naked as on those two tearful days, a long time ago, when their mothers welcomed them into the world.

'That's better,' says Lionel Atkins, the plumper of the two, picking up his towel and drying himself vigorously, from his neatly clipped grey hair downwards, past the well-groomed moustache, to the tightly stretched tanned flesh on his grisly-haired beach ball of a body. His voice has the honey-tones of an old-fashioned repertory actor; some of his detractors, if he has any, might wonder if he's entirely genuine. Lionel copes with being a widower, and enjoys being, mostly, retired, but he doesn't talk about either subject. 'It was nippy today in there, but it does you the power of good.'

'Yeah, I suppose so,' says the other, in his lightly pronounced East London accent. John Smith is slim, wirily sinewy; his head's completely shaved, and that adds to his bad-tempered expression. His wrinkled nut-brown skin has begun to sag where it had once been tight, little pyramid breasts replace his once firm pectorals and his stomach protrudes, a slight swelling rather than a gut, in recognition of a lifetime of moderate beer drinking. He runs his own business in town, Smith's Emporium, dealing in Asian fabrics, incense and a body piercing service, a growing market in Brighton's alternative subculture. It pays well enough, and allows him to pursue his passion for travelling regularly to India. 'Give me Kerala, man. I'll never get used to this bloody country. It's hot enough out here, but the sea's a fucking misery.'

'Well you see, John, for all your Buddhist claptrap or whatever it is you do, you've still got to learn to focus your mind.'

'Well thanks, mate! When I'm in need of a guru I'll give you a call.' John is smirking, both he and Lionel know that he likes to complain.

'No, I'm not trying to be clever, old thing, it's just that you need to think England, E.N.G.L.A.N.D., when you're submerged in the old briny. Remember your Shakespeare, this sceptred isle set in a silver sea. Forget those palm trees and golden sands, and then it won't come as such a shock when you brave it into our good old silver sea.'

'Yeah, right. Thanks Buddha. Still makes your knob shrink though.'

'True. Not that we need bother about genital vanity at our age.'

'Speak for yourself, granddad.' They laugh, maybe too heartily, and get on with some discreet manly towelling. Using the same code that applies between men when standing at urinals, or in the showers after a rugby match, they focus on scrupulously drying their armpits and genitals while looking abstractedly into space, without giving even a hint that they can see each other. They met at an anti-war march in London. John, the old hippie, a veteran of anti-Vietnam demonstrations, was a serial protester, but Lionel had only discovered radical politics after the death of his wife, Alice. She'd believed in leaving politics to the politicians, and had encouraged Lionel to hide with her among the silent majority. After her death three years ago, Lionel finally stood up to be counted and marched against Britain's involvement in the 1991 invasion of Iraq.

Freed from her disapproval, Lionel has also discovered a taste for public nudity. He's had enough of discretion and inhibitions. Poor Alice, he thinks, if only she could have let the mask slip once in a while. He shares his enthusiasm for nudity with his new friend John, who'd thrown away most of his inhibitions with his first inhalation of marijuana, in the summer of 1967.

'So you didn't want to be in the exhibition then?' Lionel continues, as if there hasn't been a break in their conversation. They're sitting on their towels, dusting sand, more like clay, from between their toes.

'No I bloody well didn't.' John likes to sound vehement about things, and to imply opinions that he doesn't hold. Lionel ignores his protestations. It's been five months since they started this swimming regime, long enough for two naked men to know each other very well. At first, in early spring, it had been enough just to endure the cold. They don't acknowledge that they're the only two people in the group. They never speak to anyone else, and guard their territory with fierce looks if anyone tries to make base anywhere near them. Far from being a gentlemen's club, they are more like an old married couple.

'It was quite a sight, the photoshoot.'

'I wasn't interested. Seen enough of you lot on here without wanting to be preserved bollock naked with you for posterity.'

'You can leave my posterity out of this, if you don't mind.' Lionel's playing to his invisible audience but John ignores the joke with a sniff. 'She was quite a looker that photographer. Didn't bat an eyelid about us oldies stripping off. We were quite a sight. Good on her, I thought. I don't know if they go naked much out East. Do they? You'd know all about these things, I suppose.'

'Pleased I wasn't there.' John's making a small wall with the shingle stones; there's no sand for sandcastles, and, anyway, he's really just doodling with stones. 'I don't need reminding that my body's falling apart.'

'Quite a few people made a quick escape – they didn't want to be recognised.'

'No surprise that the pervs were camera-shy,' he says, putting a new line of stones onto his wall. 'They don't think beyond sex, I guess.'

'Quite,' Lionel agrees evacuating seawater from his ears with his little finger. 'Sex is wasted on them.'

'We're just thoughts in the mind of God, they say,' John continues, watching Nico's athletic form heading smoothly towards the horizon. 'But I don't want to preach – that's your department,

Lionel.'

'You're a queer chap, John, but your mystic crap's always entertaining. It clears my head like a stiff G and T.'

'Nothing stiff about me these days, sadly.'

They're enjoying the banter, both are fluent in keeping it light – they know how to deflect when things get too personal.

'Oh we're not doing that badly,' Lionel says. 'This routine keeps us pretty trim.'

'Just as well if your bollocks are going to end up in the National Portrait Gallery,' John says, looking down at his own body and deciding that it could look a whole lot worse. He demolishes his wall and grins. 'That photographer has made a star of you mate. Rather you than me, that's all.'

'I was just doing my bit for the cause,' Lionel laughs. 'Anyway, they'll stick a few fig-leaves over our rude bits if they ever put the pictures in the papers.'

They get into their clothes and, unintentionally making a statement about public nudity, they put on their socks and vests before packing their genitals away in their white y-fronts: Lionel's freshly laundered, John's off-white and frayed round the legs. Lionel has the easier job, slipping into his things, a checked shirt, brown and beige, brown cavalry twill trousers, a dark blue regimental blazer and black brogue shoes. He's knotting his military tie while John's still unravelling a long sheet of diaphanous turquoise material.

'Bloody thing,' he cusses, winding it round his torso. Eventually they're ready – a typical English gentleman and a Technicolor monk, fully clothed in his ankle-length robe, black socks and heavy-duty brown plastic sandals.

'Same time tomorrow, John?'

'Yeah, I reckon so.'

'I'll be off then. Got to get the bus.'

'Back to the shop time for me.'

At Smith's Emporium, Conrad Adamcik, John's young, quietly-spoken Czech cleaner and part-time assistant, has been clambering around in the shop window in his pink stockinged feet, dusting the Buddhist and Hindu paraphernalia with Zen-like concentration. He's now dressing Molly, the androgynous mannequin, who gets a change of sari once a week.

'Morning,' John says, making sure that Molly's folds are straight. 'How are you today, mate?'

'Fine, Mr Smith. I have some few drinks last night but I'm OK.'

'You done the piercing parlour? I've got a couple of nipples later.'

He knows he doesn't have to ask, Conrad is an excellent worker. He's a good looking lad too, striking in fact, with his ripped distressed jeans, the pink t-shirt with 'Wild' inscribed in gothic letters across the chest, short bleached hair and interesting piercings. John thinks he's good for business, with his mix of underworld danger and gentlemanly politeness.

'Yes, all is done, Mr Smith. I'll be off to the Orb now – is that good with you? I will see you later, please. I'd like to help with the nipples, if I can.'

Conrad also cleans the pub, The Golden Orb, as well as the sex shop, Anything Goes, across the road. He makes a good enough living here, supplemented by his work as a life model for members of the local photographic club, who find some of his piercings particularly photogenic. He opted to leave Prague when his parents found a book of nude male photographs under his bed and, at an emergency family meeting, gave him an ultimatum to clean up his act or go. He left just as his country over-threw its Soviet rulers. If the world was changing, The Velvet Revolution hadn't offered him much hope of liberation, so he'd 'disappeared' to England and now he's become John's unofficial apprentice, often doing simple ear piercings and hoping, one day, to graduate to nipples and beyond.

Back at the beach, the gulls have returned to investigate as Nico emerges from the waves, hangover-free.

Chapter Five

Those fingers, so dextrous on the saxophone, are equally nimble on the computer keyboard. Alan sits at his desk, fingers darting, mind elsewhere, with the same hypnotised computer stare as all the other bright young men in the open-plan office. This is Nirvana, the commercial version of Rachel Seymour's apartment, an ideas factory, generating ideas and images for middling-sized companies, mainly brochures and magazine adverts, using the latest computer technology. Nirvana has upgraded to the brave new digital world, where product names flaunt their modernity with number codes – a dozen new Power Macintosh 6100 computers and Apple AudioVision 14 display monitors, with HDI-45 video connectors, Rachel's latest passion. Their installation, one for each desk, earlier this year, has been the most exciting day of her life – so far.

These are thrilling times for the computer industry, and Rachel is programmed to move with the times. She's planning Nirvana's next move into the growing market for company websites, made possible by the rapid development of the World Wide Web. The office, for Rachel, is the equivalent of a space rocket, launched to find new life in space. It's only a short walk from her flat, it too has a sea view, and shares her design obsession for clean colour contrasts and hi-tech gadgets. Like the flat, it's decorated white, with white plastic desks and plastic chairs in primary colours, yellow and blue, each employee contained behind see-through curved Perspex screens.

Rachel is removed, the only female, a goddess apart, in a cube, also Perspex, at one end of the room. Alan says it's like being a goldfish. Rachel hates the remark – she gives her staff a lot, she thinks, it's a good working environment, with a lot of freedom, so it's only fair that these young men allow her to make them part of her décor. She expects loyalty in return, especially from Alan. It's not her usual way, mixing business with sex; it complicates things and she likes efficient filing, straight lines and, yes, being in charge. Her pool of exclusively young male talent is at work, twelve disciples spinning dreams for all comers. The dress code is casual, and today it varies from a torn t-shirt, faded shorts and flip-flop combination, to a crumpled linen suit with sandals.

Talking is discouraged, usually restricted to whoever is on the other end of a line, communicating through headphone-microphone headsets. There is the occasional burst of laughter, or a frenzied 'Look at this. It's amazing!' – so work doesn't always dominate a day at the office, and, anyway, there's a relaxation area with drink machines – coffee or chilled water. No tea because Rachel never drinks tea, and forgot that other people might like it. Her bright young men are designing marketing images for sweat shop manufacturers, local authorities and estate agents. They initiate the ideas and designs for clients in partnership with Rachel's business partner, a nearby photographic studio. She likes to keep her team separate from the photographers. One day though, she hopes, she will grow big enough to combine both sides of the business, and achieve the financial freedom to develop her own photography.

Anything, Rachel believes, can be marketed; nothing's too serious, too boring or even too unethical – even pornography. She admits that she went too far once, when an escort agency turned nasty, claiming that she had made them look like a brothel. She hadn't foreseen the problem, but she's learnt her lesson. Now she likes her clients to be rich-and-boring-trying-to-seem-trendy types, and there are plenty of them around. These men, they are nearly always men, are safe, they go with her ideas and pay up on time. Their eyes roam, she knows they fantasise about her body too, but that's alright, all she has to do is wear the right skirt and sit the right way. She's prepared to do just enough to clinch a deal.

She only employs men. She tried out a couple of nerdy women early on, but there was something wrong with the chemistry when her style of leadership came up against female competition. She likes women, it isn't that, she just prefers her workers to be young male geeks, and they don't have to be good-looking either, geeks seldom are. As long as they shower regularly, don't mind a bit of female advice over erupting skin conditions and display a genuinely obsessive love for all things cyber, she's happy to supply them with the computer technology of their dreams.

Her company is called Nirvana because of her immediate and lasting attraction to Kurt Cobain, the decidedly geeky, whimsically beautiful, and recently dead lead singer of the rock band, Nirvana, who personified her fantasies about grungey males. One day, the hidden child in her still dreams she will employ her very own Kurt Cobain. If she's being really honest, she admits, she had wanted to make melancholy Kurt happy, make him smile, by cooking him her speciality Spanish paella and, afterwards, when she'd patted that thin little stomach, now slightly fuller, she might have saved him for the world. She's confused by his suicide, but also that she could have liked him so much, and yet found nothing in his music. Depressing, she thinks, whenever she hears Nirvana's hit song *About A Girl* – somehow Kurt never sang about her. None of her grungey computer boys would guess that she has these thoughts. To them she's just the boss and, pretty as she is, you don't mess with her.

Alan's working on a campaign for a local garden centre but he's struggling. It's a problem getting the right tone for the spring bulb section – he wants to give it a druggy psychedelic quality with *Magical Mystery Tour* rainbows, but the client wants something altogether tamer.

'I don't mind you stretching your imagination Alan, love,' Rachel had said, after taking an annoying phone call from the client, 'but I'll fucking kill you if you lose us the contract.'

They hadn't spoken much after that, and the afternoon has dragged on in sullen silence, until a brief and stolen moment when one of his work colleagues, long skinny Terry, with his pale and spotty bedroom-study complexion, shows him a magazine review of a computer game that has just got his juices flowing. It isn't just the excitement of escaping from a dungeon, Terry tells him, or just the various challenging ways you have to struggle against the powers of darkness, the real thrill is in the graphics – it's like you're really there. 'Awesome,' they both agree. Alan plays computer games like all the others, but, today, he needs the one thing that always turns him on, music. It always lifts his mood when Rachel gets him down, so he digs out his personal music system, his latest passion, the *Sony D-335 Discman* – Rachel allows personal stereos.

He needs a jazz gem to make his day. There's a rich choice of CDs in his bag: Alan is precise in his tastes. A lot of the pleasure is deciding which track to choose. He always carries a small library of CDs, some new acquisitions, others old favourites. He makes lists – it's a primary male characteristic. This morning it's a list of preferences, with a second list correlating with the first one, reordering it to fit in with his selection criteria; tenor saxophone, of course, John Coltrane, probably, romantic, today, yes, an old favourite, definitely – he's looking for comfort, a little-known live performance of a familiar piece and, if possible, with the adrenalin flow of new discovery.

There it is, a decision: his beloved John Coltrane, the tenor saxophonist supreme, in a recording of his most famous song, *Naima*, played at a concert somewhere in the South of France in 1965. That moody giant's saxophone is singing a love song to his first wife, Naima. Romantic, yes, melancholy, that too, but also a slowly developing cry from the heart. Pain mixed with sadness, released in tranquillity. For Alan, it gets no better than this. He has often wondered about this Naima, the first Mrs Coltrane. She'd inspired one of jazz's most beguiling love songs, and had helped the great man off his addictions. She'd actually saved his life, ensuring a magnificent legacy for all future jazz fans, and she'd inspired the music that Alan rates above all others. What happened to the love that whispers so delicately at the end of this long improvisation, he wonders. Naima, his love, had come home one day to be told by her husband that he needed to make a change. No explanations, he just left with his clothes and his horn. Whatever that music meant to Coltrane, for Alan it speaks of freedom

The phone rings. He answers it reluctantly, dragged back from a better place. He's looking blank, gazing through the computer screen, giving the caller one percent of his concentration. 'Yeah, yeah. Ok, I'll get the boss.' He spins round on his shiny yellow chair. 'It's for you,' he mimes, his body language robotic, his brain on standby. He can't bring himself to meet her stare. Rachel comes over and takes the phone with eyes focused on imagined profit sheets, her expression neutral and professional, her newly applied perfume filling the cubicle. He remembers it from that night in a club when their friendship had taken an extra step. Her tight brown thighs are swaggering though – even when she's working, her body is up for a dance. 'Thanks.' She walks out of range with the cordless phone to her ear, but Alan feels no pain; not even when her laugh crackles through the room. 'Allo love.' She is purring with pleasure; he gazes back at his monitor, his *AudioVision 14*. His screensaver reads: Don't give up the day job.

'Hey, look at this then,' comes Terry's enthusiastic call, as he throws the games magazine over the cubicle wall. 'They've given *Doom II* five stars, calling it a new era for survival horror. Amazing!'

'Yeah, amazing,' Alan replies without reading it.

Chapter Six

It's Sunday morning on the beach, and the so-called heatwave has lifted the nation's mood. England might be getting acclimatised to Mediterranean temperatures. The simmering and disgruntled silent majority has stopped listening to battling politicians, there are no rail strikes scheduled and, in the way of tabloid news, even Bosnia has left the headlines. England is taking an involuntary summer holiday, becoming an out-of-doors place, with its conscience on hold. Everyone, or nearly everyone, who isn't watching cricket on television, or drinking lager outside the pub, is, or so it seems, lying on Brighton's beach, now a battlefield itself with fallen weekend sunbathers, whose skins are already blushing their way towards red. Harry Pollard is unimpressed; he's seen too much blistering Anglo-Saxon flesh.

It's his day off, but he's still gone to the beach. When home is a small single room, littered with scribbled notes for songs that he can never finish, it's more fun hanging out by the sea. He's proud of the handstand that he'd just held in position for over a minute, in the background to another holiday snap. This time an oblivious German man was taking his time placing an impatient wife and three fractious children in front of the pier, too intent on perfection to notice Harry's acrobatics. An English dad is more vigilant, spotting Harry's scissor-jumping routine. It isn't the first time Harry has been compared to various pieces of human genitalia. He concedes defeat and slopes off to join Joe, as he often does when he's feeling down. Victoria is there too but that's not a problem.

Harry has dreadlocks like Joe, but he's tall and dark blond – he's a lot quieter than Joe too. Looking at them both, Victoria allows herself a bitter smile – both ends of the spectrum, she thinks. 'Does that make me versatile?' Harry's limply patting his djembe, his drum of choice, African of course. 'He'd like that. Being African, but he'll never be quite laid back enough.'

She'd met Harry when he worked in the music shop, Wah-Wah, selling dreams with drumsticks, guitar strings and plectrums, but now he just keeps his dreams to himself. She also knows that she's never featured very strongly in them. His wispy sun-bleached beard frames blistery lips set in semi-permanent confusion, their default position, and his cornflower blue eyes flinch rather than blink. He might be too frail for his dreams, she thinks. Joe has always liked Harry's not very well-hidden sensitivity. It's the foundation for their camaraderie. Joe is throwing stones aimlessly into the sea, nodding his head in time to the music. The boy's learning, he thinks, his muscles subtly flexing to Harry's beat. Their bodies co-joined by the rhythm, like lovers perhaps, but their love is sublimated, platonic and easy.

Victoria is bored, hot in her tatty black gear, she stands apart, her back to them, moving her limbs idly on the shingle, humming to Harry's beat. It helps. It always did. She would always like Harry for that, and now she wants to give him a hug. She's loosening up, Harry and Joe have both helped there. It was Harry's music that first turned Victoria on to him. She's never felt fat when dancing, or swimming, but she can't do either when she's miserable. Joe looks at Harry, who is now looking at Victoria, the two men's eyes meet and they grin. It's good to see her dancing, Harry thinks. He feels less guilty about her and her descent into depression. As lovers, they never reached the high ground, but they were good at being friends.

'I'm bored, Joe,' she says, without looking round. Male eyes find each other again and roll mockingly in sync. The beat goes on, and Victoria sighs.

'Take some time away from your head,' Joe says. 'Fly with the seagulls, get up there and soar.'

'Yeah, right,' she sneers.

'The guys at my old job are looking for someone. Why not give it a go,' proffers Harry, more usefully, perhaps, not interrupting his beat. 'You might even enjoy it. I can put in a word if you want.'

She manages to hide her smile before the others see it.

'Yeah, OK then, if you think you can. I'd really like that. I can't go like this. Can I? I feel such a scuzzbag.'

Joe shrugs. 'I like scuzz. You're OK like you are, girl, but if you're not happy then, yeah, I'm not either. Let's find you something.'

He likes Victoria, likes how she's changing, but wishes she could see it too. Loving him as he does, he knows Harry was bad for her, a bad lover, that is. He had made her feel unlovable. Maybe he doesn't know how to love. When he was with Victoria, she'd looked like the girl no one fancied – that was his doing. He just needed a regular screw, and it didn't matter too much who obliged. It was good for both of them when they split. She's getting back her confidence. She's even enjoying sex again. That's one of Joe's specialities. He has other skills too. He can see people's talents before they do themselves. Victoria has definitely found hers in his sleeping bag, but he knows that inside Victoria Buchanan there's turmoil of the darkest kind.

He goes back to the flat, Rachel Seymour's flat. He's smiling and charming, that's his style. Rachel's there alone. Freshly showered and smelling of beauty products. She's about to go out, bunch of keys and mobile phone in hand.

'Hi, there,' he says, eyes involuntarily grazing over her starched lemon shirt. His face asks if she's wearing a bra, but his voice is perfectly gallant. 'I'm sorry to keep troubling you. You lent us a towel, remember?'

She remembers, but sees that there's no towel in those large hands placed so jauntily on what look like firm hips. She wants to go but can't break through the charm barrier.

'Well, the thing is, it's Vickie. She can't get a job 'cos she feels dirty all the time, you know what I mean? I want to help her. I was thinking you might have something, you know, a dress you don't want, something that would make her look good, feel good.'

Rachel is speechless. She laughs abstractedly and waves her arms limply. What can she say?

'I know that she's a lot bigger than you, but you might have something a bit looser than the stuff you normally – you know the sort of thing. Something that anyone could wear.'

He's unembarrassed, but he has said enough for now. A silence falls, just long enough for Rachel's quick intake of breath.

'You're crazy, you know that don't you?' she laughs. 'I don't know why I'm doing this but, what the hell, you might as well come in.'

Then they're standing in the flat, just the two of them.

'You wait here and I'll see what I've got.' She's business-like again, flustered, looking for motives. Is he casing the joint? She hates herself for thinking it, no she doesn't, she's a woman of the world and, charming though he is, she's not leaving him alone to help himself.

'Look, you'd better come with me. I'll show you what I've got.'

Now they're in the bedroom, just the two of them. Rachel's embarrassed. Still in her most business-like manner, she tries to cover up the growing blush that she can feel spreading up her spine. She feels hot and she's fumbling, so unlike herself, as she opens the floor-to-ceiling wardrobes like an estate agent on a property viewing. Joe stands looking, poised, arms crossed. He's enjoying himself. Strangely quiet, feeling like she's got weights on her limbs, she rummages for a dress, shoes, underwear even. To her own surprise she's trying to match things up, asking Joe's opinion, saying too much, talking too quickly. Not knowing why, she's making Victoria look good. Joe's playing the sugar daddy, choosing couturier clothes for his mistress.

'That would suit her, but not in orange. Have you got anything with a lower neckline?'

The right dress is identified and laid out on the bed. It's a blue beach-dress: Rachel's pleased. She likes working with Joe, he's quick and knows what he wants. Oh yes, and he's attractive too – very.

'You haven't got a spare bra have you?' – he's laughing now.

'What the fuck!' she laughs back.

'Well, you're about Victoria's size even though she's big, she's not huge there. You know, she's small breasted for her weight. You're ..well, you're not small, you know what I mean. I didn't mean that...well...'

Rachel is winded, speechless again, but she just has to laugh. This man always gets her laughing.

'I don't believe you. I really don't! I suppose she needs clean knickers too!'

'Well, that would be really good if you have any. I mean, I'm not saying your knickers aren't clean, I mean if you have any clean ones to spare. No, forget it, she never wears knickers.'

Now they are both laughing but she bundles the clothes into Joe's arms, and hurries him off, out of her life. What am I doing? she thinks, but she's smiling when he's gone.

'I'm fed up with you in colours,' Rachel says, when Alan comes out of the changing booth in a pale yellow shirt and light blue summer jeans. He doesn't mind the other customers' curiosity as he's examined in his stockinged feet, expensive labels dangling everywhere. He's with Rachel, and that means being on display.

'I'd like you all black and white. Black jacket, white shirt, understated.'

He returns to the booth with a new pile of clothes.

'That's better. I like the jacket but the trousers are crap. They're too loose round the crotch. Try these.'

And that's what they bought. Alan now wears a light black jacket, white shirt open to the third button, black jeans, tight round the crotch, and black trainers. He's the perfect foil for his girlfriend, in her scarlet body-hugging dress. She looks terrific, of course, and she knows it. Alan's monochrome sets off her scarlet, in so many ways. Hand-in-hand, and with just enough designer bags to make her point in public, they saunter home, the monarchs of style.

Joe's back on the street, cruddy jeans, dirty white t-shirt, grungy trainers, same as usual. He's leaning against the lamppost, playing his flute, that same languorous tune casting its spell. Alan is with Rachel – the perfect, beautiful couple. Alan drops off his usual coin. Rachel clocks Joe. Joe plays on. Rachel's hand moves ostentatiously to Alan's left buttock.

Chapter Seven

Now it's Victoria's turn. Nothing for a long time has been so luxurious as the hot municipal shower, or that is what she thinks after she has got over her embarrassment at stripping in public, well, in front of two hurriedly changing long distance swimmers in their high middle age. All this for the price of a swimming ticket at the public baths. She has found a discarded shampoo bottle – no longer half empty but half full – and she's loving the lather. The two women leave her to it, and she celebrates. Alone and naked, in a shower cubicle, she has to keep pushing the timer button to prevent the water cutting out every minute. She's too thrilled to find that annoying. Alone, happy in her body – she doesn't feel fat or unattractive, just human, young and, yes, she has to admit it, more than a bit turned on.

Lathering in hot water is like the most sensuous massage of her life – better than Joe at his most tender, and superior by far to Harry's clumsy pawing. Her nerve ends are tingling and she shivers, sending a wake-up message to that part of her brain that registers her hunger for human flesh, her delight in her own skin and her dream of gentle hands that know how to make her feel loved. Who to invite in with her under the water? She tries to imagine each of her men, one after the other, or maybe, she grins, all together. Some happy memories there, but it's time for someone new. It's obvious that Joe will move on any day now. They both know that this is strictly short-term. An adventure in the unexpected. After Joe – yes, she has been planning that for some time – after Joe, she wants someone else who, like Joe, could be surprising. Someone who hasn't learnt sex from a manual, and who doesn't make her feel too big because he feels too small. Her hands know what to do, they are her best friends, so she lingers longingly under her tropical waterfall. He has, as yet, no face, this man, but she can see other parts of his body. She knows who he is, and will recognise him if he ever finds her.

She is still smiling as she dries herself with Rachel's thick white towel. It's her spirit that's been drooping – nothing else. It has brought her body down with it, but now in this euphoria, both body and spirit have bounced back, and she's ready to party. The hot water and the shampoo, with its essence of avocado, has sent her soaring. Just like the adverts, she thinks, just like those seagulls Joe showed her. Her body may be big, but it's young and flexible. Putting down the towel, she stretches, her stomach muscles do their bit, and her breasts sit up. She could've been a model for an Italian Renaissance painting; she's Titian's *Venus of Urbino*, voluptuous, on display, and open for business. Then it's Rachel's bra, God no, what was he thinking, hang on, it fits. And her tights, they fit too. Joe is extraordinary, she thinks, yet again. Choosing her lingerie size, that should be too much. She's ready to slip on the blue and white floral beach dress, all long and flowing and still with a lingering hint of expensive perfume. It's a perfect fit.

Bathed and dressed, she takes a few minutes to admire the result in the full-length mirror. Alone there in the women's changing room, redolent with the smell of chlorine, disinfectant and stale towels, *Venus of Urbino* is reborn.

She walks along the promenade with a newly straightened spine, tits out front, hair sleek and shiny, avocado clean, a black and blue mane tumbling around her shoulders. Even the espadrilles fit; Joe said that they would; he had an eye for such things. He knew it all, it seems, he knows her so well, too well perhaps. Too much knowledge for love, nowhere left to hide. She meets him on the beach, and kisses him as passionately as she has ever kissed anyone. She's radiant, grateful and already they both know that they're saying goodbye.

'Hey! What about you then, girl, you look the business!' He loves her like this, happy, frisky, and ready to go. She's his wounded bird made whole and now, with her feathers glossed up, warm in his hands, she's more than ready to fly. Now all he has to do is let go and watch her soar.

Harry arrives. He clocks Victoria – anyone would. They light a fire, the three of them, lagers and joints, sitting in a huddle. Harry and Victoria talk. Joe isn't listening. He puts his body where his mind is, and shifts lightly to a shingle hill, where he sits looking out to sea, playing his flute, pitching his notes on the incoming breeze.

'No we can't, he'll see.'

'No he won't and, anyway, who cares?'

'I don't want to, Harry – sorry. We've been here before and done all we can do in that department.'

Harry thinks that, before long, they will go the whole way again.

Joe said it could happen, but it shouldn't, for both their sakes; he knows these things, Joe does. Just give her some space, get her that job. Before Joe puts the flute to his moistened lips, he says something in a quiet almost inaudible tone. 'Go for it, man.' He's not talking to Harry, he's whispering to the world.

Later, Harry is walking back into town with Victoria, heading for Wah-Wah, the music shop where he used to work. The job's already set up. He's put in that good word. He watches her furtively in the shop windows. He's turned on by what he's missed, that he hadn't noticed when she was his girl. Let her be, Joe'd said, and he had. Looking at her now, he could see the pride in her body, he can tell too that she has more than outgrown him. His eyes flinch with remembered pain.

Wah-Wah smells of leather, dust, incense, clean high-end plastic and varnished wood – it's a guitar temple where instruments are sold, repaired, drooled over and discussed, at length, over coffee in take-away cartons. The walls are lined with most boys' daydreams, electric guitars, some as slickly bright as 1950s American cars, standing to attention on shelves, row upon row of famous brand names, holy to some, *Fender Stratocaster*, *Gibson Les Paul* and the heroic-sounding *Epiphone*. On another wall, a mellow array of acoustic guitars, *Taylors*, *Martins* and *Washburns*, hung by their necks, honey-golden teardrops. Drum kits of similar calibre are set on a small stage towards the back, along with a line-up of grinning electric keyboards. This seemingly limitless space also keeps a range of saxophones, trumpets and a wall's length of industrial-sized amplifiers. In the nineteenth century, the shop had been a gentlemen's outfitters, and now there's still plenty of room for discerning connoisseurs, devotees of true rock'n'roll style. It's more than just a music shop, but it struggles to make a living, staffed by ex-musicians, wannabe rocksters and air guitarists. Guitar-love is an essential to work in this place, but the wages are small, and many a wide-eyed trainee gets disappointed when rock stardom eludes them after a few weeks selling guitar strings. Staff turnover is brisker than instrument sales.

'You only need to make one or two great sales in a week,' says Jake Reilly, Wah-Wah's owner. He was a young guitarist once, and had been successful enough on London's Irish pub circuit. He still keeps his hair long, in a ponytail, even though it's turned more than a little grey, and he still wears the uniform, leather and denim. He pioneered British rock tattoos too when they were still only worn by sailors, builders and men with secrets.

Jake doesn't want to be rich – he gave up on that when his band failed to chart. He retired from the stage twenty years ago, when he was still only just thirty. Founding a temple is more his thing, he's a high priest at heart, so he's built somewhere where he can pursue his deepest urge, that is to talk and maybe, over time, to make a few conversions, or even find that star – a guitarist, perhaps, or even better, a singer, the human voice is his passion. Here, at Wah-Wah, he has created the holy of holies, the sanctum sanctorum for all the town's sixteen-year-old lads with dreams to dream, inspired to do paper-rounds to earn enough for that guitar seen in Wah-Wah's window. One man's sanctum is another's drop-in centre. Wah-Wah is a good place to have a chat if you like to talk about the latest guitar or amp news, or to hear what local bands are up to, or merely to talk music where someone will listen.

Wah-Wah is a gentlemen's club, but not for gentlemen exactly, for a particular kind of male – on both sides of the counter – classless, under thirty, nerdily well-informed, scruffily dressed in much loved jeans and with faded t-shirts that proclaim their rock heroes. They are secretly romantic, but too often deodorant-free. Jake has decided that a female would liven the mix, and with unusual good luck, today one walks into the shop.

Jake knows better than to say 'when can you start?' the moment he sees Victoria. She is definitely female but not a chick. She's big, that's fine, more than fine, she can lift weights like a man, she's got attitude, he'd say balls, and, in that crazy long dress with her blue and black hair, she has an original sense of style.

'When can you start?' he says, moments later, when Harry tells him she's looking for work.

'Tomorrow.'

'Come for a coffee and we'll fix things up.'

Jake likes women slightly taller than him; he puts his arm round her waist and she doesn't recoil. It's just as he'd thought, this woman has balls.

'We'll go to Caruso's – you coming Harry?'

'Yes, he is,' Victoria says. She feels good here, relaxed, almost at home. 'Harry looks after me, don't you Harry? Makes sure I'm OK.'

'For sure,' Harry says, smiling at Jake. 'She looks after me too, of course.'

They head off, leaving Barry and Phil, the two young sales lads, in charge. They can sort guitar strings in the absence of any new customers, Jake tells them. They're not so young or naïve not to know Jake's taste, and they eye Victoria in disbelief.

'Shit!' they whisper in unison.

'All of Harry's friends end up working for me sometime or other,' Jake says, when the three of them are sitting in Caruso's, the Italian café on the seafront. 'I'll persuade him to come back too one day, won't I mate?'

'I doubt that Jake, I'm fine where I am.'

'Still chasing rainbows – good lad.'

They find a window seat with a sea view. Caruso's owner, Vincenzo Galli, shouts a welcoming 'buon giorno' above the equally welcoming sound of the espresso machine.

'Buon giorno, Vincenzo!' Jake replies, with a well-practised and authentic enough accent.

Alfredo Cantelli, an older man, round bodied and multiple-chinned, comes over to shake his hand.

'Ciao, my old friend. Good to see you again.'

'Alfredo, good to see you too. Meet Harry and Victoria.'

'Piacere,' Alfredo smiles, bowing elegantly.

'Alfredo is a singer – once a big name in opera, weren't you, my friend?'

'In my own humble way, I suppose, yes. I'm mostly a teacher of other voices, but here we celebrate the greatest of them all, the wonderful Enrico Caruso.'

Alfredo returns to his countertop espresso, downs his caffeine shot and leaves. It's late morning, and Jake's promise of coffee has turned into three all day breakfasts – two fried eggs each, bacon and tomatoes, nothing too gastronomically criminal because this place is Italian, and Jake has faith in Italian culture. A music track plays old records by Enrico Caruso, *O sole mio* is his favourite, he often sings it to himself on a sunny day, and for a moment, he hums along with it. Victoria only speaks when she's spoken to, like Victorian nannies decreed. She's not being obedient as much as sullen, watching the reflections from Jake's knife as they flicker around the walls. There's something feline in her look, Jake likes it. She's a strange one. He's intrigued, drawn in by the challenge. He tells her about the job, it won't be too demanding until she learns about the instruments, she can do stocktaking, paperwork, that kind of thing.

'I know a bit about music,' she says, defending herself. 'I've known a lot of musicians.' She speaks while she eats, not looking up, Jake watches her dissect her bacon into geometric shapes, squares, rectangles and, maybe a rhombus.

'Are you shy with people? You'll have to deal with customers, you know.'

'No, I'm fine. I just don't talk for the sake of it – I'm not really shy at all.'

'It's true, Jake. Vickie will be fine.' Harry put his hand on her arm, and she lets him keep it there, Jake notices that too.

'So you two split up then?'

'Yeah,' Victoria's in there first, laughing now. 'We're friends though, aren't we Harry? We've been through some stuff together.'

'We have indeed.' Harry knows that she'll be fine now.

'Do you live local?'

'Yeah, well I will do. I've been staying with a friend, but I moved out today – I'm going to find a room.' She's relaxed, playing with her food, slicing and paring the tomatoes.

Her lack of interest in small talk makes no difference to Jake. He's listening to Caruso: 'This was one of his best, *Santa Lucia*, perfect.'

'I didn't know you had this thing about opera singers, Jake.' Harry often wonders if he's ever understood his friends.

'He wasn't just an opera singer, that man, he was a god. Listen to this...mare è placido...' Jake is singing, barely holding the notes, but a man inspired. 'Caruso was the singer, opera, anything.'

'You are right, Jake,' says Vincenzo Galli, a thin, bald, melancholy man with the hairiest arms Vickie has ever seen. She wonders, approvingly, if it grows like that over the rest of his body. 'Why do you think I only play these old records, they are nearly one hundred years old, but no one has ever sung better.'

'Ah, si,' Jake agrees. 'Magnificent.'

'I thought you were just an old rock freak.' Harry's intrigued.

'Well, sure, I'm that too, but singing, that's something special, no matter what style. Where would Elvis have come from without

Caruso? I tell you Harry, as much as I love rock music, I would have given it all up and sliced off my dick even, to have sung like this just once.'

'Careful what you wish for,' Victoria says, with a grin, pleased to change the subject from opera.

'Sorry love, I should watch my language.'

'Not on my behalf you don't,' she says, without irony. 'I've seen plenty of them. None sliced off though – not yet.'

Jake's laughing, he likes this girl.

'I think you and me will get along just fine.'

Chapter Eight

'It irritates me, that's all.'

A simple sentence, stating a simple truth, upsets them both. Rachel finds the most important thing in Alan's life irritating. He plays his saxophone all the time, it seems. Whenever she wants to talk or, as she says, chat, he interrupts the easy flow of communication. His music had seemed so cool at first. She'd liked having a man who revealed his sensitivity through music and she'd even liked the shining tenor saxophone itself. It spoke to her of night clubs, dancing and, yes, sex.

Alan likes to think that he's using his saxophone to sing love songs to Rachel, and, if he's being honest, showing off his virility – magnifying it too perhaps. It's difficult to play the thing without taking on some of the mannerisms of a sophisticated black man from downtown Chicago. That's what he thinks, even if he actually looks like a nice white kid from Surrey, just doing his best.

This morning, Saturday morning, the day after their crossed words in the office, Rachel has finally lost even her minimal interest in jazz. Alan's music has never been more to her than ambient eroticised sounds, and, this morning, the erotic appeal of the saxophone finally evaporates. Music has become just a noise, an interruption and an intrusion in her carefully designed living space.

Alan leaves off the song he calls *Blue Notes*. He's hurt, and retreats into that sullenness that so often looks like a sulk to Rachel but, as some men claim, is really shielded emotion. He's disappointed by her lack of interest, this flash of truth breaks the mirror of his self-esteem. He packs his instrument away, after meticulously, ostentatiously, and noisily, cleaning the emotionally emitted spittle from its barrel with a grubby cloth discoloured by several years of gunge.

'Just give us a break, that's all I meant.'

Rachel is trying to be reasonable. She too is hurt by his angry reaction, but this time she won't compromise.

'I'm going out,' he hisses, without looking at her, but he didn't mean to slam the front door. He mouths a list of expletives when he reaches street level. He would've kicked a beer can if there had been one handy, but instead, he goes to a cafe and orders a coffee. He's not good at temper displays and, anyway, he's missed his mid-morning caffeine fix.

Rachel doesn't move for some time after he's gone. She stands where she'd been when he'd left. She's feeling foolish, exposed somehow in the wrong clothes, in that simple black dress so short at the thigh. Earlier that morning she had been celebrating her bare legs, and had spent a considerable amount of time painting her toenails bright red for a weekend of fun.

It could be deliberate that he calls when Alan's out. Rachel has her suspicions when she opens the door to Joe, who is returning that towel. It's wet and manky and goes straight into the laundry bin. Standing in the bedroom with this strange man at the door, she holds on to the moment with a flickering then evaporating smile. Joe hovers – something tells him that it isn't time to leave.

'I bet you could do with a shower too, couldn't you?' she asks, picking up his directness.

'I'm sorry,' he says, unaccustomed to losing the initiative and lightly apologetic, almost, for a moment, insecure. 'Do I smell?'

'Oh, no. I didn't mean that.' She's laughing at herself now. Laughing for the first time today, and it feels good. 'Well, I suppose you do a bit, to be honest.'

'Sorry about that – it's a bloke thing, and, anyway, I can't ask you for another towel.'

'No, I mean here. You could have a shower here. Now. If you want. Not that you stink or anything, and don't think I'm some kind of cleanliness freak 'cos I'm not like that.'

She's talking too much and knows it. She's giving herself the time to shoot urgent questions to herself. What is she doing? Does she want this? How far will she go? Why does she like that smell so much? Joe would love to have a shower. Of course he does, here, in this amazingly luxurious place, with this beautiful woman and her erotically charged power play. There's no need to reply, he just smiles his smile, that smile, the one that always gets him his own way.

'I mean, you might as well shower here. You don't usually hold back, do you? You're not exactly the shy type.'

'That would be great. Really. Thanks. Are you sure you don't mind? I mean, I'm no more than a tramp and you're the lady in the big house. I mean that's never going to be right is it?'

'Some might think that,' she says, realizing that she's purring.

While they talk, their eyes are having a different conversation, quick-fired and straight to the point. He's already fingering the bottom of his t-shirt. Rachel is blushing. She can feel her face flush; her annoying capacity for colouring up always gives her away, so she tries extra hard not to look weak.

'You're not impressed, are you – by this place, by anything. You just don't care. I think that's why I like you. Maybe I shouldn't tell you that, but I like to be direct too. You don't need any of this, do you?'

'You're wrong lady. For a start, I think you're awesome; the place is fun too, I'm not knocking it,' he flashes his biggest grin yet.

She's grinning too as she shows him to the bathroom – a wet room, all grey tiles and chrome.

'This is so cool – I can't believe you don't mind letting some filthy stranger in here.'

'Go on,' she says, with a new warmth in her voice. 'Take your time. Enjoy yourself. You'll find shower gel and shampoo in the dispensers – they're not too girly for you I hope.' Now it's her turn to hover. 'Oh, yes, I nearly forgot, you'll be needing a clean towel I suppose.'

She finds him another white towel and leaves him to it. It's pointless, she thinks, pretending that I haven't got a naked stranger here. She feels ridiculous pottering around the flat. Before the bathroom door closes, Joe's clothes, his old jeans, t-shirt and trainers, hit the floor, discarded carelessly in a trail on the way to the shower, then kicked with a laugh to a corner. He's lathering himself, singing under his breath, happily cocooned in the rushing water, when Rachel, naked and still smiling, appears through the steam. They both register what they've already guessed. No surprises – they've known this would happen, right from the start.

Alan returns a couple of hours later, just as Rachel and Joe are coming out of the bedroom. Two minutes silence, or so it seems, out of respect maybe, while they all take it in. He's wearing Alan's new gear, the black blazer and jeans, white shirt unbuttoned to the third button, Rachel's arm through his. She's changed into skimpy yellow cotton – new beginnings. Alan looks fine, his eyes look a bit blurred, maybe, but he's fine. He sees the difference in Rachel immediately. She looks happy, different, not his woman any more.

She breaks the silence, it's her call. 'I'm sorry but, you know, we all move on. It's been great and all that. Really. I know I'm being shitty to you, but that's the deal, right?'

Alan shrugs. Yes, he's fine now. That coffee, and a second one, and then a walk along the seafront had clarified a decision he had probably made weeks ago.

'Sure' he agrees, 'We needed to make a change.'

Joe says nothing. His face is tactfully neutral, but he isn't embarrassed, it's not his style. Rachel gives Alan a hug just to confirm things, affection reinforced before disengagement.

'Seeya. We're going out for a bit – maybe you could sort yourself out before we get back.'

'Yeah, sure.'

'Seeya.'

Rachel smiles a new smile, one Alan hadn't seen before. It's the expression that a bored model offers to an incompetent fashion photographer. Joe takes Rachel's hand and squeezes it, he winks at Alan who returns the look with his attempt at a macho shrug. It's fine, they all agree in a momentary silence. Then the new couple go, leaving Alan standing in the middle of the flat. He doesn't watch the door; he's stopped thinking about them; a kind of yogic trance immobilises his body. Yes, I'm fine, he keeps repeating. Fine. Gradually he comes round. What should he do? Like most people about to make a life changing decision, he decides to take a shower, but he's not looking for comfort. He wants to walk through a portal, to shed his old skin for something new.

He puts some Miles Davis on the music system and, with a flick of a switch, the apartment is filled with sound. There are speakers in every room, even in the wet room. Now *that* he really will miss. As he take off his clothes, he realises that everything, even his designer underwear, she insisted on white and tight, were chosen for him, and bought for him, by Rachel. Actually everything belongs to her, she should have it all back. He kicks his clothes into the bedroom, leaving them to settle where they fall. The music plays, The Miles Davis Quintet at its most jaunty and nuanced in *Surrey With the Fringe*, enough to provoke Alan to join the musicians with a lightly whistled counter melody as he sashays under the water, enveloped in steam, barely able to restrain his urge to laugh out loud. He is, he thinks, changing right there in the shower, with Joe's soap suds still gathered round the plug hole. It's Joe, of course, who has started this, Alan can feel him still, a benign spirit invisibly playing him, laughing, watching him with twinkling eyes, amused and all-knowing, sitting up there above his head on some fluffy, and definitely punky, Rococo cloud.

Rachel had seen this too, even before it happened, she has a talent for endings, aware of them from the beginning. Now it's obvious, even to Alan, that he is moving on as he was destined to do, as he wants to do. He needs this moment of ceremonial, the purification ritual, a baptism in lather, before leaving the deconsecrated sanctuary where he has seen what feels like the truth, an incoherent but significant revelation.

Drying himself on the damp towel, he's hurrying now. Joe's discarded clothes, dirty, alien, crumpled on the floor, they will do. Anything would. Fair exchange, he thinks, grinning. How Rachel would hate that idea. In fact, these old clothes are perfect, left behind, just maybe, with intent. He dresses as quickly and as negligently as if they were his own, riding a spasm of nausea at the odour of well-worn denim and the smell of the street. It feels like no accident that Joe has left him his escape gear. Even the crusty trainers, pungent and grimy, speak to Alan of freedom. He looks in the mirror, ruffles his hair, smiles, pouts, then smiles again, trying out his new identity, or is it, he wonders, his old one. Satisfied, relieved and excited, he picks up his horn, his CD bag, putting the Miles Davis back in there too, and goes.

Chapter Nine

For a day or two now Harry has lost the urge for background photographic modelling. Maybe it was Kanti – she might have stolen something, if not his soul, with her camera. He's sitting on the steps of the deckchair cave, tapping quietly on his djembe. There's a song there, he thinks – the girl and her camera. Cam-er-a-girl, cam-er-a-girl, he drums out the rhythm and indulges this glimmer of testosterone-fuelled creativity. The midday sun makes it all the more enjoyable. He's always turned on when it's hot, it's another of those man things. His storeroom cave is at the top of the beach, on the edge of the promenade, a great position to watch the girls go by, and to imagine possibilities. This is what he does when he isn't busy.

Looking for talent, the boys in the band used to call it. Life as a deckchair attendant gives him time to develop his roving eye. The sea and sun play along with his game. Skimpy shorts, cleavage-sporting tops, and exposed midriffs saunter past all day – no one worth looking at, in Harry's opinion, comes to the beach to cover up. Sometimes groups of foreign students hang around, listening to his drumbeat, loads of beautiful continental Europeans come to England because they think it's cool, or so he's been told by some of the most eager of them. They think he's cool, the ones who hang around his bachelor's lair. He's joined that maritime elite, the lifeguard, the surfboard dude and, admittedly slightly lower on the scale, the deckchair attendant. It's so much sexier than selling ice cream.

In the liberating world of the English seaside, several well brought-up Catholic girls forget their Mediterranean consciences, and commit cardinal sins with Harry at the back, behind the pile of deckchairs, or later, just under the stars, on the beach. He doesn't fool himself about his own personal charms – he knows that he's just a stopping off point, part of the seaside tour, his services no more profound than the barman serving temptingly-coloured alcopops. He lost Vickie that way. She didn't need him to be monogamous, but she'd said she wasn't into harems. After she'd gone, he'd felt sad and a bit of a failure, but there's compensation enough on the floor of the deckchair store.

Working on his new song, a part of him, the part that thinks about sex several times a minute, scrutinises today's passing trade. Imperceptibly, songwriting turns into posing as a songwriter, soon it becomes just posing. It feels good. He feels good. Then he sees Diep, who's wearing a canary yellow t-shirt with *Brighton* emblazoned in red across the chest, blue Bermuda shorts and red flip-flops, still looking like a character from a children's cartoon. He grins and nods enthusiastically, then runs off. Later he's back, but this time with Kanti, who is, again, dressed exactly the same as her brother, who is gesticulating energetically as they walk. Obviously sharing a joke.

'Hello, Hari,' she says, still laughing. 'I have brought you a present.'

It's the photograph of him doing his handstand. Cropped to show just his torso, head and hands, he fills the frame, upside down, muscles straining, brown skin sweating, his bristly face set in terrible concentration. He doesn't recognise himself.

'You see,' she laughs. 'The typical Englishman.'

'Amazing. It's a really good picture.'

'Why so amazed?' she pretends to be hurt. 'I'm a real good photographer. Didn't you know that? And, anyway, you are good model.'

She's still quietly laughing – so is Diep. They're laughing at him, and with him, like old friends, but he's not sure if their mockery is affectionate or critical.

'I didn't think –' he's fishing for the right words. 'I didn't think you're a bad photographer, I just didn't think you could make me look this amazing.' He's still looking at the photograph. Is that really him? It's not like looking in the mirror, and anyway, he only ever does that first thing after getting up in the morning – making sure that he's still alive. The photograph makes him look adult, real even. Not how he sees himself at all, no longer, maybe, just a poser, a grown-up kid frightened of adulthood. No, here he looks simply grown up – a man.

'I'm studying photography,' she says, suddenly serious again. 'Here in Brighton. I am a photographer. It is my life.'

'I can see that,' Harry says, feeling their relationship deepen. 'You are very good.'

'Thank you. Well this is for you, it's just a first print but it's your present, Mr Typical Englishman. I hope you like it.'

'Of course I do. Thank you very much.' He's flinching, struggling to hold back his tears.

'Maybe you can help me. These chairs with the stripes, I want to picture them with, how do you say in English, with arses sitting in them.'

'Arses?' Harry's laughing now.

'Yes, is that how you say it?' She pats hers to make the point. 'You will let me photograph your chair people, please?'

'Why not,'

'Does that mean yes?'

'I guess so.'

'Is that yes?'

'Yes.'

'You English! You don't know how to speak your own language. Yes is never quite yes.'

'OK then, yes, you can photograph them, but be careful – don't let them see you.'

'That is highly generous of you, many thanks, I will make great photos here, believe me.'

She starts to work straight away. Sneaking up behind people in their deckchairs, stalking them like the sleekest of panthers, focusing on their body imprints seen through the candy-stripes.

'You see,' she says, as she changes lenses, talking in a low conspiratorial whisper, 'everyone is different. Every arse is its own person. Do you see?'

He can't see, she loses him when she turns philosophical.

'Does my bum look big in this?' he muses out loud.

'Pardon?' Kanti asks, not seeing the joke, and thinking that he's criticising her. 'What is this word bum? I don't understand. You are one are you not? A beach bum, yes?'

'I guess so.'

'There you go again.'

'Well, yes, then. Ok? I'm a beach bum. Yeah, you're right. I hang around on the beach all day, and don't do very much. Yeah, I'm a beach bum for sure, I admit it, is that better?' he smiles. 'But bum is also a word for arse.'

'Oh, so you are an arse too?'

'Some people have called me that, yeah.' He's not immune to this weird psychoanalysis. Kanti gets to him every time. Diep laughs, but he looks confused, and more than a bit shy.

'The rounder the arse the better,' Kanti giggles. 'I like the older ones best. They have great big arses. Really. Hey, look at the fat bum on those English gentlemen,' she whispers, nodding towards two middle-aged men in lycra cycling shorts and sleeveless vests. She catches them unawares and gives Harry the thumbs up. Obviously enthralled, she prowls around Harry's patch for nearly an hour. Diep sits watching, happily playing passive to her active, but Harry is uneasy about him. There's definitely something odd about his quiet intensity, something more than just shyness.

'What do you do?' Harry asks, trying to bring him into the conversation, but he gets no reply. Diep doesn't even look away from his sister. He's probably just a guy with not much going on inside his head. Probably, Harry thinks, not that different from himself. Harry doesn't try again. He's not much of a human analyst. He really doesn't bother with what lies under the skin, especially young female skin.

'This will be so good,' Kanti declares. While she worked, her face had tightened into a frown, her eyes scarcely blinking. She's relaxed again now she's got what she wants, and packs up her equipment with quick well-practised movements. She gives Diep a hug when he takes the camera cases, grinning again both at Kanti and at Harry too.

'So there you have it,' she says. 'Lots of good arses and bums today, Hari, thank you so much.' With the speed of a bird, she takes his hand and kisses it. 'Typical English bums,' she whispers, 'how I love them.'

Chapter Ten

Alan is playing his saxophone, leaning against a lamppost, Joe's spot. It seems like a fair exchange, it's a rich site for passing trade. His saxophone case is lined with coins, mostly coppers, a few fifty pence pieces but, occasionally, pound coins too. He puts it all down to John Coltrane, the man was more than a genius, he's a busker's dream. Alan's version of *Blue Train* has been really swinging today. He loves the effect on passers-by. They might not realise that they like jazz, but they noticeably lighten their step and loosen up. Sometimes, Alan thinks, some of them actually leave the pavement, levitating just for him. They're the ones who leave pound coins. The main phrase of *Blue Train* needs two beats not supplied by the sax, he fills in by tapping his foot, always his left one, but occasionally a pedestrian or two join in, helping him out with their own couple of beats, clapped or be-bopped as they almost dance on their way. Summertime in the city, the smell of rotting vegetables. Well, let's call it that; the seductive high from exhaust fumes, the peculiar aroma of pavements, the smell of humanity. Alan loves it.

Sleeping rough is beginning to have its effect – the beach is an uncomfortable bed, but it's an inspiring place to wake up every morning. His backache abates after a touch of skinny dipping, but he's no longer power-showered; stubble has sprouted on his face, he's definitely not the clean-cut guy any more, his hair has darkened with grease, and his fingernails end in black crescents. Apart from back-ache and an itchy scalp, none of this bothers him too much. The important thing is that his saxophone is shining out here in the sunshine. His music is flowing, filling the street, creating today's soundtrack – he's never felt so inspired. Joe walks by. He's always there at moments like these, jauntily nonchalant in Alan's old clothes, the gear Rachel had bought him in their final week together. There's an awkward moment.

'Rather you than me, mate,' Alan jokes.

Joe laughs, 'Yeah, right,' and throws him a coin. It's a pound.

The young woman photographer returns, he's noticed her before, a sinister presence, intense and lens-focused, snapping shots of people when they're not looking. Maybe she's a journalist, but if so, it's weird dressing like a child. He's seen what she's up to, she must have noticed, but she doesn't seem to care. When you're living on the street, or, in his case, on the beach, you're invisible, but Kanti Subhadi knows him well, she's been studying him for days now. Alan is at one with Coltrane, his inspirational guru, tied into his melody, in mystic musical union, while, unobserved, that's her style, Kanti Subhadi takes his photograph – an Englishman lost in his music.

Alan had decided not to go back to work when he left Rachel's flat, it was nearly a week ago now. What did he need that job for anyway? No rent to pay – he was free, no girlfriend, no home, no job, no boss – it's getting better all the time, he thinks. He has actually become a full-time musician, his life's ambition achieved so simply. To do what you want, he's discovered, is easy, you just have to do it, simple. Busking is a noble profession, a vocation for the initiated, smiled on from on high by the spirit of Mr Coltrane himself. If you found the right spot, at the right time, then it was always possible to earn enough money for a meal, a few drinks and a packet of cigarettes. What else does a guy need? Well, yes, but that could wait, and you don't have to buy that anyway. He's smiling behind his sax, and his mood smiles through the music.

It's summertime, slightly cool at night, but not that bad. He's enjoying sleeping on the beach, preferably under a fishing boat, away from curious legal-minded eyes, or those sinister night-patrollers, looking for whatever they can find. Winter is going to be another thing, but that's no problem for today. He can decide what to do when the time comes, that's rock'n'roll, after-all. The swim in the sea has become more than just an early morning bath, it's a daily baptism for a man reborn. He's discovered the nudist beach – it's private enough first thing, apart from a few eccentric old men, so he can strip off and keep himself reasonably clean; he can even wash his clothes in the seawater when they get too disgusting even for street life. He might itch a bit, but he could stay smart enough to busk, an honourable profession that deserves respect.

'Not bad, son,' says Lionel Atkins, looking dapper this morning in his tweed jacket, white shirt and a maroon and blue bowtie. He fumbles in his pocket, drops a few coins into the saxophone case, and listens for a moment, enjoying the performance more now that he's paid the entrance price. They are near The Golden Orb pub, Lionel's local. Alan is usually here at this time, improvising jazz standards, mostly Coltrane, naturally, but also some of his own experimental pieces, including an early draft of his new piece, *Blue Notes*. He plays leaning against the lamppost, his lamppost now, not far from his old home, grungey plimsoles, flashing a hint of toes, keeping the beat, proud to be a jazzman.

'Nice to hear a young lad with an ear for a bit of jazz,' Lionel says, with just a hint of bestowing a blessing.

Alan nods his acknowledgement with a pair of raised eyebrows, but carries on playing – he's improvising Coltrane improvising Gershwin's *Summertime*.

'George Gershwin will rest easy in his grave with the likes of you to keep the flame alight. Well done, lad. Nice.'

Lionel goes into the pub, leaving Alan with a benign quasi-Papal wave. Seems a decent sort, just a bit pompous, Alan thinks, remembering him from the beach. He looks posher with his clothes on. He segues into another Coltrane classic, *I'm Old Fashioned* and, as he plays, he can't help thinking about old men's scrotums. Will mine go like that too one day, he wonders. Do they keep growing like old men's ears? About as attractive as nasal hair. I'll get that too one day, but hey, old men still play great jazz. Maybe ears grow with musical understanding.

Lunchtime at The Golden Orb is in full swing when Lionel orders his pint. It's the usual crowd – old mates, mostly single men in their sixties and seventies, some married couples of about the same age, and a sprinkling of younger types, students just starting their day, workmen on midday break, and Mrs Webb, a ruddy-faced widow woman who always sits at the same corner table with a glass of stout, smiling at anyone who looks in her direction.

'Get us another drink, love,' she will say to anyone who catches her eye. 'I've got the coins already counted. Can't get up there very easily with these ulcers.' She usually stretches out her unstockinged legs to confirm the ulcerations. There's always a volunteer, and that's as welcome to Mrs Webb as the drink. She doesn't know that Jacqueline, the landlady, gives a free drink to anyone who does this duty and, sometimes, Mrs Webb feels hurried along by some of her over-enthusiastic helpers.

The television is muted, but a flashing news report shows soldiers with guns in a derelict Eastern European town, while Country and Western classics play on the house music system, the venerable juke box that has stood there since 1972. Jacqueline has turned down good money for it from collectors because, apparently, it's a vintage 1967 *Rock-Ola 434 Concerto,* with a window that shows the mechanism and the record dropping into position, when you pay your money. The Orb wouldn't be the same without it, she's decided – and she's right. All is well in this dark, nicotine-coloured bar, with its mid-twentieth-century oak furniture, and its beer-scented Wilton carpet, once deep red with intricate Arabic patterns, but now simply dark maroon. The appetising aroma of homemade steak pie and chips, bitter beer, furniture polish and a regular pre-business burst of air-freshener, more than makes amends for cigarette smoke and the blend of less savoury smells. 'God's waiting room,' Jake Reilly thinks, finishing his pint, before his lunch guest returns from the urinals. The Orb is handy for Wah-Wah's and it's good enough for a pint and a pie when he needs to entertain one of the visiting reps. In spite of the admirable *Rock-Ola 434,* Jake has never felt at home here. His is the only male ponytail in the bar, and it makes him either too old or too young, but the Orb is a good place for business meetings and the rep, Brian, has done him a good deal for guitar plectrums.

'Should it be plectri or plectra?' Jake wonders as Brian returns, finger-combing back his gelled grey hair, then double-checking his trouser zip. Jake stands up to leave before Brian can return to his seat. Another pint and he'd be lost forever – Tammy Wynette would steal his soul.

'Bye, Jacquie,' he calls, as he takes Brian to the door.

Jacqueline Seymour, the red-haired landlady, smiles then pulls Lionel his beer. She's a woman in, maybe, her mid-fifties, lavishly made up today with more abandon than wisdom. She has no plans to dress her age, and Scarlet O'Hara's hair salon makes sure that her hair never looks less than fiery.

'Rosemary says do you want sauce with your sausage today, Lionel,' she says.

'I think the usual would be very nice, thank you,' Lionel smiles.

Jacqueline's comment is lost when two elderly couples, a life-time's foursome, sitting in the window, join in with the jukebox in a rowdy chorus of *Stand By Your Man,* competing recklessly with the clarion tones of Miss Tammy Wynette herself.

'The music's good today, Jacqueline,' Lionel volunteers, once he's seated on the stool, his usual position, at the centre of the bar.

'Yes, you can't beat the old 'uns. Least it drowns out the racket outside. That kid's been blowing away on his friggin' saxophone all week. I'd like to get him moved on, but there's nothing we can do. He's not breaking any laws, just getting on my nerves.'

'Oh I quite enjoyed the stuff he was playing when I came in.'

'I can't be bothered with jazz. Except Ella that is. I love a bit of Ella Fitzgerald, but then she can hold a tune without keep going off all over the place.'

'Yes, quite. A great singer.'

'You still tinkle the old ivories, Lionel?'

'I try to keep in practice, yes. I've got another trip coming up soon. On the liners.'

'Where are you going?'

'Oh it's the Med again. A six-week contract this time.'

'Lovely, you lucky old bugger! All those bored widows with no one to spend their money on.'

'Well I'm not complaining. Actually you should book yourself a ticket, I shall be doing some of Ella's classics this time. *Every Time We Say Goodbye*, that sort of thing.'

'If only, darlin', I never get enough time away from this place. Not to worry, you'll have them wetting their knickers, I'm sure. You'll have to fight 'em off.'

'I won't be fighting, Jacqueline, I can assure you of that.'

He's finished his lunch when Jacqueline's sister-in-law comes into the bar. Rosemary is a few years younger than Jacqueline, well rounded, with long dark hair usually worn pinned up. Less extrovert in her dress sense than her voluptuous business partner, she's wearing a grey cotton cardigan over a simple blue summer frock.

'Oh hello Lionel,' she says, quietly. 'Have you got a moment?'

Chapter Eleven

Silence. Rachel relishes it, lying next to him in her bed, loosely covered by a white cotton sheet – it calms her body like a fresh hospital dressing. Joe sleeps the sleep of a fugitive no longer on-the-run, his hair spread out over the pillow, more Pre-Raphaelite now than street-dude. Silence. Not entirely. His slumbering breath, like a summer breeze, reinforces the absence of other sounds. Rachel finds music in the rhythm of his breath. She has no urge to move, none of her usual restlessness, she wallows in the silence, in his silence – undisturbed by the traffic that hums below the open windows, or the cries of the herring gulls, birds that never sound content. Out there, beyond the traffic and the sea birds, Rachel listens to the sea: rhythmic, gentle, inevitable, just like Joe.

'Let him lie there,' she thinks, when her built-in timer tells her to move. It's hot in the room, even though, by opening the large sash windows, she has virtually removed the apartment's fourth wall. She pulls the rest of the sheet her way, wrapping herself, Roman-goddess style, leaving her man naked, oblivious, stretched out on his back like a child, arms above his head in unconscious surrender.

She watches for a few minutes, storing the image, preserving the moment, reassuring herself that this has just happened. Then she pours a glass of orange juice, chilled from the fridge, and takes it to a chair on the balcony. This might be enough, she thinks. These moments afterwards, when nothing needs saying, when intimacy is a body memory unsullied by chatter. She rarely allows herself such tranquillity, she has never been one for meditation or prayer, but this morning, she has stepped out of time. 'Let him lie there forever, I'll sit here on guard, never letting anyone near.' 'A thing of beauty is a joy forever' – she remembers those lines now – a poem from school. She loved school – too clever or too beautiful, the combination had made her an underachiever, mostly choosing sex over exam results. That was until she discovered her business acumen – now she keeps a better balance. Thinking of Joe, she remembers her A level English texts. Keats' *Endymion*, the beautiful shepherd boy loved by the Moon Goddess who, fearful of losing him, casts him into eternal sleep. It was enough, the immortal goddess thought, enough just to look on him, knowing he would always be her lover. It is like that now, looking at the waves, subliminally counting each one as it dissipates its strength on the shingle, she feels what might be eternity – a moment, the perfect moment, repeated forever. The Moon Goddess' dream. Kept, maybe photographed one day, stored somewhere deep inside her as a memory for when, as she always does, she will destroy what she cherishes.

Then those fingers caress her neck, and she's laughing.

'Hey, what's so funny?'

She just sits and laughs, savouring this crazy grinning man, standing there in her pink silk dressing-gown with its red poppy pattern, discreet for the road but opened at the front for her.

'I just love you in pink, but I guess everyone tells you that.'

'A few – especially the ladies.'

'Do you like ladies?'

'Not when they're too ladylike.'

'That's just as well, I've no manners, my beautiful shepherd boy.'

'Shepherd? Me?'

'A schoolgirl's poem about a beautiful man.'

'That's OK then, I didn't know you were a poet, you sunbathe naked too – I like that in a woman.'

'How do you know?'

'No bikini-line – brown all over.'

'Just like you,' she puts a hand on his stomach. 'You're not exactly ashamed of your body.'

'There's nothing shameful about bodies,' he replies, imitating her whispered tone. 'They express ourselves. Mine is saying hello to yours.'

'So I see. Hello, body. Beautiful shepherd's body.'

'Well hello body, beautiful Rachel's body.'

They aren't dressing for lunch today, sitting next to each other, thighs touching, at the Perspex table, eating a mixed salad of lettuce, tomato, olives, avocado and oranges, sprinkled with Italian cheese. Two glasses of wine, white with a hint of green, Italian too; they clink and sip, looking down at each other through the clear table top, they've still not satiated their appetites.

'Shall I cut more cheese?' Joe whispers, in a low bass-tone. He's found her sharp chopping knife and brushes its edge softly with a finger. 'Hmm, perfect.'

'You're a perfectionist, like me,' she says, taking the cheese into her mouth from his fingers.

'I look for perfection,' he replies, with a flicker of grimness. 'When I find it, I'll keep it.'

They doze on the sofa, lying there pleasantly drunk, mutually relaxed, their insatiability temporarily spent. Joe stirs first, and takes another sip of wine. 'She's a lady alright,' he thinks, watching her arm slump elegantly open-handed over the edge of the sofa. She's the sleeping nude by one of those old masters. Maybe, this is perfection. A small bubble of saliva forms at the edge of her slightly parted lips, it's caught in the sunlight, sparkling. 'She's a lady alright – diamond studded.'

He shifts position, seeing the flute on the floor at his feet. 'Hello old friend.' He picks it up and blows into it, clearing the pipe, then propping himself up at the end of the sofa, he sits, cross-legged, of course, Rachel's naked satyr, the snake charmer casting his spell. It's not really his spell, it's a gift, he can't explain where it comes from, or what it is. As he plays his lonely, languid serenade, Rachel stirs, wipes her mouth and, slowly at first, her eyes flutter, blink and then open. She smiles to see him there, unable to hide his arousal, cheekily unconcerned by it. His face wrinkles with pleasure as he plays but she can't help it, the words are spoken before she remembers to hold them back.

'Don't play that now, just give us some peace.'

He stops immediately and laughs it off, but Rachel notices a hint of moisture in his eyes, and reaches out to him, she's too far away, but she manages to reach his ankles; she caresses them for a moment, holding them in silence, preventing him from leaping up, even though she feels his sinews flex. When she releases her touch, he gets up and climbs into his shorts, turning away to do up the zip. He meets her gaze and returns her smile, but he's looking through an invisible veil.

He's sitting outside on the balcony, slouching in a lounger chair with one leg draped over the arm, still looking out to sea, when Rachel joins him with two hastily poured glasses of lime juice, iced. She has put on a simple baggy t-shirt, plain white, big enough to expose one of her shoulders – effortlessly, but not accidently, she looks like a cover model from *Vogue* magazine.

'Get this down you, minstrel boy,' she mumbles, trying to retrieve whatever it is she's lost. 'Don't be upset with me, I just don't want you to put up a musical barrier between us. I had too much of that with Alan.'

'No problem, girl, don't worry about it,' he answers quietly but, they both know, not really meaning it.

Sitting there, separated in the silence that earlier she had craved, she looks at him, memorising his flesh, acknowledging the pull, but wondering who he is. Joe's beautiful, she always saw that, loving his body's ease, his freedom of movement, the mystery behind the charm. She had picked up strange men before, but not so casually these days, now that sex comes with a health warning. She's bedded guys, not knowing their name even, but enjoying the risk. A few questions and soon she knew the all about them; their jobs, their dreams, their cars and, too often, their stumbling hopes of owning her. Joe is different, he wears her lightly, too lightly perhaps, but he makes her feel that she fills all of their moments together; like she was the answer to an urgent need and that her time, their time, is now.

'God save me from beautiful women,' Joe thinks, as she plays the hairs on his leg with her toes. He watches her little brown foot with its rudely painted scarlet toenails, massaging him like a small exotic creature disconnected from them both, marauding, invading but, yes, turning him on. He envelopes the whole foot with his hand, hears her intake of breath, then lifts her into his arms.

'Hey, madam, let's make love, not war,' he whispers. That, at least, he means.

Chapter Twelve

Lionel is taking off his trousers. 'Another splendid day,' he says.

'Yeah, mate. Bloody depressing, eh?' John laughs, now naked, folding up his robe – orange today, with a red band round the edge. 'This year, summer's almost hot enough to get boring.'

It's early morning on the nudist beach; Alan is there too, doing his morning ablutions, part-swimming, part-standing in the water, dreamily staring into nowhere. Coming ashore, he avoids a group of raucous youngsters chasing each other in the surf. They've been up all night, and whatever they've been taking, it's kept them hyperactive. They see Lionel and John and line up in front of them laughing, a row of giggling schoolkids, wiggling their cocks.

'Bugger off will you, you scrawny little fuckers!' John shouts, red faced and trembling.

'Diplomacy rules,' Lionel laughs. 'They're harmless enough. Puberty doesn't come easily, poor things. It's their way of bonding.'

'They can fucking bond somewhere else,' John spins his anger round on Lionel, as the naked lads run into the sea waving V-signs. There's a pulsating vein on John's forehead – not his style, Lionel thinks.

'Don't let these things get to you, old boy. I thought you Buddhist chaps were meant to let things pass.'

'They wouldn't be so fucking lively if they hadn't been drinking all night.' John is still trembling.

'We had our day, don't forget. Don't deny them their fun.'

'Had our day, come on, Lionel,' John is grinning, pleased that he can still put his temper behind him. 'I don't think either of us are past our sell-by date quite yet.'

'I'm not complaining,' Lionel smiles.

'Had a good day yesterday. Sold a case of Indian silk to some old tart opening up a boutique in town. She wants as much as I can get her.'

'That should keep you out of queer street.'

'More's the shame. No kiddin' though mate, sales are doing very nicely. The piercings business has taken off too. You wait and see, those little bleeders will be round my place in no time bleating for ear studs and nose rings. They can't get enough of it.'

'So times are good?'

'I've got enough for another trip out East.'

'India again?'

'Definitely. Conrad, the new lad, is coming on well. I'll leave him in charge of the shop.'

'Very nice. So we'll both be off on our travels again.'

'Yeah. There's life in the old dogs yet.'

They're in no hurry to go for their swim; the naked lads are still larking around out there and the sun, already hot, feels good on their flesh. They lie on their towels, looking into blue space. John defocuses, the heat transports him East. The pebbles beneath him turn to sand, as the planet softly tilts. Lionel swats a sand fly.

'You know John, I never understand why you don't settle out there. On the subcontinent, I mean. It's where you belong, isn't it?'

'Maybe. I dunno,' whimsy has arrived on the back of his rage, and he sighs in mid-sentence. 'I miss it when I'm here but then, out there, I'm just another visitor. Travelling is my thing, I guess, but I dunno, mate. Who knows? Something, someone, might get me to settle one of these days.'

'I like to pack my case for a few weeks knowing I've got a return ticket. I like my old house, this place, you know, friends, even you, you old bugger.'

'I need my little patch too – it might not be much, but I can see it, right there in my mind's eye, no matter where I am in the world. It's a reference point – like surveyors have.'

'Time for a swim, old chap, before we get maudlin.'

'Yeah, after you.'

Their feet are negotiating the shingle, as Alan wades in from the sea, unsure about being naked in front of them.

'Morning,' the two men mutter, looking nowhere in particular.

'Morning,' Alan replies, taking a quick look at the vintage genitalia on display – John's scrotum is normal enough, he can see, reassured. Maybe old age isn't that bad, he thinks, as his testicles shrink up to his pelvis.

It's Billy Jo Spears time at The Golden Orb this lunchtime. The country singer's bullet-like diction projects *Blanket On The Ground* over a humming chorus and jangly Hawaiian guitars.

'Well if it isn't Mahatma Coat! How're you doin' John?' Monty Roberts, sixty last birthday, is a beer-paunched man in jeans, polo shirt and old trainers – he's always up for a friendly chat – more often than everyone wants. John takes the barstool next to him and smiles. He's well-known enough for his robes to make no impact on the lunch-time crowd. Brighton doesn't shock easily.

'Allo darling,' Jacqueline welcomes him from behind the beer pumps. 'A pint of the landlady's best?'

'That'd do nicely, Jacquie. Is Lionel in today?'

'He's having a quick word with Rosemary, dear,' she says, holding a neutral expression. The music changes. Frank Sinatra is singing *My Way* and, for a moment, Jacqueline looks away, moved.

'Frank's the boy,' John says, munching his potato and onion pie. 'He lives the life alright.'

'You don't do too badly from what I hear either,' Jacqueline says, her face back on duty. 'They tell me you're off to India again soon.'

'Blimey news travels fast round here. How did you know?'

'Oh, Lionel was in his usual flow this morning.'

'Just as well it's not a secret then.'

'Oh he means no harm. He'd never break a promise or gossip when he knows he should stay mum, I reckon.'

'I think I could make room for that pudding now,' John says, changing the subject. He orders cherry pie and custard, savouring its Englishness.

'Hello, old thing,' Lionel says, following Rosemary back into the bar.

Another morning on the beach and today there are more visitors than usual. Some of the regulars nod to Lionel and John, that's nudist etiquette – dignified, shameless but ostentatiously not curious. It's an all-male gathering; it's usually like that, single men, mostly middle-aged or older, establishing base camp with their clothes at a discreet distance from the next man. It's another warm morning and there is nearly a full muster of Brighton's nude swimmers. It will be different later, men will come down here for other reasons, and when it gets to evening, few of them will be swimming.

'I'll be doing mostly Cole Porter stuff this time,' Lionel explains, scratching his armpits with a military lack of nonsense. 'Always goes down well with the ladies. The gents like it too when their womenfolk get into the mood.'

'If you say so, mate.' John laughs. He's taking off his maroon underpants and folding them precisely in half, before placing them on his purple satin robe. They hobble down to the sea, it never gets easier walking on shingle. The air is warm on their skin, but they still rub their torsos as if they were cold – the default mannerism of men who take off their clothes at the English seaside.

'You should start playing again, old thing,' Lionel says, as they get to the water.

'That Tin Pan Alley stuff isn't really my scene. I prefer improvising. I do stuff on my sitar in the evenings – the guitar too – play it to keep up my spirits at night. Christ, it's brass monkeys in here today.'

Like synchronised swimmers, they dive in, grey waves bursting over them with a tangled cargo of seaweed, submerging them before they resurface puce-faced to swim – their usual routine: breast stroke between the two breakwaters then back again doing the butterfly, then a short pause when they float on their backs before repeating the pattern ten times. They do this every day without a word exchanged. The sea is their sports arena, not the place for a chat.

Jolene: country music's clean-cut seductress has silenced the lunchtime crowd at The Golden Orb. Dolly Parton meets with especial respect here, and her words are mouthed by some of the older customers, like crowds at a public funeral. Even the oldest of the locals feels a brief pang of love-lost as the Nashville queen strums her guitar. Love-lost, or love-never-found, after a lunchtime drink, Dolly Parton hits the spot.

'So tell me Mahatma,' Monty says, sporting a red shell-suit today, 'why do you wear all this foreign clobber then? Really. No offence meant, honestly.'

'I'm on a pilgrimage, on my way somewhere, even if I don't know where I'm going. I don't give a monkey's if people take the piss.' John's wearing his lime green robe, white sports socks and sandals. 'The world's not that perfect, mate, for us not to try and find a better way.'

Monty's not sure how seriously to take John, so he pats him on the knee – his way of bonding.

'The world's not so bad, you know. We've won the Cold War,

and now the one in Iraq. There's even a black president in South Africa. You can't tell me that things aren't getting better.'

'When I was young, we wanted world peace, free love and the brotherhood of man. I haven't given up yet – but don't talk to me about Iraq, it was a pointless bloodbath.'

'Well, I have to hand it to you, John, I'd never dare wear a bloody bedspread, not even for world peace – you're a brave man walking around like something out of South Pacific, and not one of the blokes either.'

'Come on Monty, South Pacific is Polynesian – you'll never catch me in a grass skirt. I'm not that much of a prat.'

'That's a matter of opinion,' says Lionel, arriving for his pint.

'Now that's what I call smart,' Monty says, enjoying this gang reunion. 'Lionel always looks like a proper gent.'

'You can't beat a tweed jacket and a shirt 'n tie when you reach our age,' Lionel says, looking at Monty's shell-suit. 'At least John makes an effort, eh?'

'Anyone for a half of the old ale then?' asks John, changing the subject.

'That's very decent of you, John, but I've got to have a word with Rosemary.'

Rosemary is standing in the doorway, behind the bar, wearing a grey cardigan and dark grey dress. She has hairclips in her mouth as she adjusts her ponytail into a bun, like a nurse coming off duty. She smiles shyly at John, as she follows Lionel into a room at the back of the bar.

'Lionel's right you know, Monty. My turn to be frank, mate. You're carrying a lot of blubber these days, you know. Come swimming with us – that'd make some inroads into that gut of yours.'

'Down the nudey beach! Not bloody likely.'

'We're all naked under our clothes, mate. Nothing like getting natural with Nature – giving your body to the sea unencumbered. The sea tells us our place in the great pattern of things.'

'Cor blimey, John, you're full of it today.'

'Believe me, mate, you'd wake up to stuff you'd never thought possible.'

Monty surreptitiously pulls in his stomach, puffs out his chest and orders them both another beer.

In the room at the back of the bar, Rosemary has slipped off her dress, and Lionel, with the most gentlemanly of touches, unfastens her bra, kissing the nape of her neck.

Back at the Emporium, John sucks a peppermint and sterilises a piercing needle. His next client is one of the cock-waving lads from the beach. John smiles as he secures a nipple in his tongs. 'Lionel was right,' he thinks, when the lad whimpers. 'They're only kids, bless 'em.'

Chapter Thirteen

The temperature is breaking some of Britain's summertime records, dominating the newspaper headlines, challenging the tabloids to come up with catchy weather-related daily headlines. 'Wot a scorcher!' 'Another sizzler!' and 'Some like it hot!' Rivers have evaporated to trickles; tarmacadam roads have melted, sticking to shoes and perfuming the streets with the smell of tar; rail tracks have buckled and hot bad-tempered passengers are getting stranded in overheated trains, when there are trains running between the twenty-four-hour strikes. Parkland grass has turned yellow, and British citizens are wilting. Only the very elderly can remember such heat. They used to say how wonderful it was in those days but, now that it's returned, they're not so sure. Britain is watching the national thermometer, waiting for it to hit the mystical number, one hundred degrees Fahrenheit, still a magic measurement in folk memory long after the nation changed to degrees Celsius. Brighton's beach is the place to be, desperate for sea breezes, crowds migrate to the seaside, to Harry Pollard's beach, for a front row view of the English Channel, transformed from its usual Northern European grey to Technicolor blue.

Harry soon rents out all his deckchairs, mostly to older couples and families, the young choose to lie on their towels, making lounger shapes out of the shingle, their bodies, in minimal swimming gear, stretched out in the sun, on display. Harry has nothing to do until people leave in the late afternoon, but he's kept an old deckchair for himself, repairing it with silver gaffer tape, reinforcing the wooden frame with string. He's a natural handyman, good with wood, and today, pleasantly bored in the heat, he's carving patterns in a stick with his penknife.

Kanti finds him there. She stops at a distance to observe him, unseen. 'A vision in brown,' she thinks. Shirtless as usual, his skin matches his old khaki shorts. He's solemn, concentrating, he could be one of those hippie pioneers that she has seen in old photographs from the Sixties. If she had to survive in the wild, she thinks, then she'd be safe with Harry. She stalks him like a hunter. Freezing her muscles, she holds her breath, concentrating her whole body into the fingertip poised to release the camera shutter. 'Don't escape,' she whispers. 'I have to take this.' She waits for the perfect moment, knowing that the shutter's action will alert him to her presence. It does.

'Hi there,' he smiles. He's back from his thoughts. He shields his eyes with a hand, holding the silence with the friendliest of grins. She's shy now – her fantasy wild man has become reality. She's not dressed shy though – a pea green t-shirt and orange shorts.

'I want to show you these,' she says, unzipping her artist's case to show him some prints. Her deckchair shots are cropped to show just the backs of the chairs, amply filled by occupants, differentiated only by their legs and feet splayed out beneath the bright blue candy stripes.

'I like the roundness,' Kanti explains, with no apparent irony, miming the shapes with her forefinger. 'I love the English on the beach. So worried about showing too much skin. Look at these feet. Black socks and sandals. High heels and no stockings. I love it.'

'They're just the old folks,' says Harry. 'Not everyone's like that.'

'I know, but this is so much more interesting. I've done some naked shots too, look. I took them on your naked beach. Even there they wear shoes and socks. Look.'

The photographs show elderly male nudists, studies in tumbling flesh, hirsute arms and backs, ancient penises on a background of soft-focus shingle. In the spirit of the French Revolution, her darkroom guillotine has removed their heads to show the old men in their true liberty, fraternity and equality. As naked as they were born, in some cases nearly a century ago – naked that is except for nylon socks and walking shoes, woollen socks and sandals, or old gym shoes with no socks. No longer smoothly pink babies, plump little peaches newly exposed to the world, age has withered them, they've been bloated and blemished, stretched and loosened by life. Kanti's artistry in the darkroom exaggerates their cragginess and, by doing so, she celebrates human grandeur.

'I love them,' she says, in a hushed tone. She might be on the verge of tears but Harry doesn't know what she's feeling.

'Amazing that they let you on the nudist beach with a camera,' he says, knowing he should've said more but Diep has arrived; he stands next to Kanti, smiling, sharing the conversation with darting eyes.

'Your brother doesn't say much. Does he speak English?'

'Didn't you know? He can't speak at all. Well, I've never heard

74

him speak clearly. He's profoundly deaf, but he's not dumb – he knows what I'm talking about. Don't you Diep?'

It's the first time Harry has seen them use sign language. Diep laughs a hoarse, disconcertingly joyful bark and returns an elaborate signed sentence.

'He'd be multilingual if he could speak, I'm sure. Don't ask me how he does it. He can lip read in Nepalese. Now he learns to do it in English – it's very complex but he's a genius. One day soon, he says, he will lip read fluently in English too. We can communicate without words anyway – we're twins. We're best friends too, aren't we Diep! Diep looks after me and I look after him. We're safe together, even here in a foreign land.'

'You're from Nepal?'

'Yes, from Nepal.'

'Cool.'

'From a very small town not very far from Kathmandu.'

'Kathmandu. Now that's really something.'

'Yes. You're right. A wonderful place. Like Brighton is too – a wonderful place. My town is called Pokhara. We grow up there, Diep and me, in the mountains. Very beautiful, big mountains. You have heard of Mount Annapurna. You can see it from our town. Very impressive.'

'Yes, sure. Brilliant.' Harry is quietly thrilled but he can only respond vacuously. 'Wild ganja growing everywhere. Amazing. Sounds like Paradise.'

'Yes,' she laughs. 'Paradise for you typical English boys. You love your ganja and your rock and roll, I know. You, Hari, are one Mr Typical English Boy.'

Kanti and Diep are laughing at him again.

'We are honoured to meet you and to take your photograph.'

'Well, it's good to meet you too. Both of you.'

'Now, Hari, can I do another picture. Please? I'd like to make a new photograph of a typical English boy.'

'Sure.' He shifts around as if looking for a pose. 'Where do you want me?'

'In a deckchair of course,' she giggles. 'Don't put your shirt on. Just as you are but with your beautiful African drum. Yes, and no shoes. You are not an old Englishman yet. Play your drum and pretend that I am not here. Imagine I am back in the mountains, picking you some nice ganja to make you high, high, what is it, high like a kite.'

Harry obeys. Slowly at first, self-consciously. His rhythms become more complex as he relaxes, and he does just what Kanti said. It doesn't take much to send him into daydream land. He sees her picking lush leaves in an idealised mountain landscape – snow-capped peaks, dark swathes of forest. She's by the side of a dusty path, pushing her way through the foliage, her fingers stripping the leaves from their stems. What is she wearing? No, don't go there. He can't help trying to imagine her without her European clothes – but he doesn't know what Nepalese women wear, so he lets her linger there, dangerously stripped of both culture and clothes, naked in a ganja bush, somewhere in fantasy land – an Asian Julie Andrews. No not that. The camera girl, yes, cam-er-a-girl, cam-er-a-girl... he can't stop the dream. She's dancing on a mountain alive with the sound of music, to the sound of his music and yes, she's naked.

'That's brilliant, Hari. Very good playing and I made a very good image of you, with sweat beads all shining on your beautiful English chest. Just as I wanted. Thank you again. You are my star Englishman, I tell you. You are very natural in your skin.'

'So you like English men?' he asks, pulling the djembe into his crotch.

'Oh, I like English women also. I am doing a project for my photography degree: it's called Englishness. I have to take many photographs.'

'Shouldn't you be taking men in bowler hats, eating cucumber sandwiches, and young ladies drinking lemon barley water?'

'But you never see that here. I haven't anyway. It's only in books, that kind of Englishness. I think you're teasing me, Hari. I know exactly what I want. The real English, real Brighton English actually. And you're just that.'

'But I'm from Burnley, Lancashire,' he grins.

'I don't care. All I know is what I can see. Here in Brighton it is all young people's music, guitars, drums, woolly hats and, how do you say, dreadful locks?'

'Dreadlocks!'

'Yes, dreadlocks, just like yours Hari. So you see, you are typical – my typical English boy, all right? You young English are all musicians. I have taken lots of pictures, look. Here is a nice boy with hair like you playing the flute on the beach, and here's one playing saxophone in the street. He's very happy, I think. They all have freed spirits. Here are more drummers too...' her voice rises through several octaves, as her emotion and her enthusiasm mount. 'Everyone plays drums in Brighton... guitars too, look. There's music everywhere, it is wonderful.'

'Too many I guess,' Harry says, shrugging. 'That's why we have to play on the street. I know some of these guys – Joe here, he's my mate. We jam together sometimes... right here. Maybe we can play in Kathmandu one day. I would love to do that.'

Whenever his dreams turn sour he thinks of the road to Kathmandu. There he could grow ganja and write songs about a better life – he might even write a love song. It's just a dream, he knows that, lying here on his bed, tonight. He has no clear idea of what Nepal looks like, maybe that's better. It's more real to him sometimes than his life as a deckchair attendant or his life in Burnley, Lancashire too. Kanti and her brother come from that insubstantial world. They might be his link to Paradise. That's karma, man, he thinks. He's back at his place, inhaling a joint by candlelight, grinning the grin of a high, excited, very laid-back beach bum, dreaming of a naked girl picking leaves.

Chapter Fourteen

Alan and his tenor saxophone share equal honours with the meandering street crowd this evening. He's playing his new piece, *Blue Notes*. It begins with a languid fanfare, mellow cries from his husky-toned instrument, linked by short florid sequences, melancholy-coloured with those distinctive flattened notes characteristic of the blues. It's a call to arms for anyone who has known what it's like to be lonely, disappointed, thwarted in desire, or just plain broken-hearted. It's going down well with his passing audience. Alan has touched a nerve. The saxophone speaks directly to anyone who has mooched down an empty street idly kicking a can, thinking that there must be more to life than this; anyone who wishes they could have more time to mooch; and anyone who wishes they knew how to mooch, or even kick a can. His saxophone case has had a record number of coins tossed into it – maybe because he's made a new connection with his music. He's learnt how to let the melody linger on his breath, lightly quivering with understated emotion.

Life on the street has helped him recognise his own hidden blues, the blues that he has often talked about and admired in his musical heroes, but only recently found in himself. It's a mixture of melancholy, comfort and pain, expressed in the lonely beauty of the tenor saxophone. Sometimes he used to wish that his life had been tougher, more like the genuinely harsh existence experienced by those great blues musicians. He knows that he's really just a middle-class white kid, down on his luck, but he knows too that this music is in his soul, even if he doesn't understand how it got there. Today, his blues are calling him from deep inside. Either he is giving this to the music, or the music is giving it to him. He knows he will never reach the pinnacle of inspiration of a John Coltrane or a Miles Davis but, out here on the street, he feels at least that he can look both men in the eye.

A mix of similarly blue sensations has lowered John's morale as he leaves the Golden Orb after supping a beer, sitting alone in a corner of the bar. Lionel has already gone on his cruise and John too is about to leave for India. Maybe he's unsettled by change, or just feeling down. He may have found this dark mood in the beer, or in

Alan's melancholy melody, or after some sneering remarks from a couple of lads, suddenly brave from a six-pack of lagers. 'Where's the fancy dress party, mate? Can we come too?' He doesn't react, he never does. Being shouted at in the street happens a lot these days, and it always hits him like a punch to the stomach. He recoils inside, but never lets it show.

When he was young, he was hurt in different ways – there had always been Brighton street gangs, groups of young men looking to pick on the vulnerable. Knife gangs, shaven-headed thugs and other bullies out, quite literally, for kicks. These loudmouthed drunks are not as violent but, today, the ridicule has made him question himself. Why do you have to wear your difference so publicly, you know it hurts you? It's my calling, well it feels like that, well, I believed that when I started all this. But did I? Did I really believe that? Why the wish for martyrdom? Maybe it's a death wish, we're all dying, it helps, maybe, to take the steering wheel from the great driver in the sky. To decide our own fate. But, maybe, I don't believe any of this crap. Am I just an old drama queen trying to steal a scene or two, desperate not to be invisible. Do you really need to walk around dressed in curtain material? Come on, mate, just look at the previous answers.

Alan's music has evaporated into the ether by the time John turns into his own street, terraced rows of shabby nineteenth-century houses with just a glimpse of a sea view, and with walls once painted cream, but now peeling like onion skins, calling out like John himself for a little love and attention. Brighton's distinctive stucco is crumbling in all these streets, with rust marks dripping from balconies and drain pipes, disfiguring the facia like smudged mascara on a weeping woman fallen on hard times. John opens a metal gate in the black railings that run down both sides of the street, he descends into the sunless darkness below, like a mole retreating into its hole. His apartment is in the basement of a house that has been divided into one-bedroom flats. Inside, deprived of daylight, it smells of incense, cats and damp – it has been his haven, his hide-away for years. He's been happy here – happy enough at least.

Dharma, a black cat, John's companion, some say his familiar, gives him a noisy welcome, industrial-strength purring and persistent infant-style whimpering, winding its body through his robes until it has found some legs to brush against – Dharma is hungry. John loves cats, Dharma in particular, he respects their dual natures, affection and ferocity, energy and tranquillity, love and independence. He would like to have similar control. Now though, Dharma doesn't need admiration, just feeding. John's strictly vegetarian food cupboard makes an exception of tinned tuna, Dharma's favourite. Soon the smell of canned fish infiltrates the already rich mix of aromas. Dharma eats rapidly and leaves through his cat flap to a world never shared with his feeder. John admires that. He too lives a secret life.

One ritual completed, he begins the others; he's a man of many precise obsessions. He pulls down the blinds and lights the long white candles that are placed on every available surface. Apart from a small bamboo table, the only furniture is an old sofa covered with Indian materials, woven from threads that glitter in the candlelight. The floor is uneven to walk on, there are several layers of rugs scattered randomly, treasured trophies from his Asian travels, colourful and patterned with abstract geometry in deep red, saffron and purple. He sleeps on these rugs and sits on them too when, as now, he is ready, not just ready but in desperate need of losing himself in meditation. He lights a taper from one of the candles and then puts the flame to his sticks of agarbatti incense, placed in a small terracotta flowerpot filled with earth, brought back from Tibet. It's time to remove his robes and, by doing that, to remove himself from the outside world. He keeps on his baggy beige underpants out of respect for the ritual.

Without his robe, he's a supplicant monk, liberated and exposed. He sounds a small carved brass temple bell, then, prepared, he sits on the rugs, crossing his legs, clasping his hands in front of his navel. It's a battle leaving the world behind, even for someone like John who performs this ritual every evening. Controlled deep breathing takes him into the zone, inhaling the incense. He savours each familiar scent, sandalwood and cedar wood; he can identify and separate each with ease; frankincense and myrrh, those gifts from the Magi, turmeric, ginger, the sharp hint of cloves and then mint and, finally, aniseed. His breathing resonates inside his head. Inhaled through his nose, he imagines it circulating through his body then, an unmeasured time later, the body-echoing exhalation through his mouth. Repeated until he loses all sense of terrestrial

80

time, a feeling of heat, even of flames, spreads through his body, starting somewhere behind his navel. It connects his mind and body. As it spreads, he senses the light, golden, but beyond definition, sitting directly above his head.

He sees the godchild, the merry prankster, the ultimate lover, then the young god himself, sounding his flute. Lord Krishna, or John's image of Krishna, comes to him at times like this in a mist of transcendent melody bringing him calm. Now in a trance, he begins to chant, his frail bass voice magnified, only muttered at first but finally trumpeted: 'Hare Krishna, Hare Krishna, Hare Krishna, Hare Hare, Hare Rama, Hare Rama, Hare Rama, Hare, Hare...' Repeated and repeated and repeated until Dharma returns for his cuddle.

Chapter Fifteen

It's a great photograph, in its smart white frame, it's been on his bedroom wall for a day now, and Harry looks at it often. It could be his first album cover, he thinks. It's that good. Sitting on blue and white deckchair stripes, he's away in a world created by pure drumbeats. Dusty hands outstretched, caught in mid-air, dusty feet blurred as they move in rhythm above the flinty shingle. His face, dusty too, framed by bouncing dreadlocks, wide-eyed with just a hint of a smile. He's looking towards some far distant spot, his face set mystically in a benign drummer's trance. It's pure Harry, but not how he has ever seen himself – not even on his good days. There on his chest shine those small beads of sweat that had enthused Kanti so much. Like spot-lit diamonds, they're the focus of the picture. In the darkroom, she'd found the buried essence of her subject matter. She'd given Harry a beauty that he didn't know he possessed. Now all he needs to do is to record that album.

'So you still like it then?' Kanti watches his pleasure, silently satisfied by the hidden surge of emotion. She's become a regular visitor to the deckchair store; Diep, silent and maybe slightly sullen, is there too. Today Kanti's here as an individual, not as half of a twin persona, it seems, here to celebrate her favourite photograph.

'Hey, of course I like it,' he says, fearful of his voice cracking with emotion. 'It's really great. I have it in pride of place on my bedroom wall. How did you do that? Getting me to look like that.'

'You did it, I was just there to record it. It is you, Hari. Really.'

He still doesn't trust his voice, so he just holds his grin while he can feel that spontaneous glistening in his eyes. He can't express thoughts like this, one-to-one in direct conversation, not without breaking down. He's never allowed himself to let go in front of other people. He's on the verge of it now, he can feel it. Something is unravelling inside, a coiled presence evaporating and, for a moment, he feels light-headed. She made love to him with her camera, his camera girl. Kanti knows this too – that's why she's here.

'Have I gone too far,' she wonders.

'Let me buy you some coffee,' he's fumbling for words, and there's still that catch in his voice.

They find an umbrella-shielded table at one of the beachside cafes. The usual trio: Harry in his sun-bleached denims, now wearing a shirt, Kanti and the ever-watchful Diep in their matching Che Guevara t-shirts, three-quarter-length white trousers and the inevitable red flip-flops.

'I love these restaurants,' she enthuses.

'So English, I suppose,' Harry jokes, he's got his voice back.

'Don't laugh at me,' she says, laughing. 'Really, it's the smell of coffee and seaweed and frying chips and vinegar. Everything in England smells of vinegar. It is so English sitting outside drinking coffee in the sunshine.'

'You have such a weird idea of England,' he's laughing too. He wants to touch her, but he's not ready to cross that boundary.

'It's quite a new thing, this eating outside and, anyway, most people think of England as rainy.' Harry knows this is a dull thing to say, but these boringly obvious phrases keep coming, covering for him. She's still the woman picking leaves in his dream. He still sees her naked here at the restaurant, knows what it's like to feel her skin.

'Why do you keep resisting? You should be proud of your country. It is a great place, believe me. I am very proud of my country.'

'Well you have a lot to be proud of.' Harry's struggling, he looks her in the eyes, avoiding her body. 'You have an ancient civilisation, a philosophy, and your own very special vegetation.'

'I don't mean Nepal. I'm proud of that too of course. I mean I'm proud of England.'

'Why?'

'It's the land of my fathers.'

'What do you mean?' She isn't naked any more. He's fully awake.

'Our father, our real father, he was like you – a typical Englishman. He had dreadful locks like you too. He went on what people call the hippie trail. All the way to Nepal. He met our mother in Kathmandu, in Freak Street. Yes, Freak Street, it's what it's actually called. I always loved that. Two freaks falling in love in Freak Street. We were born when they went up into the hills, near Pokhara.'

'Cool.'

'Yes, he was cool. They both were. I will show you.'

She takes a wallet from her beaded shoulder-bag and hands him a photograph, almost pushing it into his face in her enthusiasm.

'Look, I have his photograph. There he is with our mother and with us when we were just babies. We were cute then, don't you think? See his long hair, just like you.'

It's a small black-and-white photograph, flecked with the impurities of home-developing. Kanti's mother looks about the same age as Kanti is now, but dressed in a tie-dye t-shirt and long denim skirt. She's nursing the babies, literally, one on each breast, sitting on a rock, next to a young white-skinned man, long-haired, bare-chested, and smoking a reefer. They are like nineteenth-century pioneers.

'You see how cool he was. My Englishman father.'

'Yeah. A dude. Is he still in Nepal?'

'No. He had to go travelling again. He had many things he wanted to see, but now it has been twenty years, and so, maybe, he is not coming back.'

'Yeah, maybe.' Harry feels guilty, as if it's his fault, but Kanti seems unmoved by her father's desertion.

'That is why we have come here. Brighton is where he was born. I have come to find him or, if not, to find his spirit. Does that sound strange? That is why I am so happy that we saw you. You are so typical of my dream of England. Can you see that?'

'I guess.' Something is warning him. Behind the unchanging smile, and that open face, there is deep emotion. Kanti seems happy, sure, but this new intensity unnerves him. Diep is grinning as if has been expecting this – something Harry knows he can't give.

'Well I guess I'm flattered if I remind you of your Dad. You two haven't got any of his colouring, you don't have any European features, you know, if you don't mind me saying.' Every fumbled word makes him feel more foolish, more of a phoney cultural traveller, more of a cheat.

'No, we take after our mother, and that is good, because she is very beautiful. I want to find what we have inherited from our father. There will be things we take from him, things that are below the skin.'

'Have you had any luck finding him?'

'No. I've given up really. His name is John Fletcher. He doesn't seem to be in Brighton any more.'

Diep looks away – he might be starting to cry.

'Too bad, eh?'

'I don't think I ever really thought I would meet him in person. I thought I might find his spirit if I came to Brighton.'

'And have you?'

'I don't really know. Maybe. Since meeting you, maybe. Ah but I am embarrassing you, I can see that. I am sorry Hari. Really. You are you, and my father was my father. I can't turn you into him, I know that really, believe me.'

The erotic charge has disappeared. Kanti and Diep, naturally small, look vulnerable, like bright-eyed children. His children. Moments earlier Kanti had been an exotic fantasy figure, his naked prize beckoning him to paradise. Now she's his unwanted daughter, abandoned by his alter ego. It's his fault. He's discarded those babies and their mother, after plundering their world for a ganja thrill. He's been there so often in his dreams that his guilt is as palpable as if he had actually been that man, John Fletcher. Weird though it sounds, Kanti may have really thought that, in him, she'd found the spirit of her father.

'If I can help you both I will,' he says, but he doesn't know what kind of help she wants. He doesn't really know what he means either.

'You are very kind, we thank you.' She makes the slightest of bows and signs Harry's words to Diep, who looks serious, but there are no more hints of crying. The siblings sign together for some time. Whatever they are saying is animated with shared intensity.

'Diep says you're a kind man,' Kanti interprets the silent outburst. 'He hopes that you will be his friend.'

'I feel that we are already,' Harry says, hoping that he means it.

Chapter Sixteen

Joe is lying on the white leather sofa in his white boxers, the brownness of his skin highlighted by Rachel's monochrome colour scheme. He's watching the rise of Hitler on a satellite television channel – a gloomy presence in the gleaming white flat. Rachel doesn't notice. There's always a documentary about the Nazis or, channel-surfing, something about buying a house or cooking, on Britain's newly deregulated television network, so Joe usually sticks with Hitler. Don't people ever get bored with this stuff? He certainly is.

Archive footage of goose-stepping storm troopers flashes onto the screen with the crackly soundtrack of a rousing marching song.

'Sounds good, I love a bit of marching music,' Rachel says, wandering in from the bathroom, fresh and damp-haired from her shower. 'What is it?'

'Jeez, Rachel. They're Nazi storm troopers. Now that is just wrong.'

'Well I told you I wasn't really musical.'

'Yeah but you didn't tell me you're a fascist.'

'Fuck off and kill that television, will you?' She's laughing as she grabs the remote and presses *off*.

'See what I mean?' He's grinning now, mood changes come easily for Joe today, laughter too. He pulls her down on top of him. Her ivory satin dressing-gown obeys the law of gravity with silky speed and settles in an elegant pile on the floor. It's always best when they don't talk, either of them. Their bodies know what's right, even when they don't, so she settles on top of him, her fingers already tackling his designer-logo'd waistband.

'Anyway,' she says, through the kiss, 'there's nothing wrong with a bit of female bullying,' but she sits up, unsettled by the wry twinkle in his eyes. She rallies, her confidence restored, and settles back onto his crotch. 'I have to get all my own way when it's my morning off.'

There's a crack on the ceiling. Joe's only just noticed it, but as he lies there, as receptive as usual to her flesh on his, his sweat acting with the leather, sucking him onto the sofa, he focuses on this flaw in the flat's perfect décor. He is uncomfortable. Aroused and erotically charged, for sure, but his brain isn't engaged and, no matter how energetically Rachel rides his pelvis, he can't help thinking about that crack on the ceiling. It's threatening to open up and reveal the abstract phantoms from his nightmares. Mind and body have disassociated, and he has no choice but to follow his mind.

'I thought it was traditional to have a cigarette afterwards. Not blow a friggin' whistle.'

Joe, boxers back in place, has started to play his flute, a whimsical folksy tune that he uses as the starting point for a new improvisation. Rachel lies with her legs across his lap, stretching her body along the full length of the sofa.

'Anyone ever called you romantic, lady? I'm serenading you, aren't I?'

She tickles his stomach with her toes and giggles.

'What is it about music, I don't know. I guess I just don't get it.'

'Then why do you always go out with musicians?'

'I dunno. Maybe 'cos they're so sexy.'

'Yeah, sensitive and good with our fingers.'

He demonstrates his finger dexterity but she pushes him away, only just laughing, a flash of anger in her eyes.

'I just don't get the flute, it's like a penny whistle – a toy.'

'Never heard of the Pied Piper?'

'So where are you going to lead me, shepherd boy?' There's a harshness growing in her voice. 'Over the hills and far away?'

'Now that, woman, is not such a bad idea.'

'Well, before you do that, why don't I buy you lunch in town?'

Picking up her dressing-gown, she goes to the bathroom, while Joe dries his mouth and returns the instrument to his kiss-sore lips.

Rachel listens, smiling, and grins at her image in the mirror. Not bad, she thinks – in spite of the spot on her shoulder. Her body responds well to Joe, he's just as she likes it – hot and furious. If the music is still irritating, it's soon drowned out by the sound of her hairdryer.

After lunch, Joe drifts around town. Sauntering along, whistling quietly through his teeth, thinking about Rachel. She's cool, yes – sexy, no question – and generous too. Her cheque has bought his trim black jacket, the designer jeans, green trainers and the shiny gold waistcoat that he's wearing shirtless, and which catches the sunlight at the same time as his new gold earring and, when he laughs, the gold tooth halfway back on his upper jaw. She likes him looking good and he's happy to oblige.

He's laughing again now, inside - his face a benign smile. On his own again, walking down the street. He likes that. He's thinking of that crack on the ceiling, the best bit of the flat. Everything else is just so damned perfect. Perfectly dull. God yes, everything is much too white. The whole place needs messing up a bit – no, a lot – even the bed. He hates the way Rachel always makes it in the morning, brushing out the creases and plumping up the pillows like a chambermaid. And, stuff the flat anyway, music sounds much better on the beach. He's laughing because he knows he isn't going back.

Rachel is sitting, legs folded elegantly under her Perspex desk, with her perfectly straight spine making the back of her yellow calf leather chair redundant. She's in her cocoon. In her glass box of an office that sits in the middle of the open plan warehouse space that is Nirvana, her greatest achievement. She's successful, that's pretty obvious, and she loves success. It gives her what she considers freedom. She has got the best team money can buy in this town, and she enjoys displaying it like a prize. Her glass shell is surrounded by the team's brilliantly white desks, with alternately yellow and blue chairs, occupied by her young, mostly presentable, computer-literate men, bent over their work, oblivious to her in I.T. paradise. There has been just one empty desk since Alan left. Did he leave, she wonders, or was he pushed? It doesn't matter now.

Yes they are all young, her staff, very good at their jobs but, if she's really honest, they are as dull as so many of the young men in her experience. Men. Does she really like them? Really, no really, not just the sex, but the men themselves? What are they like – physically and mentally, their habits and enthusiasms? Has she ever liked their habits? Does she need their old clothes lying around? Socks – what's that all about? Don't even mention their pants.

Why is lavatory humour funny? Why joke about sex all the time? There's been nothing funny about it in her experience. If she had to choose between them, which one of her team would she go for? What would she look for? The casual dress rule was a good idea. She'd insisted on smart but informal – that way she could see their taste or spot their lack of it. There would be no hiding inside lumpy jackets or shapelessly baggy trousers. She encourages shorts in summer. She watches the men's tennis on TV mainly for the legs, but for the battles too. Tennis is like an old-fashioned tournament. They're fighting for her hand – well that's her fantasy. She will take the winner to bed, the loser will be fed to the lions. It's not really true. Not Goran Ivanišević, from this year's Wimbledon finals. He's sweet, a bit of a Kurt Cobain, he'd be wasted in a can of cat food. This year's champion, the American Pete Sampras, won't get into her bed. He's much too blokish and wholesome. She's enjoying this train of thought. Goran could be her new Kurt, but if not him, she's always the realist, which one of her computer boys, she wonders.

I don't need to worry about the size of their wallets – just the size of their waists. I mean it. I'm not crotch-obsessed. Not too much of a six-pack either – the vanity of the gym is so boring. Maybe I should date a body-builder one day, just to find out what makes them tick? Body hair? It's better than all that shaving and waxing. Male preening is very unattractive. Not sure about that 'men should be men' thing – that comes with problems too. Jesus! I know what I don't want. I don't want to be mum, and I most certainly don't want to be arm-candy. I don't want to be a mirror either, reflecting back a well-groomed ego.

Maybe I just want servicing. There are plenty to choose from – weeds, nerds, body-beautifuls, tramps, bores – but how much bodily fluid do I really want to be doused with? None from this lot, for sure.

So what's the problem? It always has to be a problem when you're a woman. Can't I admit I'm plain randy, and enjoy it? Is it a letting-go thing? Self-hate, they say. Joe is great, not like these lads, I know that. So why is it goodbye time?

Joe and Rachel are in the bar for that break-up conversation. The one that they both know will happen today. The bar is well chosen. Air-conditioning keeps everything, even them, as cool as a breeze. Large windows, sheltered by striped canvas canopies, look onto the beach. They're sitting on chocolate brown leather chairs around a dark wooden table, studded in weathered metal. Furniture armed against Nature. The place is ideal, and they both feel in control. Two glasses of Italian beer, shiveringly cold, accompany their civilized and mostly humorous conversation. They had already separated before they sat down.

Rachel's mobile phone rings. The ringtone is a strident, jangly intrusion. She removes her right earring – a large white plastic affair with pretensions to Fifties kitsch.

'This is just what I mean,' Joe laughs, when she finishes the call.

'What do you mean?' she asks mildly. She's pleased that he's so laid back about it all.

'I could never really go out with someone who has such a crappy ringtone.'

'What?'

'Don't you realise what it's saying about you?'

'It's just what was on the phone. It doesn't say anything about me. I'm not the phone.'

'That's just where you're so wrong. From being the smartest thing in the room, you just became Miss jingly-jangly-crap-ringtone woman. You've just told everyone that you've got no soul.'

'Rubbish!'

She still thinks it's rubbish as she leaves the bar. Ringtones are just ringtones, they come with the phone – her impressive *IBM Simon*, a portable computer, and her favourite toy. She'd never given ringtones a thought until now, but she is hurt just the same, and wonders if he might be right. For a guy who dosses on the beach, he sure knows a lot about new technologies, she thinks, almost scoffing.

'You live surrounded by computers and yet you've never thought of personalising your phone,' he had mocked in a gently insistent, almost caring way. 'Just do me a favour, right. As a leaving present, if nothing else, download something from this amazing site. The guy's a genius, and he's worked out a way of making phones personal. Do it just to make Joe happy, alright?'

He'd written the website address onto her phone with a reference code and an emoticon wink and, now that she's back at the flat, she finds herself wanting to please him, her sleeping shepherd. His voice, even his terrible music, continues to play in her head.

No regrets though, she's never encouraged that kind of thing. It's good to be home. Good to be here alone again, between men, good memories feeding interesting future promises. She pours some white wine into her favourite long-stemmed glass. There used to be two glasses like this, but one got broken. Now she only ever uses the survivor when she's between dates. It's a celebration glass of sorts. She has survived, yet again. Not caught yet, not found out either. She's still free, complete in herself. So she goes online; she is, she thinks, happiest on these evenings alone with her computer. It's a thing of beauty, the latest Macintosh, sleek, powerful and full of possibilities. She opens it up and then it all begins.

She loves computers. She loves them for being clean, electrical and, mostly, fast. They get straight to the point with just a few clicks of her rapier fingers; straight to the heart of things. She wants to find out how to change her ringtone, just for Joe, and there she is, typing in her name, address, mobile phone number and now even her email address – another new invention - all for no charge. She's given a choice of tones, ready, with a few instructions, to download onto her phone. It's so simple and, damn him, it would please Joe, so she clicks her fingers again: it's obvious which one to go for, she downloads the instructions for *A Tune for Rachel*.

This is brilliant, she thinks. There's nothing wrong with her old jingle, but there it is, a child's keyboard; she finds the notes and then there's her tune. There's more downloading and tinkering but she's enjoying this. Her *IBM Simon* is singing her song and, yes, she loves it.

Chapter Seventeen

Lionel knows how to create the perfect bowtie knot – he's always taken pride in mastering traditional techniques. He's taking his time perfecting the final touches to his tuxedo ensemble, here in his cabin in the bowels of the cruise ship Estella. For six weeks, he'll be the ship's lobby pianist. His white shirt, he starched and ironed it himself, is completed with small twenty-four-carat golden button studs, four of them shining between his collar and the black silk cummerbund that is pulled tight around his not inconsiderable waist. His cufflinks are unadorned golden tablets, elegant and understated, but enough of his stiff white cuffs will be seen when he plays the piano for the gold to catch the light. Flashy enough, he thinks, for a man who tries to hide his flashiness. Now he just needs the white jacket, the black one is for the evenings. He's ready for the lunchtime shift, but he takes a moment to double-check the butterfly wings on the bowtie in the mirror attached to his cabin door.

'Hurry up Lionel, mate, I want to take a crap,' his cabin-mate, Vince, moans. Vince is lying on the top bunk, in his less than white sleeveless vest and matching boxer shorts. 'I'd like to do it in private, I think you'd like it that way too. Know what I'm saying.'

'Nearly ready, old thing, then I'll leave you in peace.'

It's not ideal, sharing the tiny cabin with Vince Ford, the drummer in the ship's show band. Vince has a landlubber's stomach.

The Estella, one of the smaller cruise ships on the Mediterranean route, is luxurious enough for the paying passengers who are happy to be pampered in the style of those three star resort hotels commonly found on the Spanish Riviera. The various communal rooms, restaurants, games rooms, a gym, and several bars, are cheerfully decorated in bright holiday colours, with a bias towards orange and red. The walls in the main public areas are hung with framed photographs of the seaside resorts and harbours along their route, which runs from Southampton to Dikili in Turkey, and then to Alexandria in Egypt. The cruise will take in Spain, Italy and Greece too, before turning round and making its way back to Southampton, by way of Gibraltar and Spain again. The photographs imply that the cruise will take the holidaymakers on a detailed tour of some of Europe's most famous landmarks: the Parthenon, the Coliseum, the 'original' Trojan Horse, Mount Vesuvius in full lava flow, and the Rock of Gibraltar with its monkeys. Squeezed in between shopping trips round the various harbour markets, there will be a few coach trips inland, to see some of these wonders, but most of the time will be spent on board ship, sitting on deck in rows of deckchairs, eating and drinking in the themed bars and restaurants below, or shopping in the ship's very own mini shopping mall.

The central atrium, between the shops and the restaurants, is the Estella's heart. It's the meeting point and the entertainment centre, approached from all sides by corridors and metal stairways. It's brightly lit, maybe too brightly, in compensation for being below deck, and it's stocked full of plants, exotic palms and ferns, interspersed with large urns filled with red and white geraniums and giant arum lilies. In the centre of this bustling circle is a raised platform supporting a white grand piano, a sleekly elegant *Yamaha C2*, lit from above by a blue spotlight. It is here that Lionel plays piano from eleven-thirty in the morning until three in the afternoon and then again in the evenings, from five-thirty until eight, before the dance band takes over and the proceedings get considerably livelier.

He begins as he always begins – with *Begin The Beguine*, the Cole Porter classic from 1935. First a little preparatory finger stretching, a final check on those cuffs, a nervous adjustment to the piano stool, a cough and a final look around. It's busy this morning, the passengers are in determined shopping mode. He would have preferred it if more of them sat down at the tables near the piano, but at least they can hear his playing while they compare perfumes, silk scarves and cashmere cardigans in the various adjoining boutiques. His fingers feel light today, restless to get into action, as if they would play without him.

Begin The Beguine is his speciality. It's a complicated piece, and even Cole Porter himself said that he could never play it without the score. Lionel is proud to have memorised it, and enjoys performing it with his eyes either closed or whimsically focused on some imagined paradise in the middle distance. On other trips, many a middle-aged female heart has fluttered when his gaze appeared to settle on them when, in fact, he was only looking at the clock. The

Beguine is a Caribbean dance, suggestively erotic in Cole Porter's hands, sex lightly concealed under an elegant wrap. It was written when the composer was himself playing the piano on a cruise ship, the elegant Cunard liner the Franconia, on a leisurely Pacific trip in 1935. Lionel, ignoring the shopping frenzy, tries to become Cole Porter in person. Allowing his fingers to recreate that steamy mix of French and Spanish rhythmic insouciance, in his own very English style of Caribbean Creole, he re-imagines the good ship Estella as the luxurious RMS Franconia now, sadly, scrapped.

He's finishing the repeat of the big melody in its second sixteen bar appearance and about to move into the next sixteen, when he hears the tapping noise: a quiet but firm stamping sound, not a noise in fact, it's in time with his beat. It continues and then he sees her, a woman in a pale blue dress with a large white handbag on her arm, gently tap-dancing in front of the perfume shop. Lionel doesn't miss a beat, he's far too inside the music for that, but he's free enough to look over and smile encouragement. She doesn't need much, and soon she's gently soft-shoe shuffling over to him, fixing her eyes on him, firmly confident, her face lit up in approval. There's nothing too ostentatious about her little dance, it's half-hidden, underplayed but sharply rhythmical. She's now by the piano, a woman in her late middle age, slim, proud enough of her legs to flaunt them, but careless enough about her appearance to go without make-up, and to wear a headscarf on what is, presumably, a bad hair day.

'Wonderful song,' she says, in an East Coast American undertone. He can feel her breath on his cheek. 'Cole Porter knew how to raise the temperature alright.'

Lionel smiles back at his implied dancing partner, and moves into the repeat of the first sixteen bars.

'Let's begin the Beguine,' she whispers as she loosens up her act, leaving her bag on the piano; she quickens her steps, clicking her heels loudly enough to let him know that she can tap.

Unlike Cole Porter, she doesn't need the score. She sings the words audibly, but only loud enough for Lionel to hear.

'Play it again,' she pleads, mockingly desperate. 'Please, Mr Piano Man.'

'Only if you sing it out loud – I know you can.'

'If you insist, kind sir.' She's playing to her audience of one and enjoying herself. So they do it, he upping the tempo a bit and she crooning in a voice that only shows its age under pressure. They are having fun, the old geezer in the tux and the funny lady in the scarf. It's possible that some of the passers-by notice that, every now and then, the two exchange smiles. When the great melody returns for the last time, Lionel slows the tempo without slackening the rhythm, and his singer reprises her foot-stamping tap routine for a final flourish. In the movie, they would have finished to wild applause, a standing ovation acknowledging their genius. It isn't like that in the Estella's shopping atrium, the passengers are too busy buying souvenirs.

'Fred and Ginger couldn't have done it better,' Lionel says, as he does a quick segue into another Cole porter classic, *Anything Goes*.

'Not Ginger. It was Eleanor Powell if you don't mind,' she says. 'Fred Astair and Eleanor Powell, *Broadway Melody of 1940* – the best tap-dancing ever put onto celluloid. Sorry Ginger, but Eleanor Powell was the greatest – along with Fred of course.'

'I stand corrected. I don't argue with a lady who knows how to tap. I wouldn't dare.'

'You're forgiven sir. Your piano saved you.'

'I'm Lionel, by the way, and I'd forgive you anything with a voice like that'.

'Well, Sir Lionel, when you've stopped extracting the spine from *Anything Goes*, what about *Every Time We Say Goodbye*? It might just be my favourite.'

She's leaning on the piano as if they performed here together every day.

'My pleasure, I love it too,' he says, tightening up his version of *Anything Goes*, trying to save it from his obvious loss of concentration. 'I'm more of an Artie Shaw than a Fred Astaire man; the same with *Every Time*, I'm addicted to the John Coltrane recording. So gently passionate.'

'I love that too. Forgive me if I'm wrong, but isn't Coltrane's pianist McCoy Tyner? Wow, that guy could play. Oh, and I'm Kate. I'm pleased to make your acquaintance.'

'Madam, if I were wearing a hat, I would take it off for you and probably eat it too. I'm impressed.'

He's more than impressed, he's moved. The women in his life have never been like this. They've never shared his passions, not in

95

all the details. If he was going to play *Every Time We Say Goodbye,* then he was going to do the best performance of his lifetime – and he does.

When he finishes, Kate's still leaning on the piano, but now there are tears in her eyes. She finds a handkerchief and blows her nose, fortissimo and unashamed.

'Dammit, that song always gets me. Every time – I die a little. That was wonderful Lionel, I mean it.'

'I was playing for a pro, that's what inspired me. You, Kate, have definitely done this before.'

'Oh, I was so off Off-Off-Broadway, it was hanging on by my fingernails.'

She's laughing but still dabbing away the tears, as she takes a notebook from her bag. Quickly writing down a number, she tears out the page and slips it into Lionel's breast pocket, patting it affectionately.

'If you fancy a stiff one after this, I'll be in my room.'

Lionel laughs and then, when she realises what she's just said, so does she.

'I meant a drink! Now you've got me blushing, and that doesn't happen too often.'

She squeezes his arm and leaves, while he, with some difficulty, resumes his Cole Porter marathon. An offer I can't refuse, he thinks.

Chapter Eighteen

Kanti's photograph has made Harry reconsider his role as the coolest dude on his bit of the seafront. She may have bewitched him, or merely opened his eyes. He's started to write again, but he's gone off his old songs, now they seem naïve – rock'n'roll boys'n'girls, in and out of love, adolescent angst, self-centred neediness, occasional bursts of puppy joy, and insecurity behind every line. He can do better than that, he knows it. He's disappointed too with his new material. Now it sounds too adult, too detached, tired even, not his well-worn persona at all: Harry, the easy-going hippie bloke. Maybe he's too much the son of Kanti's hippie father, a couple of generations too late, uncritically impressed by the paraphernalia of post '60s cool, a facile white boy trying to be hip.

Maybe without the dreadlocks, the casually disregarded facial hair, the young man's body and libido and, of course, the tan, he's just another worn-out Englishman about to lose his youth, heir to a dying culture, and trying too hard to make banality sound profound with a few guitar chords and a drum. He can't judge, and just doesn't know if these post-euphoria ballads are any good. By giving up songs about young love and adolescent pain, he may have ended up just writing about getting laid. Maybe all songs were about that, all of his at least. He might have finally lost it.

He's sitting in his old deckchair, wallowing in the mellow light of a high summer's evening. The other deckchairs are all packed away, the holidaymakers have left, probably for fish and chips, or a few beers in the seafront pubs. Some lads are sitting on the shingle with a pack of lager, laughing and tossing stones into the sea, and a few couples are savouring the eternal romance of evenings such as this. Harry too is stirred by the power of the dying sun. He's playing his djembe, singing under his breath, and trying not to admit that he's really thinking about sex. He discreetly rests his hands in his crotch when Kanti and Diep find him there.

'You look so serious, Hari.' She holds his arm with both hands. 'Don't you like us any more?'

'Of course I do,' he begins, but then sees they're joking.

'Don't worry Hari, we don't want to be your little boy and girl! You're not Dad, honestly. You're our friend that's all.'

She looks at Diep, who nods earnestly.

'OK, OK, Diep, I'm gonna ask him.'

She lets go of Harry's arm and stands back, lining herself next to her brother in mock formality, and dipping into a curtsy.

'My brother and I would like you to come to our final show at college. Will you come?'

'Your final show?'

'Yes, our final show.'

'I'd really like that. The end of your course?'

'Yes. After the show we will be finished. Exciting isn't it. We will be honourable degree holders from one of your fine British colleges. Then we will become real artists, fully qualified. So you will come to see our work?'

'Of course.'

'We have a special opening tomorrow and we both really want you to be there, Hari. So you promise you will come?

He promises and means it. He wants to see their work, he wants to support them too. He feels responsible. Perhaps he wants to make up for the loss of their father, for them being alone in a foreign country, vulnerable in a cynical world where he has been too often the most cynical guy that he knows. He hopes to put things right for them. It could be those things but, God, is he doing this because he likes them, or is it all just about fancying a woman?

Whatever his reasons, he meets Kanti the following evening at the art college, Brighton's trendy arts palace, a shabby concrete building once chicly Modernist and now down-at-heel, and dressed up with banners and posters, still shabby, but proud of it. Kanti is waiting for him at the door, no primary colours this time, just a simple black skirt over white cotton trousers and a very wide grin. She almost hugs him, but holds back. The hug however is written on her face.

'Come with me, thank you so much for coming, I'll show you round.' She holds his hand and pulls him through the entrance hall, through a couple of other rooms until they reach her display.

He thought he knew what her exhibition would look like. He's seen a lot of her work already, but he wasn't expecting the photographs' impact when enlarged, framed and hung in a spacious white room on their own. This show is about him. There he is, larger than life, the main event in the room – 'Harry the djembe man' and 'Harry the acrobat'. He looks magnificent, epic, gigantic; his body, a palpable presence, dominates the space. He looks away quickly, his eyes welling up. The man in these dramatically lit black-and-white images isn't the disappointed and morose self-apologist that he thought he'd become. Kanti has found, or even invented, a different Harry – a man with a vision. There are other photographs too, all on a grand scale, but everything else in the room is secondary to Harry, the drummer-god, Kanti's typical Englishman.

Of course there are also the nudists from the beach, more epic images in black-and-white, each photograph expressing joy in the unexpected – Kanti's trademark. Old, often fat, naked men with shrivelled muscles and sagging flesh, displaying vintage genitals for her camera; old women too, similarly exposed, with deflated breasts and rolls of fat. Wrinkled bodies proudly on display – Kanti hasn't been recording decay, she's celebrating heroic humanity, facing the reality of mortality. Lionel is there, wet from the sea, solemn, dignified, unflinchingly and full-frontally naked; an old Greek deity, Poseidon, past his sell-by date perhaps, but fresh from his ocean kingdom.

On another wall, her latest project, the deckchair bum-shots, similarly epic in scale. Here are more elderly people, but dressed this time, their buttocks filling vividly colour-enhanced striped deckchair canvases in photographs with garishly saturated colour. The swelling curves that fill the seats are uniform, not obviously male or female, voluptuous images of physicality in repose. Underneath the deckchairs, individuality is revealed by swollen ankles, burst blood vessels, gnarled feet, bare or sandal-clad, stretched out, relaxed, careless, tense or exhausted. No beauty parade this, but a snatched moment of rest on the journey through life.

New to Harry is the series of pictures of Brighton's street musicians. Kanti has been observing buskers all summer, and her photographs, monochrome this time, are portraits, old master style, frozen in time, men and women absorbed in performance. There are innocent-faced music students, a young woman in a girlish summer frock and a hairband playing the violin, probably Vivaldi, she is seriously determined, her concentration making her frown. A long-limbed lad playing the bassoon, it has to be Mozart; his body poised, uncharacteristically elegant, elongated by the composer's legato phrase. An unshaven middle-aged man with fear in his eyes looks at the camera. His nicotine-stained fingers find life in a piano accordion, a silent melody impregnated with melancholy. A young man with a saxophone outside a pub – oblivious, lost in his playing: Alan on the day he left Rachel. Joe is there too, barefoot in the sea, playing his flute, his skin lit in the reflected light from the incoming tide, his eyes laughing, his flute a magic wand, silver rays shining in sunshine.

'You like them? I know you do because this is your world, Hari. This is my England and yours too, yes?'

'If only we could live up to your image of us,' he says, awed, hoping, or maybe daring to think that he might emulate his photographed self one day.

'So you see Hari. I love your bums – all of them. They are free just like you. You needn't have feared.'

'Feared what?'

'Oh, that my father was like you. You thought he was a bum, and you were right, he was, but he wasn't a bad man. He made us laugh. He gave us joy before he went away. The gift of joy is always there, always, once you've known it. Our father turned the switch for us, that's all any of us need. He gave me that, and I love him for it. You too could be a bum like that, if only you try hard enough.'

'What about your mother? Is she as charitable?'

'Oh sure. but it's nothing to do with charity. She loved him. That was enough. Another gift from a bum. Now she has a proper husband. He's a government officer, and she is just fine. They made more babies, and she is a rich lady, and happy. So, Hari, as you say, no big deal.'

'I'm humbled by all of this. Amazed too. I don't know what to think.'

'Well, Hari, before we go back to Pokhara, I want you to know that I love you being a bum.'

'An arse, you mean. You were right first time.'

She's laughing; he is too – time for a kiss planted respectfully on her cheek and to reach it Harry has to bow. Appropriate, he thinks.

'Now, let's go,' she says. 'You haven't seen Diep's work. It's in the next gallery.'

Not for the first time, he's forgotten about Diep who's waiting for them in the next room, sitting on a chair in the corner, impassively looking at the ground.

The room is painted marine blue, and lit so brightly that it's momentarily blinding on entry. Uncomfortable too is the loud exaggerated treble on the looped recording of herring gull shrieks. The whole space is dedicated to Diep's installation. The floor's covered with sand, except in the middle where there's a circular island of shingle, enclosed by a bright blue picket fence and, at its heart, a mountainous construction. Many deckchairs, all blue and white stripes, are piled on top of each other in disorderly chaos, the wooden frames broken, splintered, jutting out from the mound. The deckchair fabric has melted in places where the whole pile has been attacked with a blowtorch. A strong smell of burnt plastic permeates the space and Harry wants to gag. He covers his nose, feeling like a witness to an accident. Most shocking are the realistic human limbs that splay out from under the molten remains. Some of them are charred, blackened bones stripped of skin. Others lacerated and contorted fingers or toes outstretched in death's agony. Harry can't look away, he's held by their power.

'Diep won top award,' Kanti whispers, holding his hand. 'He is not so forgiving as me.'

Chapter Nineteen

John isn't wearing his robe. He isn't wearing anything. Lying on his back, body drenched in oil, he's happy to be in India. Happier still to be here on a makeshift massage table, outside his little thatched-roof bamboo house, surrounded by palm trees, on a hill over-looking the sea.

'Now you have truly left Britain behind you. I feel it in your body Jonno,' says a young Indian man, wearing a small pink-and-green chequered towel, tucked in at the front. Rajiv Namputiri has grown up in the year since John last visited the small village of Kovalam, in Kerala province, Southern India.

'You are still a man of habits,' Rajiv says, applying more oil to John's stomach, spreading it over his thighs and up to his chest. 'You were lucky to get the same house this time, Jonno, many tourists from Europe and America come here these days. They are getting braver. They like to rent remote houses away from eyes that don't need to see.'

'Sometimes I think I should buy this place from your father, Rajiv. It's where I'm most at home.'

'It will always be your home to me, Jonno.'

It is hot, too hot for talking, so John just smiles, feeling the young man's fingers probe beyond the pale of European decorum. Rajiv's Ayurvedic massage is uncompromising; John loves its recklessness.

Later, the two lie together on John's bed, with the shutters open, cooled by the swaying palm trees, nature's air-conditioning system. Their bodies had met as old friends this visit, and John's fingers take their turn to do the exploring. Rajiv is now twenty-eight; he looks more than a year older than when they last lay here in the little one-roomed woodland house, part of the family business, owned by Rajiv's hotelier father. John has been coming here for ten years, returning regularly after a promise made to the beautiful eighteen-year-old Rajiv, who manages the cottages. Now there's an ugly scar running from the young man's left hip up that side of his body to his nipple. John traces its pattern with his index finger, he finds nothing about Rajiv ugly.

'Have you had surgery?' he asks, but Rajiv just grins.

'Urumi wound,' he says, struggling for words after their shared silence. 'I have progressed to a new weapon in Kalaripayattu. You learn to be careful after you're wounded.'

'You do indeed,' John sighs. He has seen the balletic but ferocious martial art of Kalaripayattu. He has been thrilled by the athleticism and the danger, when the two fighters leap to avoid the unforgiving blade of the Urumi, a savage weapon made of a long flexible blade, part sword, part whip.

'I hate to see you hurt,' he says, retracing his finger over the wound.

'It was nothing. Just a good lesson – so really it was more than nothing. I won't get wounded again.'

'The Urumi is so dangerous. You be careful, please. For me, if not for you. I suppose it's the ultimate weapon, I can see that, but you are too beautiful, Rajiv.'

'No, not the ultimate weapon, Jonno. After the Urumi, we use these, our bare hands.' Rajiv is chuckling gently when he puts his hands over John's ears, pressing his long fingers firmly into the back of his lover's head, and pulling him into a kiss.

Reluctantly, but excited too, John has agreed to watch Rajiv perform his Kalaipayattu on a remote part of the beach. He's come to see the demonstration of Urumi sword-fighting, away from tourists' eyes. John wears plain grey shorts and a t-shirt; he keeps a low profile in India, especially around Rajiv's traditionally-minded parents. Rajiv is about to wear his kachha, the Kalaipayattu uniform, a long single sheet of cotton, wound many times round the waist like a muscle-hugging nappy, secured by a scarlet sash that leaves the upper torso and legs unprotected. John watches as Rajiv, his body oiled, ties one end of the cloth round a palm tree and then wind himself up into it with ritual precision.

The final detail is the Urumi itself, a five-foot flexible blade, razor-edged on both sides, and kept wrapped around the waist like a lethal belt. John nods a silent greeting when they meet Rajiv's sparring partner, Akshat Valodi, dressed and oiled identically, a handsome young man, fully Rajiv's equal, distinguished from his friend by his manly build, hirsute chest and thick black moustache. He has brought two small circular shields, and hands one to Rajiv.

'A pleasure to meet Rajiv's great friend,' Akshat says, with a slight bow, as he shakes John's hand. 'We will perform Kalaipayattu in

103

your honour.'

'I don't see any scars on your body, Akshat,' John observes wryly. 'You must be a great warrior.'

Akshat laughs, and holds out his arms to display his torso. 'No wounds yet, no serious ones, but Rajiv will give me one some day, I feel sure.' He slaps his hand on Rajiv's back; they laugh, with just a hint of shyness, before their faces freeze to neutral. The look is held between them, their eyes alight with warrior passion. It isn't lost on John, but he buries the thought. He decided after his first visit to Kerala that he wouldn't ask Rajiv what went on when he was back in England.

'I'll be careful now,' Akshat says, his eyes twinkling mischievously. 'Rajiv must look pretty for his wedding.'

John isn't sure what happens next. Blood rushes to his head. He sits, almost falling, on the sand; Rajiv blushing, looks away, and Akshat too is silent, head bowed. Then a rush of movement, the two men leaping, crouching, jumping twice their body height, long blades flashing, cutting the air like whips, blocked, metal on metal, by shields. Magnificent, the prowess, the peak of fitness, the athleticism and the frisson of danger. He should be excited seeing Rajiv so fluent and skilled, absorbed in his culture, reclaimed by an ancient world where John himself has no part. Rajiv looks complete without him, and John feels no excitement, no engagement in this trial of strength, just a chill spreading like poison through his body.

He leaves as soon as he can, when the match is over, when Rajiv and Akshat, sweating and panting, bow to each other and then to him. He won't remember what is said, what neutral remarks he uses to cover his grief, but he walks home alone, hurrying to find some comfort in seclusion.

There is peace in the ganja, smoked cross-legged on the floor of his hut. Drug-fuelled meditation takes him to a place beyond pain; sadly, he knows from inside his trance, it takes him beyond joy too. Maybe this is enlightenment. Free from the distractions of sex and love, his true place in the natural world. A solitary human, a tired man, joined in the eternal cycle of time – day and night, life and death, ignorance and understanding.

'I was going to tell you,' Rajiv says, nervously, when John awakens to find him standing there in the doorway. He's wearing his chequered towel again. 'It isn't what I want. I need you to know that.'

John can't answer, content enough, almost happy, that Rajiv has returned.

'My parents arranged it. It is their culture, mine now I suppose. I am not warrior enough after all, it seems. Not brave enough to tell them what I want, what I need, who I am. Not man enough, maybe,' he smiles beguilingly.

John smiles too. 'No, my friend, you are man enough alright. More than enough.'

'I don't want this to make a difference between us.' Rajiv sits down next to John, cross-legged too, putting his arm round him in a hug. 'When you come here, I will be yours. I hope you know that. It will always be like that.'

'And likewise, my friend,' John whispers, putting a hand on Rajiv's knee.

Much later, when darkness hides the world outside, Rajiv busies himself around the hut, lighting candles and incense sticks, and setting a small fire in front of the house.

'Let me dance for you, Jonno. I have brought my things. Make yourself another joint, and I will get ready.'

After lighting the fire, he sprinkles herbs into the flames and chants a plangent mantra that John has not heard before. Then, from a small leather briefcase, Rajiv retrieves everything necessary to prepare himself for the ritual. Black eye make-up, red dye for the palms of his hands and the soles of his feet, anklets strung with small bells, two earrings, one representing his male side, the other the feminine, red lipstick, an elaborate gold-coloured necklace representing a serpent sliding down his chest, matching armlets, bracelets and rings and, finally a thick gilt belt to secure his waist towel.

When he's ready, he indicates that John should stay where he's sitting, and then, with a seemingly effortless leap, he lands, his body transformed in mid-air. He becomes Shiva, lord of the dance, warrior turned dancer, lover turned healer, body glistening, bells jingling with the supple, limb-stretching movements as athletic and flexible as anything in his Kalaipayattu. He is at once, through the power of dance, the Lord who is half woman – Shiva, the eternal

105

male and Parvati, the eternal female – erotic, sublimating and unifying. A sacred lap-dance at times obscured to John's eyes by each exhalation of smoke, at other times by his own tears.

'Now come with me,' Rajiv half-whispers, taking John's hands, pulling him up and guiding him to the fire. 'Repeat my words as we make procession round the sacred fire. This is our secret yajna, Jonno.'

'My love, can you really mean this? Isn't it blasphemy in your religion?' John is moved, crying and smiling, he holds back for one last piece of reassurance. 'Don't destroy your life for me.'

'I am sure, Jonno, come with me to the fire. This is our eternal vow, before the gods. They see the spirit and our spirits are beyond gender, beyond the body. This is our gandharva, our joining, Jonno. I have to have this – we both do, don't we?'

John can't answer, he can find no more words other than the ones Rajiv coaxes him to repeat. When they are said, communication flows between their clasped hands and he's led round the fire by his dancing lover-bridegroom.

Chapter Twenty

It's a humid, clammy experience on Brighton beach tonight. Alan's musty sleeping bag softens the worst of the shingle's hardness on a back used to Rachel's *Deep Memory* mattress. If it did truly have a memory it would tell an interesting story, he thinks. Turning over again, he's still trying to sleep, but it's an intermittent pleasure between long bouts of sweaty restlessness. Too hot to lie in the sleeping bag, he uses it as a ground sheet, exposing his long-limbed body, hoping to catch any passing gusts of cool air. It's too hot to wear anything except his boxer shorts. It's getting light now, blackness turning to a faint bluey grey as sea and sky gradually come into focus. Lulled by the rhythmic lapping of the sea, he drifts into the deepest sleep of the night, finding peace in the sound of inner voices, his only companions since he started living rough.

Rachel is there, she's often in his sleeping head, soothing his body, finding his need and bringing him home released. His inner Rachel is in soft focus, warmly feminine without the edges. She's designed for his pleasure, a perfect fit for unspoken fantasies, always obliging, always impressed, only there for comfort – like the *Deep Memory* mattress. She lulls his fears, soothes his muscles, taking him to life in a meandering, painfully beautiful and unrepeatably perfect saxophone riff.

Some distance away, up there on the promenade, Nico sees everything, and nothing. In shorts and singlet, he has kicked off his shoes after his dawn run, and now stands, knees bent, arms stretched, with hands held loosely in front of him, palms facing his chest. His deep-breathing is synchronised with the rhythm of the waves, distantly lapping towards shore. He begins a Chinese moving meditation form, slowly bending down on his haunches then stretching upwards, hands rising like wings until they meet above his head. In an ancient tradition, he's greeting the rising sun. He repeats the move nine times: he has learnt to respect the number nine – it brings with it a sense of a higher, non-worldly completion. As his standing body flies like a bird, a sea eagle perhaps, riding the air currents, eyes alert to all movement, he sees the horizon, beyond the horizon too, grey meeting grey, sea and sky, sea and stone and that man lying asleep as the day breaks.

Rachel loosens her grip, she's slipping away, returning Alan to earth; now he knows where he is, and what is happening. He's not alone and, in that moment, he's too frightened to look. Someone's moving his arm, a gentle grip, professionally methodical like a mortician. He goes suddenly cold, maybe he's dead. In fear's paralysis he's helpless, this death is far from calm. He can feel the breath on his chest, it smells of alcohol, but he can't open his eyes. Through his eyelids, the dawn light is darkened by shadow. His saxophone case, always at his side, his comfort, gradually slides away from him. Then it's all action, fast. He jumps up and sees not one figure, but two. There's a crack as a man falls, a marionette puppet sliced from its strings.

'Clear off! Go while you still can.' The voice sounds American – a man in running clothes and bare feet.

The fallen thief groans, holding his head.

'Go, alright. And don't come back – I'll be watching out for you.'

'Fucking maniac,' the fallen man mutters, staggering to his feet. Probably around the same age as Alan and Nico, he looks a lot older, pale and emaciated, with pinpoint eyes. Even in the half-light, Alan can see his face – hungry and angry, like a junkie. His body's thin and wiry inside jogging pants and a torn camouflage anorak. He might not have given in so easily if Nico had dropped his guard, but their eyes meet and, wiping blood from a mouth already scab-crusted, he retreats over the shingle in a half-run, half stumble.

'Are you alright?" Nico asks.

'Yeah. I guess.'

Alan picks up his sax and checks it, as Nico makes his way up the beach.

'Hey,' Alan calls. 'Thanks! That was truly amazing.'

'It was nothing, he won't trouble you again, I reckon.'

'Well, thank you all the same.'

'Whatever you keep in that case is vulnerable out here, my friend.'

'It's my saxophone.'

'It makes you a target. You were lucky to keep it.' Nico returns, putting out his hand in greeting. 'I'm Nico, good to meet you, Mr Saxophone Man.'

'I'm very glad to meet you too, Nico. I'm Alan and thanks again.'

'No need for all these thanks.'

Nico bows, still in martial mode, then makes his way back to his running shoes as Alan sorts through his sleeping bag. He's still trembling. The *Discman* is gone along with his CDs – a cruel loss, so many rarities collected over the years, but the shock dulls his pain. What else was there to steal apart from them and his sax? A pair of old trainers, a few odd socks and a sweaty t-shirt. This is his choice, this life sleeping rough, his version of freedom, his childhood's dream: just him, a man and his saxophone, like a man and his dog, a wandering minstrel in a cowboy film, never settling for long, always moving on, beyond the sunset. Maybe the reality isn't quite so sweet. The look in that man's eye had been dangerous, he knows that. A killer moment. He would never have fought the guy off without Nico. Maybe he isn't cowboy enough to live out here on his imaginary prairie.

If he's on the run, it isn't from hell. Rachel was no devil, and the marketing job had been fun. No, it wasn't about that. He opens the case and checks the saxophone again. It's beautiful. He thinks that every time he takes it from its soft velvet cradle. His fingers were born to press those lily pad keys, the perfect foil, physical contact beyond the erotic. The saxophone shines like a sword in the rising sun, reawakening his childhood dream. Aladdin could wish for no more. Its mellow voice croons with the dawn, no damage done.

He reprises his song, *Blue Notes*, this skinny white jazzman in blue boxer shorts, sporting his first beard, adult at last, playing, or so it seems, to the retreating stars and the morning sun. He's playing too for Nico, his guardian, who watches and listens from a distance. When Alan finishes, Nico gives him the thumbs up.

Chapter Twenty-One

It's Saturday morning and, for once, there's no man in Rachel's bed. She can spread her legs, lie in the middle of the mattress and try to forget that she should have washed the sheets after Joe left. She gets there though, deciding it's fine to lie in last week's bedding; just as it's fine not to rush into the bathroom for her daily dental flossing and mouthwash. She's happy, she decides. Mild sloppiness can be tolerated today. The sun has made a dramatic entrance into her living room, casting black and white stripes, shadows and light, seeking out the single white lily in a tall glass vase on the dining table. Light can always turn the prosaic into the erotic for her.

She likes the way it rests on the flower's waxy curves, and wants to capture the moment with her camera. It's an idle day, no pressure, no man to distract her, so it's a good time to get out her professional quality camera, a new *Canon EOS 1N*, left too long in its case. She finds her tripod too and sets up her equipment. The sunlight won't wait, so she acts fast, but without hurrying, fully absorbed until she's captures the image of curves and shadows, creamy white undulations guiding the eye to a golden stamen. A fiery cross, maybe sticky with pollen.

Her mobile phone rings – that ringtone again, it still excites her – *A Tune For Rachel*. Why does she like it so much? It gets to her just below the ribs. It's playing with her. It's only a ringtone, for God's sake. Damn Joe, she grins.

It stops – it's too far away, she goes back to her shot before the sun shifts, looking for something new to rhapsodise. The sun, her personal sun, illuminates symbols for her – an unspoken dialogue that she tries to express in her photography. She's missed the call by the time she picks up the phone. She's taking her time today and throws herself down on her bed and lies there, a lily reborn, her body too, a study in curves. Holding the phone in both hands, loving it almost, she has to play THAT ringtone again – then once more and then again.

Then it rings without her.

'Hello?'

There's no one there. It's a text message, she's still not used to them – texting, another late century, technological miracle. She feels stupid – still a novice in the mobile phone revolution since texting has become the new talking.

'How do you like your tune? Hope it makes you feel good.'

The words give her a rush, first fear and then something more intense – just like the ringtone. Nothing to worry about with this guy, if it is a guy and not a machine, she thinks, excited. She doesn't know why she's allowing this spectral man into her bedroom. No need to weigh up the wisdom, it's better to follow her instinct, so she quickly types her reply.

'I love it. How did you know what I'd like?'

'That's how it works.'

'Do you know me then?'

'Not like that. It's not like that. No need to worry though.'

'I'm not worried.'

'Good. Text me when you want. It's part of the deal.'

'Wow! Really? Is this a trick or something?'

'No. Just part of the service, Rachel.'

The call comes again but, this time, she doesn't answer it. Maybe it's a hoax and, anyway, she's in love with her camera today. She sets up her tripod on the balcony for another attempt at the perfect sea shot. One day she'll get it, that definitive photograph of the sea and sky and, maybe, something indefinable on the other side of the line that joins them.

Her best photographs are a search for something beyond her comfort zone, even beyond her understanding. Maybe not today though. She's too distracted by that call.

'Did he mean it?' she wonders. A new sensation has invaded her. 'I'll test it out – fuck him if it's a sales pitch.'

The last caller has left a message – she's excited again but it's only her mother.

'Hello, love. Are you still coming to the pub tomorrow lunchtime? Hope so. Give us a ring.'

She has lunch with her mother on a Sunday once a month – no need to ring back yet, she thinks, irritable – disappointed too.

'Hello again,' she texts. 'I'm taking you up on your offer. Do you really exist?'

There's no immediate answer – that's what she'd half-expected, what she'd feared. Time to end this mystery before it makes a fool of her. She's frightened of holding onto the intangible. 'Oh yeah,' she says, out loud. 'Just a trick, the bastards.' She's disappointed because she loves new technology – so full of promises and potential excitement. It's her brave new world. Then the ringtone again.

'Glad you called. Yes, I exist. Sorry not to get back straight away – I couldn't find my phone.'

'Makes you sound almost human.'

'I am – there's man beyond the text – I promise.'

'It's weird. You know something, I can actually feel that you're there.'

'I am. I feel that about you too. It is weird, I agree, but let's not stop yet. Well only if you want to.'

'I don't. I'm intrigued.'

'Great. You know it is possible that people can sense each other over airwaves.'

'Weird. I can believe it. I feel it now.'

'Me too.'

She doesn't want to stop. How crazy is this? Drawn into this talking with text. They continue the conversation at other times through the rest of the day. It's like a first date, she thinks. 'And they call it puppy love,' she sings, getting ready for bed. Why does she always default to sentimental songs at times like these? She doesn't even like music. Feeling silly about it doesn't stop her. She puts the phone under her pillow – just in case.

Rachel's Mum, Jacqueline Seymour, and her Auntie Rosemary run the local pub, five minutes away, in the same street – The Golden Orb. Rachel likes her independence and she tries to keep a private life away from family but she likes to know that her mother's hug is only two arm stretches away in a crisis. Sunday lunchtime, once a month, is traditionally a girls' meal for just the three of them: three pies and chips, three pints of lager and then, maybe, three more pints. For Rachel, it's normal time: no more being the boss or playing the game. She can be a daughter again, a kid almost, back at the pub where she grew up – home. Nothing is going to spoil her mood today; not even the stain on her short white dress. Bloody white, she stops rubbing at it. She's only going to the pub, so what does a small stain matter? Apart from her mother insisting on washing it. She's not making the blemish a deal today, she's free, unattached. So free she practically dances in her immaculate white trainers. No stains there – even the laces are pristine from the washing-machine.

'Anyone for tennis?' mocks the lightly American accent belonging to a good-looking guy in faded denims, a crisp pale blue t-shirt and two cameras strung round his neck.

'Fuck off!' Rachel retorts, nearly losing her cool.

'Don't be like that, lady. Look, here's your photo.'

She has to look, she can never ignore her own image. There she is – shit, she thinks. She's walking down the street and she really does look like she's about to go on Centre Court at Wimbledon. She looks good, no question, but there's something odd about her. She looks so stiff, so upright, uptight too. She's like a child trying to be a grown-up, pretending she's modelling on a catwalk.

'God, she's a challenge,' Nico thinks. 'You can keep it,' he says, with a smile. 'Compliments of the Public Service Photographer.'

Before she can think of something cutting to say, he's gone – looking for another victim. Her phone rings, her smile returns. It's Mum.

'So where are you, luvvie? We've lined up the drinks.'

It's not Mum's call, it's the ringtone. It's done it again. She shoves the photograph into her bag and the thought out of her head. Nothing will upset her today, not even Alan busking outside The Golden Orb, living his saxophone dream. She gives him her warmest smile.

'How are you doing, Alan?'

'Just great thanks. How are you?'

'Fine. I'm liking your beard. Very pioneer. You know you can have your old job back if you want. I only chucked you out of my bed – not my life.'

'Thanks Rachel. I'll think about it. Seriously, I will.'

'I'll give you a month then. After that I'll have forgotten who you are.'

'Did you ever know?' he laughs, feeling wiser behind the beard. She's not winning today and, anyway, he's probably right. She remembers his body though and it still gives her a pleasant sensation.

'Grunge looks good on you, Alan,' she says, throwing two pound coins into his saxophone case. He goes straight into his reworking of Miles Davis' reworking of *Summertime*. A wasted hello gift because she never liked that song. He notices the stain. Unlike her, he thinks. Maybe she's changing.

Inside the pub, *Summertime* is drowned out by the jukebox with yodelling country star Patsy Montana singing her 1935 hit, *I Want to Be A Cowboy's Sweetheart*. The song's sentimentality goes straight to Rachel's struggling emotional core and her tearfulness rises dangerously high when she sees her mother sitting at their usual table on the customers' side of the bar, vibrant red hair clashing with her pink dress. She can be girlish here and it doesn't matter. Those mystery texts are getting under her skin and the excitement, a bit like a teenage crush, won't go away. Rachel's daughterly hug is strong enough to alert Jacqueline's antennae.

'You alright, love? You seem agitated.'

'Yeah, of course I am. Just great to see you again, Mum. Honestly.'

'You're a funny little thing, Rach. Your old mum's always here for you, you know that. Whenever you need a bit of loving tender.'

'I know. I know, Mum. I'm fine honestly.' She tries to hide her watering eyes by looking round at the customers. It's another busy lunchtime and the two landladies have got extra staff in to cover for them. There's a new barman, Conrad Adamcik, multitasking behind the bar as if he's always worked here. He only started this week. With John away, he's added another job to his list, doing the weekend lunch shifts at the pub and closing the Emporium for a couple of hours on Saturdays.

'New boy, I see,' Rachel whispers. 'Nice looking lad.'

'Conrad is sweet and ever so serious, but not one for you, love. He swings the other way, I think, if he swings at all that is.'

'Shame,' Rachel smiles. 'I'm fine though, you don't need to worry about me. It's work stuff, mostly. Maybe young Conrad can help there. I could try swinging him my way, perhaps.'

'Now don't be greedy, Rachel, leave the boy alone – he's my little godsend. I don't want you messing him up, you little minx.'

'Hello darlin', I'll give you a kiss if you take these,' Auntie Rosemary says, arriving with the lunch tray, Jacqueline's special, straight from the microwave, pie and chips, pastry over a stew of chopped steak and kidney with carrots and onions. Jacqueline has already lined up the three pints.

'So how're things, Auntie?' Rachel proffers her cheek for her aunt's kiss but Rosemary always prefers the lips when it's her niece. A kiss and a hug just like when Rachel was little.

'Rosemary's been going mad with the jukebox,' Jacqueline says, passing round the plates, 'putting in a load of old classics. Some, like this one, I'd never even heard before.' The jukebox changes to another Patsy Montana classic, *I Didn't Know The Gun Was Loaded*, complete with syncopated gun shots.

'The music in here gets worse and worse.' Rachel shrugs in disbelief.

'Even if you don't like it, love,' her mother enthuses through a mouthful of pie, 'you wouldn't believe how much it's livened the old place up. Rose knows her music – which is just as well 'cos it's never been my thing.'

Rachel says nothing.

'Talking about music,' Rosemary says, her eyes perusing the clientele, 'I'm hoping we can put on live music here soon. You know, just at weekends and special occasions, that sort of thing. I'd love that.'

'You taking up singing again, Auntie? I used to love that when I was a kid.'

'Oh no, love, but thanks. Those days are long gone, but sometimes, it's true, I fancy the idea. It never leaves you, that feeling.'

'Music and sex, people say, are the same thing,' Jacqueline says. 'Isn't that true?' Her laughter is infectious.

'Don't you mean music and love?' Rachel asks, suddenly serious. 'I'm not sure I've ever really got all the fuss about music but I like the lyrics. They're about love more than sex.' The lager is talking – one of the reasons for family reunions.

'Our little girl's growing up,' Jacqueline says, her voice quietly tender. 'So, OK, who is he?'

Now Rachel feels stupid again. 'No one, honestly. I know it's silly but there really isn't anyone. No, don't laugh – it's just a feeling. I don't know what it is. I feel different today, that's all. Ready for it, if you know what I mean.'

'You be careful, girl.' Rosemary squeezes her arm. 'Those feelings usually lead us up Queer Street and you don't want to go there, believe me.'

All three of them take a quick mental trip down that street, in a moment of silence, tucking into their pies.

Rachel's been thinking about love all day, wondering if she would ever know what it truly feels like. Then, as if on cue, she gets another text:

'How's lunch?'

'It's fine. Just Mum and Auntie Rose. They're great.'

'Hope I'm not disturbing you.'

'You're not.'

'Good. Just calling to wish you a good day.'

'That's sweet. Good day to you too.'

'Bye for now.'

'Bye. xx.'

Why did she type xx? She feels like an idiot. Now he'll think I'm just some dopey school kid.

Rosemary and Jacqueline exchange knowing glances when they're alone together clearing up.

'I recognise those symptoms, no question,' Jacqueline says. 'It's the first time she's fallen, I reckon.' They gather up the crockery and go back to the bar as Patsy Montana's voice cuts through The Golden Orb's lunchtime babble with another of her classics, *Yodelling Ghost*. At her corner table, old Mrs Webb yodels quietly to herself. She would've done it full volume if she'd had her teeth in.

'It's lovely hearing Patsy Montana again,' she says, generally to anyone who might be listening – but no one is. 'She was a terrific cowgirl that one.'

A relationship has begun without Rachel calling the shots. This man, she assumes it's a man – yes, of course it's a man – this man has arrived with an air of permanency about him. He's so assured, so confident, that he should have repelled her, but he doesn't. He knows how to hold her interest and how to turn her on without saying anything suggestive. He's an instant old friend but without the baggage, without an old friend's annoying hindsight vision. He makes her laugh, she makes him laugh too. He criticises her in a mildly subversive way and yet still makes her feel good. Even so, she wonders, letting her inner Miss Sensible plead caution, who is this guy? Does he know her? Is it one of her workers? Maybe it's just Joe teasing? But, no, this is no tease. She's intrigued, Miss

Sensible won't let her make a fool of herself but, unbelievably, she really does think she's just fallen in love. It certainly feels like love or how she's always imagined love would feel. It has happened not at first sight but at first text.

He's started sending them daily, inconsequential but witty, they make her feel that he's touching her. Dressing her perhaps, undressing her too. Either way it feels thrillingly intimate talking to him. The man she knows nothing about.

'Do you really exist?' she types one evening after they have been virtual friends, she thinks, forever. They are now spending long sessions together late into the night.

'Yup. I exist. I told you that before,' he types.

'Could we meet?'

'Is that wise?'

'Is that against the rules? Not part of the service.'

'There are no rules and this isn't really a service.'

'It's your job.'

'It's a hobby. I sold the idea to a friendly Californian – he wants to buy me too but I don't want to go to California. I like it here.'

'Wow! So you're rich?'

'Rich enough – I can buy a little house in Brighton, pay my bills and get a truly great piano.'

'Is that enough? You could make millions.'

'I'll have more ideas. Mobile phones are tomorrow's computers, there's a revolution going on out there. I like games and I like to communicate with my fingers.'

'So what's your day job?'

'I'm in the music business.'

'Another musician, blimey!'

'Sorry.'

'Don't be. I don't care. Honestly.'

'Music's not your thing?'

'That's what I used to think.'

'It's in there somewhere, Rachel. Believe me.'

'I might just like your tunes. God you're a strange guy. I don't know why I talk to you.'

'What did you do today?'

'I photographed another lily. My new project. I'm filling the flat with flowers, my models. This one was good.'

'What did you see?'

'Myself. You looking at me. It was beautiful. I'd love you to see it.'

'Shall I come round?'

'You don't know where I live.'

Of course he does, she remembers with a jolt. She had filled in the registration form with all her personal details. A dangerous thing to have done if he turns out to be that mad axe man. He could be a fantasist, especially with all that California stuff. She can hear her own breathing as she closes down the computer. How could she have been so stupid?

Then her phone rings.

'Hi, it's me. I'm downstairs.'

He has such a soothing voice, as beautiful as his music, deep and mellow, like the voice she'd imagined. She knows she has to meet him. Is that wise? Could she go through with it? She stops asking the questions and opens the door. He isn't there – no one is, but on the step is a single and voluptuously scarlet lily with a note attached: 'No hurry.'

Chapter Twenty-Two

Nico sees her arse and gets out his camera. Does she know what she looks like from the rear? If so why does she wear tight yellow trousers? She's like those sexually active baboons with inflated red glands round their anus, he thinks, but aren't they the males? Probably another of Nature's signposts gone wrong. He takes the photo, a big close up, and waits for the Polaroid to develop.

He loves the immediacy of these nearly-obsolete cameras and his new shot doesn't disappoint. Quickening his pace, he hurries after his unsuspecting model, a buxom woman in her late thirties, taking another shot as he walks.

'Excuse me, madam. I've taken this picture of you. Would you like it as a present from the Public Service Photographer?'

'What the fuck!' she says, seeing it, the tears welling up.

First blubberer for some time, he thinks, in discreet pursuit, shaken, but trying to stay objective.

'You're nothing but a bleedin' pervert. Get lost!' She's shouting now — truly angry.

'But madam, I thought you ought to see — we don't always know what we look like from behind. Some people find my services helpful. No offence meant...'

She has gone before he can finish, mingling, invisibly she hopes, with the average Sunday afternoon promenaders. Can't win them all, he thinks, pushing himself to stay professional. Then he sees his next subject, a middle-aged man whose baldness has just been uncovered when the breeze lifts the long strands of hair brushed across his pate.

'You taking the piss?'

'No, sir. I'm the Public Service Photographer — just a guy trying to be helpful. This is for you.'

Handing over the photograph, he runs for cover. It can be a dangerous job showing people what they really look like — no illusions, no camouflage.

Nico has a mission. He tells it as it really is. That's how he sees his project, showing people where they may have got it wrong, helping out and, or so he says, doing a public service and explaining it in his softest transatlantic accent. It's one of the great things about photography, he thinks; it can teach people how to see themselves objectively, catching them in the moment as they really are when they are not thinking about their looks, not standing pouting at their mirror or posing for a studio photograph. They can either take it, this slice of reality, live with it, or do something about it. It's turned out more challenging that he'd expected because he's not nearly as tough as he tries to look. There's no obligation to thank him, but he'd rather not be punched, and he hopes his reluctant models don't take it too badly. He's good at martial arts, a particularly effective form of Kung fu, but avoids having to defend himself when he can – or so he says. He's offering a one to one service, putting himself on the line, and that can be dangerous.

Next, a timid woman in her early forties, quite attractive he observes, sizing her up. More attractive than she thinks. She's dressed in a shabby grey frock, her back bent, shoulders rounded, arms crossed over her chest. Looking at her feet, she's hurrying along – someone else trying to be invisible. Click goes the camera, out comes the photo and the patter.

'Excuse me, madam, but I have just taken this photograph of you. Would you like a free copy, courtesy of the Public Service Photographer?'

'Why me?' she asks, suspicious of his American accent and smiling pleasantries. 'Are you a Jehovah's Witness or a Mormon or something?'

'No, not at all. Far from it. It's a public service, madam. Just take a look at it.'

'My God, that's terrible. Couldn't you have done better than that?'

'It's not supposed to be flattering, madam. It's to show you how you look walking down the street.'

'God, honestly, I had no idea. That's terrible. You know, I should hit you, yes, but I do look dreadful. This is amazing actually. I suppose I should thank you.'

'My pleasure, madam.'

'I think you're a bit crazy,' she laughs, 'but thanks anyway.'

'Take the photo, madam. I hope it helps.'

Nico loves photography. He doesn't just take Polaroids. When he lived in New York, he had exhibitions of his work in smart downtown galleries. This isn't just about street art; this, he thinks, is more serious, but then art for Nico is a form of politics or even guerrilla warfare. His project has added impact because he's also genuinely and undeniably a very beautiful man. His looks are too perfect for a contented passage through life. It isn't fair, a lot of people have said, he will have to pay for being so handsome. He's thirty – an eligible age, apparently – just under six feet tall, naturally muscled but not ostentatiously so, his claim to beauty is in his face. It has perfect proportions, really, features with nothing out of place. He has deep blue eyes, his admirers would call them midnight blue, and a waxen complexion that tans easily. He has the perfect suntan but, even so, his translucent pigmentation hints seductively at frailty, even vulnerability. He has always been easy to love, easily fancied at least, but that hasn't led to happiness. His mouth reveals a nervous sensibility behind momentary flashes of humour – he has learnt to wear irony as his first defence.

Nico's blessed not just with his beauty but with his lineage. He's the only son of two popular icons, paragons of Twentieth Century pop culture. His father, a Greek-Californian rock musician, his mother an Iranian-American model; both, inevitably beautiful and both, equally inevitably, dead. Both parents had been much loved, idolised even, and both had been photographed enough to live forever in coffee-table books, magazines and newspaper supplements. They are always on display whenever the media wants to illustrate Twentieth Century glamour. Nico tries to hide his history – it has not been a happy one: his mother and father were much better at receiving love than giving it. No one knows about his family tree here in Brighton and he wants to keep it that way. Brighton might just become his home. He's going to give it a go – that's why he's found himself a business here.

He gets a rough response from the young dad who's playing football with his toddler son on the beach. Fatherhood has obviously interrupted the man's football career and taken its toll on his physique. When he strips off his Arsenal football shirt, he flashes a pair of fleshy breasts and a deflated balloon of a stomach. The red cloud of anger descends when his little son spots a nice man with a camera.

'Look at the man taking our picture, Dad,' he lisps.

'What the fuck!' the man shouts, and Nico makes another speedy exit – tossing the photo onto the promenade as he runs.

'This is breach of privacy,' growls an older, big-haired woman, a self-styled Margaret Thatcher who hates Nico's photograph. She's heavily made-up and the close-up shot exposes the unflattering reality of her Punch and Judy rouge and panda bear eye makeup. 'I'm a magistrate and I've come across your sort before. You think it's clever to mock but it's not. Don't ever come in front of me in court – I know how to deal with self-indulgent dilettantes like you.'

'I was only trying to be helpful madam.'

'Rubbish. Is this an idiotic modern art idea? Conceptual, I suppose.'

'No, madam, I'm a Public Service Photographer and I thought you might like to take a closer look at your facial make-up. It might not be what you think you look like to others. No offence meant.'

She marches off with the photograph in her fist, stout legs striding in her own stormy *Ride of the Valkyries*.

Unremarkably dressed, nonchalantly understated, in jeans, t-shirt and trainers, Nico tries to hide his beauty, even his sophistication, but he can't disguise his charisma. He's making a social point. He hates the way people are judged by their appearance and hopes to show everyone their hidden beauty. Too many people dress to hide, and often, there's pain behind the camouflage.

'Come off it, mate,' someone he met in a bar once said. 'You're looks obsessed – that's because you're such a good-looking bastard.'

'Anyone for tennis?' he mocks, when he sees Rachel again – she's still in her white gear, walking along the promenade, staring at her mobile phone, texting her friend.

'Fuck off! Again!' Rachel replies aggressively.

'Don't be like that, lady. Look, here's another photo.'

God, she really is a case – beautiful but a case nonetheless, he thinks. He stays polite, knowing how to play the gentleman. Smiling, he gives her the picture.

'You can keep it. Compliments of the Public Service Photographer.'

This time she takes a second look at this beautiful young man. She can't make herself smile though.

'You're crazy,' she says, accepting the photograph while double-checking that his eyes really are that blue. Then she rushes on, it's her personal style to hurry, but she decides that she might ditch the white dress. There's the hint of a smile as she goes.

'Oi! You!' It's the young dad again. 'What the fuck do you think you're doing?'

This isn't a question, just the preliminary to a punch – a direct hit, a left hook to Nico's perfect nose. The second punch is blocked, agonizingly, by Nico's defence and the man runs off, his arm twisted at the elbow. As he hugs it, he turns white then a pale shade of green.

'What's the matter, Dad?' his little son asks.

The blood is flowing from Nico's nose but he stands his ground – he's watching the Asian woman; it's Kanti Subhadi. She's taking his photo: portrait of a wounded fighter.

'Hey, can you use my camera and take another one?' he calls. She nods, unfazed by his injury, taking the camera without comment. Scanning the elderly Polaroid, she soon works it out and takes three photographs, clinically allowing time on the composition then silently studying the camera as it slowly spits out the prints.

'For old technology, it does a good job,' she says, handing him the photographs and returning the camera. An interesting woman, he thinks, still bleeding, trying to ignore the growing pain in his nose. Interesting, she's cool and still has appalling clothes sense. Only after looking at the images does he try to staunch the blood flow.

'In my country,' Kanti tells him, 'we pull a new broken nose – shall I do it for you? It will hurt but you will have a straight nose again. You are too beautiful a man to have a broken nose for ever.'

'Go for it, you flatterer' he laughs, now tasting the blood.

'Then I'd like to get a picture of you in that awful orange t-shirt.'

Like an emergency doctor now, she certainly goes for it. Placing her two fingers in his nostrils, she gets a grip and pulls. There's a click, no small amount of pain and, for a fraction of a moment, Nico's vision fades to black.

'Thanks,' he says, regaining his colour and enjoying the understatement. Now for that photograph.'

Kanti stands passively in front of his lens, making no attempt at modelling. She knows what I'm about, he thinks, while the Polaroid image develops. This is always the difficult moment, that pause while photographer and victim await the outcome.

'Here, this is for you, courtesy of the Public Service

Photographer. Don't take offence, please, but does a good-looking woman like you have to dress like a Walt Disney caricature?'

'I am taking that as a compliment, mister, but only because you are one good-looking guy. Nothing wrong with Walt Disney. I love him. There's no mystery with Walt Disney – everybody loves Mickey Mouse and Donald Duck, they are great American symbols. So what's your problem?'

'It's not my problem, Minnie Mouse, believe me.'

'It is good to meet a fellow photographer,' she says, laughing. 'Even if he's a bit too much like me. You look for the same things, mister. Maybe we should do it together one day.'

'Hang on, we haven't even been introduced yet.'

Kanti smiles coyly. 'You are not so rude as you would like to be,' she says. They exchange contacts on their identical *IBM Simons*, the latest thing in phones, and she walks away, already looking for her next photograph. Later, when she develops the film, she takes a long serious look at Nico's bloody face. She's made one of her best portraits.

Chapter Twenty-Three

'Kiss me, Kate,' Lionel says, jokily serious, as he undoes his bow-tie, allowing the ends to hang limply from his opened collar. Kate hasn't changed since their afternoon meeting. She hasn't even taken off her headscarf.

'If you want us to get informal,' she croons, 'let's get that jacket off-a-yer. I love a man in shirtsleeves. So halfway to Paradise.'

'I'm more than halfway there, I can assure you.'

'Well, excuse me! Is that the right kind of something you should say to a lady? Experienced or not?'

'Just saying it as it is, Kate.' He's removing his jacket.

'Are you trying to tell me about something that you rather obviously can't hide any more?' She's laughing at what's happening below his cummerbund. 'So your little dog won't lie down, Mr Lionel. Time for some gin I think. Come on, sit down and kick off those shoes, for God's sake.'

Kate has one of the superior cabins on The Estella, ten times larger than Lionel's and furnished like a modern five, or maybe four star hotel with a cream-coloured three-piece suite, matching carpet and a king-sized bed; the counterpane is a respectable beige. She watches Lionel as he gazes round the place.

'Yeah, I know, relentlessly tasteful in here, isn't it? I'll fix us a couple of big 'uns to jazz up the decor, agreed?'

'I wouldn't dare criticise the upholstery,' Lionel says, spread out on one side of the sofa, shoeless and, just as the lady likes it, in shirtsleeves, gold studs shining. 'I'm staying in a dog kennel, sharing it with a sickly drummer boy.'

'Poor you,' she sympathises, with well-practised mockery. She's smiling merrily to herself, back turned, at the wall cabinet that's well stocked with gin, an ice bucket and a jar of sliced lemons and limes. As she prepares the drinks, her physical assurance wavers and she fumbles with the glasses.

'Indian tonic water to give it an air of righteousness,' she jokes, but her voice sounds distracted.

'Are you alright?' Lionel spots the change.

She's standing, muscles frozen, holding the two glasses, her face a shade paler than pale, her friskiness vanished. 'Well, no, I guess not,' she says, sitting down carefully in one of the armchairs, balancing the drinks. 'If you think you've just won yourself the girl from the front of the chorus line then I've got a big disappointment for you, honey. I'm one sick lady trying to have a bit of fun before her last legs give out on her.'

'Oh, Kate, I'm so sorry. Can I ask...'

'Cancer – not much of a turn-on, is it.'

'I'm so sorry,' he leans over and squeezes her arm. 'There are a lot of treatments these days.'

'I've done all that, honey, but thanks. No, I'm over the finding a cure bit and into let's have fun while it lasts time.'

'You're very brave.'

'There's no choice. I took this trip hoping to leave the friggin' sickness behind, but it looks like it's just caught up with me.'

'Can I get you anything?'

'You can take one of these drinks for one thing and try not to look so disappointed for another. I'm not dead yet.'

They clink glasses and drink, taking a few separate moments of solitude.

'I might as well take off this wretched scarf now – I've got nothing left to hide. So hold onto your horses.'

The scarf has been covering a bristly one inch bush of grey hair. She shakes her head letting imaginary golden locks tumble round her shoulders, Hollywood-style, then sits back and grins.

'Well, this is me, Lionel. My modelling days are over. Actually, if I last long enough, I might still do a few granny shots for a short-sighted photographer from the unambitious side of Iowa. My hair's growing back, I'm told, but radiotherapy has no style.'

'Elfin is the word that comes to mind. It's actually rather cute – very modern, short hair, seductive too. So, at the risk of repeating myself, kiss me Kate.'

'I think that can be arranged for my very gentlemanly friend.'

They don't share their thoughts once they've moved over to the bed, they don't need to. Their eyes engage but look beyond the present, maybe into the future, but probably into the past. It doesn't matter, whatever memories spur them on to this moment, whatever they express there under the sheets is real enough for both of them. Honesty enhanced by a little imagination and a lot of experience.

'You know this would be corny if we weren't two old fools

enjoying it while we can,' she says, as they sit on deck the next evening when he comes off duty. They're watching the sun set over the Mediterranean's deepening blue.

'I always liked a bit of corn,' Lionel says, breathlessly, moved. 'It's been the making of Tin Pan Alley because, admit it or not, we're all corny in our hearts.'

'Why, you old romantic, you. If you're like this with sunsets, God help us when you see the moon.'

'Ah yes, *Blue Moon*. You know I really do talk to the moon at times. I've sung too many of those songs maybe, or it might just be that I really am a silly old fool. Actually, I do share some of my more melancholy moments with the Man in the Moon. He can be very understanding, you know.'

'Can he indeed? He's kinder than Diana, the Moon Goddess virgin. She would have had you by your balls for what we've been up to down there.'

'She's only trying to protect your chastity, like a well-meaning maiden aunt.'

'She's welcome to her chastity and it's way too late for mine. I'm with your Old Man in the Moon and here he is, right on cue.'

They hold hands sitting, silenced, in their deckchairs watching the sea; golden ripples turn silver as the sun disappears behind a horizon, shamelessly hamming it up for its audience. Shadowy silhouettes now, they nestle together, indulging the emotion behind the repartee.

'Strange how the fading light makes me think of life, not death,' Kate says, after a long shared meditation. 'When the sun has gone, the world retreats and I can stop performing for it. Time to be just me, to be alive.'

'At my age, I can't help thinking about death. I don't worry about it though – there's nothing much to worry about I suspect.'

'Isn't that because you're not really thinking of death – you're thinking about life.'

'Yes. Our little life rounded with a sleep, I know.'

'Yes siree – come on get happy, get ready for the judgement day,' she's croons huskily into his ear.

'Judy Garland, Shakespeare and the Old Man in the Moon.'

'You know, Lionel,' she says, as if making an announcement, 'I only got a one way ticket for this ride. I'm paid up only as far as

Egypt. It seemed a bit optimistic to pay for a return.'

'Why Egypt?'

'I hoped some nice young Egyptians might build me a pyramid. Somewhere to rest my bones.'

'They could call you mummy.'

'No one has that pleasure. I've had my share of men and only one of them planted the right seed – but that's another story.'

'We'd have made lovely babies too – oh well. But, Kate, Egypt is very, well, very sandy isn't it? Not exactly New York City, no place for a New York babe.'

'Now, promise you won't shout at me if I make a tiny confession?'

'What now, Cleopatra?'

'Seriously, Lionel, I only got a single ticket because I didn't even intend to go as far as Egypt.'

'Where did you want to go then?'

'Well, that's the thing. Now promise me you won't shout. I thought I might end it all here. You know, I'm serious actually, just jump overboard one night. Goodnight sweet world, that kinda thing.'

'Oh, Kate, surely not.' Lionel squeezes her hand, looking for her face in the silhouette and seeing what might have been a tear illuminated in the moonlight.

'Damn you, you silly old bugger, meeting you like this, now I'm not so sure about anything.'

'Don't pin your hopes on an old man.'

'I pinned them on young men once and look where that got me. I married a fine young man, Sgt. Geoff Arnold. You can see his name on the Vietnam Memorial. We had a son, Bradley.' She sighs through her smile. 'Brad –' She needs to pause. 'He grew into a fine young man too, like his pop. He was going to change the world but then AIDS came to visit. No, Lionel, no more fine young men for me.'

'Kate, don't do anything rash. Be careful, you know. Well, I don't know what to say actually.'

'If we can't be rash at our age, when can we?' She plays with his hand in a skittish bout of Chinese wrestling. 'Oh don't worry, I'll know when it's the right time. Before then, let's have our fun. Two old fools all at sea. OK?'

'Yes, OK.'
And they do.

Chapter Twenty-Four

'I thought he'd just tuned the fucking thing,' Victoria thinks, doodling on a notepad, drawing a man being garrotted with a guitar string. She's now an established part of the Wah-Wah team and even though it's good working in the music shop, some of the younger kids get to her. One of them, Phil, is showing off his technique, trying to strum the chords to the chorus of *Made of Stone*, a song by the Manchester band The Stone Roses, one of Victoria's favourites. He's using one of the shop's best acoustic guitars, a *Washburn D-25S*, and it sounds terrible. In Jake's absence, anything goes.

'Cool,' the other lad, Barry, says, with more than a touch of hero-worship. Victoria doesn't agree.

'God, Phil!' she calls from her hideaway in the cupboard behind the counter, a space that doubles as the accounts room. 'Tune the thing, can't you!'

'I did!' he answers, rolling his eyes at Barry and mouthing an expletive.

'Well, tune yer friggin' ears then!' she persists. 'This is meant to be a music shop and that guitar deserves better.'

She's truly settled in here, but she's more than bored by invoice filing, more irritated with that than by poor Phil's guitar-playing. Screwing up her drawing and tossing it into the bin bag that she's just filled with waste paper, she swings round twice in the torn leather swivel typing chair, pulls on her black ankle boots, adjusts her black dress, tugging where it has stuck between her legs and comes into the shop with a conciliatory smirk.

'Here, give it to me.' She pulls on Phil's one unpierced earlobe and grabs the guitar from him before he clocks what's going on.

'What the fuck – '

'I'm only tuning it for you, kiddo. Calm down, OK.'

Phil and Barry submit, passively watching her like children in a nursery class. It isn't necessary to read their minds to know that they're thinking: 'Shit, she actually knows what she's doing.'

Just then Jake walks in and says, 'Shit, you actually know what you're doing.'

Victoria grins, letting her wiry hair cover her face, bending over the guitar, rapidly strumming the chords that Phil had been stumbling over. Phil and Barry smile.

'Awesome,' says Barry.

'Hey, that's really cool, Vickie,' says Phil.

'Why not play something a bit more bluesy?' Jake says, sitting down and turning on the store's amped-up keyboard, a *Roland D-70*. This is why he loves running this shop. 'What can you do?'

'You serious?' she laughs, tossing back her hair.

'Sure thing. Let's make a noise and find us some customers!'

The lads grin at each other, excited to be working here. Victoria pulls a laconic smirk. God, I've missed all this, she thinks. 'Ok, then, *Me and Bobby McGee* in the key of G.'

'Yer on.' Jake spreads his fingers over the widest G major chord he can manage and then they're away. She starts simply strumming an easy accompaniment for a couple of bars and then kicks off with a growl; then she starts singing. Her voice is deeper and a lot louder than Jake was expecting and, momentarily, he stops playing just to sit back and listen. She carries on loving the moment and loving her voice too. She knows, if she knows anything, that she can sing the socks off anyone. Jake's playing again, improvising, his eyes alight. He mimics electric guitar riffs and pumps the chords for some added volume.

Their music is filling the shop and, he guesses, the street outside. She sings louder, opening out her voice. 'Christ,' Jake mutters. This woman has some formidable equipment. They're jamming and now everyone knows that they're in the presence of the real thing – a blues singer giving it from the heart. Before they're through, there's a small audience, three or four people around the door and out on the pavement. When the song ends, there's spontaneous applause.

'Another Janis Joplin!' a middle-aged man in cycling lycra shouts.

'Who's she?' Barry mouths to Phil.

'She is fucking Janis Joplin,' Jake calls above the whooping and cheering. He doesn't want the moment to end so he plays the opening to another Joplin classic. Victoria knows where he's going. She swallows, clears her throat and comes in on cue, full volume, cutting across everything with *Maybe* – swooping high and low, sweat falling like rain from her brow. The music has attracted another visitor. Alan, saxophone case in hand, stands there swaying, head rocking, eyes closed. By the third song, the inevitable *Piece of my heart*, the sax has joined them. Alan completes the circle, with just a meeting of musicianly eyes. When it's over, Jake gives him a firm handshake and Victoria pats him limply on the back.

'That was phenomenal,' he says, breathless with shared euphoria.

'I need a cigarette,' she replies, not meeting his eyes, pushing her way out through the door at the back of the shop.

Jake follows her outside and finds her crying – dragging feverishly on her smoke.

'You were terrific,' he says.

'That's why I'm crying, man.' Her voice is choking, barely audible. 'When I sing, the nightmares return.'

'What is it, babe? Singing is what you were born to do.'

She breaks down again; there's nothing he can say so he strokes her hair when she manages to whisper, 'It kills me.'

Chapter Twenty-Five

Diep lies, face to the wall, on the top bunk in the small bedroom of a typical 1960s-style student hall of residence. Untypical of student accommodation though is the orderliness of the space that he shares with Kanti. Her black-and-white photographs are pinned to a cork notice board – deckchairs, a seascape and some elderly naked men. There's also a typed schedule for the summer months, a snapshot of a smiling Nepalese woman in an acid green sari, a monochrome photo of a young man in khaki shorts and the picture of Harry playing his djembe. Diep isn't looking at anything. His eyes are just over a nose's length from the wall as he lies motionless, in foetal position, frowning. Only a slight movement of his lungs indicates life.

He can see beyond the grey-white of the wall plaster to a mauve mountain range, veiled in mist and blurred with the green forestation at its foot, where its shape fragments further as its reflected image ripples, a mirage over the becalmed grey water of a vast lake. Diep is hypnotised, his eye movements indicate that he's looking for something. It's there. A small yellow rowing boat, and it brings the hint of a smile. Adult legs in sandals, brown skin animated by golden hair, turquoise and orange tie-died cotton shorts, a brown lightly furred chest and then, the focus of his desperate search, a laughing golden-bearded face, sun-bleached hair grown long and tied with string, blue eyes, warmly affectionate, framed by crinkling laughter-lined skin.

He's found his father, those familiar hands, long remembered, large and muscular with long firm fingers. He wants to feel them again, their warmth, the comfort of their touch, squeezing him, carrying him from the boat. He can feel the motion of those legs churning through warm water, splashing them both with its spray. The laughter returns, he has never forgotten that sound, even though he has never heard it. There's the yellow boat again. He's sitting in it now. Father and son, those hands gripping the oars, those straining muscles, still that laughter, framed by mauve-tinted mountains.

A new mouth appears and it isn't laughing. It spews fire through carnivorous teeth, gums pulled back – half fear and half ferocity – the face, stained pink around the jaws is strewn with shrivelling scarlet flowers. The dragon is protecting its temple, on guard by a rack of candles that flicker in the midday sun. Mother dragon, with nipples erect, raises her breasts in defence. The breasts too are smeared with pink dye, decorated to honour the beast, but frightening the boy who thinks of spilt blood. Those hands again, with comfort in their grip, they tighten as his father squats in front of him, eye-to-eye now, the laughing face turns gentle and the hands wipe away the boy's tears. The temple sits on an island that has barely enough space for a building. They row there on special days, always just father and son, no hurry, no need for words, just a journey for two. A private pilgrimage to the little pagoda bedecked with flags and guarded by the fiercely breasted dragon. His father lights a taper and gives it to him, placing a candle in the rack. The dragon's placated for now. Until the next time, but what will happen if they don't return? Diep's flame rises up tall, fearlessly burning in the thin airless heat.

They are back in the boat – it's all photograph clear, the mauve mountains, the oars with their bright red blades, slicing the water; the mountains quiver, tears evaporate in the light of his father's laughter. Again and again, they repeat the voyage, placating the dragon; those hands, the oar, those eyes, always focused on him, and, ringing in his head, the silence of laughter. So many times repeated with his face to the wall and his hands gripped to his chest.

When Kanti returns to the room, she sees blood on her brother's knuckles and a stain on the bedroom wall. He refuses to look at her but she climbs up to his bunk and sits by him, taking hold of his head, resting it in her lap, wiping away his tears with her finger tips. Her touch can't staunch the flow, his tears multiply and he cries a long husky howl.

Chapter Twenty-Six

They must have all come off the same coach, the forty or so teenage students who are crowding Nico's view of the promenade. Nothing much to photograph here. French students, he guesses, trying to look fashionable in the English way. White trainers, ostensibly witty slogans on skinny t-shirts and tight, very tight, blue jeans – all clones from some sci-fi condensing machine. If that's unkind, so be it, Nico thinks. Unkind can be helpful. If he misunderstands the subtleties of the teenage brain then he has always done so. Once too much the adolescent loner perhaps, he isn't interested in correcting himself now. His nose hurts. It's bruised but undamaged after Kanti's brutally effective cure. Maybe his confidence is bruised too or perhaps his body's reflexes are warning him to stand back a bit – to give the Public Service Photographer a break. He fingers his camera straps irritably but lets the Polaroid camera hang idly against his stomach, along with the expensive Canon single lens reflex camera, the *EOS-1*, that he mostly uses as a backup, and for what he now considers his self-indulgent arty shots. There's nothing to shoot today.

The French students know what ennui means and what it feels like. For Nico, though, the word is boredom – no sophisticated foreign word can liven it up. When he's bored, he thinks in straightforward American English. His credentials as the Public Service Photographer are seriously at risk this morning. Far worse than his usual victims' fashion errors is the conformity of youth – teenagers are instinctive conservatives, far from the troublesome radicals of their reputation. He pities these kids as they file past him. He doesn't know what they're saying but he can tell by their roaming eyes that, male or female, they are comparing body parts. Cocks and tits, obviously, judged through the shape of their clothes, the battle isn't to have the biggest protuberance, just the average, nothing too showy or exceptional – the cause of so much adult unhappiness, he believes. This common denominator complex applies to noses, haircuts and pimples too, everything comes under sly scrutiny. They ignore the sea and the Regency architecture and everything that their teachers have brought them to see. He can't blame them, the English coastline isn't very different to the Northern French one – it just faces in the opposite direction and the food isn't as good.

The students' teachers share Nico's opinion. The three pale-skinned women in their twenties or thirties, keeping up the rear of the procession, behind all those tightly packed teenage rears, are engaged in grim-faced gossip, illustrated by languid upper-body shrugs. One of them catches Nico's eye – maybe it was the tiger tattoo below her navel, it peeps out provocatively between her short t-shirt and her little black mini-skirt. Curiosity distracts her for a moment and a flicker of erotic interest crosses her face. The other two look too. Nico is used to furtive glances from bored women and the erotic signals that accompany them. His bruised nose warns him not to respond, but his vanity wonders if the bruising shows and, if it does, whether it would attract or repel these women.

Nico has grown up being admired for his looks, he tries not to be defined by it, but can never pass a mirror without taking a look to see if he's still the best-looking person he's met. The women, along with their students, have moved on and he knows why they're laughing – it's the international language of sex. Nothing to photograph there either, he thinks, following the three retreating bodies through the lens of his camera. French women and their clothes, he smiles, born to go together but always crying out to be parted. One of them looks back, as shameless as Lot's wife, he thinks, but well done, lady, you get away with matching those white trainers with the mini-skirt and black tights, but it's the tiger that makes it.

This guy gets away with it too, he thinks, seeing the busker, flute glistening at his lips. Joe has taken a new spot on the promenade since Alan moved onto his old position by The Golden Orb. Leaning jauntily against a street lamp, supporting his weight on his left leg, right one crossed over the other, maintaining his balance with the merest contact between bare toes and tarmac. He's in no need of a public warning photograph in his floppy white linen shirt, open to the navel, left untucked over loose black cotton trousers rolled up to the calf. He's playing a new composition, experimental for him in the use of Indian melodic patterns that remind Nico of snake-charmer music. Snake or no snake, it works its charm and, without any internal debate, he asks Joe if he can take a photograph.

'Do you mind? I'd really like to make a portrait of you.'

Joe carries on playing, his eyebrows expressing his agreement.

136

This isn't a Polaroid moment, it's more of a revelation. Nico unpacks his SLR camera, fusses over lenses, just like in his Manhattan days. He circles the flautist, stalking him with martial flexibility but he can't get it right. The photograph won't match the mental image. Joe smiles when he takes the flute from his mouth.

'You alright there, man?' he asks, humour in his irony.

'Either you, the sun, or both of you, are in the wrong place.'

'You want me to move the sun? – no problem.'

'You know, I do believe you could,' Nico says, not entirely joking. 'I really want this picture, do you mind? Can you move over so the sea's behind you?'

Joe shrugs amicably and moves his stuff over to the edge of the shingle. 'Here?'

'Perfect.'

Nico is already on his knees, camera to eye. Joe begins to play again. He likes this guy. He knows what he wants and says it. Joe sees straight away that Nico isn't just very beautiful, so he's happy to be charmed too. This interesting stranger can do whatever he thinks necessary. He's an artist, for sure. Nico takes twenty or thirty shots, moving like a gymnast, shifting on his haunches, lying on his back or even crossing into Joe's body space for an extreme close-up. Then he's satisfied. The image through the viewfinder is the one he's waiting for – man, music, the sun and the sea. He sees the special quality in Joe and hopes that the developed picture will capture his anarchic spirit. He packs away the camera but stays listening to the music, captured by the serpentine melody until it comes to an approximate and unhurried ending. In Joe's music, endings are pauses in eternity but, today, they sound like a beginning.

'That was wonderful, man,' Nico says, clapping and bowing in respect.

'You're welcome. Just toss a coin in the case and we're quits.'

'Sure, here's a quid. OK?'

Joe nods and shrugs, grinning. 'Whatever you think it's worth, man. Thanks.'

'I tell you what, why not let me buy you a coffee or something. How about that?'

'Wow, so my music's worth a quid and a coffee – I must be getting better.'

'OK then, let's make it a beer.'

They're talking like old friends before they introduce themselves to each other, sitting in a seaside bar with two pints of chilled American lager.

'Pleased to meet you, Nico.'

'Likewise, Joe.' Nico bows graciously, forgetting his nose injury.

'We've nearly met so many times,' says Joe.

'Yes, we have,' Nico agrees. I've photographed you before, but always from a distance.

'I know.'

The exertion has opened Nico's nose wound and blood trickles over his smile, it tastes like real life, he thinks, licking it away. A kindred spirit, for sure, Joe thinks.

Chapter Twenty-Seven

Alan's frightened before it happens. Lying in the dark – away from the promenade but invisible, he hopes, he snuggles, shivering even though he's cold, psyching himself out of his growing panic. This isn't his paradise beach, his shipwrecked desert island. He feels alone, vulnerable and, yes, scared. The beach will be impossible when the cold weather comes. Some of that chill has already entered his heart. He's uncertain now about joining Brighton's growing population of street sleepers, once unheard of, or ignored in British towns. Homeless vagrants used to have a romantic aura. True or not, they were seen as 'gentlemen of the road', eccentric free-thinkers or just late night drunks – nothing to worry about; they were, Alan assumed, happy enough, enviable even.

There's a new trend in 1990s Britain, caused by social security policy cuts directed at unemployed school-leavers. Now, in Britain's cities, young people are often found sleeping in doorways, mostly young men but young women too. Runaways, troubled teenagers who have fallen through the government's threadbare safety net, finding transient comfort in alcohol and drugs, often paid for by hurried alleyway sex. Alan has seen it often enough but he has ignored it. Until now, he has been a young man, like many others, absorbed in his own comfort zone. He has virtually stepped over their bodies lying on the pavements. Not his problem. On his saxophone he could cover the Willie 'Long Time' Smith classic *Homeless Blues* and feel heart-felt solidarity with all those bluesmen who 'couldn't find no place to go'. The blues were always in his head but, tonight, they are deep in his palpitating heart.

It's probably a rat, he thinks, hearing scampering sounds on the midnight shingle. Rats and the lapping of waves. He can't settle, he's seen his bogeyman in every shifting shadow. When he finds out for sure that it isn't a rat, it's too late.

His nostrils' memory tells him that the old enemy is back, the man with the pinprick eyes. No point in fighting, even if it's to save his beloved horn. This time the man makes no mistake, the saxophone is snatched and kicked out of reach and whatever light there is catches the glitter of a knife.

'Don't come fucking looking for it, OK,' comes the low-pitched voice, a harshly sibilant whisper. He leans down close, his breath burning Alan's skin. 'Through me you will pass into eternal pain, put thy mouth in the dust, you hear. Lie desolate, yes, desolate on the streets in lamentation.' The mumbling rises in pitch as his words are punctuated by three kicks to the ribs and a finishing shot to the groin.

Later, Alan huddles, wide awake in a shop doorway, still shivering inside his sleeping bag but sweating in the humidity. He's spent his last night of freedom on the wilderness beach. This doorway supplies a roof, a concrete mattress on a central Brighton street, where all-night lighting and the occasional passers-by, mostly young people staggering home drunk, make him feel safe enough. Sleep comes as it always does, but his dreams are restless, on the verge of consciousness, until his body relaxes, submitting to a welcome sensation of warmth. Then there's laughter:

'That's better.'

'Yeah, much better.'

'Better in than out.'

Alan opens his eyes to see three grinning lads urinating on him, shaking themselves dry and running off whooping. The warmth goes cold; Alan is soaked, hair, head and body, and he wells up, repulsed and humiliated. He gets to his feet and looks at himself in the shop window. This is the true desolation of the street. He has nothing more to lose so he returns to the beach and dives, fully clothed into the sea, barely visible in the breaking dawn. Willie 'Long Time' Smith is singing in his head, telling him what he already knows, that he ain't got no place to go.

Chapter Twenty-Eight

Harry's room would win no interior design awards. It has a double mattress on the floor, strewn with unwashed bedding, a coverless duvet, crumpled as he'd left it. The sheet, once white, now grey, retains his body indentation. Clothes lie on the floor of a doorless wardrobe, under an unoccupied rod lined with redundant metal hangers. He can usually distinguish between clean and dirty clothes with a sniff to the appropriate area, although it isn't always an easy decision. There's a chair-shaped object in the middle of the room, its function obscured by a heavy military greatcoat and a few pairs of discarded jeans, legs splayed in crusty rigor mortis. On the floor there are tumbled piles of music journals, *NME* mostly, the *New Musical Express*, Britain's coolest music paper, turning yellow. Newer editions lie opened on the classified ads pages. Some escaped socks and underpants, shot down perhaps, trying to get away, are scattered round the room on the wood-effect laminate flooring.

The walls, paint-deserted wood chip, are decorated with unframed rock'n'roll posters, reflecting his eclectic obsessions; The La's, his Liverpool heroes, Radiohead, his taste's heroes, The Smiths, symbols of his Mancunian gentrification, George Harrison, his childhood guru, sitar-duetting with another idol, Indian master-musician, Ravi Shankar. It has been Harry's unfulfilled dream to play with these guys. In a central position, over the boarded-up fireplace, there's Kanti's djembe photo, her challenge. It has shaken him out of his stupor. Harry's writing a song.

Since the old armchair is out of action, he's got used to the floor and, today, he's lying chest down in the crinkled boxers and t-shirt that double as nightwear and sloppy daywear when he has no plan to go outside. He's writing lyrics, scribbling on a notepad with a plastic ballpoint pen, reactivated after a lengthy period lying dormant on the floor by his bed. His djembe sits on its side, allowing him to check a few rhythms. After a burst of writing, he reaches for an acoustic guitar, a vintage *Eko Ranger* from the 1970s, given to him as a lad by a musical uncle. He isn't a great guitarist, he knows that, but he can strum chords and that's how he's always worked out his songs. The process is mostly about alternating different chords to see what's the best order. Then he tries them all over again, in a different key, and then returns to his writing pad to alter the lyrics. 'She has gone' becomes 'Where did she go' – he doesn't like two notes for 'gone.' He changes it again. 'Gone' comes back and it's held for two beats. That's better – until the whole phrase is cut. The creative process for Harry is a mix of the languid and the frenzied – very few of his songs have a painless birth and most of them lie slumbering, drowning even, in the womb.

Harry isn't a prolific composer; this is his first song in months. It's inspired by the Subhadi twins' exhibition. Rattled at first and, as usual, doubting himself, he has taken up the challenge. Kanti's photographs, especially the one here on his wall, have elevated him to a heroic level that he still can't take seriously. If not a hero exactly, then at least he looks like a man, as good as the next guy, and that's good enough. Kanti, part child, has seen the man hiding behind the fearful adolescent. She has focused on his physicality, using laboratory skills to exaggerate the monochrome exposures, giving his flesh a simmering silver tone, animating the sinews and veins, emphasising the shadow lines on his face and pinpointing the bristles of his beard. He's no self-regarding Narcissus, but he's remained quietly startled by this view of himself. He's inspired, even with a residue of doubt, to live up to Kanti's image.

He's challenged too, scared even, by Diep's installation. Was this a personal attack? Was he Diep's hatred figure – his voodoo doll? It made Harry feel like a symbol of British imperialism hiding behind the mask of well-meaning hippiedom, trampling Nepal's traditions under sandaled feet and turning an ancient culture into just another stop on England's hippie trail. He isn't Diep's father and yet he feels guilty as if he himself had abandoned these children, after taking his pleasure on their mother. The guilt builds on his new sense of manhood. It's not enough sitting on a beach dreaming of his mythical Asian nirvana – wallowing in his cannabis-fuelled, soft porn imagination.

He hasn't seen Diep or Kanti since the exhibition. Maybe Diep has changed things permanently with his violent masterpiece. Harry wonders if there was some of her brother's anger hidden behind Kanti's laughter too. The flayed limbs in Diep's installation have coloured the way he sees both of them. Things have got complicated – maybe too complex for someone who has always defined himself as just a bloke.

Even though he hasn't actually seen them since their show, he

142

sees Kanti differently now, with eyes that have been trained by her camera lens. Now he can see beyond her small girl's frame and her primary colour clothes and beyond his fantasy of what lies beneath. He's underestimated her. Her small-boned skeleton belies and camouflages her womanliness. Her eyes, once seen as just lively and joyful, reveal a deeper light. As he sees her more clearly, he understands her less. He's turned on by her, that at least is obvious, but he still doesn't know if he's happy about this.

She's the inspiration for this song and he's working on it with a passion he hasn't felt since coming to Brighton. He sketches in the final chord progressions and declares it finished. It's the first song he's written that has more than four chords.

Chapter Twenty-Nine

Rachel erupts into her office this morning. No one says anything, no one dares, but everyone looks and more than a few eyes meet. No longer a vision in white – the tennis dress and other similar mistakes have been dumped in an Oxfam bin. Today she's wearing a petrol blue silk dress, bare arms, hem cut just above the knee, cleavage on proud display. Even more remarkable are the very high-heeled petrol-blue shoes. Rachel has been shopping and, in spite of the sophisticated stitching and expensively dyed silk, she's never looked less dressed-up since the day she ditched her last school uniform. The unspoken fuss and the raised eyebrows are all to do with her body language. She walks into the office as if she's just given up underwear. Basking in the obvious attention, Hollywood style, she catwalks shamelessly to her work bubble.

'OK, boys, back to work. I'm pleased you noticed though – this girl thought it was time for a change.'

'It can't be lost virginity,' one of them whispers, but it's definitely something to do with sex – even her make-up has more than a hint of showbiz.

'From virgin bride to Madame Babylon in one easy step!'

'Whatever she's getting, she's enjoying it.'

They're laughing when she comes back from 'freshening up' and she knows what they've been saying. Schoolboy geeks, she thinks, but she's enjoying the attention. She's had one or two of them over the last couple of years, the juiciest fruits from her tree, but, for now, she's had enough stumbling adolescent sex – part frenzy and part ego-therapy. Through her Perspex window, today, they all look five years younger to her and not in an attractive way – bless them.

Her mobile sends its text alarm, a pleasing pair of chords that her virtual friend describes as a plagal cadence. His latest ring tone. The message is from him – he usually texts her around coffee time – it's been a morning-after thing since they'd started those long late night chats. She kicks off her shoes and curls her feet up into her chair to read it. She's got over that abandoned lily. She's been taking photographs of it every day – watching its gradual decay. Her text friend isn't just a no-show, their conversations have got more frequent and even more intimate. He's testing her, she thinks, maybe even grooming her. They've agreed to postpone meeting, even to postpone speaking over the phone. Texting is the thing now for Rachel. He wants to talk, he says, but she's not so sure. There's a magic in these texts. Better to keep it like that until they actually meet. Maybe it will always be like this. She's testing him too.

'You feel good today.'

How does he know that? He's known her right from the beginning. From that first day, she's felt that he not only understands her, but that he's there with her all the time. He can see her, she believes. Maybe, he's always known her. Crazy stuff but she doesn't care. She's intoxicated by him and she's never felt like this before.

'I'm feeling great – but you know that already!!' she writes, enjoying the exaggerated second exclamation mark. Everyone uses exclamation marks these days so why not double up on the feeling.

'Yes, I knew.'

'I don't know how but I'm fine about it. Mystery man!!' Maybe doing the double punctuation twice is overdoing it. She won't do it next time.

'Not so mysterious – just careful. What is all this about exclamation marks?'

'God, you're good at this!'

'You don't need to exaggerate – you're fine as you are, Rachel.'

'I love hearing you say my name. You never tell me yours.'

'Don't I?'

'YOU KNOW YOU DON'T.' She uses capitals even though she knows it shows that she's desperate.

'You didn't ask. I'm Emmanuel.'

'God is with us!'

'I am no god, believe me.'

'I'm not sure that I do!'

'There. The single exclamation is much more effective.'

'Yes, you're right, Emmanuel.'

'Thanks, Rachel.'

'You're not such a secret now.'

'No. I'm your music guy, remember. The man who gave you a song. Emmanuel Kaspar Gulan.'

'Wow! Exotic or what!'

'My parents were Polish but I'm English, a Brighton boy like your Joe. Joe Edevane, our mutual friend.'

'You actually know Joe?'

'I've met Joe. Your ex-boyfriend. This was his idea. I don't know him though. He's some fixer, that guy. The best.'

'This is so weird. Did Joe tell you about me?'

'No. I know about you from you.'

'I've told you nothing, well not much.'

'You don't have to say much, but you tell me about yourself just the same. I think your photographs would tell me even more. I'd love to see them.'

'Any time, Emmanuel. Your music tells me about you. I'm not an idiot, you know. I run my own business. I even make money.'

'You're a businesswoman. I'm a music geek. A match made in hell!'

'This doesn't seem much like hell.'

'No, it doesn't.'

'I liked your exclamation mark too! But you're not just a music geek – you're a computer geek too.'

'I told you I've given that up.'

'Crazy man – you could be rich. The man who gave away a million dollars!'

'It's not about that.'

'Now I feel bad.'

'Don't – you know what you want.'

'Do I?'

'I think so.'

'I used to know.'

'What does my music tell you?'

'Things I don't understand.'

'That's the falling fourths. That tells me that you're a romantic. They're dying falls.'

'Clever git! I don't know what you're talking about.'

'You feel them – those dying fourths.'

There's a pause – a palpable silence. Emmanuel with her. She doesn't want to break the spell. She can feel that he doesn't either. She doesn't reply, it isn't necessary. This is deliberate, this silent communion, these breathless moments looking at her phone. She wants to kiss it.

'I have to go now. Talk again soon.'

'Yes, soon!' She nearly types a second exclamation mark but

146

changes her mind and puts down her phone like a wreath on a memorial. Then that plagal cadence again.

'!!'

She replies with a smiley. 'Emmanuel,' she whispers just to hear the sound of his name. 'Emmanuel Kaspar Gulan.' She repeats it under her breath, behaving like an adolescent. It's unavoidable and much too enjoyable, so she takes a moment to bask in the swooniness.

Her professional self returns after a coffee and she gets on with work. Today she has to rally her staff, to get the job finished for a company specializing in luxury bedding. It's a question of being sexy enough without making it pornographic. You can't sell beds without sexual overtones but no one ever buys a bed admitting that they're looking for a good time on it. She's decided to use photographs of pleasant-looking but dull enough couples, lying sleepily under a duvet together, wholesomely covered and cosy. He exposes a nipple and she's covered up to the collar bone. No obvious nudity as long as everyone knows that under the sheets, they're naked and gagging for it. She's often discussed acceptable body parts with her team and she's only once had to alter one of their campaigns for obscenity. Not even the slightest hint of body hair is acceptable for her clients. She's still thinking of nipples and more when Alan walks in.

'Is this a bad time?' he says, noticing disapproval.

'It's not that, Alan, it's the smell of stale crotch that gets me. If you want to come back to work then maybe a little scrub down with some soap might not be a mistake.'

'Oh, sorry. That bad, eh?' – Alan can still smell the urine but hoped it was only in his mind.

'Worse actually but, hey, I'm over the shock now. You alright? You look terrible.'

'I'm OK – a bit short of cash for hygiene.'

'So what do you want to do? Come back to Mamma?'

'Well I could do with the money, to be honest. I'd like to try and do the old job again and keep up with my music if I can.'

'Your busking, you mean?'

'Yeah. The busking.' No point in playing up the hard luck story, he thinks. He may have lost his saxophone but he's still playing it in

147

his head.

'You'd get more money if you didn't smell like a sewer.'

'Thanks for the helpful advice.'

'You're welcome. So, let me get this straight. You want to come back part-time? Do just enough to get some dosh but not enough to spoil your street-cred?'

'I know it sounds bad, Rachel. I've always liked the work here, you know it was never about that. I'd put my all into it when I was here, I promise, but I want to keep going on the sax – I need to.'

'Well, for old times' sake and because I sort of love you still – don't get me wrong though, my bed's definitely off limits. We'll sort something out if you can clean up and get yourself some clothes that aren't contagious.'

'Brilliant. Thanks Rachel.'

'You will have to get yourself a room – living on the street just won't work if you're coming back here. Is that a deal? Can you do that without thinking you're selling out?'

'Yeah, sure. Brilliant, Rachel. You're great, you know,' he adds, meaning it but also wanting to sound positive. 'You look great too, by the way.'

'Thanks, but don't think you're coming back to me, OK? That's over – loved and filed away in the archive.' Rachel manages to control the rising blush by laughing it off. She can never quite erase images of her former lovers naked and, under the crud, Alan is looking good, she can tell. She puts some ten pound notes into his hand, like paying off an old debt.

'A hundred pounds should fix you up with some clothes. I'll give you the deposit for a room too when you find one. Keep the beard though, it suits you. Now get that stinking body of yours out of here. Vamoosh.'

Alan runs his finger lingeringly over his old desk and raises a grubby hand in salute to his old colleagues, and only then does he realise he's trembling. He leaves hurriedly, relieved to get outside, free from Rachel-Zone where he's nearly sold his soul. The job will help expel the demons, that's as important as the money, he decides, but they're still there, mocking him from within.

Clothes shopping is a lot quicker without Rachel's expertise. He just needs new jeans, a couple of t-shirts, some boxers and trainers, nothing much different from his pre-Rachel clothes, ordinary guy gear. Then he goes to the swimming pool – not for a swim, of course, he's had his share of that. It's the cheapest way to get showered. There's a locker for his new gear, a bin for his old stuff and soap in the communal showers. Under a cocoon of lather, he sheds his old street skin. He scrubs until he's sore, until even his nostrils forget the ordeal. He hasn't a towel, he forgot to buy one, so he shakes himself dry like a dog and, when no one's looking, finishes the job crouching under the flexless hair-dryer that's unhelpfully fixed to the wall. He has to accept that he's really too much of a geek to survive on the streets and anyway, he's useless at self-defence. Later he goes back to Wah-Wah's and clinches a deal with Jake Reilly.

'Great to have you on board,' Jake says.

'You sure part-time is OK?'

'No problem. I can't afford you full-time.'

'Nice to see you again,' says Victoria.

'You too,' says Alan, eyeing the saxophone cabinet.

Chapter Thirty

John has told Rajiv not to come on the long journey to the airport. He prefers saying goodbye in private, at the small rented house, so briefly their home. Rajiv has made excuses to his family, lied to them, told them that he was helping a friend, so that he could hide away with John for the last week of his trip, and before the family wedding celebrations begin. That week has passed, John packs in silence, his hands trembling while Rajiv lies on the bed watching, willing himself to remember every gesture, filling his memory with this man, the most unlikely of lovers. So unlikely that their relationship has been a secret easily kept. Once he'd dreamed of going with John to England, to the land of sparkling rain, castles, red-jacketed soldiers on horseback, red buses and red telephone boxes. England, where all lovers were free and where no one married unless they were in love. John has dreams too but he has seen too many disappointed immigrants, arriving in hope, but soon trapped by poverty in his often cold-hearted country.

Rajiv's image of England is as illusionary as Rajiv's castles, they've both always known that; fairy tale buildings built on clouds. When they first met, Rajiv asked John if he lived in a castle with a butler and servants and hogs roasting on a spittle in the kitchen. John loves the irony but cherishes the dream too. Rajiv is his Indian Prince Charming, with magic charms and mystical beauty who, just possibly, could conjure a new world for them both. Even now he believes that his Indian dream has more reality than Rajiv's England.

They have held back from the ultimate test; John knows that and feels like a coward. Why does he come to India every year and never commit to staying? What holds him back? If he had insisted on staying, would Rajiv have submitted to this traditional marriage, given in to his family's authority? Disappointment makes John feel old – no match for a charming princess in the realm of his Prince Charming. It might have been better to end it all now, but his mystical marriage to Rajiv is real enough, sealed over sacred flames, their love rising in smoke to a spiritual zone far above their bodies.

They have both seen visions of the land where their spirits are united – it is no further away from India than it is from England and now, their marriage consummated, celebrated with fire, it's easy enough for them to go there whenever they think of each other. Rajiv is there now as he lies watching John closing his case. He's sure that his Hindu gods have blessed their ritual even if Hindu priests would have condemned them. He believes in a religion that offers hope beyond human understanding. Whatever the bonds are between him and John, he knows that what he feels is sacred and that it lives beyond barriers of geography and priestly prejudice. He's crying, he knows that too, but he's only sad in this, his physical state. Their spirits will never be separated.

'Well, my love, time to go.' John's calm now. Their parting is almost perfunctory. 'Give us a hug and don't cry any more.' The hug too is restrained, they're frightened of going too far, fearful of being pulled back and then not having the strength to carry on. It has to be done now, John kisses Rajiv on the forehead over the mark of their ritual ashes, their eyes complete his words. The monsoon rain chooses this moment to deluge, incarcerating their hut behind water, as torrential as their emotions but not powerful enough to keep John from leaving. The car has arrived, the taxi from the village – time for Rajiv to hide. The beginning of the long pretence comes as a chilling shock when Rajiv hears the car pull away.

John has one last stop before the airport at Kochi. His trips from England to India are financed by his ability as a salesman. Every year he buys reams of silk and cotton to sell in England, to anyone wanting to insert some Eastern exotica into their décor. His middleman and friend, Prabodh Bharadwaj, is a Kochi tailor who handles the Indian end of John's fabric importing enterprise. There isn't a lot of money to be made out of this business, but it pays for the travelling and keeps him out of debt, enough for a simple life in Brighton. Prabodh has already dispatched some of the cloth to England but, as is their custom, there has to be a farewell exchange of gossip over hot milky tea.

'Not so cheerful this time, my friend?' Prabodh says, sagely nodding his head. 'You look troubled, John. Sad to go, I think.'

'It's always difficult but, yes, more so this time. I'm getting old. Maybe time to settle down – to decide which continent to die in.'

'You must choose where your eyes will close happiest, John. Don't carry your sadness away with you.'

'I know. I know that Prabodh, but thank you. I always like your advice but I also need your practical skills. Have you a smart city suit that would fit me?'

The man arriving at London's Gatwick airport looks very different to the one that had left weeks earlier. John, his grey hair grown back, wears a new grey suit with a cream-coloured shirt open at the neck, his feet shod in black city shoes. He's home, he thinks, he wonders, he hopes.

Rajiv has kept the yajna fire burning since the night of their gandharva ceremony. Without John, it's important to keep the ritual flame alive. He lights two ceremonial candles in the fire, places them in a lantern and transports them to his parents' house, where his father has kept a fire burning for him since he was born. Alone, he joins the flames, youth mixed with maturity, and he intones a secret prayer.

'So the old man's gone?' It's Akshat Valodi's mocking voice. 'You have to get over it, Raj, it's time you became a man.'

'You might look like a fine man, Akshat, with your big black beard and your hairy lund but you have no idea what it takes to be a man.'

'I know enough to feel your pain, my friend,' Akshat whispers, humbled. He encloses Rajiv's head with his outsized, boyish hands and joins Rajiv in prayer.

Chapter Thirty-One

Victoria sneers when Jake puts an old record on his state-of-the-art, spider chassis turntable – his new *Michell Gyrodec*, gold-plated, brass weighted, silver finished dream machine with oil pump bearings. He's had an idea and it's obsessed him since the day Victoria broke down after out-singing Janis Joplin. He's going to risk it today, even if she hates it. She's got to him; she's now, as that old song went, under his skin. Not her thing, old recordings of classical music. Classical music has always meant boredom to her. Parents' music, her father used to play it to make her feel stupid, or so she thought. It can't have held any meaning for him because he never showed any other signs of sensitivity. Funny how classical music buffs always seem so uninterested in life, she thinks. It doesn't belong in her world and, anyway, she knows nothing about it, just as she knows nothing about her father's golf club, or where he goes every Tuesday night.

Jake insists on the music, ignoring the sneer. He has shown her round his flat. Nothing surprising there, she thinks; it's typically male, in an ostentatiously prosperous way. A kitchen full of gadgets that look unused, a concentration on black leather in the upholstery department, and modern art on every available wall, not so modern that you'd miss the emphasis on the female nude – post-Picasso grotesque, more Francis Bacon and no less grotesque. Large women, mostly, with legs splayed and breasts cascading, lie on beds, on the floor or, in one picture, spread-eagled on a rock. No wonder Jake had been so keen to invite her back to his place. So far though, he's behaved like a perfectly boring English gentleman – he could even be a friend of her father's. He mixes dry Martinis with olives in replica art deco cocktail glasses, and shows her a seat at one end of the king-size leather sofa. Now it's time to demonstrate his hi-fi equipment – a bank of sound studio machines which have enough flashing lights and control slides to impress even Victoria who, generally, is impressed by nothing much at all.

'I want to play you something very special,' he says, sounding unsure of himself.

She's been expecting the worst, something chilled, middle-of-the-road porn, easy-listening to get her into the mood. He might just be naïve enough to think she can't predict his bedding plans. No, she's wrong about the music. He chooses an ancient 78 rpm, revolutions per minute, gramophone record made, he tells her solemnly, on the first of February, 1904. It doesn't throw him when she shrugs unenthusiastically. Ignoring her reaction, he fills in some more unrequested information. The recording date wasn't the only geeky fact at his disposal, far from it. The recording was made in New York; that is enough, more than enough for her, but he continues anyway.

'It was made in the Carnegie Hall, New York's great concert hall, not in the hall though, that would have been too much for their equipment in those days – actually it was made in Room 826.'

'Wow,' she scoffs, spreading her legs Francis Bacon style. 'I don't really care if it was recorded in the men's room while they were having a shit but if it turns you on. Fine.'

'Yeah, I know, I'm boring you but, humour me, OK, stick with me on this one, I want you to hear this.' He slips off his shoes and untucks his shirt – for her benefit, she assumes. He's a lot older than her but he isn't unattractive. His stomach hasn't started to spread in the usual middle-aged bloke way. He looks after himself, she can tell, nice backside too, muscular and not too big. He's even trimmed some of his chest hair, just enough, not too much.

He'd furtively undone some more shirt buttons while he was fixing the drinks. She saw him do it. She's trying not to be harsh. She likes the man and, for all his B-list Lothario mannerisms, he looks good in an Italian kind of way. Blue eyes, black stubble with a touch of grey and hair that somehow works in a pigtail. He isn't too tall either, she likes moderately-sized men, a snug fit she's found. Watching him playing personal dj for her, she wishes he didn't wear business suit socks with his jeans but, apart from that, he's doing OK. God, she thinks, why am I such a bitch? I'm not exactly, the front page of Vogue, sitting here in my old black frock.

She's just right, Jake thinks. He has wanted to invite her here since that day when she sang her heart out in the shop. She's not like his other women, the ones he invites round after a first drink and a couple of rounds of small-talk. The ones he only needed for a night and who probably forgot him as quickly as he forgot them. It's taken weeks to invite her – not his style at all. She has what his Irish grandmother used to call spunk. Balls, even, he thinks, and he loves ballsy women.

'So listen to this – put your prejudices to one side just for a moment, OK?'

'Go on then? Surprise me.'

The turntable enables the use of early twentieth-century diamond needle styluses and Jake has a collection of these too. The gramophone record is still in its original brown wrapper with a hole in the centre to show the record label. This is a sacred moment and Jake is suddenly less Lothario and more altar boy. He's as fastidious as a heroin junkie with the needle until contact is made with the record grooves. There's a sound burst of amplified crackles and then the room is transported to the ambience of Room 826, Carnegie Hall, New York, on that morning in February 1904. The muffled sound of a harp introduces the plaintive crooning of a baritonal bassoon singing a melancholy melody. The accompanying harp line is punctuated by separated plucked string chords, heartbeats, sounding fatefully for the outcome of this musical misery.

'It's like *The Godfather*, very Italian,' Victoria says but silence is demanded, sneers forbidden. The bassoon makes it to its dying fall. The harp accompaniment starts again but this time, instead of the bassoon, a man's voice. At first it sounds weirdly distant, from pre-history, but Victoria's ear adapts rapidly. This man's high but dark-sounding tenor, so tremulous with emotion, is almost a cry. Un cri du coeur, she loves that French phrase. A cry from the heart, she knows all about that. It goes straight to her heart and, helplessly, her eyes water. It gets worse, or is that better? The voice rises to a mellifluous high note that is held for longer than she thought anyone's lungs could take, but then, no letting up, it moves, still no intake of breath, upwards to a gigantic climactic melody held at the very top of the voice. When it has finished, she says 'What the fuck!' – she's never heard anything like this before – never actually listened that is. Never heard the human voice so dangerously seductive. She doesn't bother to wipe away the tears or worry about sniffing back the mucus.

'Enrico Caruso,' Jake whispers, in awe of the singer and thrilled by her predicted reaction.

'He must have been a beautiful man to sing like that,' she says when she finds her own voice again.

'He was,' Jake agrees, 'in his way.' He flicks through a bookcase

155

and takes a thick tome, opens it on a remembered page and passes the book with a smile. No, he's not beautiful, not conventionally anyway. A small fat man with a round face, a round chest and a round stomach. Broad shoulders, short legs and a dimpled chin, but Enrico Caruso, she sees straight away, had an instinct for beauty. It's in those dark eyes. Looking at them, her eyes water again.

'He was beautiful,' she says simply, handing it back.

'You remind me of him.'

'Well, thanks! I look like a middle-aged man do I? Flatterer.'

'You have his shaped face. Sorry, love, but it's true. That's how I knew you had a great voice – right from that first day in the shop.'

Victoria grins, blushing. 'Fix me another Martini,' she says, covering her emotion, 'then play that fucking song again, will you!'

He does, and again. Both the record and the Martinis are repeated many times. Afterwards, neither is surprised that their musical evening ends in bed, and neither is surprised that Jake is tied to the bedposts.

Chapter Thirty-Two

'No, Mr McGuiness, put that away, OK, love. I don't do toys, especially when I don't know where they've been,' Rosemary says, lying naked on the bed in the back room of The Golden Orb. Her body, well-maintained over her more than fifty years, looks much better in the nude than in her limp cotton cardigan. When her hair is untied it's a grey mane, thick and long, Lady Godiva markers pointing to breasts voluptuous and toned enough to keep her nipples pointing her admirers in the eye. When naked, she knows how to bend her knees so that her favourite identifying marks are exposed to advantage. She believes, superstitiously, that they're the secret of her erotic success, those two identical moles sitting above her left hip bone. The twin stars of her constellation brighten her early evening prime. One of her customers, a retired Classics professor, calls them Castor and Pollux, the Roman twin gods, the patron deities of sailors and other travellers, who guide their followers home. Physical confidence and indifference to her clients' taste gives her real style in the sex business.

Mr McGuiness, who always prefers to keep his socks on, is also naked but considerably more excited than she is. He puts the offending sex toy back in his raincoat pocket, with only a slight visible dip in his enthusiasm. Brian McGuiness, skinny and with no other noticeable muscle tone, looks forward to his weekly session with Rosemary. As with many an elderly widower, she's the only outlet for his still lively libido. Rosemary isn't fussy about the allure of her clientele. She couldn't do her job if she looked for sexual thrills with her senior gentlemen. She and Jacqueline started this little side-line when the finances were tight after the pub landlord, her brother Derek, Jacqueline's husband, died. They'd decided to take over the running of the Orb together but Jacqueline dropped out of the sex business early on. 'You've got more stomach than I have, Rosie,' she'd said. 'I just can't look at them. Poor old buggers.'

Rosemary has always been the patient one. She's a pragmatist. If she needs to do this to make ends meet, she thinks, then needs must. She convinces herself she's fulfilling a social service and that's also why the police have mostly turned a blind eye. You could hardly call this bawdiness, she thinks, looking at Mr McGuiness. She gives him a comforting smile – she's genuinely fond of some of her gentlemen. They keep her mind off sex.

'Now, come on, honey,' she chivvies, 'stop fiddling with your raincoat and get onto the bed.' Mr McGuiness does what he needs to do, then fumbles his way back into his clothes, the tweed uniform of retired gentlefolk. He pays up without any conversation, he never talks when he's here. Carefully and slowly, he counts out the notes for an impatient Rosemary who's already wearing her dressing gown. Back in the bar, he feels good and finishes his pint of mild, chatting amiably with his friends.

'I thought I'd never get him to boiling point this time,' Rosemary says to Jacquie, returning to the kitchen for a cup of tea. 'A nice hot bath and then I'll take over the bar.'

'Monty was asking if you were busy later. Shall I tell him you can't fit him in?'

'Oh, put it like that and I suppose I'll oblige. Anyway he's a friend of Lionel's and he's eye candy after old Mr Mac Gee.'

'I don't know how you keep doing it, I really don't, Rosie. You know you don't need to. We're doing nicely enough these days just with the pub.'

'Don't tempt me, Jacks. I think I'm getting a bit old for this game – especially when Mr Mac Gee keeps getting out his fluffy old thingummy.'

'P-lease!' Jacqueline laughs, pretending to throw up. 'Honestly, Rosie, you're the patron saint of dirty old men.'

'And of fallen women, I reckon. Nothing a hot bath won't cure, though. Tell Monty, Rosemary will be available for roly-poly in an hour.'

'OK, love. I'll change the sheets. Think about what I said though. There are only so many saggy scrotums a girl needs in a lifetime.' Precisely none, she thinks, trying not to imagine Mr McGuiness' testicles.

Back in the room, bathed, revived and in her comfortable pink towelling dressing-gown, Rosemary helps Monty off with his jacket. He's nervous. The cocky little jokester from the bar is quiet, his arms and shoulders stiff with tension.

'Relax, Monty, you feel all stiff, love.'

'I wish,' he says, smiling nervously.

'Oh don't you worry, we'll soon sort out that little problem.'

He lets her take off the rest of his things, lightly joking as she works like a nurse preparing a patient for surgery. He has a bit of a stomach, for sure, but there's scope here for some fun. She likes Monty, he's quite sensitive once he stops trying to be funny all the time. He's clean too and that makes a nice change. She starts to unzip his trousers but his hand rushes to stop her.

'No, I'd rather do it.'

'OK, my love, whatever you like, but there's nothing to fear, I can be very careful.' He lets his hand drop and she carries on – she even takes off his socks.

Back in the bath, she scrubs her legs with a long-handled pink plastic bath brush and works up a considerable lather. A spontaneous smile came to her face when Monty kissed her goodbye. It's still there. He's sweet. A little fat bundle – someone to cuddle, yes; that smile grows. Her sister's words have stayed with her and, without actually thinking it through, she refused his money when he tried to pay. He's nothing special to look at but, alone in her bubble bath, she feels cherished, loved even. Well, something like that. She had to guide him all the way but he'd treated her with respect and, later, affection. It felt like a date even though she knows that it isn't true love, not in the *Some Enchanted Evening* sense anyway. It wasn't exactly sexual chemistry either, maybe she's helped too many men on their way to that messy moment of release. No, it's not love and it's definitely not lust but whatever it is, she decides, it will do nicely enough for now.

The bathroom, her private haven, is a small, tall-ceilinged room, walls fully tiled in black and white with a large water heater that is a perpetual fount of hot water. She can soak in comfort and refill the bath as often as she likes or, on occasions, after some of her less savoury clients, as often as is necessary. The warmth on her body, the steam on her face and the light touch of the brush – pure luxury. She wriggles her toes and greets each one individually. 'Hello, little toes, did you have fun too?' Her voice echoes from the ceiling, like it did in church when she was a child, the star of the choir, a little angel, or so the choirmaster had said when he fondled her hair. She always loved singing. It felt good in her head, the notes vibrating in her palate. She always knew when she was perfectly in tune because her voice then filled the whole church, ricocheted and then came back to her like a dog wagging its tail. It's been a long time since she has felt like singing, but the echo inspires her. Lying

159

back with just her head showing above the water, she fills her lungs and lets rip. 'Meet me in St Louis, Louis. Meet me at the fair!' She has the rich mezzo soprano of a balladeer and the jazzy edge of a cabaret singer. 'Meet me in St Louis, Monty! Meet me in the bar!'

'You sound bloody marvellous, Rose!' Jacqueline calls from outside the door. 'No need to ask you how that went then.'

'I'm taking your advice, Jacks,' she replies, laughing, like the singer she is, from her diaphragm. 'I'm a whore no more!'

She shifts under the bubbles and the suds on her hips subside enough to reveal her moles. Castor and Pollux shine like stars through shifting clouds on what might well have been an enchanted evening after all.

Chapter Thirty-Three

There have been too many people having too much fun on the beach today, and Harry is suffering from humanity fatigue. All the deckchairs have been hired out. The shingle beach is a mirage of blue-and-white stripes; between the chairs and all around them people are lying on towels, stripped to their swimming gear, glowing red under a varnish of sweat and suntan oil. Laughter, bad-tempered parental shouting, the screeching hilarity of over-excited children running out of control, Harry's had enough. He's normally a man of tranquillity and patience but, today, he's over-heated, impatient and, yes, irritable. Were there really that many jokes in the world to keep this crowd laughing for a full day? Even if there were, how many jokes can anyone hear before laughter opens the door to depression or jaws ache from over-use?

Harry wills the languid summer tide up onto the shingle, pleading with it to wash the crowds out to sea, everyone, even the little toddlers, delighting in their endless games of filling plastic buckets with stones. He doesn't want a mass drowning, just a marine miracle. All these people and their deckchairs would be washed up on a remote shore, like shipwrecked courtiers in Shakespeare's play, *The Tempest*, the only play he's seen. There they would become exquisite spirits, lost forever to a realm of ecstatic silence. Something like that does happen when the sun loses its heat and the evening light calls the crowd away into town, guiding their long march back to the train station, no strikes today, and then, still joined thigh to thigh, squashed into trains going home.

The sinking sun exhales a cooling breeze, soothing Harry's, if not savage, then over-heated breast, as he sits, bare-chested, djembe between his knees, on a hillock of shingle, beating out a serenade, over the empty beach and the silver-flecked water, to where the sea tumbles over the waterfall that, to Harry, is the distant horizon, the way to Prospero's island or, even better, the road to Kathmandu.

He greets Joe with a nod, but doesn't interrupt his drumming. Joe sits next to him, flute in hand, barefoot and bare-chested, in cut-off denim shorts. Without a word, he joins the music. Harry has the measure of Joe's flute meditations, and he tempers his playing to a soft finger-pad shuffle. Joe sits straight-backed, in lotus position. Harry is slumped, back curved, hair obscuring his face. Their music

161

sounds like a divine invocation – maybe it is.

Nico sees them – they're silhouettes in a Hindu temple. He's coming from the promenade, summoned by the call of the flute. If not a god then a serpent, he's drawn noiselessly to the music over the shingle. Putting down his cameras at Joe's side, and kicking off his canvas espadrilles, he carries on down the bank of stones, untucked white shirt hanging loose, baggy white cotton trousers rolled up to the shins. He reaches the newly exposed sand, still wet from the retreating tide and shining in the low sun's light. He too becomes a silhouette as he strikes the first stance in his personal ballet – his Tai chi pattern, black curly hair ruffled to life by the breeze. He moves slowly, in slow motion even, each body-shape dissolving into the next – an illusion of shifting stasis. The music's limpid melody line, supported on languid drum rhythms, transcends movement and time.

Yogic too is Joe's flute technique, straight fingers aligned with his arms and legs. His physical symmetry has an elegance just short of contortionism. Harry's djembe picks up Joe's gently accelerating heartbeat as he watches Nico in the middle distance. Joe's heart synchronises with his – it's no more alien than the shadows formed by his own blinking eyelids. The three, formlessly absorbed in the music, are controlled by each of Joe's long-held breaths. When he inhales, Joe believes that he breathes in the world in its entirety, both its good and its bad. Sanctified friendship is personified in the music's melody and pulse. Fear is there too – fear of loss. It might be a summer evening's lingering farewell, but Joe knows it's more than that. The flute has a power that he only partly understands. He might inhale the world with each breath, but his music, floating on each exhalation, returns something to that world like a secret benediction that he has no right to bestow.

'Fucking hippies!' a jeering shout splinters the calm. Five lads with lager cans and alcohol attitudes have found, they think, easy targets.

'Play something we can sing along to, mate! Give us a blast of *You'll Never Walk Alone.*' The loudest of the jokers is also the biggest, and he doesn't wait for an answer before launching into a rowdy chorus of his favourite football team's anthem. The others join in, laughing, looking round for support.

'Come on, y'wankers, try playing some real music!' The ringleader

162

grows braver by the second but Nico, long distance, has seen them and, cat-like he springs. He doesn't get to the top of the beach before Joe turns his face on the enemy with fiery eyes that silence the song and send the drunken lads running. Later they say, sobered, that they'd felt their flesh actually burning.

The sun is burning brightly too as it glows in its descent behind the sea, igniting the waves with scarlet and painting the sky blood red.

'Wow,' says Harry, shaken. 'There was something powerful going on there, man. The ground rumbled when those kids ran off.'

Later he still can't work out exactly what happened, but he's pleased that Joe and Nico, are on his side. The sun sets, its loss of heat hardly felt on this humid night. The fading light is watched in silence, moodily even, by three solemn faces: Joe, Nico and Harry. Later, Harry goes home, moved, but also disturbed by their silent communion. If they weren't my friends, he thinks, they'd scare the shit out of me. Nico and Joe stay where they are – soon invisible in the dark.

Chapter Thirty-Four

The sun has risen on the nudist beach. The air has hardly cooled during the hours of darkness, wet shingle stones turn red in the pink light and the tide begins its gradual retreat over mirror-like, foot-printless sand. It's John's first visit here since returning from India, and he's glad to be alone as he walks down to the water. It's his attempt at a painless re-entry to English life. A large herring gull cocks its head, scrutinising him for soft body parts, sharp-eyed for a quick snack. No great loss, John thinks, but he doesn't like the look of that beak ominously tipped with red. Wet pebbles massage the soles of his feet, welcoming him back, uncomfortably, reminding him, if he needs reminding, how much he misses the sandy Kerala coastline, where the green of the palm trees meets pale yellow sand washed by that vivid tropical blue. Beautiful too, he admits reluctantly, these red stones leading to brown sand, and then the mistily silver English Channel. No bath-warm tepid water either: the English Channel welcomes him with a cold slap. The gull flies over his head, expressing disappointment with a shriek. No more lingering, no more regrets, John sprints into the waves and dives, body-careless, into an unfriendly salty void.

Lionel sees the lone figure swimming between the breakwaters. His old friend has returned, and he's missed the old sod more than he'd expected. He's been back in Brighton for a week, and he too has taken his time getting back to old routines after his adventures at sea. It's a melancholy return for him too. He misses the Mediterranean, the music-making and, most of all, Kate. Something has died on the beach or been washed up dead. He spots the brown-freckled skin of a fish being torn apart by a new influx of gulls. A good supper wasted, he thinks, that was a nice piece of cod. He hopes the gulls make a clean job before the sun and the flies do their worst. The humidity this morning rivals the Med and Lionel has abandoned his English tweeds for light cotton trousers, beige, under a pale blue seersucker jacket, matched with a plain cream shirt. The special summertime lightweight tie, a loosely knitted biscuit-coloured cotton, seems sensible enough on a man who likes to either dress up or strip off completely. Soon his clothes are lying in a pile on the shingle, as neatly stacked as if they were in his bedroom cupboard.

The sun licks the water off their skin as the reunited friends lie on their towels, recovering their breath. There were few pleasantries out there at sea – a few smiles and grunts, and then unspoken camaraderie as they clocked up their lengths between the breakwaters. Now, lying here together, they've already caught up with each other, even though no words have yet been exchanged. There's an involuntary sigh from John, masked by a cough and a seawater sniff. Lionel hums lightly under his breath, and discreetly fingers an imaginary piano.

'So how was your trip?' he asks, as if it's no great matter.

'Fine, thanks. Good actually,' John replies, in an equally matter-of-fact tone. 'How was yours?'

'Fine too, thanks. Good to be back tickling the old ivories. Yes, it was good. How was business?'

'Good. Yeah. Mr Bharadwaj has dispatched a new haul of fabrics. It should get here next week. Keep me going for a bit.'

'Well done Mr Bharadwaj. It's good to have a reliable chap over there.'

'Yes, he's a good man, Bharadwaj.'

'I see you've grown your hair back. Very distinguished. Going for the matinee idol look, eh?'

John laughs grimly. 'Yes, something like that. Time for a change, I think. So did you meet any fair maids on your cruise? Your usual romp with the current Miss Saga Holidays, I expect.'

'Oh nothing very much. It was mostly me and Cole Porter and a shared cabin – a poor chap with digestive problems.'

'Nice. Delhi Belly on Cruise Med. Messy.'

'I was fine. It wasn't the food and I'm a good sailor. Always have been. Poor old Vince though, he may be a rock'n'roll drummer but he's not as hard as he thinks. I even put on a few pounds,' he says, rubbing himself down with his towel. John's dressing too so they return to an easy silence. It isn't customary or manly, they think, to look at each other when they dress, but this time it's different. Lionel can't help watching, intrigued, as John puts on his grey trousers, followed by a fairly reasonable, if slightly slick, outfit: a blue dress shirt, black leather shoes and the jacket half of a summer suit.

'Forgive me, old chap, but I can't help noticing a certain change of style.'

165

'I told you it was time for a change. Meet Mr Bharadwaj's finest off-the-peg fashion.'

'I think I approve of your Mr Bharadwaj.'

'Don't start putting me off, mate. I wanted a change, not to dress up as bleedin' Noel Coward.'

'No fear there, old chap. You're no Noel – I'd say more footballer chic.'

'Watch it, mate. You saying I look like a spiv.'

'As Pontius Pilate said to the Pharisees, what I have written, I have written.'

'You cheeky old bugger,' John laughs. 'You know, it's actually good to see you again.'

'Likewise, old friend. Maybe a few halves down The Golden Orb? For old times' sake.'

'You're reading my mind.'

'It's good to be back.'

'Yes.'

Chapter Thirty-Five

Kanti and Diep are twins, female and male, not identical, but they aren't so very different in their bodies. Once they were saddened by their gender distinctiveness. They share more features than not – high-cheeked heart-shaped faces, the same pale skin type, an iridescent mix of the light brown and gold with a hint of vanilla and thick jet black hair like most Nepalese. Their most distinctive shared features are their large wide eyes, set under rounded brows and heavy lids that often rest half-closed only to flash wide open, startlingly, with pupils so dark brown, they are almost black. Their similarities outweigh their differences and, male and female, they're both beautiful. Diep is slightly taller than his sister, and his torso is as skinny as a piece of string. That's what Kanti told him after she allowed him to see her small breasts for the first time, after the period of secrecy that had followed their almost synchronised puberties. They'd kept their bodies apart for a year, sleeping in different rooms for the first time, bathing separately, always covered from each other, even though they both shared the same furtive curiosity.

They'd got over their shyness around their eighteenth birthday, when they got used to the process of physical change that had threatened to pull them apart. Once over their growing pains, they were as they'd always been. Their mother didn't know or, if she did, she made no comment, when the two of them reintroduced themselves to each other's bodies. Diep, now lightly hairy and sinewy and Kanti, rounded and soft. Being naked together felt natural once more; dimly understood fear and unwanted shame dissolved after they'd stood naked with each other again. Diep had stared, hypnotised by his sister's womanly bits, she'd followed his eyes as they moved over her torso and she, in turn, smiled at his limply dangling lingam. They had focused on each other like artists sketching a life study. It was Adam and Eve meeting for the first time. Their sibling eroticism was unacknowledged, platonic but pleasurable. They'd returned to their paradise garden, their bond renewed. Away from disapproving eyes, they'd stripped off again to swim together at night, rededicating themselves to each other in the sacred waters of Lake Phewa.

Since coming to England, they've shared a room again, living together, uninhibited, beyond shyness and, or so Kanti had thought, without secrets. Now she doubts if that's true any more, and remembers what it was like to feel lonely. Diep hasn't left their room since the day he skinned his knuckles on the wall. She has been bringing him food that he seldom eats and, feeling desperate and helpless, she's watched his tearful decline into depression. He's stayed on the upper bunk for days, in his midnight blue silk pyjamas - a parting gift from their mother, who knows how to heighten beauty with colour. They've now finished their art course and they should be celebrating, but the moment has passed unmarked and, since then, they've both been paralysed by Diep's gloom.

Kanti's been denied her share of joy in their moment of success. It has, maybe, often been like that – a hidden struggle to remain optimistic. She'll stop making plans, she decides, tearful herself. She'll stop setting herself up for disappointment. They were meant to be deciding what to do next, an exciting time, whether they should go home or stay here in England, extending their visas. There's a lot to organise, a joy in itself, but that too is denied her. Since Diep ran from the art college in tears he's cried every day, refusing to communicate, lying on his bed, a foetus in the womb of his own misery. Kanti has tried grasping his head, pushing her face into his, and forcing him to read her lips. She's shouted at him in frustration. She'd never found his deafness a barrier before, but now she's often crying in frustration, wishing he would tell her what's wrong.

Two naked children, a boy and a girl, are splashing in the lake, laughing, squinting in the sun, when they see Father, the tall blond man gesticulating from the shore. He's there with their mother, they're naked too, apart from beads and henna tattoos. He's calling them in, to eat round the fire. Mother is stirring the pot, but her breasts are still home for them. They lie in the tent, four bodies together under a mosquito net. Kanti is hugging her father's golden-haired leg, her brother snug at his mother's nipple – their parents entwined, her head on his shoulder.

She wants to tell Diep so many things. What she's feeling, what she's been saying to Harry and that brightening feeling in her heart.

Maybe today, Diep will see this. She's returned to the room, in her orange t-shirt and red shorts, still stinging slightly, but amused in her sadness, by her meeting with the Public Service Photographer. The smile hasn't quite left her lips when she sees Diep. He's sitting up, legs dangling from the top bunk, looking at her, and the slightest of smiles transforms his face. She grasps the moment and leaps up onto the bunk beside him. He turns away just as he did when they were children, but she finds his feet and, also like when they were kids, she tickles his soles, laughing at her own mercilessness. She laughs as loudly and as wildly as he does – wriggling on the bed in an agony of affection.

'Maile tapailai samje!' she repeats, screaming the words joyfully but also accusingly. I missed you, she keeps saying, until they can take no more and collapse panting next to each other, grinning at the ceiling. When they get their breath back, he speaks with excited, animated hands. 'I'm sorry, I'm a bad brother. I have been with my black demon but now he's gone.'

'Thikai cha, thikai cha,' she says, verbally and in signs. No problem, no problem. Then she puts two fingers on his lips to absolve his crime. She shows him the Polaroid photograph of her and tells him that Nico says she looks like Minnie Mouse.

'Minnie Mouse,' he signs. 'I love Minnie Mouse!' When he sees the photograph, he laughs like a braying donkey.

'Nico says I should stop dressing like this. He says I am beautiful, truly, little brother, and then I mended his broken nose.' Diep stops laughing. 'You are beautiful, little sister. But poor Minnie Mouse, I shall miss her.'

'No more little Miss Minnie Mouse and you, my brother, must stop being Mickey. No more big American dream.'

'It was childhood's dream,' Diep says.

'Oh, Diep, does that mean we're grown up?'

'My demon told me childhood is over.'

'Then we must dream a new dream, Nico's dream, maybe. He is American, maybe he has a real American dream for us.'

She goes to the full-length mirror and starts to ape her Walt Disney character, as Minnie Mouse begins her final striptease, giggling and throwing her clothes at her brother. When she's naked, she stands in front of her reflection, looking at her body, appraising it objectively.

'It is a good body, I can see that,' she says. 'That man has a good eye.'

Diep leaps from the bed, pulling off his pyjamas to stand next to her, grinning, naked too, grown up perhaps but back where their dream began – back on the banks of Lake Phewa.

Chapter Thirty-Six

'Very smart, Alan, love the beard,' Rachel says, hoping to keep her enthusiasm ironic-sounding without putting him off. 'Blue jeans are never a problem round here. Nothing wrong with t-shirts either. Is that Burnt Siena?'

'I dunno. It said orange on the label but thanks, I did my best.'

'You smell better too. Is that *Java* or *Caveman*? The sweet smell of guys' deodorant. Lovely.'

'Someone left it in the bathroom at my new place. I thought of you when I was having a shower.' Alan resists telling her anything else about his retreat from street life, and tries to put his shower-time Rachel fantasy out of his mind.

'Nice – boys sharing stuff. I hope you'll be very happy there.' Poor Alan, she thinks, he never had any taste.

'You're looking pretty spectacular yourself, if you don't mind me saying.' Their reacquaintance is recrimination-free, and a bit of edginess was only to be expected from the woman that he'd once thought as his life-partner-to-be. He isn't being arch though about her new style. He's no expert, but he knows the dress is expensive; pale red flowers and a touch of green on an ivory cream background. A Japanese look on silk that moves with her, and doesn't just hang there without an agenda. He likes the way it's always trying to slip from her shoulders.

'Great dress. Really shows off your figure.'

'Well thanks, Alan. Enough said maybe.'

Actually she's pleased that he's noticed, and she goes back to her own desk with just enough of a spring to let the dress show what it can do. Alan smiles. She was always queen of the strut. Physically they can never have any secrets from each other, they've had too many enjoyable experiences between those crisp cotton sheets. Something stirs inside his new blue jeans, but he puts it down to normal guy stuff, nothing at all to do with reawakened lust. The memory of lust past is exciting enough for now.

He gives his work colleagues the usual office-macho gesture, a mix between a nod and a shrug, but it's not quite the same here now. They return the sign awkwardly and return to their work. The new bearded Alan has grown a few years on them. Is he Lazarus returned from the grave? They don't know what to think, but they smell mortality and recoil. It won't be the same as before. He's not worried about it and kicks off his trainers to let his toes stroke the stiff synthetic carpet. The modern world welcomes him back with shots of static electricity. He has his old desk too so, after revolutionising his life, it's almost as if he'd never been away. Almost. He thumbs through the new marketing brief – a campaign for J & F Builders Ltd, manufacturers of 'PVC fascias, guttering, cladding and window board systems'. Nice. He rolls his eyes, pleased he's only working here two-and-a-half days a week.

His denim bulge isn't lost on Rachel, it brings back pleasant memories. Alan's body had never been the problem. It was out of bed they'd irritated each other. They were like terriers on leads, wanting to run in different directions, always ending up snapping instead of having fun. He's good at his job and, for a time, out of office hours, he'd made her feel good too. No, there isn't a problem having him back at work, but the zip on his jeans will stay strictly out of bounds. Today she's just enjoyed a nostalgic detour.

Ten minutes later they're both busy clicking away on their keyboards.

'Rachel, you know you don't have to see me.'

'Don't be daft, Emmanuel.'

'I could just be your virtual lover.'

'You're already more than that.'

'There might not be any more.'

'I know differently. You won't get out of this so easily so don't even try.'

'I'm not trying – just giving you a let-out clause.'

'I've already read the small print.'

'OK then. We have a deal.'

'Yes – a deal.'

'Only if you're sure, Rachel.'

'I am.'

'We just have to name the day.'

'Can't wait!'

'So?'

'So what?'

'When can we meet?'

'Next week. Sorry it's not sooner.'

'Computer stuff?'

'No, music.'

'Fine. Next week is good.'

It isn't, of course; she wants it to be now. 'Friday?' she suggests, wishing it could be Monday. She's decided to play the long game, and to keep her cool.

'Friday then.'

'Exchange photos? Just in case?'

'No. Let's do it the dangerous way.'

'OK, Emmanuel. All or nothing.'

'All or nothing. Agreed.'

Playing for danger always excites her. She's burning for him now. If they were meeting tonight, she would have looked just right, but she can wait. He might be an old man with an axe, she knows that, it's the risk with virtual friendships. He isn't old, she has no doubt there; well, he might be old but would that matter? He's a modern man, on her wavelength, she's sure of that. Their conversations often run into the night, but he's always sharp, one step ahead, always says the right thing, alert to what she tries to keep hidden. He never asks what she's wearing, or the colour of her hair, but he knows who she is. He can see she wants more than a nice house and a father for her kids. She's typing out her life when she speaks to him, her impatient fingers stumbling over the keys.

When he's gone, she feels like they've had sex, in some ways they have – good sex too, but much more than that. She's opened up for him, more than she has to even the friskiest of her lovers. As for the axe, well, maybe that's a risk worth taking – excitement should be tinged with fear. She's not frightened of being bludgeoned to death, she's always been brave, but there's a nagging fear that she's about to see beyond the mystery. Their meeting is inevitable, unstoppable but when it happens, it might ruin everything. Oh well – all or nothing. Red toenails might be good after all, she thinks. No, it doesn't matter what she wears. She wants to see him now.

Alan is typing intensely too. It's easy to lose interest in window board systems, so, for a break that has already turned into a quest, he begins a detailed comparison of saxophone manufacturers on *Yahoo*, the newly-launched computer search engine which promises to revolutionise the twentieth century's access to knowledge. Life feels good to Alan, pleased to reunite with a world bursting with invention, but surer than ever that he can no longer live without music. He's stopped having nightmares. The thief in the night has retreated, replaced by dreams of a silver machine. If he can save enough money out of his two jobs, it would be useful to know the price of a *Selmer Mark VI*, the horn of his dreams.

Chapter Thirty-Seven

Lionel likes walking, and loves Brighton's urbane clifftop promenade that divides town and beach, allowing pedestrians to savour both environments, the wild and the partially civilised. He isn't taking this walk to admire the view, he has an idea that needs some exercise before he gets to The Golden Orb. Being the son of a military family, he believes that tactical problems are best worked out with a stiff walk. It's too easy to wallow in personal dilemmas at home in his large and lonely Regency house. Sitting with a gin and tonic in his usual chair has led him to many a wrong decision in his life, and he doesn't want to make that mistake again. It's definitely time to take that walk.

Last night, with the inevitable glass of gin, he had mourned the end of the cruise, and his return to the solitary, if not monastic life of an aging widower, endowed most of the time with a frustrated but youthful libido. It isn't just a matter of sex, but he's never underestimated its importance. No, he misses Kate. Often, since she left the ship in Egypt, he has tried to imagine what she's doing. He thinks of her every day, especially in the mornings, waking up, his loneliness renewed.

This morning, he smiles sadly at the thought of that feisty American woman striding round the burial grounds in the Valley of the Kings, looking at pyramids and contemplating death by looking it in the face. If only he could be as strong, he thinks, crunching his cornflakes, unable to concentrate on the morning broadsheet - ethnic cleansing in Bosnia, AIDS cases reach four million, opinion polls point to a change of government, and England has beaten South Africa in the cricket. It shouldn't be Kate Arnold entering his head over breakfast. Alice should have been there, smiling across the table – that had been their plan. Beautiful Alice, his Alice, his wife for more than thirty years, the companion who'd loved him enough, even if she'd never liked music in the house. After time, they'd lost the habit of sharing and he was excluded when her cancerous decline had become private, silent and grim. Had that gaunt dying face blamed him? Since coming back from this last trip, he's been wondering if he would impregnate all his women with cancer.

These days he finds it difficult to remember Alice. Her

photograph's on the mantelpiece, of course, but he's long forgotten how that face looked when alive. She's become a melancholy icon for a sinner's penitential prayers. Maybe their dead baby poisoned what they might have had. He still sees the child, grey in her arms. He sees other bodies too, hundreds, thousands, lying in heaps, long ago now, Belsen-Bergen, 1945. The bulldozers, the mass graves, the despair – no job for a soldier celebrating victory. He tries to forget, but he still sees their faces. The 11th Armoured Division, the lads, his mates, relieving Belgium, and then the Netherlands – enough to be proud of, but he still remembers the horrors and never talks about it. Better to think of those women who'd tempted him from the marriage bed, the comforters, those sheltering arms. They were always laughing, having a good time – he searches for memories where he's laughing too. Kate might just be one in a long chain of those women. No, it was more than that. He might be in love with Kate. Without her, he feels truly alone.

Walking along the promenade to The Golden Orb, he indulges foolish daydreams that hurt – the most painful is him, in his youth, meeting young Kate like young people do. Love should be easy – it just walks in. If he'd only known Kate when they were both young – war or no war. The thought keeps returning to wound him. He might not have been such a dutiful civil servant, he might not have been so conscientious over his pension rights, either, or the mortgage, he might even have tried for a life as a musician. With Kate anything was possible. In another life perhaps. In another life with Kate – but, reality kicks in. He's an old man and she's dying. She might be dead already. Dying alone when he should have been at her side. She's touched his life, disturbed him, made him dream those old dreams again. No point in dwelling on the might-have-been. If he can't live with Kate, then he could live with Rosemary. That's why he's taking this walk. He knows his weaknesses. He's always needed a woman, somewhere to hide his tears. Yes, he'll marry Rosemary, if she'll have him, even though he doesn't love her. Over the years, it's always been more than a prostitute-client relationship. They laugh together – the sex has been good too. That was more than he'd ever had with Alice. Today he'll ask Rosemary to marry him.

Conrad is behind the bar at The Golden Orb. Pierced, Polish and bleach-haired, he's a trusted alien here in this most English of pubs. He has a sympathetic bedside and bar-top manner. You can talk to Conrad, tell him your secrets, even if you're Mr McGuiness and your favourite sex toy has just packed in. Conrad encourages the confessional among his elderly customers, like a sensitive urologist after an outbreak of chlamydia.

'Maybe I can recommend things for you at Anything Goes, Mr McGuiness, I work there this afternoon. I think I can sort you out.'

'That's kind of you, lad, it would help, keeping it discreet, you know, not so embarrassing.'

'OK, I see you over there later.'

'I wondered where you were,' John says, coming in for his pint. Conrad pours him his usual.

'I'm always here if I am not at the Emporium or over the road, you know that, John.' He lowers his voice, 'I help out the old guy when I'm over there later. Poor man, I feel sorrow for him. It's not so easy when you're old.'

'Quite.'

'Sorry I mean very old not –'

'Well, anyway. I dunno, you never stop working.'

'It's the money. Three jobs pay more than one. It's simple arithmetic, John.'

'I'll think about it. A bit of a rise, maybe. Let's see how things go.'

'I like being at the Emporium. It's my first priority, John. I want to learn all the piercings. I hope one day to do the whole body, not just the ears.'

'OK, we'll talk later.'

'I didn't recognise you, mate,' Monty says, sitting next to him at the bar. 'Blimey, you look different. You're quite a handsome bugger on the quiet.'

'And you're full of beans, Monty,' John smiles. 'What's put the spring in your step?'

Someone activates the jukebox and the wheezy sound of a bluesy harmonica announces the queen of country music herself. Dolly Parton tops The Golden Orb charts most days and today; after that first pint of ale, someone usually chooses her anthem to high emotion, *I Will Always Love You*.

'It's not so much what as who,' Monty replies in a confidential whisper. 'Old Monty has been having a bit of fun in your absence, mate. The old plonker's never had so many outings.'

'Good for you.'

'You're looking great, John,' Rosemary says, coming into the bar in a new floral frock with her hair, blow-dried bouncy, loose over her shoulders. She's been freshly sprayed with a perfume that shouts female.

'You too, Rosemary. Your hair suits you like that.'

'Well thank you, but you really do look great John. You've softened your edges. India's turned you into an Englishman.'

'He was hiding his flame under his sari, Rose.' Monty blushes when Rosemary puts her hand over his and presses it onto the bar.

'India gave me time to think. The make-over's no big thing. Just a new suit and some hair.'

'Well, you look very nice. I almost fancy you. I probably would if I hadn't got my Monty now. That's right isn't it, love?'

'What is?' asks Lionel, breezing up to the bar. 'Gosh, Rosemary. You look wonderful.'

'Well it sure is a day for compliments,' John mutters, as Dolly Parton promises eternal love.

'A pint of the usual, please Rosemary,' says Lionel, pleased that she's here but already worried, beginning to wonder if she'll agree to his plan.

'It's lovely to see you again Lionel,' she says. 'Had a good trip?'

'Yes thanks. The cruise was just right, thanks. Me and my fingers, you know. We did Cole Porter proud and Mr Gershwin had nothing to be ashamed of either.'

'I'm pleased you're back, Lionel, because I've got something special to tell you.' She pushes back her hair and pauses for breath.

'Funny you should say that, I've got something I want to tell you too.'

'Monty and Rosemary are an item, that's the big news,' John announces, recoiling from more tales of boy meets girl.

'Oh, stop it John, you're so embarrassing. That's not what it was about at all,' she says, laughing, giving him a playful slap on the arm. 'We've been doing up the dining room and I want to show you something.'

'Another drink, anyone?' Conrad asks, ever the barman diplomat.

Rosemary walks Lionel through to the room at the back of the pub, giving him more than enough time to rearrange his thoughts as well as his expectations. Well, it was never actually love, he thinks. A silly idea. He's much too old. He's found his smile again by the time they get to the dining room.

'Well, you and Monty, fancy that, it's lovely news. Congratulations.'

'Yes, thanks, Lionel. I was going to tell you but John beat me to it. He's left his Mr Charming hat back in India. I've been thinking and now that I'm seeing Monty, I've decided to give up my gentlemen. I would've told you first, of course, but you were away.'

'Well, Monty's a very lucky man,' he says, meaning it. There will be no marriage for him now, and no more sex behind the bar. Time for another rethink and another long clifftop walk.

'Oh I know it's not exactly young love and it's only funny old Monty but it's a bit of fun and that suits me. Anyway, that wasn't what this is about. It's much bigger news. I want to show you my acquisition.

Lionel's lost for words – he takes a moment and, hiding a few tears, he walks over to inspect the new white baby grand piano. He's impressed – it's a four-foot-eleven *Samick from South Korea*.

'We're bringing live music back to The Golden Orb,' she says, putting a hand on his shoulder. 'We've got the licence and now we need both you and your fingers. Will you join us? Will you be our pianist?'

They both know the answer. He sits at the keyboard. His fingers have already decided.

Chapter Thirty-Eight

Two small children in Walt Disney costumes – Kanti and Diep are excited. They're shopping with their parents at Pokhara's outdoor market. Mother and father are in city clothes, with city-serious faces. John Fletcher, their father, laughs; Kanti and Diep like him best that way. He takes a photograph of them, carefree once more, in their party clothes. His long blond hair is tied back under a broad-brimmed hat; he's wearing a winter-dark coat, a rucksack on his back. Only his golden beard tells the twins that it's him. He wants to look happy but his face tells the truth. When they arrive at the station, family laughter has faded. John Fletcher gets on the train. Mickey Mouse and Minnie Mouse stand on the platform – excitement past, now they're merely confused. Tears will come later.

Today, ten years on, here in the centre of Brighton's fashion-shopping centre, Kanti, in new jeans and a simple grey t-shirt, is armed with her *Canon EOS-1* fitted impressively with an *EF* zoom lens. It's her favourite, she tells anyone who asks. Diep has an equally formidable wide-angle on his older *Canon EOS 650* – he too is wearing jeans and a grey t-shirt. They're still, almost, identical but they've discarded their Disney t-shirts. The Public Service Photographer has won.

'I feel brave now,' Diep says, curling his little finger round Kanti's.

'You have always been brave, little brother, you make me brave too.'

Nico arrives, as promised, ready to surprise them. He's also in jeans, body-hugging and bleached, designed by *883 Police,* according to the label on his right buttock. He's in a white t-shirt, the brand worn by Marlon Brando, it clings to him like skin. His *Polaroid 600 SE* camera, known as *The Goose,* hangs from his shoulder. Round his neck there's his SLR and, like Kanti's, it's a *Canon EOS-1,* also sporting a thick macho lens, a New York purchase, his *EF 28-80f/3.5-5.6 USM.* Lenses are major talking points for Kanti and Nico while they're waiting for Joe.

'Is this for visiting royals or just Hollywood stars?' Joe asks, cameraless, the last to arrive, looking at the others waiting for him like paparazzi. He's in knee-length denim shorts, blue t-shirt, gold waistcoat unbuttoned and loose – scruffier than the others but a lot cooler too

'We were waiting for you, star-boy,' Nico quips. He's trying to ignore the blood surging to his head.

He plans to wipe away all traces of Kanti's disneydom in a newly-decorated Georgian shop called *Sato* in a smart shopping district. This part of town was once a network of tiny fishermen's cottages, but now the only fishnets are stockings. It's boutique heaven or hell, depending on your tolerance for shopping.

Nico knows how to receive gushing welcomes without showing impatience, he's lived in Los Angeles. He smiles blandly when Luisa Sato's kiss grazes his cheek with theatrical artifice. Luisa, the boutique's glamorous young Japanese owner had rushed or, rather, glided out of the shop, setting off the chain of bell chimes that dangle welcomingly in the doorway. Luisa, fashionably pale, has crisply-cut short black hair and there's not a stitch of denim in sight. Clothes are her passion and to prove it, she's wearing a short pink dress that looks as if it has been made from strips of Formica, vertically hung like Samurai armour. She smiles at the others, saving her kisses for Nico, her hand delicately brushing his forearm.

'This is Kanti,' he says, getting down to business. 'We have to do something about her urgently.' Nico lets the skin round his eyes crinkle as Luisa gives Kanti a welcoming bow, sussing her out, head to toe.

'This will be fun, Kanti,' she says, without too much of a smile – smiles are uncool in these quarters. 'You are beautiful but you wear the wrong clothes. It's lucky that you've met Nico because he's a genius at these things, believe me. It's a gift he got from his sensational mother.'

'Let's leave Mom out of this,' Nico says, repressing the edge in his voice. 'People should celebrate who they are, that's all I'm saying. I'm just trying to help them find out who that is.'

'I celebrate who people are too,' counters Kanti, 'but I'm the worse person for clothes wearing. I celebrate the body.'

'The right clothes on a person say a lot about their body,' he says, meeting Kanti's intensity full on. Now, it seems, everyone is looking beneath each other's clothes. Luisa smoothes down her Formica dress, fingers armed with sharp baby-pink nails.

'When people hide their bodies, they're hiding themselves,' Nico says, enthused. 'If you're built big or little or whatever, then celebrate it, don't hide – express who you are. It's not a trivial fashion thing. Believe me on this.'

This is Nico's mission and it helps that he's rich - a celebrity orphan. Actually he's very rich. This isn't shopping for shopping's sake, or spending for money's sake. As the Public Service Photographer, he's stalked the streets of New York, Los Angeles, then London and now Brighton – it's his unsung charity work but it's also, he hopes, street art.

'Hey, but anyway,' he says, thinking he's said too much. He doesn't want to upset his new friend Luisa, whose face too easily expresses disdain. 'I love clothes, especially yours Luisa. Design and beauty are my passions, I guess.'

'Let's see what we can do then,' Luisa says, still on the verge of smiling, as she guides them into the store. She's anxious in case Kanti changes her mind about buying *Sato* clothes.

Joe isn't upset being left alone outside, he's done clothes shopping enough with Rachel and that has more than satiated his interest. For Rachel, fashion wasn't about self-revelation, it was camouflage and dressing her boyfriends was a sartorial attempt at cloning. In Joe's opinion, they'd got on best at skin level. Memories of her body lighten his mood; they liven his body too. Unkissed and soft under his lips, down there her womanliness was daringly dark – mysteries Rachel has yet to acknowledge.

He sits ruminating on a stone bench, under a silver birch tree, in this civilized pedestrian shopping precinct turned urban woodland. This is where the serious business of glamour attracts a flow of stern-faced women in the dappled morning sunlight. His mouth, voluptuously lipped, curves seductively, giving him, simultaneously, both a sensitive pout and a meditative smile. He's thinking of the bodies he's loved, bodies he's dressed and undressed. There are other bodies too. His face's default setting is happiness but troubling thoughts furrow his brow. He's unsettled behind his mask.

Luisa Sato makes copies of designer clothes. Before each fashion season she studies style magazines, analysing the new designers' work then creating her own Luisa Sato originals at a greatly reduced price. Her boutique, *Sato*, is small enough to feel exclusive but intimate. Kanti, who has no issues with her body, strips, sexlessly, to

182

her underwear, in the middle of the shop, patiently trying on anything that Nico suggests. Luisa, finally, gets her to change in the curtained cubicle.

'She would look great in anything here, am I not right, Luisa?' Nico says, serenely at ease.

'Absolutely. I love seeing my clothes on beautiful Asian women,' Luisa says, smiling coyly. 'But don't tell anyone that I said that.'

'I can buy two outfits. That's the idea. I'm not a rich English lady,' Kanti says, asserting herself.

'Don't worry about the money – I've an arrangement with Luisa.' Nico says. 'This isn't about high fashion, I promise,' he says. 'I'll make you look like nothing Walt Disney ever even dreamt of. Trust me.'

Nico is sitting on a golden plaster throne, upholstered in white. Diep squats on a step at his feet, with the cameras pyramided on his lap. His eyes never leave Kanti. If Nico is calling the shots and Luisa is doing the running, Diep is their audience of one. He claps noisily when Kanti appears in an ivory coloured mini-dress, short-sleeved with a plunging neckline and cut square out of stiffened cotton. Nico understands the surge of pleasure this dress produces in her. It loosens her limbs, feminising her, opening her to new possibilities. He can see that, and she knows he can. When their eyes meet, she has to use all her self-control to stop blushing.

'Brilliant,' coos Luisa.

'Beautiful with these,' Nico agrees, picking up a polished gun-metal necklace of three large co-joined tubes and a couple of matching, bondage-style bracelets.

'You can take the boy out of New York...' says Luisa, 'but, well, you know.'

'Nico, you are one very clever man,' Kanti says when they leave.

Luisa Sato allows her face to relax when they've gone, going into the yard behind the shop and, solemn-faced, slumping onto a scruffy plastic chair, kicking off her shoes, then lighting a cigarette. It would be much easier being a sophisticated Japanese fashion-designer, she thinks, not for the first time, if she hadn't been born in Kent.

The shopping trip continues round small back street shops and rowdy market stalls, Brighton's speciality. Nico, not saying very much, picks up a garment here or points out a pair of shoes there – he's a master at work. Diep remains tirelessly enthusiastic and Kanti, for once, enjoys being at the wrong side of the camera. Joe follows them, he's carrying all the cameras now, tailing behind but the smile has returned behind his lips.

'You're one crazy man, my friend,' he says, when Nico falls behind the others to check he's alright. 'Where did you learn this stuff?' he asks, rubbing Nico's bicep affectionately, reinvigorated by his friend's young American optimism.

'Oh, along the way,' Nico says, with an evasive smile. 'It's my hobby, I guess, maybe my weakness. Mom's legacy perhaps – I grew up in fashion shops.'

'Don't even think of trying it out on me, OK?'

'No need, Joe, I'd have nothing to add.'

'Clothes find me, these days, it seems.'

'That's what's so great.' Nico puts an arm round Joe's shoulder, a hug disguised as a machismo flourish. Joe returns the affection with a fake punch to the belly.

Kanti stops, waiting for them, passes her carrier bags to Diep and rummages through her leather shoulder bag for a stiff brown envelope. 'This is for you Nico.'

Nico whispers 'wow!' He's impressed. It's a monochrome print, Kanti's latest, his portrait, head and shoulders, a modern Rembrandt – a dramatic low-lit study in darkness. The eyes are pools of emotion, the beginnings of a grin animates his face, and the nose, swollen and distorted, drips blood.

'A souvenir,' she says, serious now, as is Diep, who looks over her shoulder. 'Nico, you were still one pretty man even when you got, the word is, I think, splatted.'

'Hey, Miss Mouse, I do believe you've seen right through me.' His expression, not for the first time today, shows just a hint of fear.

'As I told you, Nico, I like it when I see under the clothes. It will be your turn next, Joe, if you let me.'

Joe has qualities, she thinks, that don't translate into photography. Not easily, anyway.

'Now it's your turn, Diep,' Nico says, bouncing back. 'Denim jeans, for sure, a black shirt, I think, and a grey jacket; crumpled linen would be great.'

'You're making him a man,' Kanti whispers.

'He's a man already,' Nico says, proud of his day's work. Some of that photograph's mood has made it onto his face.

Chapter Thirty-Nine

Hove Lawns, a manicured recreation space, is a grassy oasis between a traffic-congested road and the gentler confusion on the lanes for roller-skaters, roller-bladers, runners and strollers on the promenade. This popular stretch of grass on the seafront is already, by mid-morning, dotted with dedicated low-key recreationalists tossing frisbees or navigating complicated multi-stringed kites. Keeping a safe distance, a wobbly toddler shows her parents how well she can walk, until gravity reclaims her and she crashes to a delightedly soft landing. A winged statue on a tall plinth presides over the place, holding an olive branch in spite of a recent protest when her Grecian dress was splattered with red paint. She's Peace and her spirit usually prevails here. If she could approve or disapprove, the Peace statue would definitely smile on the group of twenty people practising Tai chi, with Nico, their instructor, body proud in his white singlet and shorts.

The only uniform is bare feet; Nico insists that everyone in his group learns to connect with the earth by developing a sensitivity of touch through the soles of their feet. Otherwise, the Tai chi students wear whatever they want - just sawn-off jeans and tribal body tattoos for three young men, two of them with shaved heads and one wearing his dreadlocks in a ponytail that swings weapon-like with every movement. They've bared their torsos, not to maintain suntans but to show off elaborate body decorations and, just maybe, to display their potential to three French women, off-duty teachers, also bronzed and athletically-built, in bikini tops and shorts. One of them, when she stretches upwards, reveals beneath her navel a small tattooed tiger, rampant with protruding claws. It doesn't go unnoticed. Nico's classes attract beautiful people even though he usually concentrates on the others, the less well-endowed.

He will have words afterwards with the middle-aged woman in skin-tight pink three-quarter length stretch-pants and a baggy orange t-shirt. She's a classic case for the Public Service Photographer. Shorts and t-shirts are in the majority, some with illustrated jokes on the breast, as tired as the colours of the sun-bleached fabric. Most of the students are veterans of Nico's Tai chi classes, now held here, when the weather is fine, every Saturday morning. Soon, when the building is ready, he will open his new gym but this is still a secret. Some of the students are clients in his personal-training business, mostly his Public Service Photography victims, or, as he likes to think of them, his discoveries. A few, including the tattooed lads, have come along for the first time today, thinking they'd have a laugh, thinking that the dance-like, tree-hugging movements are easy. Soon they're struggling, muscles complaining. Their laughter increases as they tire, they're beginning to look uncool to the French women. Nico soon silences them.

'This may look peaceful, gentlemen,' he says, amicably enough. 'You're welcome here if you come in respect, but don't tempt me,' he adds with a subtle hardening of timbre. 'Don't tempt me to show you why Tai chi is a martial art.'

'Cool,' smirks the man with the ponytail, before finding himself lying on his back.

'Last warning,' Nico grins. 'Get on with it or go.'

They stay, their laughter sobered. The others smile at this summary justice. Joe's at the back of the group, no shirt, faded denim shorts, a novice but already the most fluid of the students. He and Nico exchange mischievous glances. 'Gentle strength, hidden power,' Joe says, under his breath.   One day, Nico thinks, Joe will be teaching me.

'On the seafront with my camera,' Rachel texts.

'What are you looking at?'

Emmanuel surprises her with a text message. God with us, she thinks. He's always there in her mobile phone, always ready to talk.

'The Peace Statue'

'Never seen it.'

'You can't miss it. Come on, I don't believe you.'

'I've heard about it. It's a big angel.'

'Yes. It looks great against the sky. So blue today.'

'Is it?'

'Course it fucking is! Just what Saturdays should be like.'

'I'm expecting a passionate photograph then.'

'Now you're mocking me.'

'Not at all. You really sound like you've just seen an angel.'

'Maybe I have.'

She gets no reply. Would that happen if we were sitting face to face, she wonders, frustrated. We wouldn't have to talk all the time. We'd be happy just being together, feeling each other's presence. It's like that when he texts. She goes back to her camera, her *EOS-1N*, with her latest acquisition and new inspiration, the *Canon 100-300mm USM* lens. Photography is winning her quality time now she's a single woman again. The sky is very blue today, and her shots of the Angel of Peace have a rapturous quality. She, or maybe he, looks as if she's descended from Heaven. Male or female, the angel looks radiant – at peace. When she's happy with the composition, Rachel has to wipe her eyes to get the focus sharp. She's crying. Stupid woman. What's happening to me? It isn't sadness, it can't be, but the tears won't stop coming.

'Sorry. Phone call,' comes the text, ten minutes later.

'No problem,' she lies. Sniffing, she wipes her eyes and sees Joe in the Tai chi class. He's a beautiful man, she'll never forget that - one of the best. She's fascinated. His movements look like they've nothing to do with musculature. She likes men. It's about beauty as much as sex. She appreciates the finer points of their bodies. With Joe, she might have been distracted by the sex and only now truly appreciates his beauty. His skin shines like polished mahogany against the grass. He's the earthly equivalent of the angel, she thinks, and, with her zoom lens furtively attached to her camera, she waits, trying to predict the sequence of his movements. She's hoping that he will repeat one particular gesture, one arm raised while the other, palm upwards, retreats to the waist. She's rewarded with a photograph that twins her shot of the statue. Both are bestowing blessings. Joe's so-often laughing face is serious. She moves closer, but gets closer still with the help of her zoom lens. She captures the sunlight illuminating the sweat on his brow, crowning him king.

She's packing away her camera, squatting on the grass, when the Tai chi class ends. Joe sees her and nods, smiling recognition, but he's talking to the girl with the tiger tattoo, putting on his t-shirt with Tai chi grace. They leave together, Joe's familiar laugh is carried to her across the grass on the breeze and she feels a sharp pang of regret. The class ends with ritual bows, after the bond of communion they're individuals again. The three lads, humbled, saunter off in silence, humbled and thoughtful after Nico's handshake.

'Hey, I suppose it would've been more polite to have asked

before you photographed my class,' Nico says, sitting down next to Rachel; he's appeared out of nowhere, like an eagle diving from the sun. She recoils like a naughty schoolgirl, she's always hated criticism. Nico though is smiling.

'I can hardly talk,' he adds. 'If you remember, I've photographed you too without permission. Great lens you got there, I see. The *300 USM*, nice. You're the girl in the tennis skirt, right?'

'Shit,' she swears, turning from the attacked to attacker. 'You were that bloke who told me not to wear white.'

'Yep. Good to see you in green. Much better.' She takes the compliment, putting her camera in its case.

'Thanks', she says, almost shyly. 'Actually, I hate to admit it, but you were right. I gave the dress to Oxfam.'

'It will look lovely on someone else.'

'Well, you look rather fetching in white.'

'Thanks.' Nico enjoys the scrutiny. She should play tennis, he decides, she'd be great at returning the ball.

'What's all that Public Service stuff about then?' she says, relaxed, sitting here next to him on the grass.

'I'm like you,' he says quietly, dropping the banter. 'I appreciate beauty. That's why we're both photographers, isn't it?'

'I wasn't taking photographs of the group. Just my ex-boyfriend.'

'Joe?

'Yes.'

'Thought so. He's definitely a beautiful man.'

'It didn't last between us. He's probably out of my league.'

'You and me too,' Nico thinks, shrugging sympathetically.

'I have to confess,' she says, 'that I was tempted to do some shots of your class. It looked so serene, yes, beautiful, in fact. I think I could really get into Tai chi.'

'I'd be great to have you,' he says, getting to his feet and handing her his card, aware that she's sussing out his body, from the legs upwards.

'I do believe, kind sir, that I already have your business card,' she says, with gentle mockery.

'I'm not making a pass, honestly,' he says, 'but, forgive me, I need to tell you that you're a beautiful woman.'

'Wow, so direct!' She's breathless for a moment, receiving the compliment like a punch. 'Well, that goes for me too,' she says, forced out into the open. 'I'm not making a pass either but you're a beautiful man, Nico Melas.'

They linger there, stretched out on the grass under the statue of Peace. Rachel likes the idea of a friend who doesn't want to take her to bed. Nico hopes they'll be friends too. Brighton is throwing up interesting people, he thinks, opening its arms to lonely travellers. It might even cure the pain in his heart.

Chapter Forty

'I'm turning into a cliché but it doesn't matter,' Rachel thinks, jogging along the promenade in her new apricot-coloured running shorts, white singlet with apricot and yellow splash patterns, and new running shoes with the inevitable apricot racing stripe. She sighs, still pleased, somehow, with her superficiality. Is it really necessary to look so good all the time? It's the apricot hairband – that's one accessory too far. Her jogger's pony-tail is cute enough without it. 'I really might be genuinely superficial, profoundly so.' She's talking to her latest accessory, Nico, the man with the perfect body, who's jogging along next to her, in white singlet and running shorts.

'Don't knock it, Rachel, superficiality is an underrated virtue. Profound superficiality might be the secret of true happiness.'

Nico has become her personal trainer, he even has the words Personal Trainer printed over his left breast – just above his heart, she notices approvingly. Nico really is perfect. She has booked her perfect beautiful American man who, for a couple of hours a week, devotes himself entirely to her. Maybe she should get him to wear something apricot too.

Running next to him, he pacing himself to her speed, she enjoys her power over him, even when she starts to get breathless while he remains annoyingly relaxed. It's a sexual thing, she'll never turn him on and that's fine – better in fact than all the usual sports-trainer perving. With what she hopes are discreet sideways glances she looks to make sure that they really are the attractive couple that she wants everyone to see. They run past a bus shelter and she approves their reflection in the glass. That's the important thing, she admits, they could have been an advertisement – a man and a woman, fit, beautiful and young, the perfect couple, everyone's dream. No need for him to wear apricot, or to love her, but it's good he's her friend. Anyway, she decides, his white gear stops him upstaging her.

'Why do I still feel like shit then?' she says.

'Dig deeper into that superficiality, Rachel.'

It isn't Nico's fault. He's charming and focused, funny too. He encourages her, praises her level of fitness. When they stop on the grassy area by the Peace statue, she's winded and he looks away discreetly. He's a true gentlemen and she likes him. She bends over, gasping for breath, head and arms hanging loose, fighting the nausea. Nico, with paramedic calm, is taking boxing gloves and a punch pad from his rucksack.

'OK, before you get your breath back, I want you to punch me, keeping your heart rate up.'

'I'm fucking dying here,' she says, still gasping.

'No, you're not. You're loving it.'

She's loving the boxing gloves, and smiles through her pain at Nico standing there, boxing pad in front of his chest and legs flexed to take the strain. He's always so laid back; friendly but, yes, she gets it, indifferent. She wants to kill him – not literally, but when she starts to punch, both of them feel her ferocity.

'Always so angry,' he thinks. 'She makes it all personal. If she could control that, she'd make a great fighter.' People often get personal with Nico. He arouses feelings in strangers, not just because he's almost unnaturally handsome, but because he gets under the skin. He gets in there, it's him who makes it personal. Personal but detached. Feeling her anger, admiring her energy, he can't break out of his introvert's cocoon. He was like this as a child. His mother had adored him with more than a touch of worship. His father too, unusually for those times, had openly expressed his love for their only child. All the kissing, fondling and hugging had been enjoyable enough. He'd learnt to accept it as his due, but as a child of famous and glamorous parents he'd only got loved on special occasions – when public duties or rehab allowed them some family time together.

'Harder, Rachel. Keep going now, great.'

His parents had loved him, certainly, and they were good at showing it. It was cool for a kid to have a rock band father, a rock idol dad, a sex symbol pin-up pasted on all his friends' walls, and a whole rock band for uncles. Cool until that day. A father there in the bath as cold as the water, long time dead. Naked body, bloated, discoloured, too naked for the eyes of a father's son. Floating in vomit with a glass-eyed stare. His father still never leaves him.

'Come on Rachel, another minute. Give it all you've got.'

'Smug bastard,' Rachel laughs, punching with more than her remaining strength. It might be blood that clouds her vision, she'd heard of that, the red mist. Nico may be nice, but he's too pretty, and she wants to punch him in the face. This is exciting, the exhilaration of body and brain. She's found new strength in herself in these last moments before she can punch no more.

'Brilliant, Rachel, you've done really well. Now take a rest.'

She needs no advice there and falls, lungs heaving, onto the grass.

'One minute and then we'll start again, OK?'

'Fucking bully,' she's laughing between breaths, relaxed in her spasming. 'Yeah, sure, OK.'

He never saw his mother's body – not like that or in any other way. She will always be that woman in coffee table books and Sunday newspaper magazines, the glamorous face of an era. The romantic dead, the perfect couple: heroin and alcohol. He wants to love them like the rest of the World does, but childhood memories tarnish their image. He's still trying to lose these memories. He really would like to be profoundly superficial.

'Right, time's up. One more round and you're done.'

Human bodies, even strong ones, look frail to Nico. He knows what happens to them in time. Rachel has finished the routine, now she's lying on the grass as he manipulates her through a series of extreme stretches, pulling each leg forward until the whole limb nearly touches her torso. She's strong and flexible but she feels fragile in his hands, breakable even. She grins through the pain and he grins back. It's these moments of trust that he cherishes. He knows her body well, its tautness, those alert muscles, tight buttocks and firm skin. He likes the way her stomach heaves when she's breathless, she has a beautiful diaphragm but, most of all, he loves the smiling trust as well as the fire in her eyes. She's a fighter, this woman.

'So Nico,' she says, when they're sitting in Vincenzo Galli's seaside café, their regular après-exercise retreat, trying to ignore Enrico Caruso who's singing in Italian about broken hearts, with a sob in his voice. 'Can't they play anything a bit more up-to-date?' she says, irritably.

'Don't knock Italian songs to an old New Yorker,' Nico replies with a nuanced grin.

She's beginning to learn that intolerance looks unattractive, so she changes the subject. 'This public service photography stuff is kinda weird, Nico. Honestly.'

193

He doesn't reply for a moment, he's looking out to sea. They have the perfect view from here and the English Channel is dressed for the occasion, as blue as anyone can remember. Nico's eyes moisten imperceptibly.

'I'm just a sucker for beauty, I guess,' he says, stirring his coffee with his thoughts. He can talk to Rachel, mystery-free, and it helps. 'People get defeated by their looks. Well, you might not know this, you're too attractive to understand.' He half-closes his eyes the way it usually works on both women and men – not on Rachel though.

'I'm not stupid, you know.'

'That makes it worse. A lethal cocktail, beauty and brains.'

'You're laughing at me, you bastard.' She hides a smile behind her coffee cup, caffeine revived. 'You're a kind-hearted guy, but I still don't understand why you're doing it. If I'm not bad-looking, then you must have the same problem – only more so.'

'Hey, now you're making me blush.'

'Crap, Nico, you know you're handsome, very handsome.'

'I guess. Yeah, of course. I've been told it so many times.'

'Poor you!'

'It can get boring. You must know that. Always the honey jar for passing bees. It doesn't always make me feel good about myself.'

'But why the public service photography?' She's pushing him and he's enjoying it - almost. Self-revelation isn't his style.

'Well, I suppose I hate seeing people feeling unattractive when they're with me. OK, now I've said it. It sounds crap, I know. The fatal gift of beauty and all that stuff, but I suppose I want to repay the compliment. No, maybe more than that. I dream of a level playing field, I guess, where everyone feels right in their own bodies. The world is an elitist beauty parade and believe me, Rachel, beauty parades are minefields.'

'That's lovely, Nico; for a bullying bastard, you're quite a softy.'

'Well thanks. It's also an art project, I suppose, but before I get too high on my moral horse, I'm hoping these people, my victims, will come to my gym. That's my latest project. So, maybe no great principles after all. I'm really just another pimp touting for business.'

'That's fine by me, I'm a businesswoman, don't forget.'

'I'm pretty inspired by it actually. I call it a gym but it's really a dream factory where everyone can find their own beauty.'

'Wow, that's quite an ambition. And you really you own a gym? How perfect is that.'

'Yes, I really own it, bricks and mortar, a roof over my head. I'm a lucky guy, I came into some money – it's an investment, I guess.'

'I'm a big fan of money.'

There's Rachel's ring-tone – she has a text.

'Hey. What you doing?'

'I'm with Nico.' She smiles apologies across the coffee table.

'Nico?'

'My personal trainer.'

'Ah, OK. Now I'm jealous. It's definitely time we met, you and me.'

'Not long 'til Friday,' she types, followed by a smiley face. She can't hide when she's talking to Emmanuel. Nico clocks her expression. He knows what she's feeling. He didn't want to feel it again – not after New York. This time it's unintentional, an accident maybe, a secret too, and it's arrived with a danger warning. As he told Rachel, he's grown used to minefields.

Chapter Forty-One

Alan's new home isn't much – a room without a view. There's a window, so accuracy could claim that there is a view of sorts, especially for enthusiasts of rust-stained concrete. Alan has rented a room that calls itself a flat in a similar concrete block to the one he's now watching from what can be called his window. There's a shelf and a wall cupboard that could be described as his kitchen, because there's also a small workable cooker and a miniature fridge. Both could look almost new with a bit more cleaning, he could hear Rachel say. The room would have been perfectly square if one of the corners hadn't been requisitioned for a tiny bathroom with cosily positioned facilities: a shower, basin and water-closet. 'So no bidet, then?' Alan had asked the agent, who hadn't realised he was joking. 'You'd have to pay a lot more for that, I'm afraid,' she'd replied, without irony. Bidet or no, Alan's happy. The flat is cheap, more expensive than sleeping on the beach but a lot more comfortable. It has a single bed and a wardrobe made out of reinforced cardboard; there's a table too and a chair.

Alan has a home but no saxophone. He's kept a space on the table for his new instrument, a first priority now that he's getting paid. It isn't a place to entertain friends but no problem there, he'd only had a social life when he was living with Rachel, and that had ended, unregretted, as soon as she threw him out. Moving in doesn't take him long. He unpacks his three carrier bags, hangs up two pairs of jeans in the wardrobe, and puts his jacket on the chair. He's bought two pairs of socks and some underwear as a neighbourly gesture to his office colleagues. They have a place in a drawer along with his three t-shirts, the cutlery, a dinner setting for one, a tin-opener and a corkscrew. He's forgotten about towels again, but he does have a new toothbrush, some toothpaste, a rediscovered luxury and, even better, his favourite, some dental floss. He would have to buy a towel. 'Just maybe,' he thinks, smiling, 'maybe I should ask Rachel if I could borrow one.'

That was how this all began. Did Joe know that all of this would follow on from his cheeky knock on Rachel's door? 'It's almost creepy,' Alan says out loud to the concrete view. There's not much more to unpack: teabags, milk, a packet of Garibaldi biscuits, a white mug burrowed from the office and a metal plate he'd found on the beach. None of these things say first pay-cheque moment – that glowing feeling is reserved for the package at the bottom of the last carrier bag – a box of saxophone reeds, bought from his new workplace, Wah-Wah's. 'So it comes to this,' he says to the space where his saxophone would sit. 'I prostitute myself for you my friend.' He remembers the day when, as a newspaper boy, he spent his first pay cheque on a collar and lead in anticipation of the pet dog that never materialised.

Alan's always dreamed in lists, cataloguing the things that he needed for happiness. There'd been that dog, then the football, a brief obsession that one, then he'd discovered computer games, *Donkey Kong* and its successors. He has outgrown as many games as he's changed shoe sizes. His computer game wish list had been constantly altered, with old games ticked off, and new ones anticipated, but the dream that never went away had begun at school, when a teacher brought a saxophone, a legendary *Selmer Mark VI* to class, and let Alan have a go on it.

It'd been love at first blow. He'd managed a reedy note when all the other kids had just made rasps or squeaks. The saxophone dream had been born that day, and it's never faded. Sheet music became the next obsession, he'd wanted to see it written down before he'd realised that jazz doesn't work that way. Then his lists became catalogues of jazz cds – a connoisseur's collection, now lost, stolen, presumably dumped, John Coltrane thrown into the sea – unplayed. The job with Rachel too had been a dream come true. He could play with computers all day and get paid for doing it – paid money to spend on his lists. His dreams are less pleasant tonight. He's alert for danger and, even behind a locked door, he jumps at any sound. If he can ever afford a new saxophone, he decides, there's one old standard he'll never play again. *Strangers In The Night* has a new meaning.

'I'd love to,' he says, when she asks him to join the band. 'Or rather I would if I had a horn.' He's been dreaming about this all week.

She didn't know what had happened to him on the beach; when he tells her, she recognises the nightmare that had kept her awake on those nights when Joe hadn't been there.

'Oh man, that's horrible,' she says. 'I got freaked out on the beach once. Some crazy man with a knife tried it on, Joe saw him off, it was pretty awful. I still dream about it sometimes.'

'Yeah, me too.'

He has only been at Wah-Wah's for a week now but he and Victoria have got over their mutual shyness. She hopes he doesn't remember what she was like, a moody malcontent, she knows, that first day when Joe brought her round to borrow the towel. They get on, they're getting to know each other well enough, but actual friendship might take time. They're two introverts in a goldfish bowl. The relationship is workmanlike rather than spontaneous perhaps, but there's been mutual respect since that first jamming session in the shop.

'Don't worry about the saxophone,' she says. 'Jake will let you use one of the stock instruments, no problem.'

'Really? You sure?' He doesn't dare hope for this.

'What will Jake do?' Jake says, smiling benignly. Victoria usually gets her own way these days. When he hears what's happened, Alan learns that, sometimes, dreams really do come true.

'Tell you what,' Jake says. 'A weird guy brought an old horn in the other day. I could tell it wasn't his to sell, but I gave him a few quid to get shot of him. Take a look. Have it if you want.'

There'd been no need for Jiminy Cricket, no need to wish upon any star, Alan recognised the case immediately. In bed tonight, like a child before Christmas, he has an idea.

'Yes, the Bill Evans arrangement of *When You Wish Upon A Star,* with Freddie Hubbard on trumpet. It'll make a great sax solo.' He works out his part in his head, humming himself to sleep.

Chapter Forty-Two

'Excuse me, Mister!'

Lionel hasn't noticed the woman shouting at him. He's walking home from the bus stop, down a street near the seafront, where large terraced houses linger, showing their age, like distressed gentlefolk. With crumbling off-white stucco and peeling paint, Brighton's Regency houses have their own special style and wear shabbiness as glamour. One of them, his, is much too big, he knows, for a man who tries to keep the past in its place – covered in dust, fossilised, seen but not heard – a past, his past, is also a prison from which he's failed to escape.

'Excuse me, Mister!'

He's absorbed in gloomy late life thoughts, and only registers that someone is calling him after the third or fourth attempt.

'Excuse me, Mister – do you remember me? From the beach? I took your photograph. I'm Kanti.'

Lionel does remember – it's the girl who'd dared him to pose naked.

'You look like a proper English gentleman with your clothes on, Mister. Nice jacket.'

'You look good too – very nice,' he says, putting down his carrier bag. She's wearing a black top with matching leggings, decorated with randomly-sized scarlet dots - one of Nico's favourites. Lionel's been buying groceries, ready-made meals from the supermarket. He is, he admits with some sadness, always too ready to stop and chat. It's a lonely person's weakness, and being old too often means lonely. Kanti wonders if he's blushing or if he has high blood pressure. He's sad, she decides.

'You live round here? – It is nice. Proper big houses. Nice.'

Diep appears, like a genie, out of nowhere. He has the camera equipment slung over his back. The boy wasn't there before, Lionel thinks, beginning to get suspicious, but ashamed of his reaction. There's a feeling in Britain that society isn't what it used to be, when people knew their place, and respected their elders, when spinster aunts could cycle to church past village greens where every young man played cricket. Today you have to be careful of muggings, he's heard, but he hates such talk – these are nice young people. Don't let me get cranky in my wretched old age, he prays to nowhere in particular.

'You remember my brother, Diep?'

'Pleased to meet you, Diep'

Diep gives his distinctive laugh, and holds Lionel in a twinkling stare. He's wearing new black and white shorts, cut just above the knee, the latest style, and a white, nearly see-through short-sleeved shirt. Nico has allowed him to keep his red plastic flip-flops – they're his unique selling point.

'We saw you from the bus and remembered you naked, so we wanted to talk to you again.'

'Your pictures were very good. I went to the exhibition. Very good actually – very naked too, of course.'

'You were not embarrassed, I hope, Mr Lionel – you have a fine English body when naked – people admire you, I am sure. It's very brave being naked in public.'

'You are very kind. I've no illusions about my appearance – but no, I'm not embarrassed.'

'I do more photographs – I am working on a new project, that is why I followed you off the bus.'

Lionel wonders if he likes the idea of being stalked by these two – charming though they are. There's something fleetingly sinister in Kanti's directness. Easy charm comes easily to the insincere, and he begins to feel vulnerable again. She puts her portfolio bag down on the pavement and takes out her latest work – three monochrome prints.

'These are all naked people – naked where they should be dressed. I am very interested in this.'

Lionel is interested too. Amazed even, when he sees his friend Rosemary, naked of course, legs splayed, sitting in a deckchair, a small dog at her feet, licking an ice-cream cornet that she holds down to it, while the sea creates surf on the beach behind. The colours have been exaggerated to give the piece an air of unreality.

'Remarkable!' Lionel pronounces enthusiastically. 'I know this lady, how strange is that. It's a remarkable photograph, it has an epic quality. Very clever.'

'Thank you, mister. I met the lady on your beach. Do you like the style? I photographed her in a studio and added the seaside afterwards. I'm pleased with it.'

'I hope Rosemary likes it too,' he says, smiling, remembering that body fondly.

'She will love it, I know she will. She's one brave woman coming like that to my studio. I admire her a lot.'

Diep laughs loudly at a herring gull attacking a black bin bag, spilling the contents over the pavement. He shows Kanti, with guttural enthusiasm and a flurry of hand signals. She doesn't find it funny but laughs anyway, wanting to end the distraction. Lionel now realises that Diep is deaf. Poor lad, he thinks, sorry to have doubted him.

'Your friend is deaf?'

'My brother, yes, he's deaf, but he reads lips. You will get used to him, Mr Lionel.'

'Just call me Lionel. I'm very happy to see you again, miss...'

'You must call me Kanti. I am hoping that you will let me photograph you again – maybe in your home, if you trust me not to kill you or steal your treasures.'

'Well, I don't have any treasure, my dear, and I really don't think you're the murdering kind.'

'Can we come then? That's wonderful. Can we come to your house and photograph you, Lionel?' Kanti hasn't let up the pressure. From the first she'd been determined to have her way. It is her work, it's serious, and nothing will stop her, but she likes this old man too.

He's definitely getting cranky these days, he decides. Half an hour later, he's naked in his upstairs living room. It's a large tall room with old furniture, not old enough to be antique, but weathered enough to give the house a respectable if neglected atmosphere. The air is opaque with dust and impregnated with the aroma of stale face flannels, or worse. Lionel has long forgotten about the finer points of housework and, anyway, he doesn't care. He's posing in front of his grand piano, once a good one, a Blüthner with ivory keys as yellow as his teeth. Kanti issues instructions like a film director and, whether he wants to or not, he's watering a large cactus with a black plastic watering can, his clothes lying in a conspicuous huddle under the piano.

'I think it looks better with your glasses on,' Kanti calls from behind the camera that she's fixed onto its tripod.

'That's good, I always feel naked without my specs,' he jokes, but

201

she doesn't understand. 'Ah, now I can see you again.'

'I like what I am seeing very much, Lionel – you make a very good naked man.'

They work fast, Kanti likes it that way; her photographs are made in her head, long before she sets up her camera. Lionel dresses with his back to them, and Diep packs away the equipment with practised fluidity. Old-fashioned courtesy didn't stop Lionel from stripping full-frontally, but he feels more comfortable dressing, doing up his flies at least, in private, facing the wall, while Kanti checks her shots with an expression that resembles anger.

When they've gone, he wonders if he's made a mistake by being so trusting. He's revealed his body and his home to people who are little more than strangers. 'Well, it really doesn't matter that much,' he says. Like most people who live on their own, he talks to himself. 'I'm not going to worry about any of this old junk.' As he usually does when he needs encouragement, he sits at the piano and plays his favourite Cole Porter song, *Every Time We Say Goodbye*. There really is nothing to worry about. His fingers, nails down on the keys, stroke the length of the piano in an elaborate glissando. 'Silly old fool,' he whispers. 'Who cares!'

Two days later they're back, waiting on the doorstep when he returns from his swim.

'I have something to show you Lionel,' Kanti shouts, running up the street to meet him.

'Excellent, I've been looking forward to seeing what you made of me.'

'I am hoping you will like it, Lionel. You will be glad to know that Mrs Rosemary likes hers.'

'Yes, she just told me on the beach.'

'She is nice woman. She likes my picture and the one of her man, Monty. He's funny, you wait until you see his picture.'

They're in the kitchen, Lionel is making tea, remembering at the last moment, and not for the first time, that Diep is here too. He adds another cup and saucer as Kanti spreads out the photographs on the old pine table. Art and teacups, a civilised artistic soirée, very Bohemian, he thinks. The mood is enhanced by the sound of a violin being played next-door. A plaintive melody, French classical music, Franck or Fauré, he guesses. Kanti's nudes now cover the table, animated by the melancholy background music. There are some photographs of Rosemary, saucy seaside postcard studies with 1950s-style Technicolor nudity. Monty's there too, the colours equally exaggerated, a retro advertising poster. He's standing on a metal ladder, with his back to the rungs, in a full-frontal display, one hand on his hip, the other holding a paintbrush – splashes of yellow paint and a cheeky grin animate his face.

'Now that really is what you'd call The Full Monty!'

'So funny, Lionel!' she laughs, not knowing what he means.

'You know all of my friends now.'

'Yes, I am getting to know you all very well. And here is the photograph of you, Lionel. It is great, I think.'

She places it with the others like a winning card. Diep, grinning, sounds his agreement in his own form of guttural Nepalese. Lionel thinks he looks so much more naked at home than he's ever felt on the beach - older too, he thinks, especially now he's sepia-tinted like in an intense Victorian daguerreotype. Solemn-faced and statuesque, it references early nineteenth century pornography but he just sees an old man, and sighs.

'It's wonderful,' he says, after a meditative pause. 'You've done something very special here. Not beautiful perhaps, but definitely poetic. You make me feel, I don't know how to explain it, you make me feel real, somehow. Mortal too. Thank you for that.'

'I am so happy you said that, Lionel. It was my ambition to make you real. To show you as you are. You make me very happy.'

With the tea things in place after another of their visits, Lionel thinks 'no' when Kanti first mentions it. He'd got in some cakes specially for them, éclairs bursting with cream crowned with dark molten chocolate. Unusually for him, he's even wiped down the table with a clean dishcloth. He looks forward to their visits, but he likes living alone – or so he tells himself when she asks him again.

He had lodgers once, but they got on his nerves - sad divorcees mostly, men on a melancholy downward spiral who had wanted him to share their grief, making their loneliness palatable. He'd thought that the company might have been good for him, but he'd stopped letting out rooms in this down-at-heel five storey house when the last tenant had, with an unnecessary lack of consideration for others, slit his wrists in the bathroom. He hadn't wanted to share someone else's grief quite so palpably. So, never again, he'd decided, but, in spite of that, he says 'yes' to Kanti.

'We can share a room, Diep and me. We always do that, then Diep's room is a studio. Can we do that?'

'There's plenty of room, you can both have studios if you want.'

Diep shouts something, possibly in English, probably in Nepalese, with such uncontrolled enthusiasm that he not only astounds Lionel, but challenges his Englishness too by hugging him uninhibitedly and kissing him on the forehead. Lionel thinks Diep has just said something like 'Ba'aa' but he doesn't know what it means.

'You are so kind Lionel,' Kanti says, with almost English decorum, thrilled that her plan's come together. 'I know that we will have a great time living here with you in your house.'

Lionel wonders but it's too late now, and he offers the attic rooms as studios, as well as two bedrooms on the fifth floor. The twins rush up the stairs ahead of him as the violinist next-door begins another doleful melody – and those tears come again.

'Go to the top of the house and I'll show you the studio,' he calls but they're already up there making plans. They will sleep up here too, they tell him.

'Yes,' he says to himself, 'a good decision, this. Open the place up for fine young people. A new generation. Kate would like that.'

Chapter Forty-Three

Alan feels like a bank manager might feel – like a city-slick broker about to clinch a dodgy deal, another of the smart-suited ones, the 1990s thrusting élite. He'll never be one of them, of course, but walking down this commuter-time street, he's on his way to work with his saxophone case carried like a briefcase. There's a spring in his step and he swings the saxophone as he goes. If he could whistle, he'd be whistling a happy tune. He's truly going to work in the best sense. He's not heading for Rachel's office, or to the oasis that is Wah-Wah's. It's rehearsal day with Victoria and Jake and he's heading towards their apartment. He hasn't played in a band since school, when he'd got together with a few mates to do a very poor but precocious imitation of a 1940s swing band. Since then his saxophone love has turned to addiction. Friends had said that it was ruining his life and turning him into a weird introvert but today, introvert or not, he's partying like never before, and it feels far from weird.

He looks at his reflection as he passes the black mirror-like window of the sex shop, Anything Goes, just to check that he really is Alan. There he is, for sure, walking down the street where he used to live with Rachel, the self-appointed saviour who never knew who he was. If she had, he thinks, she would have been very bored indeed. She'd made him a great lover, almost, dressed him and undressed him for the role, but she'd never touched the spot that his saxophone reached. This morning he feels terrific, pre- and post-coital rolled into one. The two of them, his saxophone and him, are out for the time of their lives.

There's that flute again, Joe's back in his old place, the lamppost vacated by Alan these days, but where they'd first met in the early summer. Maybe it wasn't the towel that started all this, Alan thinks, seeing Joe again. It had probably begun right here in the street, when he'd first heard that flute arabesque. He puts his hand in his pocket and feels for a pound coin – it's payback time, but money won't do it.

'Hey, thanks Alan,' Joe calls, his melody paused. 'Good to see you looking so bouncy.'

'Yeah, thanks Joe, bouncy's the right word.'

'It's the way to be. I'm bouncing too. So no hard feelings? OK?

You know – you, me and Rachel.'

'You saved my life, Joe, believe me. Love her as I do.'

'Glad for you, man. Everyone finds their normal in the end – it's the rule.' Joe says it with confidence, but wonders if he'll ever find his normal and, if he does, if he could face it.

The flute is still playing in Alan's head when he gets to Jake's place; it haunts him up in the lift and says its smiling goodbye when Jake opens the door.

'In here, man – come see.'

The second bedroom makes a fine studio. A new partition wall divides it into a soundproofed recording space and a very flashy control room on the other side of a double-glazed window. Jake spends a lot of his hobby time here, mixing tracks, or even just sliding buttons and connecting cables for the hell of it. He's tied his ponytail into a bun – he always does this when working with headphones, and doesn't care if it makes him look like an old lady. He's invisible to himself when his ears upstage his eyes.

'Go through and sort yourself out. Harry's in there,' he says, opening the door to the live room.

'Hi,' says Harry, adjusting the microphone, a *Coles 4038*, over his drum kit.

'Hi,' says Alan, exploring the room like a territorial animal inspecting new terrain.

'How perfect is this,' says Harry.

'Very,' says Alan. He's falling in love again, he thinks, running his hand over the microphones; all classics, Jake had made sure of that. His is an *N-Dyn RE20*, he sees. Perfect. He gives Jake the thumbs up. Jake grins back from the control desk on the other side of the window. He's slung on tracksuit bottoms and wears a baggy white cambric shirt open at the chest – enough cover but not too restrictive. He likes to feel free when he's making music.

Victoria's in professional mode too when she comes through from the bedroom. She looks intense, almost bad-tempered. It's the way she deals with excitement, Jake thinks. They go straight into rehearsal. Jake has already recorded the keyboard part for the first song, wanting to do the whole thing today, if they can, at what he's billed as a trial rehearsal. Harry and Alan settle down immediately and improvise their parts around the backing track.

Victoria sits on a barstool and adjusts her microphone, another classic, Jake's treasured *Rode NTI Condenser*. She knows nothing about mics but she's dreamed of this moment. Time to soar, she thinks, just like Joe said, time to soar like a seabird. She smiles seeing how far Jake's placed the mic from the stool. He knows the size of her voice. She taps it and gives Harry a grin. He will know how I feel, she thinks. This is what it's all about. Then it's to work. She sings, warming up her voice, ignoring but liking the surprised looks from the boys. She strums rhythm guitar and floats her voice, listening to Jake's track on the headphones. Her hair is pinned up with a comb, she wants her body free too. She's naked under the roomy black summer dress. She ditches the stool, standing up is better. Her stomach and buttock muscles liberated to support the voice, her lungs unencumbered air pumps; her head resonates like a bell. She was built for this. Jake knows that too, as do Harry and Alan. Linked together by headphones, all four are claimed by the music. This is going to be great, they think.

Alan has worked out his saxophone solo, a counter melody to Victoria's heartbroken lyrics. He's choreographing his body to swing with his imagination, dreaming his way into the song. His face, usually so inexpressive, is an animated portrait of passion. 'She sounds like a saxophone, like a jazz riff,' he thinks, thrilled by the sound. She's singing as if he's actually playing her on his sax. Together they could make the purest music. So much better than sex, he thinks – better than sex or maybe it is sex.

'I never knew,' Harry thinks. He's turned on but not like when they were in his bed, fumbling half-hearted lovers. She was never like this when they were together.

'I never knew,' he keeps thinking. 'I'm such a prick.' He tries to remember what it had been like, what he hadn't noticed at the time. He tries to remember but he can only recall the orgasms and, he knows well enough, his orgasms have never changed. He really had thought that he was doing her a favour – fucking the fat girl en route to elsewhere. His groin shrivels. 'What a prick. I was just bonking, she was making love.' He can hear the pain in her voice. She's spitting out scorn, a cry of battered love – the pop diva's classic mix of vulnerability and strength. Vocalising her pain in the universal voice of agony. Harry's almost scared; he's never known this woman.

They play for a couple of hours, inspired, individually turned on.

They play the piece dozens of times, repeating phrases and subtly altering them, without much talk or even making eye contact. While Victoria paces intensely round the studio, the others come in and out of the control room, listening and appraising, developing the musicians' language of grunts and nods.

'I think we're in business,' Jake says, understating his excitement. 'Let's call it a day.'

'That was unbelievable!' says Harry – Alan agrees. Victoria smiles sullenly when they give her a hug. They can feel that she's shaking. There will be no party, no celebration, it's beyond any of that. The pub would be so inappropriate.

'Can we meet up again next week?' Jake says. There's a catch in his voice, but he maintains the business-like tone.

It's all been said by the looks on their faces. Now it's finished and a difficult silence hangs over them. Alan and Harry can do nothing more than just pack up and leave, like visiting plumbers at the end of a job.

'See you around,' Alan says.

'Yeah, definitely,' says Harry. 'Amazing, eh?''

'Yes, amazing.'

And they go their own separate ways.

Jake takes Victoria to bed; if he doesn't hold her, she will collapse. She hasn't said anything since they finished recording. She's trembling, silently crying, hanging on to him like a terrified child. Lying together for comfort is all they can do and it's a long time before they speak.

'Shit, Jake,' she says, sobbing. 'I told you this'd kill me, I can't take it. I can't do it, honestly. It'll kill me,' she manages to say, between gasps. 'Don't push me, promise me that. Don't let it kill me.'

'Try telling me,' he whispers consolingly. 'What is it, love?'

'Jake, honestly, don't go there. It's buried pain. Buried pain should remain just that, buried.'

'I'll do anything, you know that.'

'Well, you know what to do.'

They turn to their bodies and try to appease the agony. It takes most of the night. Their bodies react lustily, thrusting to kill the pain that fights back, frightening in its ferocity.

At dawn they lie panting, silently acknowledging some kind of battered truth. Calmer now, Victoria staunches her tears in the pillow.

Chapter Forty-Four

It's a balancing act, Jacqueline thinks, sitting in front her dressing-table mirror, adjusting her make-up before going downstairs to spruce up The Golden Orb's public bar. The red hair has been a great idea, she'd been sure of that the moment she'd noticed she was more grey than blond. The trouble is that her latest red, brash in its boldness, clashes with her rouge. Is it too red? Rouge should be red and, just like lipstick, the redder the better. That's the artistic policy of the young redheads who design Brighton's most avant-garde hair at the Scarlet O'Hara Hair Salon, down the road from the pub, underneath Rachel's flat. They, of course, are young, firm-faced and shameless. Jacqueline only shares one of these qualities, but goes along with their experiments in anarchy. She has to decide what this charade is about. Is it just a naïve attempt at trying to look young, when she knows she looks over fifty? Or is it more about creating an acceptable fifty-year-old persona?

She sits here every morning, like an actor painting the face of an imaginary character, her own invention, Jacquie, the pub landlady with a heart of gold. It mostly works. She's popular with the regulars, the old folk who watch her strut the boards behind the bar every day, glamorised by the juke box and the daily tipples that go straight to their heads. In the right light, to her old gentlemen she's a country singing star, the latest sensation from Nashville, Tennessee. Who knows, maybe even dirty old Mr McGuiness has started to dream about her, now that Rosemary has given him up.

In the daylight, up here in her room, she wonders why she bothers. One cheek is redder than the other, is it the light? She looks like an old tart, she decides, and those lips, so kiss-me-quick – but there's no one she wants to kiss. Not in that way. It's a soulless act wearing a big heart on your sleeve, when you've no interest in the consequences. That's why she preferred it when Rosemary took care of that side of the business – looking after the gentlemen while she looked after the bar. Maybe they'd made a success in the sex industry because neither of them was interested in sex.

The difference between Jacqueline and Rosemary is that Rosemary isn't squeamish. It'd been alright with Rachel's father, Derek Seymour, good enough to have given her Rachel before he'd got too demanding, always pawing her, even when she'd rather have had a cup of tea and a doughnut. Bugger tea, though, she'd thought, so she'd poured herself a large gin and let him get on with it, while she thought of that doughnut. He'd known that she was bored, and she hadn't blamed him when he'd started to look elsewhere. She's never been drawn to those insistent male organs – difficult to keep tame or so their owners claim. It has been a very long time since the last time, and she suspects her body would reject the intrusion like an unsuccessful heart transplant. No more foreign bodies for this lady. No thanks very much. When Rachel's dad passed on she hadn't made a fuss. She was sad the dirty bugger had died, but glad that his plonker was finally zipped up. The happy family bit had been a con. No, not quite. Family really meant Rachel and her and, well yes, Rose. They'd always been more than sisters-in-law – they were family with or without old Derek. Since he's been gone, she has become Jacks, Rose's old man – well that's how it feels and, maybe, it's how it has been from the start. Still, she has to keep up appearances, she knows her job, so she tones down the rouge and adds another layer of scarlet to her lips. She purses them to the mirror and kisses the air. Business is business, after all.

The offspring of Jacqueline's unwelcome coupling comes into the bar before her mother has opened up. Both like this time best, when the pub is empty and just smells of fresh coffee and furniture polish. Anyway, Rachel feels like talking, and Jacqueline loves any time spent with her child.

'Is it a bad time for a coffee?'

'No, of course not, love. Actually I'm ready, all dolled up, beer pumps set. We've got half an hour for a chat.'

'Start the stopwatch then. quality time with Mum. Perfect.'

'I never have enough time with you, my love.'

As she pours the coffee, Jacqueline regrets skipping the nail varnish – her fingers look naked and, yes, they look their age, fifty-five and used to washing up. Rachel, however, looks perfect to her mother's eyes. A new summer dress, purple satin with large pink roses. Classy kid, she thinks.

'False eyelashes? Nice,' her daughter laughs, pulling a grimace.

'Part of the uniform. Don't knock it.'

'They scare me. Like spiders eating your eyeballs.'

'Rachel, for God's sake. How do you think that makes me feel now.'

'Sorry.'

'Well, you're looking great. Very pretty. Do I hear the fluttering of cupids above that sweet little head?'

'You might,' Rachel blushes, but she's happy that it shows. She's just finished texting Emmanuel, and isn't ready to go into work. If he's a real man, and not just a series of letters sent through the ether, she will tell her mother about him soon. They never talk about boyfriends, but this time it's different. She's longing for that mother and daughter moment when she can talk about his eyes, the way he puts his arm round her, and the moment when his breath tickles her neck. Yes, OK, she thinks, it's time to get corny.

'So what's he like?'

'Not telling.' She laughs coyly, part teasing coquette, part schoolgirl, but the truth is there's nothing to tell – nothing her mother would understand. She does feel his breath on her neck, she can feel it now. She feels him next to her all the time, but she could never explain that to anyone and especially not to Jacqueline, the ultimate in hard-nosed realists.

'How's business?' asks the hard-nosed realist.

'It's going really well. I'm going to have to take on some more guys, if it carries on like this.'

'My sweet little girl, businesswoman of the year. I can believe it alright. You always get what you want, my little chip off the block.'

'Thanks, Mum, I'm not always so confident, you know. I needed to hear you say something like that. To tell me I'm great, to convince me. Like when I was little.'

'You're welcome, Rach, but you're always great to me.' She pats her on the shoulder and lingers, feeling the satin.

'Nice bit of schmutter – the little girl's definitely in love.'

'I always thought falling in love was kind of soppy. Too easy, a lazy way out for a girl. I got that from you, I reckon. You never went for that, did you – the girly romance thing. I've been happy enough with someone to fancy and to have some fun with but this time it's different. It's made me feel, oh, I don't know, like a fool.'

'He's not making you feel like a fool, he's making you feel like a woman, my love. And it suits you.'

'He makes me happy, I guess.'

Jacqueline kisses her cheek.

'Enjoy it, Rach, it doesn't come along every day. If he breaks your heart, I'll have his balls on a plate, and that's a promise. Anyway, time for work, my sweet,' she says, patting the cheek she'd just kissed to remove the lipstick residue. Rachel takes her mother's licked-finger administrations without comment. Sometimes it's good to feel mothered.

'I've got to open up and you've got a whip to crack at all those handsome young men who are making you rich. So get along with you, my girl.' She gives Rachel an affectionate slap on the bottom and shows her out. Kanti is waiting at the door.

'Ah, it's so good you are open but, excuse me, is Mrs Rosemary here? This is the right place I think.'

'Yes, it is. Rosemary's not down yet,' Jacqueline says, scrutinising this beautifully dressed young woman. Not another tart looking for work, she thinks, suspiciously. 'How can we help?' she asks, with a glacial smile.

'Look, I'll be going,' Rachel says, leaving hurriedly. There are some aspects of her mother's business that she doesn't want to know about. Jacqueline blows her a kiss, but keeps a stern face for Kanti.

'I have Mrs Rosemary's photograph. The one I promised her. I've done the final prints,' Kanti says, unfazed by the hostility.

'Photograph?'

'Oh yes, my photograph. It's fine Jacks,' Rosemary says, coming to the door. 'Come on in, Kanti love.'

Rosemary takes the photograph out of the envelope, smiles at it and passes it to her sister-in-law. Jacqueline isn't easily shocked, but this is one of those moments.

'Do you like it? I do, very much,' Kanti says, including Jacqueline in the most radiant of her smiles.

'Good God, you're naked!'

'Yes, naked. The real me. I love it. Thanks so much, Kanti. It's fantastic, honestly.'

'And what about you, Mrs Rosemary's friend? Do you like it too?'

'It's, well, it's, it's extraordinary. Truly extraordinary. I don't know what to say. Except, yes, it is a very good photograph and, well, Rose, there's no denying it, you do look extremely naked.' Jacqueline has to take another look, then look at her sister-in-law, and then at the photograph again. 'It's extraordinary,' she says again.

'Amazing.'

'Yes, Jacks, that was the idea. Naked and free. Free to be who I am. Bless you, Kanti, it's wonderful.'

'I'm very glad that you see it like that. I will include it with my very best work when I have my exhibition. I will put it on the wall with your boyfriend, Mr Monty.' Jacqueline's shock is sinking in further. 'And also with the naked picture of lovely Mr Lionel, your old gentleman friend.'

'Bloody hell, Rose!'

'You should get one too, Jacks, honestly. It feels incredible doing it and you've said several times now that it's an amazing photograph.'

'Oh yes, please do. I would love to do you too. You would be truly great naked, believe me. You're not as frightening as you look, no, forgive my English, but, I forget the word. Ah yes, you are formidable.'

'You know what,' Jacqueline says, laughing her deep smoker's laugh, 'you know, I do think I'll go for it. Yes, what the hell, I will.'

Chapter Forty-Five

Victoria jabs irritably at two fried eggs that have stuck to the frying pan. She severs a yoke and swears like a godless Italian mamma: 'Coglione! Fucking things!' The yellow blood seeps across the pan, so she attacks the second egg and hacks it to death with the fish slice. 'Stronzo, puttana! Fucking Caruso!' Then she scrapes the ruins into the bin and starts over again with fresh eggs. Their shells are savagely cracked with a knife, she opens them and lets the contents drop neatly into the pan. 'Bravo,' she whispers.

Italian opera phrases help, she's discovered. Enrico Caruso has done it to her again, even though she'd cursed Jake at first for putting on 'his fucking music all the time'. Today it's the 1902 recording of *Questa o Quella* from Verdi's opera *Rigoletto*. 'Not as good as the 1904 recording,' he'd said. 'In 1904 the voice is perfectly clear and ringing, but in 1902, you can actually hear him clearing his throat, like the chain smoker he was.' Victoria had rolled her eyes, but her black-dog humour cleared like a toddler's tantrum when she heard that eerily real frog in Caruso's throat from ninety years ago. She admires Jake's nerdish insensitivity – if you like it, go for it, she thinks.

Why did he think she'd still be interested, when she'd been like a woman in mourning since the recording session. She'd cried herself to sleep, nearly haemorrhaging with tears, and had woken feeling no better nor any wiser about why she was so unhappy. This morning, it's as if she's committed a murder, or broken something especially precious. Maybe she has. Jake had got up much earlier, leaving her asleep, hoping that her mood would evaporate in sleep. It hadn't. 'Bless him though,' she'd thought, 'he's so good for me – a touch of groundless optimism is what every girl needs.' When she'd come into the living room, he'd given her one look and laughed.

'You look like something out of the *Mad Scene* in *Lucia di Lammermoor*,' he'd said, pressing a firm kiss on her lips. Instinctively, she'd recoiled: 'What the fuck, I haven't even brushed my teeth yet.'

'Your hair could do with a brush too.'

'Fuck you,' she'd laughed, in spite of herself. 'And what or who is *Lucia di Lammermoor* anyway? Don't tell me, you'll only make it worse.'

She did brush her hair though and changed into the Japanese silk

215

dressing-gown that he had given her – one of his many impromptu presents.

'Fucking man,' she smiles as the two new eggs fry obediently in the pan.

'Questa o quella per me pari sono,' she sings along with the words, not realizing that she knows them by heart. It's one of Jake's favourites. She has no idea what the words mean, but she's cheered by the jaunty swagger in Caruso's delivery. 'God,' she thinks, 'this crap actually makes me feel good. I really must be crazy.' Jake changes the record to the 1904 version and, even from the kitchen she can hear what he means. The voice is freer, brighter, with a thrilling steel in the high notes. Tenderly coaxing the eggs with the fish slice, she goes the whole way with Caruso, opening up her voice right to the top of her range, as she butters the toast and places the two perfect eggs, definitely sunny side up, onto plates with sliced tomatoes and a few sprigs of parsley. She sings Caruso's second verse too, as she pours the coffee, reaching the highest note when she's putting the finished meal onto a tray. Bringing it out onto the balcony, she sees Jake standing there open-mouthed, silent movie style.

'Where the fuck did you learn to do that?'

'It's only fried eggs. I'm not an idiot.'

'No, who taught you to sing like that? It was bleedin' sensational, Vickie.'

She's as surprised as Jake is, and the black dog decides it might be time to leave.

'My-a only teacher was-a Signor Caruso,' she laughs in a stage-Italian accent, pushing past him with the tray.

Jake follows like a millionaire calculating his bank balance, but this isn't about money – this time, he really believes that he's found a star. 'Fuck,' he mumbles under his breath to the universe, 'who brought me this woman? What did I do to deserve this?'

It's a quiet Sunday morning, with rolling black clouds scurrying over an otherwise pure blue sky. Tinkling breakfast china mingles with the sounds of the sea, a solitary church bell and a man shouting for his dog, a white one.

'I'm sorry about last night,' Victoria says, coffee-revived.

'Forget it, you were great.'

'No, I mean afterwards. I was crazy, I know. It was all too much.

Too raw, too exposed. I just can't do it, Jake. It was like going mad. Like your Lucia di whatever.'

'You're an artist, my love,' Jake says, giving her a kiss tasting of toast. 'It's tough, I can see that, but you have the gift, it's obvious every time you open your mouth but, this time, just then, you were something else. Amazing. God, Vickie, you've got a very special talent, but it makes you fucking difficult to live with, I tell you. I'm totally into that though, I'm astounded, in fact.'

'Jake, I don't know if I'm strong enough to keep feeling like this. Seriously. I loved that session, loved the singing and doing it with you guys, but I went somewhere that I don't understand. It was terrifying, like I'd found all the grief I've ever felt but reinvented and relived at twice the volume. Grief over things I still don't recognise, grief for the future as well as the past. Honestly, Jake, it felt like it was killing me.'

'But you're OK now? I mean, just then, out there singing like a fucking goddess?'

'Dunno about the goddess, but yeah, I think so. The terrible bleak feeling's gone. God, Jake, you have to help me with this.'

He puts his arm round her and tries to absorb the trembling. She grasps his hand with both of hers and squeezes it until it hurts.

'I hope I'm not crazy, Jake. Honestly I do.'

'You're not crazy, girl, just touched by genius.'

The man with the white dog has gone onto the beach and the church bells are peeling their Sunday best. Victoria and Jake hold their position, hands clinched, almost ready to jump.

'Fucking genius, my arse,' she laughs. 'Let's finish our breakfast and do what normal couples do on Sunday mornings.'

They don't mention it because it feels too corny, but they both notice those black clouds being blown off to the East.

Chapter Forty-Six

Dharma pumps John's chest with his paws, sinking his claws into the flesh, and waking his human friend only when he draws the first blood. John strokes the cat absentmindedly, already associating this painful awakening with his disturbed dream. The morning dawns with increased melancholy and even Dharma, his semi-loyal companion, can't lift the gloom. The animal gives up, sensing insincerity in the stroking hand, and leaves noisily, maybe even sulkily, through the cat flap. John lies in bed sleep-tired, still only half-awoken from that dream, and reluctant to join daytime reality. It's Rajiv's wedding day, he'd remembered it with the first of Dharma's scratches, the one that had drawn blood.

All week, he has been trying to bury thoughts of this day, when even his weakest and most unrealistic hopes of a life with Rajiv would be permanently crushed – in spite of Rajiv's hopeless protestations that it would change nothing. It feels like bereavement lying there, warm from the night, but with the spreading chill of realisation. His separation from Rajiv will be made formal today on the other side of the world, and nothing will alter that fact. There's no point in getting up, but he does, he needs to let some air into the incense-stale basement where he's been hiding now for nearly twenty-four hours. Even this, his English home, is about to go when the lease ends at the end of the month. If he were a young man it would be a fresh start, but this morning it just feels like an ending. He can taste his own bile, and his flesh is sticky where his sweat mixes with the droplets of blood on his chest.

He splashes himself with cold water at the sink, looking at the gaunt old man reflected in the shaving mirror. Still only in his Indian cotton pyjama bottoms, he goes out to the little back yard, where Dharma returns with another offer of love, weaving insistently between his legs. Up there, three floors above the basement flat, the metal fire escape leads to the sky. Shivering in the shadows, he looks up at the blue, as if through a telescope. Up there, and beyond, lies India, in another time zone, in another reality. He won't resent that ceremony being celebrated so far from his reach, or let his spirit sink into pettiness or anger. Or so he hopes. He's trying to be rational, even spiritual about it.

Back inside, he lights a candle and kneels at his hearthside altar, struggling to find the peace to send positive thoughts to Rajiv. John hopes that it's possible to walk away from submerged anger and nagging sexual jealousy, even in the most superficial of meditations. He'd been taught that once and, today, he's desperate to find a tranquil place beyond his body. Dharma takes no pity on him and starts a relentless call for breakfast.

Without enthusiasm, unrefreshed by prayer denied, John goes to the beach. It's later than usual, so he has to walk through groups of naked sunbathers, mostly middle-aged males, human walruses lying under an angry sun. They watch every new arrival with half-glances. John knows well enough that the image from his shaving mirror isn't what these men desire. Lionel's clothes are lying in the usual place; he's already in the sea, a solitary figure counting laps between the breakwaters. John undresses, numb to his body, like a prisoner about to be strip-searched. The sea is cold and brutal, but he welcomes its undiscerning embrace.

Joining Lionel, his strokes are faster and more aggressive than usual, so he catches up, and the two finish their ten lengths together. They return to the beach in silence, and the conversation is fragmentary as they dry themselves.

'Another day,' Lionel says, without conviction.

'Yeah, another day.'

'Something keeps us at it.'

'Yeah but don't ask me what it is.'

Then the music starts on the next beach. Joe and Harry are beginning their morning raga – the flute and djembe greeting the morning sun.

'Bloody music gets to me.'

'Not yourself today?' Lionel observes, trying to float the conversation.

'Maybe not. There's something about that flute – it draws stuff out of me that I'd rather keep inside.'

'He's a bit of a wizard that kid.'

The music silences them again as they adjust shirt cuffs and shoelaces. The flute takes John back to India and that last night with Rajiv. He will be dancing with his new bride, probably even at this moment. The flute makes that thought difficult. When he stands to adjust his belt, he tries to hide his trembling fingers.

219

'Still can't get used to you in civvies.'

'Civvies?'

'European dress.'

'Yeah, well, that's how it's going to be from now on.'

'Forgive me, John, but are you alright? Nice jacket.'

John puts on his blue denim jacket and smiles grimly. 'Thanks, it's new. Sober enough I think.' The trembling has moved to his voice. Lionel notices.

'If I can help, old chap. A trouble shared, you know.'

'Thanks, Lionel.' John is about to say more, but his voice won't do it, and he looks away squinting, trying to stop the burning in his eyes. He should have stayed in bed. 'I'll be alright, it's just a difficult day and that music is getting to me. Thanks for being a friend though, Lionel. I mean it.'

'Tell you what, come to dinner. I'm having some friends round. It might help to have some fresh faces. Take you out of yourself, that sort of thing. Come if you want. You can help me celebrate becoming a landlord.'

'A landlord?' John's voice returns.

'I'm taking in lodgers. I was persuaded by a very insistent young lady. Tonight's my last night of freedom.'

'Now I have to come,' John says, thinking it will be his first night of unwanted freedom. His eyes are ready for those tears and he turns away to hide them. 'Bless you Lionel, you're a good friend.'

'You're welcome, so come tonight. Take your mind off whatever it is.' Lionel squeezes John's arm; even physical contact has never been their way. 'It can be a queer old world,' he says. 'That's why we need friends.'

Chapter Forty-Seven

When he played drums with his old band, The Burnley Boys, it had been, well, normal, Harry thinks, sitting next to Joe on the beach with his djembe. It had been just four blokes together, school friends playing the best instruments they could afford by saving up birthday present money and doing paper rounds. They'd been good too, even if they hadn't ever made a hit record or sold out a venue. Burnley blokes, ordinary lads – he misses them, the lack of complications, awkward thoughts, difficult people and confusing emotions. His new friends are unpredictable and, at times, frightening. Even Joe is beginning to scare him. At first he just thought of him as a muso, one of them, but a bit of a rogue. A guy who lives by his wits, who always comes back smiling. It's that mouth. Even Harry, no great expert on the aesthetic, knows that Joe's mouth is special, but he's only just realised that Joe's smile might not be a smile at all. It might just be the shape of the lips, set to look like he's always smiling even when he's far from happy. Worse still, perhaps he smiles when he's angry.

In the two years that he has known Joe, he's never thought to ask him about his life, where he comes from, if he has any family or even how long he's been living rough. Joe isn't like that, it's not part of who he is, his past is irrelevant, he's just Joe. Harry identifies with that too – it's a bloke thing. They've swapped girlfriends more often than they've exchanged anecdotes about their lives. In that way Joe's an honorary Burnley bloke too. 'But I wonder sometimes who he is,' Harry thinks. He probes deeper these days. 'When he's away in one of these musical trances, he can be quite scary for a little guy.' They can improvise together without preliminaries; Harry always knows what to play, but doesn't understand what's hidden in Joe's music. Maybe Joe really is a snake-charmer and Harry the snake, curling and uncurling, his poison neutralised, at his master's command. He's fine with that, whatever happens, he loves Joe. Joe's a mate.

Last night it had been Victoria thrilling him, but also unnerving him. He'd thought he knew who she was too but, like Joe, somehow out of his reach and now, magnificent in her way too. She'd made a great drummer of him last night. It was never like this in Burnley, musically bewitched and out of control. He isn't sure if he likes it, or if he can live up to the challenge. This is even without Kanti and her brooding brother. If he isn't working today, he thinks, he'll ring round the old band members and try to get together with them again. Maybe meet them down the pub, like normal blokes.

'There we go,' Joe says, taking the flute from those still smiling lips. 'The earth's back on orbit. Job done.' Yes, he's smiling but his eyes are weary.

'Yeah, if you say so, mate.' Harry doesn't want to hear this stuff, not today; he looks at his watch. 'I've got deckchairs to put out.'

'I'll come with you.' Joe looks slight, just the little guy, standing there blowing spittle from his flute. 'I'm heading your way.'

'You don't say much do you?' Harry kicks a pebble off the promenade as they walk.

'What do you want me to say, man? You did some great rhythms this morning. You summoned gentle demons and made them dance. It's all in those fingertips of yours. You don't need me to tell you that. Is that better, crazy guy?'

'Yeah, sure thing. Gentle demons dancing.'

'Is that what you wanted to hear?'

'I was going ask you what planet you're from?'

'I wish I knew, man!' Joe laughs. 'I wish I knew, for sure. I guess like us all, I'm from Af-ri-ca. I feel it in me bones, man.' They laugh – back in sync, almost Burnley lads – almost but not quite. Look away, Harry thinks, and Joe would evaporate.

'I played with Vickie's band last night. With her new fella and your friend Alan. It was amazing, Joe – quite seriously, Vickie has turned herself into a rock'n'roll legend, or Jake has. Something's happened, honestly. You'll be truly surprised.'

'Nah, I always had faith in that girl. She just has a long road to travel. Like this one, running along in her fancy running shorts.'

'You've had them all, mate, I'm telling you,' Harry laughs, lightening up, admiring Rachel's form as she runs towards them with Nico at her side.

'Hail fellows well met,' Joe calls. His sparkle returns; he straightens his spine, flexing his muscles and his wit. 'Two gods sent by Apollo himself, wings on their heels. How you doin'? Bringing me a message from Olympus?'

'Don't they just ring you on your hotline, Joey?' Rachel answers, letting her voice sound casual, wishing Joe didn't get to her every time. 'No need for humble messengers.'

'Humble, are we today?' Joe says. 'But whatever, you're looking great, babe.'

'I feel great thanks, Joe.' As usual, she sounds as great as she intends to sound whenever she bumps into old boyfriends. 'Nico is getting me into shape.'

Nico remains silent, standing there, hands on hips, an athlete in repose. He smiles and nods in Joe's direction.

'There was never much wrong with your shape, girl,' Joe says.

Rachel is about to answer when Emmanuel texts her. 'Sorry –' She moves away. 'A message, I'd better get going. Thanks Nico, bye guys.' She's off.

'I'm loving that ringtone,' Joe calls after her, his mouth really is smiling now. 'Emmanuel's the man, I tell you.' She raises her hand in acknowledgement. 'He's the man, alright,' he repeats under his breath.

'You've really loosened her up,' he tells Nico, who's still standing there smiling, watching – at peace with the world, it seems. That's what he hopes it looks like.

'I don't think it's me, some new guy has got her bouncing,' he says, watching her moving away, light-footed, animated by her man.

'Well, yeah. Good for her,' Joe says, watching her too.

'How are you, Nico, Mr Kungfu Master?' Harry asks, trying to cut through the unsaid. 'I tell you, I feel mighty safe knowing you guys.'

'Well, thanks,' Nico says, inclining his head, objective again, assessing Harry's physique under the sun-bleached tank top and board shorts. 'You're bigger than both of us. Strong too, by the looks of you.'

'Harry's a gentle giant,' says Joe. 'He needs looking after, don't you Harry?'

'I could be fitter, I know that.'

'Nico gets everyone fit.'

'I can't teach you anything, Joe.'

'That's your great teaching, man.'

'I think not, but thanks. Well, Harry, let me know if you want to come along sometime. My gym's open. Come and test it out. I like teaching guys who could be athletes.'

All three of them look athletic enough to turn a few eyes as they saunter along the promenade. Harry feels good again, almost normal, one of the three musketeers. He's part of an A-team, a junior member, no doubt, but a part. It's a great place to be on a hot summer day. The whole town appears to be out on the prom today. Promenading, letting the sun and the sea work nature's cure on their souls. The crowd is even larger when they approach the pier. The nation's at play, it seems. Then they see the police cars, the crowd barriers and the line of ambulances.

'An IRA bomb,' someone says. 'It's in a bicycle chained to the railings.'

'It never ends,' Joe says, grimly, not just meaning the killing of children with bombs.

'Hello Hari,' Kanti calls, some time later. Not knowing about the bomb – it's been defused and destroyed – she's been waiting by the deckchair store. 'So you've met my friends. This is so great. Hello Nico, Hello Joe.'

'Hello, Miss Mouse,' Nico says, smiling affectionately – glad that she's joined the family. 'Still looking good, I see.'

She's wearing the saffron yellow mini-dress that he chose and, yet again, Harry has to reassess another of his friends.

'Wow, you look fantastic,' he says. Maybe too fantastic for a simple Burnley lad, he thinks.

'Yes,' Nico adds, 'I've told her: no more Minnie Mouse.'

'Nico is not just a friend, Hari, he's a photographer with a very special eye. He has made me a different woman.'

'Time to go, I think, Nico,' says Joe, in a stage whisper.

'Agreed,' says Nico, but before their diplomatic retreat, Diep arrives from the beach, in swimming trunks, dripping seawater, a towel round his shoulders.

'Now we all here,' Kanti enthuses. 'Diep too – I'm so happy.' For all Nico's efforts, she's Minnie Mouse on her birthday.

Diep looks equally excited and actually speaks, or at least gives an approximation of speech. The word repeated several times sounds very like 'swimming'.

'Great, little brother, yes – swimming. Diep is learning English fast. But, excuse us, we must go pack. We're moving today and I come to tell you, Hari. We want you to visit us in our new house, don't we Diep. Will you come? All of you, yes you too Nico and you Joe. I want to take photographs of all of you in our new studio.'

Diep definitely says 'studio' and then 'we pack'.

They are both talking at once. Then Harry notices that Nico and Joe have gone.

'Come back to the gym,' Nico says, after a while – a comfortable silence has grown between them. 'It's just along the seafront here.'

'It was news to me back there, this gym. Impressive that – you're good at secrets.'

'I thought you knew everything.'

'I know very little and understand less.'

'It's no secret. Come see. It's a good place, believe me.'

'I've no doubt about that.'

The conversation is superfluous because they both already knew they were going there. Nico has anticipated this moment since before the building work had started. He's nervous, silently excited – it feels like a new beginning. It seems like that to Joe too.

Chapter Forty-Eight

It would've been more romantic to have met in a restaurant, at a pre-booked table, in a dark corner, oak furniture, perhaps, candles definitely, a small glass vase with a single flower, an orchid, white but with faint purple veins and a flush of pink, a starched white tablecloth with matching napkins, an armoury of heavy silver cutlery and tall, fragile stemmed wine glasses to toast their meeting in golden wine. That would have been special – better than the end of the pier, perhaps, but Rachel's disappointment is nothing compared to her excitement.

'You need to be free to escape,' Emmanuel Gulan types. 'You might hate me.'

'I'd rather hate you over French onion soup and a glass of champagne,' Rachel replies, her fingers skipping friskily over the keyboard.

'It would be like booking an escort. Instant romance.'

'Instant isn't that bad.'

'I'm impatient too, you know.'

'That's so nice to know, Emmanuel. I'm like a puppy let loose in the park.'

'I'll come running, as the singer sang.'

'You're making me pant.'

'I can hear your breath.'

'I heard yours once.'

'Really? When?'

'Silly man! When you rang. The night you chickened out.'

'It was too soon. My mistake. Forgive me.'

'The flower was nice. I nearly tossed it in the bin!'

'I'll make up for it tonight.'

'Now you're making me nervous.'

'I'm nervous too and it's not my style.'

'I've never been on the pier.'

'Living in Brighton all your life. That figures.'

'I never liked funfairs. All that false jollity.'

'It's anonymous there. We'll be strangers. Strangers on a train.'

'Now I'm really scared.'

'Are you joking?'

'Mostly. I am scared but not of you. Supposing it doesn't work out.'

'What would we have lost?'

'Could we ever go back to being just like this? Could we? When the mystery's gone?'

'That's like all relationships.'

'Maybe why mine never last.'

'Don't be scared. Embrace the mystery of mysteries. It isn't the end of things. It's the beginning.'

'We have already begun.'

'See what I mean.'

'Yes, I know. Emmanuel – God is with us!'

'Now then! No gods. No magic. Just mysteries. Two people meant to meet.'

'Yes. Meant to meet. I feel that too.'

'You still wearing red?'

'Yes. Red hot.'

'I'll wear a red shirt.'

'Like a secret society.'

'Our mystery of mysteries.'

'I want to see what's under your shirt.'

'I'm seeing that puppy in the park.'

'Woof woof!'

'See you at six.'

'Yes. Six. Emmanuel I'm scared.'

'Me too and excited.'

Rachel's hands are shaking by five o'clock. The boys must go now. She'll make an excuse, tell them she has a meeting in the office, and they should all clear off. They should go for a drink. Celebrate. God, she thinks. I'm hysterical.

'Celebrate what?' Alan asks.

'Oh, I don't know. The mystery of mysteries, anything. Here's some money celebrate with me.'

'You alright?' Alan is momentarily worried.

'Yes, I'm fine. Go on, you lot. Get lost!'

She gives them money, a celebration bonus, and is glad that they leave so quickly. So much for their work ethic but if they'd stayed any longer, she'd have cried. She fumbles for condoms in her desk drawer. She always keeps a stash there, just in case, living in hope, she used to call it. She finds them, with a bottle of perfume, at the back of the drawer. *Mystère De Rochas* – an impulse buy that she'd only used once. She needs to calm down, her hands are shaking and she drops the condoms, scattering them over the floor. Shit. Control yourself, Rachel, you're going crazy. She puts the contraceptives into a zipped compartment in her bag, and is already worrying about the impulse to bring them.

What is this about? Is it really just to get laid? She opens the perfume, her hands are still trembling. She sprays her neck, her wrists and then, her hysteria growing and her actions speeding up, behind her knees and into her cleavage. Her mother had told her that a French designer said that a woman should put perfume wherever she wants to be kissed. Rachel sprays it into the air and walks through the mist. The perfume covers her body. Everywhere, she smiles, perfect. She goes to the washroom, but when she comes out of the cubicle, she sees that her face is white. She washes carefully around the perfume points and then washes down there. Just a precaution. Better than regretting it afterwards. She focuses on calming her hands. Deep breathing helps, she remembers her gym teacher saying. She tries it. Bloody hell, it works. Now for that last touch of make-up. She's as steady as a surgeon wielding a scalpel. Her lips have never looked so perfectly red.

It is less than a ten minute walk to the pier, so she leaves the office at 5.47, walking briskly, enjoying the adult sound of her high-heels, just like a grown-up on a posh night out. She checks her phone. He might have left a message and she's missed it. Nothing. The early evening is darker than usual. Summer clouds, black ones, circle overhead. Shit, shit, shit. She keeps a smart little black raincoat wrapped up in her bag. Very Audrey Hepburn. Shit. It really is going to rain. It's only slight, a summer shower.

The change in the weather hasn't deterred the crowd that's gone to the pier to experience the town's scariest funfair attractions, the thrill rides. The end of the pier, after the pavilion of gambling machines and fairground stalls, is host to the rides that Rachel has always dreaded. Only the truly brave, or the very stupid, dare endure being swung up into the air over the sea and plunged down again with face-distorting g-force. The place is a cacophony of rock music, heavily woofed in the bass to cover, or so Rachel presumes, the worst sounds of terror. Above the music, above the shouting and above the laughter, is the constant chorus of screaming, as people are hurtled above her head on what look like frantically animated industrial cranes. She hurries through the thrill-seekers, towards the very end of the pier, where Emmanuel said they should meet: by the final railings, overlooking the sea and, this evening, exposed to an intermittent surf spray. It's just turning six on her phone when the rain comes down as a deluge. Shit. She looks for the red shirt but just sees kids in anoraks, and fussing parents racing for cover. She's getting wet. She puts on the raincoat. Shit, again. Shit. I'll text him. He won't see my dress. He'll get soaked in shirtsleeves.

'Hi, it's raining. I've put on my black coat. I can't see you but I'm here.'

'I know,' comes a voice. Emmanuel is standing behind her.

Chapter Forty-Nine

Nico's gym is called simply Nico's Gym. It's built into one of the Victorian arches that stretch in rows under Brighton's clifftop promenade. Originally fishermen's storerooms and boathouses, they're now part of Brighton's popular marine playground. The Arches were carved out of the cliff-face by the entrepreneurial vision and hard graft of Brighton's nineteenth-century founding fathers and their army of navvies. They now house nightclubs, bars, novelty souvenir shops, workshops for canoe builders, windsurfing clubs and, sprinkled among them in this sun-worshipping bohemia, artists' studios and an outdoor stage for live rock concerts. Lightly-clad people of all ages worship here at this shrine to youth. Most of these establishments open out onto the promenade but Nico's Gym is a private club, its members are selected by invitation only, the fees negotiable but cheap.

It looks impressive from outside, with its curvaceous Victorian window frontage, glazed with bottle-bottom glass, and its entrance protected by a silvered steel door with an encoded entrance security system. Inside, there's a large circular open space with a domed ceiling constructed with bricks and nineteenth-century steel girders, painted white but made colourful by flowing streaks of rust, hints of clifftop vulnerability in this ultimately unforgiving maritime environment. The bottle glass window panes make an illuminated mural on the inside, picking out, filtering and distorting water-reflected sunlight and giving new colourful dimensions to the white plastered walls and the shiny floorboards, stained with light brown yacht varnish.

'Wow,' Joe exhales and shrugs, impressed, smiling good-humouredly at the five or six gym visitors, men and women, barefoot Judo-style, even the man in a wheelchair, dressed in white pyjama outfits secured by white sashes tied round the waist. They're practising Tai chi and various martial arts patterns. One of them recognises Joe – it's Conrad on his day off. He returns Joe's smile with a slight head bow and continues a series of Muay Thai kickboxing moves. His kicks and punches are delivered into space with fiery-eyed ferocity.

'Conrad is very talented,' Nico says. 'He's brought his Thai boxing here with him. He's much better than he thinks – no thanks to me.'

'One of your finds?'

'Well, no actually, he just joined himself up at one of the seafront classes. He's a very determined young man.'

'Hey,' Joe whispers, subdued, as if he's visiting a temple. 'This is awesome and, yeah, so gleaming new, amazing. I feel like a tramp here, a right slob spoiling the ambience.'

'You're spoiling nothing, my friend. Believe me.'

'It's so squeaky clean here; I bet your showers are brilliant. Is it cheeky if I get myself a bit of a wash?'

'Help yourself, Joe. Be at home, OK. My space at your disposal – clean or, well, cruddy.' Joe laughs, no pretence. Nico's smiling, then he grins, American style – he can't help it. Joe being here makes the place complete.

'Do anything you want here, just like I do.' Nico gives a proudly proprietorial gesture with his arm. 'Here, take one of these.' He hands him a thick white towel. Joe grins, remembering when he'd last borrowed a towel like this. 'The showers are through here.' They go up a polished steel spiral staircase to the empty changing rooms and beyond to the showers. 'See you when you're ready. There are some spare uniforms in the changing room if want one. You'd look good in white.'

'There you go – always the stylist – thanks, man.'

Nico leaves him alone in a cavernous tiled space where rows of extra-large chrome showerheads indicate that this is a communal wet room. Joe's soon lathering himself in soap smelling of orange, lavender and Quillaja bark. 'Nice one, Nico,' he thinks, 'the acceptable face of civilisation.'

'Don't worry, you get used to it,' says a female voice. 'There are separate cubicles but no one uses them.'

'I'm fine, lady, if you are,' Joe says, unfazed.

'It's great here, isn't it,' she says, turning on the water. She's one of the students, a large middle-aged woman.

'Yeah, perfect,' Joe agrees his head covered with lather, his manners immaculate. He's delighted by Nico's power to surprise. The woman stands at a discreet distance, leaving him in his imaginary rain forest.

'Afternoon all,' says another newcomer, a young man, his pale body in the early stages of firming up. He enters the shower with the help of a crutch, after taking off his prosthetic left leg in the changing room.

Downstairs, Nico, the undoubted leader, watches his students, silently walking among them, making minor adjustments, straightening a back here, a leg there, repositioning renegade feet. He knows their bodies intimately – in more detail than if he'd been their lover. He fetches his camera and surveys the room for new shots. Some here are already featured in the black-framed photographs that line the walls. The gym and the photos are part of the Public Service Photographer project. Some in their twenties but others middle-aged or older, the students are the fruit of his work around Brighton. The framed photographs are grouped in pairs, an 'after' image of each uniformed student and a 'before' of them captured unaware by his roving camera. Conrad is the exception here. There is no 'before' photograph of him, just a series of kickboxing action shots. Wearing satin boxer shorts, his wrists and feet bandaged in traditional Thai style, Conrad's physique is emphasised and celebrated, his very white skin studio lit with dramatic shadows. The last image on this wall is Joe, playing his flute on the seafront on the day that they met. Man, Music and the Sea, it's called. It's Nico's masterpiece.

Joe is now washed and uniformed, a barefoot warrior in white. Smiling at Nico, he enters the studio, tentatively, unusually so for him. Vigilant too, like a true warrior. He does a lingering tour of the exhibition. Nico watches, sitting on a high stool at the drinks bar, next to a weapons rack stacked with Chinese swords, spears and hand axes, his unofficial armoury. Joe reaches his portrait, stands in front of it for a minute, then turns towards Nico and bows, oriental style.

'An orange juice?' Nico says, sipping his own.

'Yeah, thanks. This is amazing. These pictures, not just the one of me. You're a magician, Nico.'

'Some of them here were reluctant at first and others, of course, just tell me to get lost. I got a few bruises that way.'

'The photograph of me is phenomenal. I've never had anything like that before,' Joe says, suddenly solemn. They refuse eye contact, looking instead at the floor. A link had been forged on the day of that photograph – an instant connection, a spontaneous friendship, electrically charged and, they both think, dangerous. A mystery might be resolved tonight. Joe looks up from the floor and finally meets Nico's gaze. Uncompromisingly, they hold the moment with shared, but unspoken knowledge.

'Cheers, man. Mutual respect,' Joe says, deliberately breaking the spell, and offering Nico a forearm handshake.

'Yes, mutual respect.' Nico rides his emotion, holding onto Joe's grasp and returning the muscular squeeze. A metaphor made material. They loosen the hold, smiling recognition.

'Here, let me show you round,' Nico says, the urbane New Yorker once more.

'There's no hurry,' Joe answers.

'This is also my home but I don't tell people that.'

'Cool.'

Nico's scared of saying too much or too little. He wants to be alone with this guy, to keep him here when the others have gone. It might be all that he wants and, now, he still struggles to look Joe in the eye. It's never felt like this before, never this painful. Some of the students are leaving, bowing and exchanging pleasantries as they go. The others take their cue from Nico's subliminal session-ending strategy and the class comes to a close. Conrad has showered and changed into his work clothes – jeans and a white t-shirt with 'Born Queer' in black lettering across the chest. He's off to start the evening shift at The Golden Orb.

'Good to see you again, Joe,' he says.

'You too, man.'

'Thanks Nico,'

'My pleasure.'

He doesn't linger, Conrad was born tactful too, and the signals are strong. When he's gone, Nico raises his eyebrows. 'I thought you said you didn't know him.'

Joe shrugs and grins. 'He's a dude. We've had some fun together, I thought you'd get on with him.'

The last one to leave is Nico's latest recruit to accept the Polaroid truth test. She's a woman in her forties, now changed back into a summer frock, a black slip over a white shirt, courtesy of Luisa Sato.

'I can't thank you enough, Nico. I feel so different these days. Ready for anything, almost.'

'No almost, Anne; you are ready for anything – full stop.'

'Well, I'm definitely ready to tackle the weekend shopping,' she

233

jokes, blushing, suddenly awkward in the company of these pleasant young men, who are obviously distracted.

When she's gone, Nico adjusts the lights, reducing their strength to a glow that compliments the golden rays of the evening sun, penetrating the wall of bottle glass. The boisterous world outside is muffled, turned to abstraction.

'Here, let me show you,' Nico says, no longer hiding the emotion in his voice.

They go through to the back of the circular room; there's a small door immediately behind the spiral staircase, beyond it is Nico's living space. This is home, a subterranean room carved out of the cliff and lined with bricks.

'I think it was a beer cellar in the old days,' he says, unable, somehow, to keep from sounding like a nervous estate agent. 'It's my cave, my hideaway, my nest. You're the first person, the only person, I've brought here.'

Joe is already walking round this windowless, stone-floored chamber. 'Wow' he says, then whistles his approval. Nico shrugs and points at the rudimentary furnishings. There's a bed with an Oriental hessian covering, almost like sacking, simply embroidered with dark red cotton. There are piles of floor cushions, faded green and yellow satin, that match the old two-seater sofa, once à la mode, but now torn and frayed. A museum piece, Sixties style.

'A souvenir from New York,' he says. 'Come, sit down.' Joe takes the sofa, but Nico lies back on the bed, his feet touching the floor. He stretches and spreads out his arms, willing himself to relax. This is good, amazingly good, he thinks.

It feels like home but Joe's still the guest. He stands up again and walks round, taking in the details, still the warrior en garde. On one wall, there's an industrial shelving unit with books, box files and a collection of objects from the beach, driftwood, feathers and a wicker lobster pot. On the other wall is an old wooden door sitting on beer crates, working as a desk for the computer, a state of the art laptop, a *Macintosh Powerbook 500*. There are more framed photographs over here too, old rock concert posters and framed pages from fashion magazines featuring his parents.

'Mom and Dad,' Nico says, sitting up, pulling an expression somewhere between irony and pathos. 'The famous dead! God bless 'em.'

'They look famous enough,' Joe agrees, sitting on the bed, sensing warm blood coursing through Nico's body. 'Famous and glamourous. Definitely out of my league.'

'Dad was a rock star and Mom was beautiful. They gave me life and, oh yes, a heroin habit straight from the womb. I loved them dearly, of course,' he says, with a whimsical snigger. 'Well, actually, I still do. I just don't want to be like them. I keep their photos as a warning. These too.'

There are yet more photographs, two young men, one of them the young Nico. 'One of the less famous dead,' he says, with a sad smile. 'A New York friend. The plague.'

'I'm sad for you.'

'Thanks.'

The two of them stand for a moment – soldiers at a memorial after the wreaths are laid.

'I love this place, man,' Joe moves away into the centre of the room. 'It's as you say, a cave. Hidden away, but it feels like we're at the centre.'

'We are. My escape to reality.'

Joe laughs. 'I like that.'

They return to the gym and find that the bottle glass window has turned black with the night,

'I call it the Gymnasium. It must be my Greek heritage – in Ancient Greece, gymnasiums were special places,' Nico says, dimming the lights until they glimmer like candles. 'The gymnasium was where young men came together to learn. I'm still learning here, man. Every night, behind locked doors. That's when I'm free. Free from hurt, free to feel hurt too, but also free from disappointment, from being judged.'

A long silence begins, it's far from awkward. They hold it, taking its weight together, muscles flexed, listening to its voice.

'Stay if you want.' Nico whispers, tasting the mystery. 'Make it your cave too. There's enough room and, anyway, it's already claimed you.'

'I believe it has,' Joe's whispering too. His mouth is smiling but this pleasure's serious. Neither knows who made the first move but whatever happens next is inevitable.

Chapter Fifty

Lionel's spending the afternoon in his dining room, making changes. He's not used the room for dining since Alice held her last dinner party here, weeks before her death. It had been a sombre event, when her penchant for plain cooking finally matched the guest list, the more conservative members of the accounts committee she'd chaired at her Methodist church. Methodism had been a late life conversion, one that Lionel had felt unable to support. Today, he wants to erase those painful memories. In surgical gloves and a paper mask, like a forensic scientist, he boxes up Alice's china ornaments, mostly porcelain figurines of country folk, and dried up potpourri dishes.

He's removing decades of dust, and worse, the evidence of personal failure, with the help of unused buff-coloured dusters. It's a shame to get them dirty, he thinks, but the smell of lavender-scented furniture polish, married life's aroma, focuses his mind. Making the mahogany wood shine again brings back those uncertain times, when the house was resplendent but oppressive under the supervision of Alice, who took polishing, like most things, seriously. He enjoys ignoring her household hints as her voice re-emerges, like the ghost in Hamlet, telling him not to forget to dust the tops of the doors. Goodbye Alice, he thinks, with amused melancholy, finishing the job with a jolly multi-coloured feather duster, and the antique Hoover vacuum cleaner bought, he remembers, in 1962, but not used since the lady of the house moved on to tell St Peter how to polish those pearly gates.

Poor Alice, he'd never appreciated the effort that she'd put into making their home an efficient, if soulless, living machine. After her death he'd often thought of selling the old place, and finding suitable bachelor accommodation, but his natural conservativism and a touch of self-mortification told him to leave things as they were. Staying has come at a price. He's endured painful memories here: guilt and, more than he admits, loneliness. You don't need to have had a happy marriage to miss the company of a dead partner, he decides, standing on stepladders, feather-dusting the swagged curtain pelmets in the tall dining room windows, and counting the desiccated spiders' corpses hidden there.

Kanti and Diep will be moving in this evening, and it's time to make real changes. The first job has been to remove the framed wedding photographs that perpetuated the lie. Poor Alice, he thinks, as he often does these days, we could have been happier with a bit more imagination.

Jacqueline rings the doorbell, partly out of neighbourliness, and a lot to do with curiosity. She has promised to help spruce up the place – all five floors – public bar friendships are meant to be like this, she thinks. It's a community of friends, that's the idea. When Lionel opens the door, he doesn't recognise her. The garish make-up has gone, along with the red hair. She now looks like she is, a woman of, say, around fifty-five, with neatly cut light brown hair, pale lipstick and just a hint of eye makeup.

'It's only me,' she laughs. 'I've always looked like this under the slap.'

'Very nice too. You can be quite the lady when you want.'

'More of the lady and less of the landlady, you mean. Well, why not. You've had a bit of a makeover too, love. I never thought of you as a Mr Mop.'

'Needs must, Jacqueline.'

'This is quite a house,' she says, sizing it up from the hall. 'You didn't tell me you lived in such style.'

'Not sure about the style but it's certainly big, I'm afraid. You sure you still want to help?'

'Just try to stop me. This will be fun,' she says, putting on the cotton housecoat that she uses round the pub when its closed. The pattern, clusters of falling pink rosebuds, reminds Lionel of a summer storm. Apt, he thinks, as she plunges into action mounting the stairs, two steps at a time, carrying a bucket with her cleaning equipment, the pub's cylinder vacuum cleaner under her arm. Cleaning is a military discipline and a pleasure for Jacqueline – Alice would've approved.

'You'll find plenty of bedlinen in the linen cupboard,' Lionel calls.

'Don't you worry, I've got it all in hand.'

Upstairs, for the rest of the morning, with many crashes and thumps, she dedicates herself to cleaning the bedrooms and the two bathrooms – she loves epic battles, especially ones she can win. Downstairs, Lionel enjoys the sound of chaos in retreat. He's still gathering up the Alice memorabilia and sorting it into either charity shop bargains, antique collectables or just plain rubbish.

'I won't miss any of it,' he says, when the man with a white van drives the black plastic bin bags out of his life.

'You won't regret it, Lionel, believe me. We've all been cutting the crap recently.'

'Yes, indeed,' he thinks, liking the idea that he's cutting the crap. That's exactly it. Old age demands looking beyond the crap, seeking clarification beyond life's clutter, deciding what's important and what's just a collection of bad habits and, yes, crap.

Later, Jacqueline and Rosemary come round with the food – a banquet for the Subhadi twins: vegetarian curries and side-dishes, recipes from a Nepalese cookbook, cooked in The Golden Orb's kitchen. They've changed into party frocks – a classic black evening dress for Jacqueline and a green chiffon gown for Rosemary – both Luisa Sato originals. Their new clothes were bought on the advice of new friend Nico Melas, recommended by their ever vigilant barman, Conrad Adamcek, who's running the pub tonight in their absence. Monty's here too, in a baggy blue suit with a flashy kipper tie that hangs snugly along the line of his paunch – these days he likes to go wherever Rosemary goes, even though she'd like a little more space. John's here too, in his Indian suit, hair slicked down, freshly shaved, quietly, maybe sullenly, taking in the scene like a cat locked in a strange room.

Kanti and Diep are upstairs with Harry, who has helped them in with their luggage; art portfolio cases, camera equipment, a couple of rucksacks and two long-haul suitcases.

Lionel has sorted the wine and set the table with what was Alice's best china, glass and silverware – wedding presents saved for special occasions and, therefore, hardly used. He is taking a moment to wish his solitude farewell, and to welcome himself to what feels like his new home. He hides his feelings with some unnecessary last minute cutlery-straightening, like an old-fashioned society butler.

'Welcome,' he says, standing, meaning to continue but, uncharacteristically nervous, sitting down again, smiling emotionally at the assembled company round the long dining table, now sparkling with candle-lit crystal and silver. There's an implied compliment in the fact that everyone has dressed for dinner in the old fashioned way – Lionel's way. Except for Harry, that is, who thinks smart is jeans and a t-shirt. Diep, in a new white shirt, is even wearing a tie, and Kanti is debuting her black cocktail dress, the very image of international sophistication.

'I wanted you all here tonight to celebrate a new beginning,' he continues, still sitting in his place at the top of the table.

'This is a typical English diner party, Lionel, thank you so much. I feel we are really in England now,' Kanti says.

'I want you and Diep to be happy here – it's your home now.'

There's a babble of conversation and laughter – the good humour helped by the stack of bottles, lined up along the dresser. Lionel smiles like an old tribal chief as he looks round the table, the whisky aperitif has pressed his emotion button.

'I'd like to drink a toast to my late wife Alice. It's been so long now since she died, that I can't even remember if I liked her.'

'Lionel, that's an awful thing to say,' Rosemary says, nearly choking from a mixture of amusement and shock.

'Let him finish, Rosie,' Monty chips in. 'It was his marriage not yours.'

Jacqueline laughs, nodding.

'We muddled through,' he continues. 'Let's raise our glasses to Alice, God bless her.'

'To Alice!' they echo, standing, only slightly embarrassed, emptying their glasses.

'Good for you, Mr Lionel,' Kanti squeezes his hand.

'Yes,' Rosemary agrees. 'Let's not invent saints and martyrs. I'm sure Alice was a lovely lady but, no offence meant, bless her, she would have done better with someone, let's say, more settled in their habits.'

'Yes, indeed,' Lionel laughs. 'We should never've tied that knot.'

'Knot?' Kanti asks.

'Got married, my dear. Anyway, I'm putting the past behind me today.'

'That's just wonderful,' Rosemary says, squeezing Jacqueline's hand; they exchange moist-eyed smiles.

'I met someone once who said it was too late to find hope in fine young men,' Lionel continues, warming to speech-making. 'I'm sure she meant fine young women too. I want to restore that hope by opening my home to these inspiring young people, Kanti and Diep, wonderful young artists, both of them.'

'You are a great man, thank you so much,' Kanti says, standing up, almost shouting her enthusiasm. 'Let me make some toast for you too, Lionel, father to us all.' Lionel's touched and sets his jaw firmly. He's sitting between the twins and, when general conversation returns to the party, he turns to Diep.

'I hope you understood what I've been saying, Diep,' he says, exaggerating his articulation. Diep makes a guttural sound and then, probably, 'Yes.'

John, from across the table, has been listening, and he furtively wipes his eyes.

'Diep has been learning English,' Kanti says. 'He is getting so good at lip-reading that he understands more than I do. My brother is a genius boy, aren't you Diep?'

Diep laughs from the back of his throat and says, 'No. Not genius. Happy.'

'You are John, is that right?' Kanti says, alert to the melancholy man facing her over the table, and making to draw him into the circle. 'You have a fine English name, like my father. He was John too.'

'Oh really? An expat like me.'

'Yes, our father was also John, a fine English man like you, who loved Asia. A lot like you in fact. He loved Nepal – India too.' Her eyes shift to Harry, who is sitting next to John.

'I'd love to go to India and Nepal,' Harry says, limply.

'I go to Asia every year,' John says.

'That's great,' says Kanti. 'Hari will go to Kathmandu one day. It is his dream.'

'You're the drummer from the beach, aren't you?' John says. 'You and the flute player. I hear you playing there most mornings. It's inspiring, like a morning raga.'

'Thanks, man,' says Harry, chuffed.

'John plays too,' Lionel says, joining in. 'You play the sitar, don't you, old chap.'

'Yes, a bit – just improvising on my own. Nothing fancy.'

'Join us some time, if you want,' says Harry, feeling less like an alien now. 'I really like the sitar.'

'Yes, maybe I'll take you up on that one day. I go swimming near there every morning.'

Diep is signing to Kanti, and grinning in John and Harry's direction.

'John,' Kanti says, 'Diep thinks you are like our father. He says you must be a very nice man.'

'Oh mate, thanks. Far from it I fear, but it's a sweet thought.'

After a deep drink from his wine glass, John makes his decision – alcohol, weariness and emotion take over, giving him the words. It's time to tell them a story. He hadn't intended to, he isn't even sure that he wants to and, for a moment he thinks no, control yourself, you old fool, let the moment pass. There's so much affection round this table, too much sincerity for him to sit here carrying the lie. When he finally decides that he doesn't dare, he's already breaking the news, hearing himself saying what he has dreaded since childhood. The table falls as silent as a prayer meeting. He talks slowly, simply explaining who he is, what he is, and then tells them that Rajiv, the man that he loves, is getting married today. It's told so quickly and over so unexpectedly, that it's almost anticlimactic. There's nothing more to hide. Feeling vulnerable and exposed, truly naked, he looks round the table at his old friends. Friendships must be reborn in this moment. The silence lasts only a few seconds but long enough for his life to change permanently. Then everyone claps. Then everyone cheers.

'I always thought you were a bit queer, Mahatma!' Monty laughs. 'Good luck to you, mate, it takes all sorts.'

'Yes, of course we all guessed,' says Rosemary. 'I don't think anyone's surprised, but it's great that you've said it.'

'Well, I'll be blowed,' Lionel laughs. 'I'll be blowed if I knew. John, old thing, I never guessed, not even an inkling, mate, but it's fine by me. We must all love who we love, however we do the loving.'

'All love is a celebration,' Kanti says, her face shining. 'I knew you were a fine man, John. You are a man of love, like my father John. It is good saying things as they are.' She pauses, unsure what to say, when she sees his doleful expression. 'But you are also very sad. We must help if we can. We must be your true friends.'

'Here's to John,' Lionel says, raising his glass. 'New beginnings, old thing.' The others join in an impromptu seated toast while John looks down at his feet. 'It'll make no difference to our swimming club, old boy, I want you to know that.'

'Thanks Lionel, good. Life as normal then.'

'The only way, old chap.'

While they talk, Diep is growing increasingly animated, bombarding Kanti with a vigorous onslaught of signs and his own form of excited Nepalese.

'Ladies and gentlemen,' Kanti announces, when he's finished. 'Please allow me to speak. Diep always knows what to do. This boy, your boy in India, John. What is his name?'

'Rajiv,' John says, barely able to say the word. 'Rajiv Namputiri.'

'Well then, we should light a fire for Rajiv Namputiri. For John and Rajiv. Here in Brighton, on the beach, tonight. Hari can help us – he is good at beach parties, he's the best beach bum in England.'

After dinner, instructed by Diep and interpreted by Kanti, they light a marriage fire on the shingle and let the flames burn tall. There's beer and laughter and music too – Harry has brought his djembe and he plays with a great unleashing of energy, long and loud. Everyone recognises the universal rhythms of primeval celebration, and the dancing is infectious. It's a party like any other, but John can't speak, he stands by the fire, so close his skin nearly singes. Through the flames, and through moistening eyes, he sees Krishna. It might or might not be Joe Edevane dancing, playing his flute, but John feels Krishna's spirit. It's the melody he's heard many times before, here on the beach and, illusion or not, he believes it's a form of the god.

'Krishna, help me,' he silently prays, 'consume this grief with your dance of fire.'

It should be a sacred immolation, in honour of love, he thinks. If only he could be brave enough. If this is the time, if this is Krishna's message – but he knows it's not. The test is to go on. Diep comes to him, his eyes moist too, reflecting the fire. 'Ba'aa,' he says, hugging the man who wears his father's name. Then he says it again with a quivering smile. 'Ba'aa, Father,' or that is what John chooses to hear. It's so unexpected, this young man's hug, those arms trembling with feeling, squeezing an old fool like him, who can only stand there, body frozen but, maybe, no longer untouchable. A long-defended barrier collapses, it's a form of immolation, perhaps, and John returns the hug. Both stay locked together like this for some time, seeing in the fire those they have loved and lost. Their tears flow, wetting each other's shoulders, and then, through the fire, Krishna again, his face crinkling with mirth.

Chapter Fifty-One

Emmanuel's smiling nervously. It had been his idea to meet Rachel here at the end of the pier, but he feels out of place, even disorientated in such a playground atmosphere. He's a man her age, maybe thirty, about her height, maybe an inch or two taller; he's slim but not skinny, a good body, she guesses; his thick dark hair is cut short but not too short, she likes the way it flops over his forehead, interesting too his very pale skin. This is Emmanuel Kaspar Gulan, at last. Just how she's imagined him, well, almost. She hadn't predicted those lips, rudely luscious on such a sensitive face. He's wearing a rain-splattered red shirt, pectoral-wet, and much more revealing than the black-rimmed sunglasses. She hadn't imagined them either, but she likes the vampiric hint. He's very pale, handsome enough, attractive enough but, more than that, and extraordinarily, he is, in the flesh, definitely the man who had set her alight with that first simple text message. She wants to hug him but doesn't dare. This might be enough. It might be better to just hug the moment, to stand here looking at him, this man, to memorise him and to lock him away in her brain, where no one could take him from her. 'God, Rachel,' she thinks, 'you do actually love this guy.'

'Emmanuel?' she says, her body trembling, her breath almost breathless, as she struggles to say something interesting.

'Yes, that's me. You must be Rachel.'

'Yes,'

'Well, howdee, as they say on the range.'

'The range?'

'Sorry, a bad joke. Cowboys, it doesn't matter.'

'Oh right, I see. Yes, I suppose it was a bad joke.'

'Yes, it was,' he's struggling to control feelings too. 'I told you this would be awkward. You can go if you want, I half expect you to anyway.'

'Don't be silly, Emmanuel. Why would I do that, for God's sake.'

'Because you don't like my jokes, maybe. Or because I'm blind, perhaps.'

'Blind?' She hadn't noticed. She'd thought the sunglasses odd but hadn't thought blind. Blind. Repeating it to herself helps. Blind. She hadn't thought of that.

'Yes, blind. I can't see. I never could see, so I'm sort of used to it. It's easier for me than for you, I reckon. Blind isn't good news, I suspect. Not what you wanted. A bit of a shock.'

'Blind,' she says again. 'You're blind. I'm getting it. You can't see. You can't see anything – anyone. You can't see me.'

'Yes, it's true. Not being able to see often comes with blindness. It's one of the symptoms.'

'This place must seem crazy to you. The funfair, the rides, all that screaming. That must be so confusing.'

'Not really. I know about the pier, about the rides. It's all about laughing and screaming and that other sound, the watery one. That's the sea, I believe.'

'Hey, watch it.' They're laughing. 'Oh, I didn't mean watch it literally. Well, you can't actually watch anything, can you? Oh, I'm sorry, I don't know what I'm saying.'

'It's OK. I'm a blind man in a world where language was written by people who can see. You can tell me to watch it, I don't mind. You can say 'look out' too and, if you know what I mean, you can say 'I see'.'

'You're not totally right on that anyway, you know.'

'Not right about what?'

'Language being written by people who can see. The man who wrote *Paradise Lost* – wasn't he blind?'

'You read Milton?'

'I'm not stupid, you know. I read it at school. I had to. I just remember he was blind, and that he wrote wonderful rolling sentences that made me cry, even though I didn't always understand what he was saying.'

'I don't want to make you cry and I do know that you're not stupid. It's just that no one reads Milton these days.'

'I suppose you read with Braille?'

'Yes, I see with my fingers.'

'I see,' she says, looking at his pale tapering fingers. His fingernails are short and manicured. Ready for action. 'Oh no, I've just said it,' she laughs. 'I didn't mean to say 'I see'. I meant I know. I know about Braille but I don't see – sorry again – I mean, I don't understand, how you can use a computer.'

'Oh, that, my computer talks to me; it's simple. Now, tell me something. Do you want to have dinner with me? You can say no.

244

Better to be honest straight away. Better for both of us if you left now.'

'Of course I want us to have dinner. Anyway, I'm hungry. First you think I'm stupid and then you think I'm superficial.'

'I think you're beautiful,'

'Now I know you're blind!' She's giggling now. 'Can I kiss you or is that premature?'

'Kiss me quick, as they say. This is Brighton Pier after all. Kiss me before the rain starts again.'

She hugs him, drawing him close, squeezing him, feeling his muscles relax. He's blind, she keeps telling herself, trying to convince herself that it makes no difference, and that she won't let it make a difference even if it does. This moment has been delayed for so long. He's hugging her too and she gasps, involuntarily knowing that his fingers have begun to see her. He touches her face, feels her smile, the curves of her ears, and detects the moistening around her eyes. He lets his fingertips run along her jaw line, examining the tightness of the skin as it joins the thin vulnerable neck that fits neatly into his hand. This is Rachel, no doubt. The person he too has loved since that first text. Loved but feared, unsure how she'd take his blindness. Then he finds her pulse, the jugular vein, her heart is racing under his touch. She won't reject him, he can tell now, so he draws her mouth towards his. As they kiss, her fingers too learn how to see. Fingers lead the way, then their tongues, searching, meeting, exploring and lingering as their bodies press close, their arousal perfectly visible to both.

'Still hungry?' he asks.

'You've whetted my appetite.'

'So I take it we have a date?'

Rachel touches the side of his face and rubs it softly.

'We need an intimate table for two – somewhere where no one can see us.'

'I've booked a restaurant with a view of the sea. Would you like me to show you the way?' he says, taking a collapsible white cane from his pocket.

Later, Rachel believes that they both really do see the sea, the stars too, as they walk slowly, arms entwined back to her flat. She persuades him to come up with her, and then she finds out what it's like to be seen by a far-sighted, delicate-fingered lover.

Chapter Fifty-Two

A woman, or rather the American lady, as Ali Hassan, the young Nubian waiter calls her, is sitting in her usual position at the table next to the indoor palm tree, in the terracotta orange restaurant of the Al Moudira Hotel, Luxor. She's seen the pyramids, tombs and temples, sailed down the Nile on a yacht, and she's taken some memorable photographs, mostly concentrating on erosion, contrasts between the clear blue sky and haggard gold-coloured rocks. Kate Arnold can't engage with the archaeological splendours of Ancient Egypt, it's just sand and ruins, she thinks. She prefers sitting here and, when he has the time, talking to Ali Hassan, wondering at the beauty of his skin and, even more beautiful, his optimism. She should have come to Egypt when she was young. It's too late now to engage with unfamiliar cultures. It's different talking with Ali Hassan.

'I dream of going to the United States,' he tells her. 'I will find a waiter's job at the great Hotel Ritz-Carlton and pay my respects to the Statue of Liberty.'

'My country would be honoured to have you,' she says, wishing him luck with his American dream.

'You must come to have dinner there one day and I will give you the best table, like here.'

'Ah yes, a table with a view of Lady Liberty.'

'Yes, I have seen photographs.'

Kate feels a long way from home or, rather, a long way from feeling at home. She isn't dead yet, even though she's prepared herself for the inevitability of that not wholly unwelcome prospect. Maybe the pills have worked, or maybe it is Ali Hassan, the new fine young man in her life. He helps with his hope and ambition, charming her to think of future possibilities and daring her to hope too. That is liberty enough. She has come to Egypt to die, but those tombs weren't intended for her. Death demands more respect than hitching a lift on dead pharaohs, Kate realises that now. She had shipped herself here when she was too frightened to jump into the sea. It might have been cowardice not to end it all quickly, after her last night on the cruise with Lionel. But no, it would have been foolish, an unreliable method, and probably messy too if there'd been sharks around. She's crossed the world to sit in an Egyptian restaurant, talking to a Nubian boy, listening to the Italian hotel pianist, Mario Lazzati, who plays American music badly. She's rediscovered George Gershwin in Luxor. It was Mario who decided to play it for her, but he just can't get the swing in *They Can't Take That Away From Me*. With what life she has left, she wants to swing a few more times, or even just once more, before making her exit. That was why she wrote the postcard to Lionel.

It wasn't entirely a surprise when he saw the postcard of the sun setting behind the pyramids. His well-worn optimism allows Lionel to hold out for the improbable. It cushions the probable too. It was meant to be. He likes to think that he has known it all along, known that Kate hadn't died. Maybe his subconscious has been preparing the house for her arrival without telling him. He tries to stay calm, to convince himself that this really was what he'd expected, but he knows that it wasn't so much expected as prayed for. He is, he knows this too, not so much a wise old man, as a silly old fool. So he stands for a long time by the hall mat, postcard in hand, emotions frozen, not daring to believe what he's just read.

Kanti and Diep have let in the light, brought the old place to life, and lit it with hope. Maybe that's what brought him this postcard. He can hear them at work upstairs in their two studios, making things new, reinventing his world. He goes to sit at the piano, his comfort zone, and rereads the card. 'Is it too late for a request? An old Yankee woman on her way to England wants to hear some more Gershwin.' He lets his fingers run over the keys, softly swinging his version of *They Can't Take That Away From Me*. Time for a piano tuner, he thinks.

Wah-Wah has a noticeboard for business cards advertising music lessons, local rock concerts, bands looking for band members, musicians looking for bands and, at the bottom, piano tuners. It's a quiet afternoon at the music shop and Alan's on his own. Since Victoria gave up the job, he now works as Jake's number two. When he gave Rachel his notice, she'd squeezed his arm and said 'good idea' but there had been no choice. Music has claimed him full-time.

Victoria giving up the band had been a set-back, but he's over the disappointment. His future is all about one man and his saxophone, he knows that, and he'll go wherever that takes him. Harry, even though he's more used to these things, was disappointed too. 'She's had a kind of breakdown,' he'd told Alan when they last met. Jake is looking after her, so now Alan is the new face of Wah-Wah. He's becoming a local hero with the town's aspiring musicians. He likes it here. He might even love it, life in a refuge for music's fellow travellers. The work is interesting enough without being too busy and he has time to play his saxophone when there are no customers or, sometimes, even when there are. He can be shamelessly boring here, he can talk saxophone to like-minded musicians, one bore to another, and never find it boring.

He's got a small group of followers these days, jazz groupies, mostly, aspiring saxophonists and enthusiasts who get a kick out of hearing live music. Marie-Louise Freneau, is particularly keen. She's a French teacher, here for the summer but thinking of staying. She wears tight t-shirts and even tighter jeans, leaving a gap for her midriff to expose the tiger tattoo that roars from just below her navel. Even more interesting to Alan is the fact that she also plays the soprano saxophone. He'd met her through Joe, that man knows everyone. Amazingly, or so Alan thinks anyway, she's a Sidney Bechet enthusiast. He'd let her play one of the shop's soprano saxophones, not quite testing her out, more intrigued. She'd played *Petite Fleur* in Bechet's 1954 version. She was note perfect. No hurry, he thinks, but a female music nerd, attractive too, who, so he hopes, actually respects his playing. He might be onto something here.

Today he's writing a new middle section to his song *Blue Notes*. It has a deeper melancholy these days. The inspiration still comes from his heroes, John Coltrane in particular, but now it comes via his heart, or from somewhere inside himself where thoughts, usually vague and undeveloped, turn into saxophone abstractions. They're only notes stumbled upon by accident, but they're powerful enough to take him by surprise. This might be the beginning of his own distinctive voice. The new melody sings of loneliness but arrives like a spirit with a message. Maybe it will always be just him and his saxophone and, maybe, that's not as bad as he'd feared – not, after all, a weakness, a lack of maturity, a nerdy adolescent male thing, or even a lonely thing. These twelve new bars point his way forward in the whimsical, worldless way of revelations. He plays it through again from the top, without noticing Lionel standing in the doorway.

'Oh sorry, I didn't see you. I got a bit carried away.'

'That was beautiful,' Lionel says. 'An unexpected treat. Aren't you the lad who plays outside The Golden Orb? I've enjoyed your style.'

'Do you play too?'

'The piano, a bit of jazz, some blues, but also Tin Pan Alley. I'm looking for a piano tuner.'

'Someone's got a card on our board. You could give him a try.'

'I didn't realise you worked here. I thought you were a street kid. A talented one of course. I remember your Coltrane improvisations. Very clever, if you don't mind an old man's opinion.'

'It's good to know someone was listening.'

'I suppose you wouldn't consider playing with a few old fogies some time? A group of us are getting together regularly at the Orb. We're doing jazz mostly, and we could do with a drop of new blood. Think about it.'

Alan does think about it – for a second or two. They agree to give it a go. 'The Golden Orb on Thursday evening then. See you there.'

Jake, in a suit and tie, makes way for Lionel at the door and pulls a face when he's gone.

'Christ! Two ties in Wah-Wah's, that must be a first.'

'You going to a funeral?' Alan asks, guiltily putting his saxophone behind the counter, daunted by this suited version of Jake Reilly.

'No, the opera. I'm taking Vickie to London, the Royal Opera House, would you believe.'

'Does she mind?'

'Don't be so bloody cheeky, you. She'll love it.'

'You've brainwashed her, Jake. But don't tell me – it's still music. It's all one, I know. Even Italian opera.'

'Yeah, that's right, especially Italian opera. Vickie and me, we're into big passion these days and not just the way you're thinking.'

'So is she OK? You know, better.'

'Honestly, Alan, mate, I can't tell you how much better. It's been a long process, but she's set alight, it's fantastic, believe me. I'm still pinching myself, honestly, mate. She's terrific these days.'

Victoria has changed, she might even have recovered from the depression since discovering that she could sing note for note with all of Jake's Caruso records. When she sings these Italian opera arias, her voice doubles in volume and strength, and she has no problems at the top of her range, singing notes she hadn't even realised were there.

'It only seems too high until you get there,' she tells Jake, 'like mountain climbing. When you're up there, it feels just great – on top of the world.'

It feels like her own voice. It also feels like it is who she is, who she was meant to be. She can never be the new Janis Joplin, she has decided, it'd be her short-cut to an early grave. She has found an untried part of her personality by singing in Italian, and her black dog can't follow her there. It turns her on too. Now singing often ends with her taking Jake to bed, the only way down from her high. It's as if Caruso may have changed his gender for Jake, as a reward for all that loyalty over the years. L'amore italiano leaves him exhausted on the bed – the two loves of his life united in one very insistent young woman.

She had only stopped singing Italian tenor arias around the flat after her first singing lesson. Jake had arranged for her to sing for Alfredo Cantelli, his old friend from the seafront café. Alfredo, a retired operatic tenor, is now a singing teacher, the best in Brighton. He'd often invited Jake to his flat on the seafront where they indulged their mutual Caruso obsession, sharing favourites from their collections and talking opera into the night. Alfredo Cantelli, small, round and ebullient, like Caruso himself, had looked interested straight away when he saw Victoria's physique. After a few courtly platitudes, he'd got down to business, playing progressively rising chords on a grand piano silhouetted by the sparkling view of the sea. Victoria was awed and inspired by the burnished sound of the full-sized *Steinway* grand piano, as Alfredo pushed her voice to its highest limits and beyond. He then got her to sing that Caruso aria, *Questa o Quella,* where all of this had begun. Kicking off her shoes, she'd sung undaunted by what was in effect an audition. Signor Cantelli had chuckled while he played the accompaniment. 'She's phenomenal,' he thought, 'this magnificently large young woman, standing there in her jeans and baggy black pullover.'

'You have a lot of potential,' he'd said, concealing his excitement. 'If you work hard, you could sing all the great roles. You have a big voice, Victoria. One day, you could be a dramatic soprano but you have to stop singing Caruso.'

'What's a dramatic soprano?' she'd asked, making sure that that was what she wanted to be.

'It's the best.' Alfredo's forefinger and thumb link in a symbol of perfection. 'Perfetto. You will have to learn how to use your voice but, and I shouldn't be saying this, you've mostly got all you need naturally there already. You can sing low C's and high C's and all the notes in between.'

Signor Cantelli had agreed to teach her, and to coach her until she could pass into music college. When Jake and she got home, they'd celebrated in bed with the latest interesting device that Victoria had bought, on Conrad Adamcik's advice, from Anything Goes.

In Egypt, the sun sinks behind the pyramids. Tragic love turns ecstatic in the last act of Verdi's *Aida* and Victoria knows this is what she has to do. 'Morir! Si pura e bella' sings the dying slave girl with the huge voice. 'To die! So pure and lovely!' agrees her handsome Egyptian lover, who has been incarcerated with her in their pyramid tomb. He isn't Enrico Caruso, and the slave girl isn't Victoria Buchanan, but they're doing well enough. In the stalls at the Royal Opera House, Covent Garden, Victoria holds hands with Jake and knows that he's crying. 'Fuck it,' she whispers, 'I can do this.'

'Yes, love, fuck it – you can – and you will.' Jake hopes that he'll still be around when she gets there.

The sun sinks behind the pyramids again, the real ones this time, a long way away, as Kate Arnold's flight takes off for London.

Chapter Fifty-Three

They're late for the swim. Actually, Rosemary was late and Monty had been waiting for her outside The Golden Orb. He hadn't seen her since yesterday when, to all their amazement, she'd joined their swimming club. Lionel and John are already on their way back to their clothes, wet, mahogany brown and invigorated. Monty hesitates for a moment too long before taking off his underpants.

'It's alright mate,' John knows what he's thinking, 'you're quite safe, believe me. You'd be a long way down my hit list, that's a promise.'

'Oh, he's not that bad,' Rosemary says, patting Monty's bald head affectionately, but, in mid-sentence, in mid-head-pat, she makes her decision.

They run off to the sea together and, like young lovers, Lionel thinks, if rather rounded and wobbly ones, they're holding hands when they reach the water.

'Sweet,' Lionel says, still watching them. John shrugs. He isn't looking.

'I must tell him,' Rosemary thinks, and it seems appropriate to tell him here, standing naked, ankle deep in the sea. No one can accuse her of not being open.

'So, there you have it,' she says. 'It's about me — not you. Still friends?'

'Of course,' Monty says. 'I'm over it already,' he lies, diving into the sea. Swimming helps. Thrashing through the waves, he lets his body vent his anger, his hurt and his grief. Hiding in the foam from his man-made whirlpool, he can sense his body's instinct for survival. Rosemary takes a gentler swim, still pondering her new self-discovery. She smiles after each breath, every time her face emerges from the waves.

'Ah, new love,' says John, watching now.

'Time to go, I think,' says Lionel. 'I've got to get back for the piano tuner.'

'I've got to start packing.'

'Where are you going?'

'I've had notice to quit. The lease is running out on the flat. Sad after all these years but, you know, new beginnings. Dharma the cat will be more upset than me.'

'You should've said, old thing. I'm sorry.'

'Don't be sorry, Lionel, I've been shedding more layers than an Eskimo stripper. It feels surprisingly good.'

'Shedding the past is quite energising, I know. I've felt much better getting shot of the old stuff from my place. Just got the basement to do now.'

They both have the same thought, but it's Lionel who acts on it.

'Move in, old chap. It would be lovely to have you there. You'd have your own entrance, and you can do what you want down there – whatever takes your fancy.'

Then and there, they agree terms and shake salty hands on the deal.

John dawdles on the promenade; he's watching Lionel getting the bus. Friendship, he thinks, is kinder than love. Friendship, he's discovered, maybe too late in life, is also a form of love. Coming out. It's an awkward expression, he thinks, but it's a good phrase – better out than in, out of the shadows, out in the open. He's alone still, of course, it doesn't make being in love any easier. He's getting old too, but he's contented enough with who he is; happy, if that is the right word, to have got here to his own kind of queer equilibrium before it was too late.

Two young men are practising Tai chi out on the beach, by the water's edge. They are Nico and Joe. John's free now to acknowledge beauty wherever he sees it. They're silhouetted against the sun, their bodies moving in slow-motion. Time has felt like this for him too. The silhouettes speak to him of infinity.

'You like Tai chi?' Harry asks. John hadn't seen him there until now.

'Yes, I'd like to try it, I think.'

'They're the masters, Nico and Joe,' Harry says, watching too. 'They're started teaching me – taking me on a journey. They're special, I reckon. You should ask them about lessons.'

'I think I will.'

'Still up for that raga? I was serious about liking the sitar. I told Joe. He's up for it. Come along if you want. We're usually here at this time.'

John's pleased that he'll finally meet Joe, the man behind those flute melodies that have, so often this summer, invoked the spirit of Lord Krishna himself.

Rachel can't describe the feeling. Maybe tingling would do. Can you enjoy withdrawal symptoms, she wonders. She still feels the yearning, but she's satiated too. She's so high on whatever it is that she might never come down again. She doesn't want to anyway. Emmanuel's sleeping next to her, lying on his chest, unconsciously pinning her to the bed with a splayed arm and leg, his head turned towards her, his breathing not quite a snore, he's at peace, she thinks, and at home in her arms. She lies there enjoying his breath; it's sweetly warm on her face. She's happily imprisoned until he wakes. When he does, he grunts a smile as his sightless eyes open – they're blue, she discovers – they look into an infinity that she's only beginning to understand. She kisses them shut, closes her own, and then lets her fingers see all of him. 'Carnal knowledge has never felt so complete,' she whispers, much later, up close, her lips on his ear.

'I have a job to go to today,' he says, after their shower, letting his fingers run through her wet hair.
'Computer stuff?'
'No, I told you I've sold that idea.'
'I could've marketed it for you. I'm really good at that.'
'I know, but it's just a hobby for me. I should bore you sometime with another of my ideas – using fingertips instead of keyboards. Great for blind guys.'
'That doesn't sound boring at all,' she says, loving this man more all the time.
'A joke, Rachel,' he says, smiling. He wants to kiss her again.
'It's not a silly idea, you know. But, anyway, enough of that. I'm not going in this morning. The boys can get on without me.'
'I really do have to go, Rachel,' he says, reluctant to pull away from her lips. 'They're depending on me.'
'The music business?' She's watching him reach for his clothes.
'Yes – boring, maybe.' He stops, hands on hips, and looks at her through his sightlessness. 'It's not California but it suits me. I've got everything I want here; well, if you'll have me that is.'
'That's a done deal, Emmanuel Gulan, didn't you realise? For rich or for poor.'
'Is that what it sounds like?' he asks, nervous again.
'I guess it is. Amazing that, I'm not going nowhere, that's a

promise,' she says, even surprising herself, kissing him before he realises that she's so near. She's caught him naked, still about to dress.

'Wow,' he says.

'Come back to bed.'

Much later, she watches him putting on his trousers. He finds his clothes easily, last night he'd placed them precisely on a chair as if he was packing a case. Rachel is fascinated, loving his orderliness.

'I'll be free at lunchtime, can we meet later?' he says, finally dressed, but unable to hide the happiness coursing through his body. She really did propose to him just then. To be sure, he keeps rerunning her words. A done deal, yes, she even said 'for rich or for poor'.

She fastens his belt and imagines them married, buttoning his red shirt and brushing out the creases against his chest. She can see them now in a Silicon Valley mansion perhaps, but, if not that, anywhere will do, as long as he's there too.

'Text me when you're ready,' she says. 'Just like before.'

'I will. Complete with exclamations marks, of course.'

Jacqueline has borrowed the white van from the white van man, so that she can drive John's stuff to Lionel's basement. She's always loved driving, and if the pub business ever went bust, she's decided, she'd try to get a heavy goods vehicle licence and become a lorry driver. It would have more credibility, she thinks, now that she's lost the red hair and rouge. She's revving the engine outside The Golden Orb, when Rachel comes down the street.

'Do you fancy a ride?' she calls. 'I'm helping Lionel get rid of some old rubbish and then we're moving John into his basement.'

'Glamorous offer,' Rachel laughs. 'OK then.'

Harry has given up his job as a deckchair attendant – it was a matter of resigning before he was sacked.

'Where do deckchair attendants go in the winter?' Kanti had asked.

'Where indeed!' Harry is thinking. 'Do they have deckchairs in Nepal?' Maybe he would have to go to the Southern Hemisphere – Bondi Beach perhaps. Or maybe just give it up now. There's no future in deckchairs, not for him, he'd be better reforming the old band. The guys are still in Brighton, he's got some new songs – the time's right. Inspired by Victoria, embarrassed by her too, he's been writing every day since that rehearsal. She could blow him away with her songs, and then give it all up for opera. Crazy woman. What has he done? Apart from the deckchairs, and getting laid when he felt horny? Could he ever be as crazy as Vickie? 'Chuck it in,' Joe had said recently. He drops round the deckchair shed most mornings. 'You don't want this job. If you want to be in a band, do it. Don't just sit here dreaming bands and the rock'n'roll life. You're a drummer boy, get used to it. It's your destiny, man.'

'I resigned,' Harry tells him this morning. 'The band might be getting back together, and I'm going to work with Alan at Wah-Wah. I'm finishing at lunchtime.'

'Well done, drummer boy.'

It's been good sitting in the sun all summer, looking at girls and getting an impressive suntan, but what's happening to Harry the beach bum? The answer is there, in front of him.

Kanti looks great, no, more than that, she looks beautiful. The new sharp haircut and the new dress, thin and figure-hugging – she's never looked better.

'Very cool,' he says, in a voice like a wolf whistle.

'It's thanks to Nico. My American dreamer. He puts clothes on people. I take clothes off people. My job is easier, believe me. He is a master.'

'I've given up my job,' Harry tells her. He's heard enough about Nico. 'I've decided to spend more time with my drums.'

'Oh Hari, I'm so glad. So very glad, so happy about this. You can be the great drummer now, just like I know you can be.'

'I can only try.'

'When you finish today, you must come and see the new studio. It's all set up, and it is very great indeed. Come and see, later, Hari. Please.'

Lionel and John have cleared the basement flat. It's been unoccupied all the years Lionel's lived here, only used to store boxes and unwanted furniture. It's connected to the house upstairs by a staircase with a lockable door, and has its own front door, with a private yard at the front and the back. Without the clutter, it's a perfectly preserved example of early 60s interior design. Zany geometrically-patterned wallpaper, pale green paintwork that has scrubbed up like new, and smart stone-flooring. There's a living room with an open fireplace, a windowless bedroom, and a kitchen and bathroom, both with porcelain fittings that date back more than fifty years. 'It's perfect for an old geezer,' John said when he saw it.

'This is perfect,' says Jacqueline. She and Rachel are helping with the boxes. 'Even you, John, can be happy here.'

'It might be perfect for me,' he says, assessing his new home, holding Dharma who's growling in his travelling cage, 'but Dharma's the fussy one.'

'He'll be as happy as Larry,' Lionel says. 'Just wait 'til he finds the mice.'

The staircase door has been left open and they can hear music from above. A limpid melody echoes through the empty house and even, it seems, silences Dharma.

'The piano tuner,' Lionel tells them.

'Beautiful,' says John, the emotion in the music challenging him to stay calm. He walks into the yard to hide welling tears. New beginnings can be sad, he thinks.

Rachel, too, is affected by the unexpected beauty of this music. Jacqueline notices immediately.

'Are you alright?' she asks, putting her arm round her. 'What's the matter, my love?'

'Nothing –' Rachel quickly wipes her eyes. 'It's the music. It's so beautiful.'

'It's a Chopin *Nocturne*,' Lionel says. 'The one in E Flat Major. Lovely isn't it.'

'I didn't think you liked music,' her mother says – even she can feel its power.

'It's wonderful,' Rachel says. 'So sad but so joyful too.' Her tears return as Chopin's melody seeks out new depths of tragedy.

'Ah, those dying falls,' Lionel sighs. 'The piano tuner's doing a great job up there. He'll be finishing in a minute. Come and listen if you want.'

Rachel is still tearful when they go up to the living room, where she stands, like a shy schoolgirl, at the door. 'Come on in, my dear, I'm sure he won't mind.'

Before she sees who's playing, she already knows that it's

Emmanuel. He's sitting at the grand piano, still in that red shirt, wearing his sunglasses, looking directly at her.

'I knew it was you,' he says, letting the last chord die as she comes over to join him.

'I knew it was you too,' she says, lowering her voice. 'Your voice was in the music.'

'That's because I was talking to you,' he answers, reaching for her hand.

'I didn't know I liked music,' she says.

'I knew, Rachel. It's where we began.'

'Play it again, please,' says Lionel. 'I'm sure we'd all like to hear it.'

Rachel stands by the piano as he plays; Lionel and Jacqueline find seats.

'So this is her man,' Jacqueline whispers to Lionel. 'She's fallen the whole way this time.'

Chapter Fifty-Four

Chopin's Nocturne snakes its seductive way up the stairs into the two attic rooms at the top of the house. It follows Kanti and Harry as they climb from Lionel's living room, past rooms that have been unoccupied for years, past their shared bedroom, to what has become Kanti and Diep's studios, two large rooms with bare floorboards, white walls and a connecting door. There are sash windows with views over roofs to a silver sea. Kanti is wearing a silky silver dress, and Harry, led the way by her insistent hand, is inspired, almost, to poetry, but probably a song, comparing her to the sea on this summer morning when even the air seems to sparkle. Diep, in paint-splattered blue pyjama bottoms, with primary colours splashed over his torso, mumbles a neutral greeting, briefly interrupting his work.

In his studio, the walls and floor are already streaked with paint – bright oranges and reds, and a vivid mauve-pink, the principle colours of his new sculpture. The same height as Diep, five-foot-eight or so, an intricate plaster humanoid, a deformed Modernist dragon, stands in the middle of the room, umbrella'd by a two-tier plywood pagoda that is as yet unpainted.

The dragon, crowned with a warrior's helmet, has multiple arms and legs with reptilian hands and feet. It might be howling or laughing or, maybe, both. Its mouth, exaggerated like a circus clown's, gapes open, with cheeks upraised, displaying pointed teeth and an extended tongue, as violently red as a Cubist flame from a Picasso nightmare. The body, like the head, is smeared with mauve-pink paint: the remains, perhaps, of a bloody meal. It's draped with necklaces and strings of bells, but is otherwise naked; its prominent female breasts are firm and pointed, with rouged nipples that are also eyes. The groin, similarly rouged, supports a large and angrily erect phallus. In its largest hands, held out to the front, is a tiny yellow rowing boat, in danger of being crushed by the scarlet claws. In the boat is the focal point of the sculpture, a small frightened boy, painted blue, holding his head in terror.

'Not finished,' Diep says, almost intelligibly, signing as his words form, his face now animated with pleasure, as he shows Harry what he is doing. 'It stands in water. Flags here. Many colours.'

He almost skips as he fetches a large circular hoop that's been propped up against the wall. Placing it over the sculpture, he stands back, indicating the sculptural equivalent of a picture frame. It's a replica of Brighton beach, the grey-blue sea and the grey-brown shingle is dotted with blue and white striped deckchairs. He then fetches more sculptures, intricate primary coloured statues, each placed into position with priestly care. A large plaster Harry, a nude figure sitting on a rock, djembe between his legs. Then another, two naked men, obviously Lionel and John. They stand to attention behind Harry. Then two more nude figures, Joe and Nico – a flute player and a dancing man locked in ancient martial poses. Diep places them to the side of the group like figures in a Christmas crib. Finally, in the centre, between Lionel and John, a larger statue. Diep and Kanti, also naked, also standing to attention, joined at the hip and staring into the void or, maybe, into a mirror.

'Tell him it's very powerful. Sad but beautiful,' Harry says to Kanti, who is signing between them.

'You've already told him,' she says.

'I'm happy you like.' Diep puts a clenched fist into the palm of his hand, and bows with a rapidly spreading smile. Then, quite clearly this time, 'All my father.'

They leave him and go through the joining door. It's a journey from darkness to light. Kanti's room is a white-walled, white-floored photographic studio with a small stage and a lighting rig. One expanse of wall is hung with her photographs, portrait-sized prints of her nude studies.

Amongst them, Lionel by his piano, an old man, mind and body in balance, his life engraved on his flesh. Rosemary, voluptuous, a nude mystic, meditating, at peace with herself. The camera, or rather the lighting, lingers lovingly over the twin moles on her thigh. Monty, fat and unsure, like a grinning child, is an innocent still finding his way. Jacqueline, aggressively but joyously naked: she is marching forwards to the camera, breasts swinging free; she's crossing the world, head thrown back in laughter. Then Kanti's latest work – John is on his knees in deepest melancholy, his candlelit body sinewy lean like a Medieval martyr praying for release. Victoria and Jake are here too, gladiatorial and unrepentant, with a touch of leather. Then Conrad, the eternal wise child, studded and tattooed but serenely pale, displays his latest piercing with full-frontal pride. Alan emerges shyly from the sea, lost, a

Shakespearean lover on an alien shore. Nico, on the beach, a splendid statue bursting to life, exquisitely naked in mid-Taichi movement, one foot at the water's edge the other mid-air, his face lightly shadowed with doubt. Joe is there too, crossed-legged on the shingle, his body front lit, but half-silhouetted by the sinking sun, the flute, of course, at his lips. His eyes, not laughing now, intense and fiery, maybe sad too, burn through the camera lens like a sunset. Kanti's self-portrait with Diep hangs at the edge of the group – the naked twins stand to attention, solemn and innocent, Byzantine icons or Buddhist temple statues, they're holding hands, just as they stand in Diep's sculpture, ready to jump or, maybe, to be reborn.

She's the naked girl Harry's imagined, no fantasy, no daydream, now unveiled and he can't look away.

'It's the Final Judgement,' Harry says, trying to sound detached. 'Everyone judged, defined. You photograph skin but you're looking beneath it.'

'Oh no, Hari, not really. I can only see what they give me. I shall do Rachel and her wonderful piano man next. They will make a romantic picture. Or, better, if they let me, I might do them each alone.'

On the other walls there are the photographs of Harry. The revelationary images of his true self, he thinks, moved to see them again.

'You never asked me to get my kit off,' he says. 'I always expected it.'

'You never asked me to take mine off either,' she says, with mock coyness. 'You needn't worry, though, because I shall.' She's smiling as she runs her finger from his mouth to his navel. 'I was, I hoped, saving you for later.'

'And why is that?' he asks, smiling too.

She looks down at the floor. 'I shouldn't say. It isn't what Nepalese ladies are meant to   admit – and, anyway, not in public.'

'You've got to say it now – we're not in public.'

'I suppose I will,' the coy smile returns. 'But I'll be sad if this spoils things between us.'

Harry waits, nervous too. He doesn't want to lose her, but he might just be adult enough this time to make sure that he doesn't.

'I didn't want you to be one of my naked people, not part of my

261

project – they are as they are, undisguised, human, I love them all, but not in that way. Nakedness isn't about sex, not always,' she says, after a very deep breath. 'Oh Hari, how do I say this? But sometimes it is. When I see you naked for the first time,' she's giggling now, 'I want it to be in my bed.'

She dissolves into nervous laughter, like a Japanese Geisha blushing behind a paper screen. 'Now I want to run away,' she says. She either wants to run away or into his arms, but Harry gets to her first.

'Don't run,' he says, embracing her tiny body. 'I won't run if you don't.'

'One moment,' she says, disentangling herself. She goes to the door, turns the key in the lock, then steps out of her dress.

Harry takes off his t-shirt, but Kanti does the rest. She unbuttons his shorts and, as they drop to the floor, she emits an involuntary gasp.

Downstairs in the basement, Jacqueline and Lionel are still helping John. There are just a few boxes left, and of course, an imprisoned and very angry cat. They pause in their work to listen again to the piano. The music has descended on them like a magic spell, enchanting them with its melancholy.

'He seems a nice young man,' Jacqueline says, sighing. 'He's a good pianist too.'

'She loves him,' John says, his voice still husky with emotion. 'Mutual I think.'

'They're lucky,' Lionel agrees, holding on to some of his own private thoughts.

'Bless her, my little Rach. Who would've guessed. You know, nothing was ever good enough for her. That's all changed. Bless them both.' She's giggling. 'Forgive me, but, well, I was going to say love is blind.'

'It's all you need,' says John.

'You don't seem to need anything more anyway, John,' says Lionel. 'Just a few pillows, rugs, candles and a cat. Buddhism has a lot going for it.'

'Always the mystic,' John quips, trying to settle down an angry Dharma who's still hissing from inside his cage.

'New beginnings, old thing,' Lionel says, squeezing his arm. 'New beginnings for us all. Now where do you want this?' he asks, lifting the statue of Krishna.

Prabodh Bharadwaj, John's business contact in India, hasn't been idle since his friend left for England. Rolls of cotton and silk fabrics have been dispatched, and he's now composing an old-fashioned explanatory letter in his elegantly precise handwriting. The last cargo will take two weeks to arrive in Brighton but, there is more. The Kochi tailor isn't just John's trading partner, he's his friend. There was nothing they didn't discuss that last day together, sitting with the bottle of whisky that they'd substituted for their usual milky tea. It was as John's friend that he'd given this young man a job, when he'd arrived destitute at his door. It didn't take much to loosen his tongue. Rajiv Namputiri had left home to avoid an unwanted and inappropriate wedding. The lad would benefit from a holiday, Prabodh decides, and the cost would be negligible when added to John's shipping bill. Best kept as a surprise, the details could be sorted later, he thinks, dropping the letter in the post.

Chapter Fifty-Five

'This way,' Emmanuel says, hurrying Rachel down a dimly-lit side street. 'I'm going to show you something you've never seen before.' He taps his white cane rhythmically as they go – Rachel resists guiding him, he won't want that, his steps are confident, but she can hear his anxiety.

'You're scaring me again,' she says. 'I'm scared of me, not you. Scared that you can take me anywhere you want.'

'I'll never take you where you shouldn't go, that's a promise.'

They're in a graveyard away from the street lighting, it's dark, and the graves are ghostly shapes, shadows of a shadow, under the towering silhouette – a Gothic building.

'Don't be scared, it's fine. I know where I am.'

'That's what I'm frightened of,' she laughs, as he squeezes her hand. She feels hot against his touch.

'It's alright, I have a key. We're not doing anything illegal.'

'Shame.'

He leads her to a heavy wooden door. 'This is exciting,' she thinks, 'but stupid. I love this guy but he's crazy.' It's like a horror movie without the bats – so far. Then she sees one, flying low. 'Fear can be cosy in the right company,' she thinks. He opens the door and guides her into an unlit church that smells of candle wax, incense and dust.

'I can't see a thing,' she whispers, quietly thrilled.

'I can see exactly where I'm going. Come on, I'll show you.'

It's now totally dark for Rachel, she can only walk because Emmanuel takes her arm and leads her into the blackness.

'Here, sit here, you'll be fine. I want you to see something. Trust me – just sit here until I come back, alright?'

'Yes, of course. Fine, but you have to admit it's a bit scary. Just a little bit.'

'That's the point,' he says, but there's kindness in his voice. 'Now stay there, OK. All will be revealed. Trust me.'

She does. She's trusted him since those first text messages, so no reason to change now that he's walked her into a scene from *Dracula*. Alone, on a wooden pew with what feels like a carved arm rest, she listens to what she hopes really are Emmanuel's footsteps walking briskly away from her. Then she hears a door open and what sounds like feet on stone steps. He's above her now, she can hear him high up there, near what must be the ceiling. She feels cold for the first time this summer, and her little cotton frock is now scanty cover. She can't hear him any more; she can't hear or see anything, and then she feels the biggest body shock of her life. It's a thunderous sound, louder than anything she's ever heard, she thinks. It shakes everything. Her buttocks and legs vibrate with the solid oak pew. She could be on one of those end-of-pier terror machines, but this is more than excitement, it's sublime.

Above her, in the organ loft, Emmanuel, organist for this parish, has, quite literally, pulled out all the stops for a performance of his favourite among the works of Johann Sebastian Bach, the *St Anne Prelude and Fugue* which he now plays, using all three organ keyboards, full volume, accompanied by volcanic bass notes from the foot pedals. Using all four limbs, hands and feet, his whole body is music-animated.

'That's my tune,' she says to the unseen ghosts, the watching vampires and the spirits from hell. 'What the fuck!' The phone ringtone that she loves so much is magnified ten thousand times on the giant organ. What was a tiny tinkling sound, now truly overwhelms her, sitting here, enveloped in the glorious church-rumbling sound that, she will later find out, is the key of E Flat Major. Rachel will often cry joyful tears when she hears E Flat Major – which is often. It stays with her after the organ is silenced and the echo drifts away. She can still feel it when Emmanuel is back, sitting next to her in the dark.

'I want to share everything with you,' he whispers, hugging her. 'This is my world. This is what it looks like – what it sounds like too.'

'And what it feels like. And it's not really *Rachel's Tune*,' she says.

'Oh yes it is, but it's also J.S. Bach's tune.'

'I don't like music, as you know, but I'm loving this J.S.Bach. Magnificent, joyful and tragic. Like being caught in a tangle of conflicting emotions. It takes you somewhere, somewhere where everything is resolved. Resolved completely, finally, so ecstatically that, at the end, you arrive where you've always been heading. Loud too. Wow!'

'Wow to you. You're quite the musicologist when you get started,' he says, bathing in their shared body heat.

'I loved feeling you in the dark, seeing you in the dark. Your body in the music.'

'I brought your friend here once and he said that you'd appreciate my world.'

'My friend?'

'Joe Edevane.' He said I should meet his photographer friend. Someone with a true eye. That's you, Rachel. You can open my eyes. I can open your ears.'

'I hope I'm good enough for this,' she whispers, to herself as well as to him.

'We will both be stronger,' he says. 'Love makes lucky people complete.'

'Yes. Oh God yes, Emmanuel Kaspar Gulan. If I was texting that, I'd type three exclamation marks – maybe even four.'

Chapter Fifty-Six

Live music is coming to The Golden Orb and the pub has been given a celebratory facelift – a new coat of whitewash on the walls where the stains were most obvious, some window-cleaning at the front of the building, and a chrysanthemum flower in a jam jar on every table. Jacqueline embraces change like any successful entrepreneur, she's even bought herself a trouser-suit for the occasion. It's more than just about the music because today is a bit like a wedding. It's not official, but everyone knows, or assumes, that Rosemary and Jacqueline now share a bed.

'It took a long time to get here, Jacks,' Rosemary says.

'Too much sex probably,' Jacqueline says. 'Too distracting, my love.'

'That wasn't sex, it was business,' Rose laughs, enjoying Jacqueline's hand on her thigh.

Conrad has moved into Rosemary's room. He's the son they never had, they say. He's working full-time at Smith's Emporium and is now qualified to pierce any body part suggested to him by his growing list of clients. Some of his customers are from the photographic club where he's still the star life model. One picture made it into to a popular glossy magazine that's still available in Anything Goes. Conrad doesn't work in the sex shop any more, but he still pops in for a chat. He sometimes serves behind the bar at the Orb, and his celebrity status has made him a draw for some of the pub's new clientele. It works, Jacqueline thinks, having a man around the house.

Every Thursday night from now onwards, the resident band Flotsam and Jetsam is booked for The Golden Orb Jazz Night in the reopened back dining room. It's the biggest sensation to hit the pub since Rosemary retired from the world's oldest profession. Flotsam and Jetsam is a five piece band: Lionel Atkins, piano; John Smith, bass guitar; Alan Norton, saxophone; Monty Roberts, drums; and, on vocals, Rosemary Seymour. They will do jazz standards, the best of Ella Fitzgerald and Rosemary Clooney with an English accent, and a special emphasis on the music of George Gershwin.

Controversially, the band has resisted the pub's speciality. There's no Country and Western on their playlist, but, in the public bar, a few die-hards keep the juke-box going. Dolly Parton would've had more grace than to upstage Flotsam and Jetsam's opening night, but old Mr McGuiness makes a special gesture of protest – still fondling his trouser pocket, he spends a little more than he can afford on the jukebox's Dolly Parton collection. These ten songs are old Mrs Webb's favourites too. Dolly Parton has brought the two together and now Mr McGuiness is Mrs Webb's principal drinks waiter at her corner table and, just maybe, more than that too.

'This is for you, dear,' he says. They clink their glasses to his first choice, *Starting Over Again*.

Maybe Flotsam and Jetsam aren't the greatest band to do the pub music circuit, but they have a special quality – underneath the quintet's smart performing gear, four tuxedos and a little black frock, courtesy of Sato's boutique, is maybe the true secret of their success. The five still have their all-over tans, topped up every morning at the nudist beach where, after a swim, and John's now regular seaside sitar raga, the band plan each week's playlist. Alan, now an honorary old geezer, is allowed to keep his swimming trunks but after a while he hasn't bothered. Nothing's too embarrassing, he says, for the greater good of his saxophone. He's Lionel's lodger too. He has a room with a view of the sea and a houseful of music fans.

Alan has convinced Lionel and the others to let him have a go at arranging Gershwin's *They Can't Take That Away From Me*. He's thinking of John Coltrane's soaring tenor sax solo in an old 1957 recording and, tonight, he lets his saxophone soar too, introducing cascades of subtly languid fast notes into Gershwin's moodily romantic masterpiece. Rachel, sitting between her mother and Emmanuel, doesn't miss the meaning. His sax was always more important than the sex. Emmanuel's fingers play an imaginary keyboard in the palm of her hand until she closes it around them. He raises her hand to his lips. She's persuaded her mother to run Sunday lunchtime piano recitals once a month here at the pub. Emmanuel will be playing Chopin and Bach next week and, if no one else comes along, at least he knows that Rachel will be there.

Harry's here to show support for his friends. He's living with Kanti in Lionel's house too, where his collection of drums now includes a Nepalese tabla. He plays ragas with John, and with Joe when he's around. He and Alan are now joint managers of Wah-Wah so that both can take time out for their music. There's a rumour that Harry's band, The Burnley Boys, will play its first gig here at the Orb in the autumn, after recording an album in Jake's studio. Kanti leans against him, her head on his shoulder. 'This is so English,' she whispers.

'England's whatever you want it to be,' he says, hoping that it's true. Diep is here too, and Kanti is quietly thrilled when she sees his feet tapping in time to the rhythm. There's much hope here in the land of their father. Here, Diep will be safe. Let it always be so, she prays to unspecified gods. They've found their English family – it's assembled here tonight in a not so typical English pub.

'Alan's got real talent,' Jake says, coming from the bar with a tray of drinks. Two pints of beer, two glasses of lemonade and a large gin and tonic. Victoria, sipping her gin, actually looks happy, no, more than that, she looks remarkable in the black dress with its daring neckline, designed to show off a single string of pearls and a magnificent cleavage. Jake gave her the pearls when she got into music college. 'To show them you're a prima donna,' he says. 'Prima donna assoluta,' he adds. 'Whatever,' she says, rolling her eyes at Harry.

Marie-Louise Freneau is here, her tiger tattoo still on display; she's found a seat at the front with a good view of the saxophone. 'Alan est merveilleux. Très cool – un jazzman anglais,' she thinks. Alan, proud and more than a little hopeful, acknowledges her with a Gallic shrug and throws his melody to the piano.

Lionel speeds it up without changing the tempo, and shows the tune how to dance. There, of course, is Kate Arnold.

'It was worth the trip just for this,' she says to Marie-Louise. They share more than just that front table – they both love bourbon and jazz. Kate mouths the words when Rosemary sings 'they can't take that away from me' but she changes 'that' for 'this'. Lionel's fingers acknowledge the truth and race triumphantly the length of the keyboard. 'For you Kate,' he mouths back to her.

Rosemary runs with the lyrics, giving full-throttle to the torch song defiance. No one will take this away from her either. She smiles at Monty, he's behind her, softly brushing the cymbals, and she lets her hips swing to his beat. He's taken it well, thank god, she thinks, but her eyes find Jacqueline who, a rose in her hair, is swinging her hips by the bar.

Monty takes things as they come. Being alone among friends will do for now, he's decided. When Rosemary's solo comes to its mellowest low note, his drum solo begins – first distant thunder under her words, then it erupts into mayhem. 'Give him a chance and this little man can go wild,' Rosemary thinks. 'Flotsam and Jetsam, indeed. Don't underestimate any of us.' Monty invokes lightning in his final flourish, bringing cheers from the audience and a blood pressure flush to his cheeks.

Then it's over to John – the bass guitar starts its duet with Lionel. It's their daily swim written in music, throwing ideas to each other, testing how far they can go without drowning. John has survived. Maybe it really had been Krishna in the flames that night and maybe, who knows, maybe some of his prayers have been answered.

Tonight, standing at the back of the room, he's there. Motionless, intense, in black t-shirt and jeans, he's every inch the young European. Here with a beer in his hand, Rajiv Namputiri has found his English castle – his eyes follow John, just as he did when they made their vows with a dance, on the other side of the world. Maybe English laws will allow them to stay here together, but that's a problem for another day. For now he's The Golden Orb's new barman and, tomorrow, he'll dance as Lord Shiva on the beach, to Harry and John's morning raga.

'How's the nipple piercing?' Conrad asks, playfully brushing Nico's chest.

'Painful,' Nico says, smiling defensively. He doesn't finish what he was going to say because something dark has entered the room. They both feel it, like a sudden drop in voltage. Simultaneously, martial arts instincts flexed, they see the man in the torn camouflage jacket. His eyes, still pinpoints, catch theirs from across the room, like a criminal caught in the act.

'Through me you enter the city of woes,' he shouts above the music. 'Through me you will find eternal pain!'

The audience ignores him – they might not be able to hear him. Either the music is too loud or just too enjoyable. 'Abandon hope, all ye who enter here,' the barking prophecy continues, but Rosemary wins the battle of voices. Just another drunk, most people think, but watchful eyes are alerted.

'You will excuse me, I must extract that man,' Conrad says, coiled for action.

'I'm with you,' Nico says, already moving.

'No, leave it to me. Please. You taught me well – both of you.'

'Be careful, he carries a knife,' says Joe, who's here too, standing, almost hiding, in the shadows with Nico.

They watch him, parent-like, as Conrad creates a minor scuffle, hardly noticed, that quickly ends with the man demobilised, arms knotted behind his back, voice silenced, Conrad's arm hinged round his throat. Rajiv, literally springing into action, has arrived to help and, in seconds, the man has been slipped away. With no interruption to their set, Flotsam and Jetsam play a world premiere – the first performance of *Blue Notes*; the composer, Alan Norton.

Chapter Fifty-Seven

Joe didn't go back to the cave. Nico wasn't surprised but it hurt. Three months passed with no sign of him – until tonight when he is lying lifeless on Nico's bed, his body outlined under a crisp linen sheet. His face, frozen, eyes closed, still smiling, exposed, silhouetted on a plump white pillow in Nico's dimly lit bedroom. On the floor, the gold waistcoat lies with the rest of his clothes; on a table, there's his flute and a small leather case. Nico arrives late – maybe too late. He stands in the doorway momentarily breathless, eyes fixed on Joe's motionless body. After all that, this. No, it can't be.

Joe shifts in his sleep and Nico exhales, nearly gasping, but he can't look away. This is how it would be and how it would feel, like New York. Not again. Trembling, he wants to switch off, to stop the pain. He lets his body slide down the closed door, sitting slumped, barely propped up, on the floor. Joe moves again. His face, lids closed, looks at Nico, then through him and beyond.

'He's back,' Nico thinks – even his thoughts find it difficult to believe.

Nico looks round the room and sees the small case. It's made of old leather, battered, tied up with string. On the top there are white stencilled letters. EDEVANE. He'd seen it once before in the deckchair store. There's a pile of clothes under the table – street clothes, grimy, he's seen them before too.

'Have you come home?' Nico whispers under his breath. Joe moves again, his head turns away.

A few old clothes, a case and a flute – Joe's worldly possessions are here. Joe Edevane, Nico keeps repeating – it's a mantra that calms the shaking. Joe Edevane, a strange name, Nico has only thought of him as Joe. That's all he knows about the man in his bed – the sleeping man, his flute, those clothes and, yes, that case.

If Mrs Edevane had shared her secret before she died, it would be in the case marked EDEVANE. Maybe there's no secret. There might be nothing to know. Nothing more than Nico can see lying there on the bed. What else does he need? He knows nothing about Mrs Edevane, and not much more about Joe. Open the case and look inside, maybe you'll find explanations.

Nico's not tempted, he's not looking for answers. There's that picture on the wall. Kanti's photograph of him — eyes en garde, nose swollen, blood pouring over his grinning mouth. Underneath she's written the title: *Alive*. 'Yes!' he whispers; it's a shout of joy. When Joe opens his eyes, Nico hands him the flute.

'Play me that tune,' he says, smiling.